The Wolf
The Royals Of Presley Acres: Book 1

Roxie Ray
© 2023
Disclaimer

All rights reserved. No part of this publication may be reproduced, distributed, or transmitted in any form or by any means, including photocopying, recording, or other electronic or mechanical methods, without the prior written permission of the publisher, except in the case of brief quotations embodied in critical reviews and certain other noncommercial uses permitted by copyright law.

This is a work of fiction. Names, places, characters, and events are all fictitious for the reader's pleasure. Any similarities to real people, places, events, living or dead are all coincidental.

This book contains sexually explicit content that is intended for ADULTS ONLY (+18).

how much other people liked my food, my recipes, and my little finishing touches.

"That should do it for brunch." I wiped my hands on the rag I kept tucked into my apron string for easy access, then turned my attention back to preparing meals for the Hollifield family. Cassidy hired me from time to time to prep lunches and dinners to make their hectic lives easier. I was happy to oblige, especially since she paid me so well.

"How's it going in here?" Cassidy asked with a dazzling smile as she rounded the corner. "It all smells so delicious."

Cassidy was the type of woman who could make friends with a bullfrog; she just had that golden personality that drew people to her. I supposed that was part of the reason she held these fancy shindigs so often.

"We just finished up." I turned to face her. "I hope you and your friends enjoy your brunch." I loved putting them together, and her friends were my clients, but occasionally she had others in—sometimes the higher-ups in the pack—and it always made me nervous.

A crash caused us both to jump.

"Oh, shit. I'm so sorry." My newest hire, a younger girl in college, swooped quickly to the floor. "I'll get this cleaned up."

I crouched to help her. "It's all right. If you don't break a plate on your first day, it's plain bad luck."

She smiled at me and wiped a tear from her eye. "I'm so embarrassed."

"Don't be. We all screw up around here." I gestured to the other staff who smiled and nodded. "The true test of a waitress is keeping your attitude in check and never letting the client see that you fucked up."

"I've already got another plate ready to go." Adam stood at the kitchen door. "Come on."

The girl stood and dumped the broken pieces and ruined food into the trash. "Thanks for being so understanding."

Smiling, I wiped my hands on the rag tucked into my apron. "Of course."

"Sorry you had to see that." I returned to Cassidy's side. "The kitchen life isn't quite as glamorous as you'd think. Hopefully, this won't change the way you look at my food."

Cassidy squeezed my shoulder. "Are you kidding me? Anything you touch in the kitchen is a masterpiece, Liza. You'll make someone a very happy wife someday."

Damn it. *Here we go again.* I would never tell her my real opinion—that I didn't think women had to find a man to be happy. I was happy just as I was, and I certainly didn't need a man to make it so. I could cook for myself, please myself, be myself, and I had no one to answer to. I sure as hell wasn't going to fuck that up by adding a man into the mix. Besides, there wasn't much for a man to do unless he cleaned the gutters at the house and the business premises. And I could do that myself, I just chose not to.

Her lips curled into a sly grin. "It's really not that difficult, Liza. If you'd simply attend one of the lunar mating ceremonies, we'd have you matched up in no time."

Lunar mating ceremonies were a meat market free-for-all, and I wanted no part of them. Cassidy, without much respect for boundaries, had a tendency to encourage me to find a mate, and this certainly wasn't the first time she'd pushed a ceremony on me. It was probably because we were around the same age, but Cassidy was already brewing baby number three while I hadn't even started looking for a man. I wasn't sure I ever would.

I was as single as they came, and I didn't mind it at all. My sole focus was on my catering business, and I considered myself a happy, successful, independent woman. I didn't need more.

Sighing, I huffed out an exasperated breath, but it didn't quite have the gusto it deserved, either. "I appreciate your concern, Cassidy. I'll think about it." Mostly as my brain grumbled through it. "Right now, though, you need to go get ready while I make sure the table is set for brunch." And that was the end of it. Period. Big fat end of subject.

It helped that she didn't argue with me and rushed off to touch up her makeup, so I took a reassured breath, but then reality hit. Who was I kidding? After she spent the next twenty minutes trying on every maternity dress she owned until she found one which matched the theme and the expected attire of her guests, she would find me and thrust me into the spotlight. Hightailing it out without notice was my only hope.

I joined my staff on the large patio where brunch would soon be served. Small cans of fuel were set up beneath the chafing dishes to keep the dishes warm.

"This looks fabulous, guys." I adjusted a vase of flowers that adorned the center of the table, pulling a petal with a browned edge from one of the red roses. "Guests should start arriving at any moment. Let's get out of the way." The tablecloths were pressed, the silver had been shined.

My staff nodded and made their way back into the kitchen.

I stepped back and admired the setup. The table was laid with snowy white linens, and each plate had a custom-crafted spread of food. Proud of my accomplishment, I took a few moments to gaze at the arrangement. We handled details. All of the details. This was a no-worry setup for which we were paid premium rates, and in my humble opinion, we earned it.

Car doors slammed in the distance—my sign to move back into the house.

It wasn't as if I didn't know the women who would be in attendance today—I worked for a lot of them—but coming from a middle-class family didn't exactly lend itself to mingling with the rich unless it was work-related. We just didn't have a lot in common. They were the invited guests, and I was the help. I was fine with that, but I was courteous because some of them were my clients.

"Hello." I waved to the women and smiled as I slowly made my way from the patio to the kitchen.

"Not so fast." Cassidy blocked the door, grabbed my hand, and pulled me toward her onto the patio. "Liza, I'd like you to meet Persephone Keller."

A tall, black-haired woman turned to face me and held out her hand. Her smile was friendly, although cautious, as if she were sizing me up before she offered me a genuine welcome. She wore a sleeveless silk sheath dress with a high collar. Regal. Elegant. Dripping money from her diamond earrings.

I was well aware of who Mrs. Keller was, so I gave a slight curtsey to the alpha's wife to show my respect, then gently shook her hand. "Wonderful to meet you, Mrs. Keller."

The Kellers were like royalty in the shifter world, and Persephone Keller was the queen of the south. She was a leader who commanded any room she graced with her presence, and her strong personality intimidated most people. I wasn't sure why, though. As the wife of the alpha, Persephone Keller was in a position of power that deserved a certain amount of reverence, but the way I saw it, as long as I put my best version out into society, I had no reason to be daunted by her temperament.

She inclined her head slightly but didn't make eye contact. It was as though she was dismissing me by not acknowledging my presence—a swift reminder of my place in Presley Acres. I didn't take offense to it, though. In the shifter world, everyone had their place, and I gladly accepted mine.

I turned to Cassidy and widened my eyes. In no world did the help rub elbows with the queen. I couldn't believe she'd brought me out here in my white clothes, my apron still attached around my neck, to meet Persephone Keller. We'd have to discuss it later. For now, I was heading to my comfort zone and settling in until the event was over. "Well, if you ladies need anything else, I'll be in the kitchen."

Cassidy patted my arm before turning to Persephone. "Liza has been with us for years now. She really is a lifesaver in the kitchen." She chuckled. "I don't know what I would do without her."

I eyed Cassidy again, still wondering what she was up to and if I could skip the pleasantries. If it were up to me, I would've turned and sprinted to the kitchen like an Olympic runner. I had important work to do, and being in a crowd dressed as I was among all of Cassidy's high-profile friends made my stomach queasy with nerves.

I couldn't relate to any of them. As a child, I'd been on the outside, watching from afar. The children from well-off families stuck together through our days as children, then as teenagers and well into adulthood. I had nothing to talk to them about. I was fairly certain they didn't want to hear about my newest recipes or the moon-shaped burn I'd received from my cast-iron skillet.

Cassidy raised her eyebrows and spoke like this was any other conversation with any other woman in the pack. "The Keller Pack will be hosting the lunar mate ceremony this year, and Persephone was just saying how she needs a caterer for the event."

Oh. This was business. That made my presence more reasonable.

Persephone finally looked directly at me. For all of her status and nobility, she wasn't a woman who chose words carefully. She cocked her head to the side, sizing me up.

After a moment, she nodded. "Cassidy speaks very highly of you and your skills. Some of my other friends have mentioned your professionalism, as well. Would you like to cater the event?"

Holy shit.

I clamped my lips together. No way was I going to allow them to flop open in shock in front of the queen of the south. *Was this really happening?* If I catered the lunar mate ceremony, it would be, by far, the largest event I'd ever been hired to work. I'd catered weddings for many of the pack members, but this would be an event that would bring hundreds of shifters from all over the country, and they would be eating *my* food. Not only was it a huge undertaking, it was also an opportunity I couldn't pass up. It went without saying—although I would have to say it—that I was more than willing to take it on.

I wanted to accept gracefully, promise to do a good job, and thank Persephone for the opportunity. This was for my business, and it would elevate me to another level, but instead of managing any of those things, I could only muster a simple sentence: "I'd be honored," which was also true.

Persephone nodded and smiled as if she'd just won the lottery. "Wonderful."

I cleared my throat and nodded, too, now back to business. It was time to put my admiration away and do the job I needed to do. "If you have a moment, we can discuss the budget and I can create a couple of mock-up menus for you to review."

I glanced at Cassidy, who was smiling from ear to ear. Certainly, if it went well, she would take all the credit for recommending me, and if it went badly, she would lament how she'd given me a chance. Either way, she would come out smelling like a rose.

Persephone waved her hand through the air dismissively. "There's no budget." She narrowed her eyes as if she couldn't imagine such a concept as budgeting. It felt a bit as if I'd made my first mistake, but I bounced back with a smile as she continued. "Just put together a quote and I'll pay whatever."

Wow. I shouldn't have been surprised but I was. These people, the ones throwing the mating event, were shifter royalty, and they had a level of wealth I'd never understand.

No budget. I repeated the words again in my head. I was grateful, though. Having an unlimited budget would make my job catering for the ceremony a lot less stressful.

"Okay. I'll need a couple of days to draw up a contract for you, then I can get to work." I curtsied again, though I wasn't sure it was necessary. "Thank you."

As I turned to leave, I mouthed *thank you* to Cassidy. She responded with a wink and returned her attention to the multiple guests who were seated around the large brunch table. "All right, ladies. Who's ready to begin?"

I stumbled into the kitchen, almost unable to believe what had just happened. I'd met Persephone Keller, been offered a job, and in the space of one short encounter, my business had been drastically elevated because, against all odds, Persephone Keller had taken a chance on me.

This was the opportunity of a lifetime, and I planned to make the most of it. I was busy spinning ideas in my head: filet mignon in a creamy mushroom sauce—meat was always a hit with the packs—a brisket seasoned with au jus and the secret blend of herbs and spices that I always used.

By the time I returned to the kitchen, my cheeks ached from the smile I couldn't have wiped away with foaming soap and a squeegee. But then it occurred to me that Cassidy was a lot sneakier than I'd given her credit for. She'd found a way to ensure that I would have to attend the ceremony I mostly wanted to avoid like the fucking plague.

Of course, I'd be in the kitchen managing my staff, but it would have the distinction of being the first mating ceremony I'd actually attended.

The whole concept disgusted me, and I shivered at the idea of even being in the same city as one of those ceremonies. I had many goals in life, but finding a mate wasn't one of them. The thought that I would find the one person I was destined to be with at this ceremony was absolute idiocy. Prior to this moment, whenever someone suggested that they'd found true love at one of these things, I rolled my eyes and laughed out loud. Much the same as this moment.

I surveyed the kitchen, grateful my catering staff had already left for the day.

It took about an hour to finish prepping meals for Cassidy's family, but she had enough meals to last the week by the time I was done and could hang up my apron, so to speak.

I was exhausted, but as I headed out of the kitchen, my mind was still buzzing with ideas for the lunar mate ceremony. I had a real chance to get my name out there with this thing and I wasn't going to blow it.

This is it. A now or never moment. I'd spent years working my fingers to the bones, learning, trying new things, taking chances—some panned out, some didn't—and it was finally paying off. The future was mine for the taking. I had a quality product and extraordinary, professional staff. Most of all, I had talent. Those were all things I could control. I could cook in my sleep. I would just be doing it on a much larger scale.

I hopped in my car and headed back to the office to start drafting a contract for Persephone. This was the kind of thing that couldn't wait. I wanted to have the details locked in, the budget—or lack of one, in this case—in writing and approved so I could start working. Plus, punctuality and timeliness were signs of professionalism, and I certainly didn't want Persephone to doubt that I was at the top of my game—the kind of professional who could be counted on to deliver with efficiency.

As I drove, the idea of a fated mate continued to float around my mind. I just didn't buy that there was a person in the world who would stir something so potent inside me I'd never been aware existed, that it would lead to the great love of my life. At least those were the words Cassidy had used to describe her mate.

I'd heard others describe fated mates as soulmates connected by some unbreakable bond. Someone who could supposedly bring the best out in their mate and unlock passionate emotions that transcended time and space.

I hadn't bought it then, and my mind wasn't easily changed.

Chapter 2 - Ty

One Month Later

"I've been in touch with our logistics department, and they've found the source of the shipment issues." Bill looked at me with unblinking eyes as if he could scare me out of my anger, but I was certain he had no idea of the kind of anger I could summon if I needed to.

Now, though, I reined it in, ran my hand through my hair, and glared at the manager at Keller Motors. "Well, spit it out. What's the problem?" Answers. I needed fucking answers.

Bill took a step closer and thrust a handful of papers in my direction. "Instead of printing by date, they've been printing in alphabetical order. Things ordered on the first of the month by Zimmer have been printed out at the end. So, we aren't dealing with first in, first out, and everything is printing out of sync."

"Son of a bitch." I pulled in a loud breath through my nose. It was probably one of those kinds that should've been called a cleansing breath, one meant to calm the fire, but my fire raged. I snatched the paperwork from him and compared our client information to the dates of the part orders. The whole fucking system had broken down, botched by some incompetent asshole. "So that's why we're receiving all of these returned products." No one wants to wait a month for product that was supposed to be delivered overnight. Of course, there were fucking returns. "What are we doing about this?"

Bill looked down at the sheets in my hands, then met my eyes. He was a man who owned his mistakes, and this was his. Even though he wasn't the order entry guy, he was the manager. The overseer. *His* mistake. After a moment, he crossed his arms defensively. "First, let me just say how sorry I am, sir. I should've been on top of this. It shouldn't have happened, and it certainly should've been caught before these shipping errors were made."

Apologies meant nothing without a plan to correct the situation. I nodded. "Yeah, and?"

"I've got my IT guy working to correct the program as we speak. Everything *should be* running smoothly from this point forward." I'd spent my entire life without qualifiers like *should be. I* needed a man in charge who could guarantee results. As I was about to inform him that his days at Keller Motors had come to an end, he held up one finger as he read his phone screen then looked at me. "According to the email that just came through, it's fixed."

I sighed. He'd just saved his job. "This type of fuck up can't happen again, Bill. Each time we have to process a return and then re-ship to the proper address, it slows production time. And what does that affect?" I wanted to hear him say the word.

Bill scowled. "Profit." And that affected his bonus the same as it did my family's bank accounts. "I've already put a secondary checklist in place to ensure this doesn't happen again." That was a good thought, but it didn't excuse the fact that it had taken a month to catch and a couple million dollars to fix—so far—and if he'd been doing the entirety of his job like he should have, this secondary checklist would have already been in place.

"I appreciate your diligence." He'd been with the company for a while. My father would say we owed him our loyalty since he'd been loyal to us. I didn't subscribe to the same philosophy as my old man, but there wasn't much else I could do but give the guy another chance. "I want to give you a chance to make this right. You've been a fantastic manager, and I don't want to lose you." I lowered my voice because the lie hurt. "But if something like this ever happens again, I'll fire you." There wouldn't be a third chance. "I depend on you to keep things running smoothly. This type of mistake is unacceptable, so I hope your computer fix is indeed fixed. I have a business to run and a reputation to uphold. Next time, this shit will be dealt with swiftly."

He nodded and cleared his throat. "Yes, sir. Thank you for giving me a chance to make it right. The shipments will go out on time, even if I have to do the deliveries personally." And that was why my father was as loyal to Bill as Bill was to us. "Guaranteed."

I shook his hand, then walked him out of my office. He veered off into the plant, and I went to the parking lot.

My family owned several businesses in town, and Keller Motors was just one of them. We had the parts factory, a tanning and beauty salon, a car lot, a grocery store, a bookstore, and a few other things I didn't do much with. I spent most of my days putting out fires my father was too busy to handle and attempting to keep the businesses moving smoothly, despite the fires still burning.

I usually enjoyed the work and interacting with the employees. Stupid shit like this, though, made me want to retire at the ripe old age of forty.

Now that the shipping issue was settled, I took a deep breath of fresh air and slid my sunglasses on. The sun was shining, the temp was warm, too gorgeous of a day to be stuck inside a manufacturing plant, and for a moment, I felt sorry for our employees. But we paid a fair wage, allowed plenty of paid time off that could be used at their convenience, and we were providing jobs to the inhabitants of Presley Acres, Texas, that simply wouldn't be available if we weren't around. If we gave the whole plant off for every nice day of the year, not a lot of work would get done.

The Kellers, my family, were pillars of the community. All around in our town and neighboring ones, shifters and humans alike respected the work we'd done for the city and for the pack. We acted with the thought of all the people in Presley Acres and made sure that shifters and humans lived in harmony in town, working together, playing together. For the most part, there was harmony. Of course, there were times that keeping peace was difficult due to fear, some egos, the ever-present machismo.

My phone buzzed, and I pulled it from my back pocket, looked at the screen and considered shoving it back where it came from. The eye roll that came from seeing my mother's name on the screen was involuntary. After all the stress at Keller Motors, the last thing I wanted was to deal with her high-strung nit-picking. Ever since we'd been chosen to host the lunar mate ceremony a month ago, she'd become an absolute tyrant who couldn't be reasoned with. I'd been keeping my distance and had a wealth of excuses at the ready for whatever favor or chore she had for me today.

Any other time, she was a great mom. The kind who loved unconditionally, the kind who did what she thought was right—and she usually was—without thought of consequence. She was the kind of woman others looked up to. But for the love of all that was good in the world, someone needed to confiscate her fucking phone. This was probably the tenth time today she'd called to make sure I'd picked up my suit, scheduled a haircut and a car detail, and at least five other things. But I sure as hell didn't have time to do any more of her bidding.

I usually looked forward to the ceremony, though I'd never found a mate, but this year it couldn't pass quickly enough. I was a long time past ready for it to be over.

Against my better judgment, I answered the phone. "Yes, Mother. What can I do for you now?" There was a twinge of guilt at speaking to her this way, but I was fast becoming immune.

"When are you going to be home?" Her voice was high-pitched and anxious. Likely, there was a problem with the flowers or the caterer, and she'd reached her limit for a day.

But her tragedy was my quick fix, so I laughed. "It's so good to hear your voice, too."

"Don't smart mouth me, Ty; I'm not in the mood," she scolded. I could practically see her clenching her teeth. "You need to make sure you're home in time to get ready."

I cleared my throat and focused on saying all the right things—the things I'd practiced after the last call that would end this call quicker. "Yes, Mother. I'll be home in plenty of time. I'm actually on my way to get the haircut now." She just needed reassurance. This was an easy call.

Her breath quickened, and she let out a soft moan.

I'd failed. My mother was losing her shit.

"Mom, you have every detail taken care of, including me, and I'm no easy task. You're formidable. Everything will be perfect because nothing would dare be imperfect. You don't need to worry." I paused to make sure I could still hear her breathing on the line and that she hadn't fallen over from either the fit of her dress or her anxiety. When I heard her sigh, I continued. "The ceremony will be the most extravagant this town has ever seen."

That was all it took. She erupted.

"I'm not worried about any of that!" she yelled into the phone. "I know how to throw a party and, of course, it will be the most lavish ceremony that anyone has ever attended. I'm throwing it." Confidence wasn't an issue that plagued my family. "My worries lie... elsewhere."

Fuck. Elsewhere usually meant me, and I didn't have to guess why. She was assuming this would be another year that I wouldn't find a mate.

This wasn't one of those conversations I was going to get out of easily, and I had an appointment to get to. I hopped into my car and started the engine. "Don't worry about things you can't control."

"How can I help but worry, Ty? You're forty, in case you hadn't noticed." She said the number like it was a curse to be this old and single. Maybe back in the day, but not now. Nevertheless, Mom had to have her say, although she did pause and soften her voice. "If you don't find a mate tonight, we need to discuss other options."

"Other options? Like, I should choose a mannequin?" I knew damn well she meant that I would need to consider choosing my own mate instead of counting on fate to do it for me, but teasing her was too much fun. Of course, she was right—she usually was—but I didn't want to think about that right now. "I'll see you soon, Mother." I tossed my phone onto the passenger seat and sped to the barbershop.

Other guys like me had switched to the salon by now for one of the four-hundred-dollar haircuts that were preferred in my circle of friends, but I liked to keep it old school.

Tradition.

Routine.

Things that lasted.

Unfortunately, the newest trend must've been barbers. I had to circle the building twice to find a parking spot. Of course, the one day I needed to rush, the barbershop was super busy.

"Ty, good to see you." Stanley, the gray-haired barber who'd cut my hair since I was a boy, looked up from the cut he was giving to a guy about my age. I didn't know the guy, which was a rare occurrence. "I'll be done here in a few."

"Sorry, I'm late." I smiled and shoved my hands into my pockets. "I got held up at Keller Motors."

"No worries." As expected, Stanley finished up the other cut and cleared his chair for me. "It's only a few minutes."

Averting my eyes from the long line of men waiting for a haircut, I took my seat.

"Doing something special for the big party?" Stanley draped a cape around my neck. "Or just the usual?"

I stared at my reflection. This cut fit my face. "Yeah, just give me the usual. Pretty sure my mother's heart will stop if I walk into the ceremony with something different." I tried to imagine the look on her face, but I'd save that for her birthday.

Stanley chuckled. "That party is all anyone's been talking about today. Are you looking forward to it?"

We had this conversation every year, but this year the pressure weighed on me. I pursed my lips. "Eh. I could take it or leave it."

"Is tonight the night, Ty?" The voice came from behind me, and I turned to see one of the elder pack members sitting a few chairs down. He probably meant well, but it was the kind of question that pissed me off.

It was no secret that I'd attended multiple lunar mate ceremonies. It was also common knowledge that I'd gone home alone each time.

Unclenching my jaw, I cleared my throat. "There's always hope."

"Yes, indeed." Stanley smiled at me in the mirror as he sprayed my hair with water. "Never stop believing. Your perfect mate is out there."

I wondered whether that was true. It had to be. It had happened for nearly everyone I knew. There was no reason it wouldn't happen for me. Nothing made me different.

By the time I made it home, I was nearly starving to death, but I bypassed stopping to grab a snack from the kitchen, even though my stomach had been rumbling since before my meeting with Bill at the factory. Instead, I ran upstairs because my mother would lose her mind if I wasn't in my suit and ready to party in T-minus five.

While I was dressing, though, and counterproductive to speed, my mother had me on speed dial and kept calling every ten seconds until I finally decided to answer. "Yes?"

"Are you on your way?" She breathed heavily into the phone. "Please don't tell me you're going to be late for an event our family is hosting."

"Mom, if I do nothing else in my life, if everything else I ever do is a disappointment to you, I promise I'll be on time for the party." I let out a low growl because sarcasm didn't dispel enough frustration. "It would help if you'd stop calling me every damn minute."

I hung up the phone and tossed it onto the bed. I'd just lied. Not that I wasn't ready in plenty of time to be punctual, but I was hesitant to leave. My gut churned as I imagined being hopelessly unable to find a mate. Again. Failing. Again. I imagined the whispers. How quickly the gossip would spread. Of course, it would be turned around to somehow be my own fucking fault. That was how gossip and rumors worked.

I couldn't blow off the ceremony, though. I'd spent a few too many nights alone jerking off instead of looking for a mate. But tonight, there was a chance I could find a woman to do it for me, even if it wasn't forever. So, I pressed forward and finished getting ready.

When I left the house, I had to speed. I arrived at the Presley Acres Country Club with only a few minutes to spare.

I tossed my keys to the waiting valet.

"So nice to see you, Mr. Keller."

I nodded. "Hey, Roy." Then I walked up the steps, maybe with a bounce in my step, a hope, and the anticipation of a man on a mission he certainly had the ability to complete.

As I walked into the house, a middle-aged woman with shoulder-length, gray hair met me in the foyer. "This way, please."

She escorted me to the library—as if I didn't know where the fuck to go when I'd been coming to this place to my whole life—where my mother was speaking with one of the staff members. "The lighting is wrong. Fix it."

"Ma'am, your son has arrived." The escort left us alone, and Mother turned to face me.

"Ty! Thank goodness, you made it on time." That was absolutely how important this was to her. Appearances were everything. She hugged me tightly, then pushed me away to arm's length. "Let me get a good look at you."

I stood still and let her inspect me.

As she adjusted my tie, I forced a smile and pushed my shoulders back, standing to my full height. "What do you think? Do I look good enough to mate?"

It was an odd question to ask my mother, but now that it was out there, I couldn't take it back.

She rolled her eyes and continued to look me over from head to toe. The tension radiating from her body was so thick it made my blood pressure rise.

Sometimes even mothers needed consolation. I cupped her head in my hands. "Stop worrying."

She squeezed my hands lovingly, then tossed them aside. "If only I could, Ty."

A laugh bubbled out of my throat as I leaned forward to kiss her on the cheek. "Fate will do its will, and we just have to let it be." Those were the words she'd said to a lonely teenage boy many moons ago.

She grabbed my hand and took a deep breath. "Are you ready?" It was as if she expected me to be nervous. I smiled to let her know it wasn't the case. I was steady. Of course, I was never unsteady.

"Ready as I'll ever be."

The escort returned and led us to the ballroom's double doors. "Wait here. Once you hear your name called, I'll open the doors for you, and you can make your entrance."

What the hell? Was this a lunar mate ceremony or Cinderella's ball? And if it was Cinderella's ball, what the fuck did that make me?

I glanced at my mother and raised my eyebrows, the question unspoken but obvious between us.

Holding her hand up between us in a stop-traffic kind of way, she mouthed the word *breathe*.

All right. I supposed we were doing the grand-entrance thing.

The announcer's loud voice came over the speaker system. "And now, will you please direct your attention to the main ballroom entrance? Please welcome your host for the lunar ceremony, Ty Keller!"

I stood tall as the escort quickly opened the double doors. Stepping into a room filled with shifters, I gave my best smile and held my hand up in a wave. I knew how to be cordial, even when battling surprise. There were twice as many shifters as I expected. "Thank you all for coming."

Once the applause died down and the voices were little more than a low murmur, someone grabbed my arm and tugged. "Right this way. No time to waste."

Mother dragged me across the ballroom to a tall woman dressed in a long, purple gown. "Ty, I'd like you to meet Stephanie Aldrich."

I stared into her eyes. Nothing. Not even a dick twitch. There should've been at least that.

"Nice to meet you, Stephanie." I shot Mother a look, and she took the cue to move me through the crowd to the next target.

My mother introduced me to woman after woman, but there was no pull, no tug in my gut, no real reaction at all.

"This is Gladys Underwood. Her mother and I went to school together. We were sorority sisters." Mother stood back, watching closely for any type of signal that meant there was even a sliver of attraction between the two of us.

Gladys, though strikingly beautiful, seemed shy. I reached for her hand. "Wonderful to meet you, Gladys."

She blushed. "I've heard so much about you, Ty."

I would have wondered what that meant, but my mother was nearby. Not really much to wonder.

I glanced at my watch, and my heart dropped. I'd only been at this for fifteen minutes and it already felt like an eternity. "Please, excuse me."

I walked toward the door; Mother hot on my trail.

"Where do you think you're going?"

"I need a drink." The bar was just outside on the terrace, and I couldn't get there fast enough.

"Tyson." I turned to face her because she'd put *that* kind of emphasis on my name.

"Oh, come on, Mother. I need a drink. Or is that not allowed? Do I have to dehydrate on top of being tortured with these horrific introductions?" If I was honest, they weren't *all* horrific, but no one had yet made me consider mate-bonding.

She knew it, too. It explained her scowl. "Fine. Come straight back, though." The implication was in her tone—if I took too long, she would send someone after me. It was graduation all over again.

I gave her the same nod eighteen-year-old me had given, then hustled to the bar. "Scotch. Neat."

The bartender nodded and poured the amber liquid into an old-fashioned glass. I knocked the smooth, buttery Scotch back and motioned for another. The second took the edge off.

Ahh. That was better.

"One more."

This time, I picked up the glass and brought it with me. I mingled in the ballroom instead of returning to my mother's side. In one corner, there was a group of guys about my age, and it looked like they were all hiding out, huddled together, and—like me—wishing the night would end. "So, this is where all the fun's happening."

I knew a couple of them, but they all laughed and greeted me with smiles, a couple off-handed waves, and some nods.

"Where've you been?" Jace Windham was my age, a couple inches shorter, and whereas my hair was black as night, his was more of an aged-whiskey brown. Still dark, but not *as* dark. We'd known each other since we were kids.

"Oh, you know. Trying to find someone I like enough to put a ring on it." I slapped Jace on the back with one hand and gripped his shoulder closest to me with the other. "What about you? Any matches tonight?"

He pointed to the corner of the room. "Not me, but that guy looks like he's ready to go tits up."

I glanced across the room at a guy who looked moderately familiar, and a woman I'd never seen before. They were staring longingly into each other's eyes, dancing so close that with just a few less clothes, they could've been fucking in the middle of the ballroom.

"Huh. Well, looks like someone found their lunar mate." I raised my glass in a toast and tried not to be jealous. "Cheers to 'em."

Jace grinned and clinked his glass against mine. "Cheers, indeed."

I glanced around the room once more, hoping I'd find some spark of soulmate recognition between me and one of the other women, but I was fairly certain I'd met them all, and, alas, no spark.

Like she sensed I was trying to find my way to the door as discreetly as possible, and this was just a stopgap, my mother reappeared. "Would you look at that?" She pointed to the same couple I'd just seen.

"Yeah, I see it." I crossed my arms. This was my defensive position. All women looking for a mate would bounce off me like kryptonite.

She massaged her neck. "Others are already pairing up. You need to meet more women." Her desperation—probably for grandkids—made her voice shake.

"There's my boy." Dad maneuvered through the crowd and threw his arm around my shoulder, giving me a shake like he was letting me know he'd saved me from whatever my mother had planned. "I've been looking for you. Come have a drink with me."

I'd never been so relieved to see his face. I held up my glass and smiled.

He snorted because he knew what I was facing with my mother. I'd faced it at every ceremony for the last several years. "Well, let's have another."

I wasn't going to and couldn't argue with that. My old man was known for his ability to lighten the mood in any situation. And boy, I needed it right now, so I was eternally grateful for his intervention.

I turned just in time to see Mother's jaw drop. She huffed and stomped off, presumably to fuss at some of the staff for their lack of competence. It was something I would hear about later, but I couldn't take more introductions tonight. There was no one left, and I wasn't in the mood to spend time with a woman with whom a relationship would go nowhere.

"Can you believe this?" Dad gestured at the ballroom. "Your mother went a tad bit overboard with this one, don't you think?"

There were topiaries in the center of the tables. Crystal goblets and glasses. Elaborate silks draped from the center of the ceiling to the walls in wide swoops. Mom did nothing in half measures. But I understood. This was important to her.

Dad was right, though. I took a sip of my Scotch. "It's a little much. Yes."

My dad shook his head as we walked to the bar. "That woman never sits still." He placed his order at the bar. "I spend ten hours a day chasing her ass around the house, hoping I'll get a moment of her time. It's better than having a personal trainer."

"You knew exactly the kind of woman you were marrying." I rolled my eyes. My mom and dad were made for each other. Every once in a while, she slowed down enough for him to catch her. "Don't even pretend like Mother's type-A personality is a shock."

"A shock it most certainly is now." He swirled the ice in his glass. "But I can still complain about it any damn time I want." He smirked, smug because he'd won the point.

Talking to Dad was a lot easier and often preferable to talking to Mom. At least, right now it was refreshing to not be asked about my fated mate. I was grateful to have one parent willing to cut me some slack.

"So, this is where you're hiding." My cousin Jacob pulled up a bar stool.

He was five years younger than me, but he'd had no trouble finding a fated mate early on. *Lucky bastard.*

"Yeah, we needed a break." My dad chuckled and raised his glass.

"A break?" Kelis, Jacob's mate, wrapped her arms around his neck. "You've only been here half an hour. If you don't have more stamina than that, no wonder you can't find a mate." Bold. I supposed that was part of the attraction between them.

I held up my Scotch. "Oh, I have the stamina. Don't you worry your pretty little head about that, Kelis."

She wasn't my favorite person. She was a well-known gossip, and seemed almost proud that she'd been called *the town crier*. Not that I was one to throw stones about how someone lived. I'd grown up pampered. Went to the best school. Had the best clothes and shoes. The right car. Despite all that, I hadn't gone full-on snob. Kelis had. She stuck her nose up at anyone she deemed unworthy of her attention, which was most people.

The speaker system crackled, and my mother's voice vibrated through the crowd. "Dinner will soon be served. Please make your way to your assigned tables."

Sometimes my mother's timing was impeccable. This was one of those moments. "Oh, look at that." I set my glass on the bar. "We don't have time for an in-depth discussion of my mating skills." I shrugged, not sorry one fucking bit to end my conversation with Kelis.

She rolled her eyes. "Maybe next time."

I smiled but thought I would rather cut off my left arm and beat myself to death with it before I spoke to her about mating.

Dad and I made our way to the dining room. The country club was equipped with room enough for a lot more people than this. Come to think of it, she'd probably planned it that way.

As I pulled my chair out so I could sit at a table of women I had no intention of dating or mating with, I felt it. The tug.

In my gut.

In my chest.

I couldn't move.

Couldn't think.

I glanced around the room, checking faces for that recognition, for the woman responsible for my wolf growling deep in my chest. *"Mate."*

Chapter 3 - Liza

"Any better?" Adam eyed me and reached out as if he were going to touch me. At the last second, he pulled his hand back. "Your head, that is."

My tray teetered on the edge of the counter as I supported it with my hip. "The medicine's helping some, but my head's still pounding." For a few minutes, earlier, I'd kept one eye closed to block out some of the light I thought might have been contributing to the pain, but then I rammed my hip into the corner of a prep table. Keeping both eyes open was optimum for my safety.

I'd been so busy managing the preparations for the lunar mate ceremony, I hadn't realized just how much pressure I was under. I wasn't eating well—a bite here and there from an hours-old sandwich—nor was I sleeping well. I was too detail-centric about this to manage more than a few hours at a time. Three hours of sleep wasn't enough for anyone, especially someone who'd been hired to cater the most important event of the year.

To put the cherry on top of my stress sundae, three members of my kitchen staff had called in sick with colds. It was that time of year, inconvenient as it was for me. Now, not only did I have to oversee and manage every aspect of the evening, but I also had to dress like a waitress and serve the guests. I'd started as a server, so it wasn't out of my realm, but definitely not preferred.

"I've never seen so many shifters gathered in one place." Piling my tray full of appetizers, I glanced at my staff, counted heads, made sure I was covered, and that everyone had an assignment. They were keeping up, even though we were still short two staff members. I made a mental note to do something nice for them once the event was over and we could relax. Assuming, of course, we were able to pull it off and I didn't have to worry about finding a new career.

"I saw a couple connecting for the first time." Adam giggled like he'd never seen anything of the sort before. "It was like some kind of fairytale moment. They saw each other across the room, their eyes locked, and some invisible magnetism pulled them toward one another. Fucking magic." He shook his head. "Lucky bastards."

"I'd like a little bit of that magic to make it through this dinner." I rolled my eyes because I was seeing the promised land, and it looked like one of those SleepMagic mattresses with a down pillow and blanket. "We can fawn and 'ooh' and 'ahh' later. Let's get back to work."

"Some of these guys are looking so goddamn good tonight. Men sure look good in tuxedoes." Sabrina, my best friend, walked into the kitchen, slapped her tray on a stainless-steel prep table, then fanned herself with a napkin. She'd been serving hors d'oeuvres, and now needed another tray. Fortunately, there were several already plated under the portable heat lamps.

She was my best waitress—probably the best waitress I'd ever employed—so I was more than grateful she was able to work the ceremony with me.

"Oh, yeah?" I shrugged because I had yet to leave the kitchen. "I haven't noticed." And I certainly hadn't had time to gawk at the attendees. Tuxedoed or not.

Sabrina lifted a new serving tray from the counter and arranged the plates to her liking. "Are you kidding me? You have such tunnel vision." She shook her head and sighed, like my not noticing was a personal affront to her. "How in the name of lightning and thunder could you not see the magnificent and majestically tight asses accentuated by snug fitting slacks and missing jackets? You might need an eye check, woman."

I chortled. If there was one thing for which Sabrina had developed a fond appreciation—more, a passion—it was the male physique. "I'm not blind, Brina, just busy. There's a difference." I could definitely appreciate a well-rounded, tight male ass as well as the next girl. I just didn't have time to do it often or to spend a lot of time discussing it.

"Well, in that case, I can assume you didn't see Future Alpha Ty, either?" This time she fanned herself with a hand. Unfortunately for Derek, another server, the hand belonged to him. He jerked away and shook his head.

I gave her my usual blank look. "Nope. Wouldn't know him if I saw him."

That was the truth. I'd never met him in person or even seen him at a distance. Maybe I'd seen a grainy picture in a newspaper or something at some point, but I could have passed Tyson Keller on the street and would never have known.

"Oh, Liza, he is *divine*. You can't miss him. He's the one all the women are staring at. Hoping for. Wishing for. Probably praying for." Sabrina tucked her short, blonde hair behind her ear. "He's tall with black hair, and he has the deepest gray eyes I've ever seen. Gucci himself probably fit that suit to Ty's body, which is grossly unfair to those of us who can't get close enough to lick all those acres of luscious muscles."

I wrinkled my nose and squinted at her. "Lickable muscles? Doesn't ring a bell. Or maybe we don't find the same things attractive. Otherwise, I would've noticed him."

"Baby, if you don't find Ty attractive, you have to be blinder than I thought. He's a dark-haired Jensen Ackles He's decadent. Like silky caramel and chocolate." She made a show of licking her lips. "Definitely edible." Then her grin morphed into something that could only be described as naughty. "Biteable at least."

I'd never met Ty and hadn't even been in close proximity to him or his family until I met Persephone.

We didn't go to school together since he was a good ten years older than me. Plus, we certainly didn't run in the same circles. Ever.

Even during the full moon runs, the pack was segregated. The high class ran together while others had their own cliques and did their own thing.

I wasn't one for pack runs, anyway. For whatever reason, I'd never felt the call of the moon like everyone else around me. This was another of the prime examples that highlighted my differences from the other shifters, and another reason why I was alone.

But lickable muscles, a biteable ass? It piqued my curiosity, and I wondered if he was as ethereal as others had made him out to be. Since I was here, I could probably catch a glimpse.

It had been said before, I couldn't really remember where, that when Tyson Keller walked into a room, his aura was like its own entity—something that could be felt by everyone in attendance.

I supposed I'd get my chance to find out since I'd be serving the dining room all night, but I couldn't afford to be distracted by tight pants and a nice ass.

Not when I was up to my eyeballs in mushroom caps and grilled peach chicken.

I didn't want to grumble at her, but this all had to go well. My livelihood was at stake. "Sabrina, maybe less gossiping and more serving?" I quickly finished filling my own tray and moved toward the door. "We can debrief and drool where appropriate after dinner. Right now, getting this food out to those tables in a timely fashion is the only thing in the entire world that matters to me."

My business was on the line. It would take one dropped fork, a misfolded napkin, the slightest screw-up at all to turn Persephone against me, and, therefore, the entire upper echelon of society. My business would go to hell, as would my life and any prospect of having one from this day forward. I was not about to let that happen. "Let's go, ladies and gents."

With a deep breath, I opened the door and stepped out into the formal dining room. I was ready to serve the guests with grace and confidence. I was about to be the best damn waitress they'd ever seen.

A gentle murmur of conversation competed with the string quartet playing in the corner. Every eligible shifter lucky enough to have received an invitation from Persephone was in attendance. No one would dare decline such a prominent request from the queen of the pack. The queen of the entire area.

And show up, they had. In their best suits, ornate dresses with shoes—oh, the shoes—looking like they had stepped out of a fashion magazine.

I took a quick glance at my drab uniform and wished for a moment that I had the opportunity to play dress up like this, with the hair and the nails and the shoes. Then I remembered how much time and effort that always ended up taking and scrapped the idea completely.

I smiled graciously every time a guest complimented the food. It happened often. "Thank you." I never really knew what else to say. Probably, they weren't looking for much more out of me, either. I was the help. I was supposed to blend in with the table linens and wallpaper.

One of my regular catering clients nodded and took a sip of her wine. "This salmon is delicious, Liza."

I smiled at her. She was always so kind and complimentary. I often thought I could serve her canned tuna on a cracker, and she would love it, but the salmon was always a particular favorite. "It's one of my favored recipes," I replied. "It's locally sourced and marinated for twenty-four hours."

Locally sourced was the new in and hip thing, but I always tried to shop locally.

Murmured compliments circled the table, and the husband of one of my other regular clients added, "Please, do let the chef know that I particularly enjoy the way the flavors meld together so perfectly."

His wife slapped him on the shoulder, looked at me, and rolled her eyes. "Pardon Jeffrey. He's so obtuse about the help these days." I was the help. She looked at the shoulder she'd just slapped, laid an elegant hand on his shoulder, then hissed, "She's the chef, you idiot."

Oh, damn. I only wanted to serve the food, not cause marital strife.

I smiled at poor Jeffrey. "It's quite all right. I had to fill in for some of my staff this evening." I placed another appetizer on the table.

Then it was time to become part of the room again and not someone who socialized with the guests. I was grateful they were enjoying the meal. As I moved away from the table and on to another to finish delivering what was on my tray, I remained silent, but watched as some of the staff floated to their tables. So far, everything was running effortlessly. Thank goodness.

I turned and walked back to the kitchen, waited until I was through the swinging door, then let out a loud breath before walking to the table where the trays were lined up. I would have to start plating more, but right now, I needed to get back to business. "I need more appetizers." Like anyone was paying attention to me, I added, "Everyone seems happy with the salmon."

"Of course, they're happy with it." Adam grinned and loaded my tray for me. "You're the badass bitch behind it all. The woman behind the salmon. And the beef rolls, the lava cake… it's all you, girl." He snapped his fingers and winked at me.

I loved Adam. I could always depend on his unfiltered commentary to lift my spirits. His words propelled me forward.

Adam came to work in a fantastic mood, and when I was busy doing other things, he kept the flow in sync. "Tell me, boss lady, are you feeling the pull… the ting of desire in your chest? Is your fated mate sitting in the dining room waiting for you and his filet mignon?"

I rolled my eyes. "Don't drink the Kool-Aid, Adam. I don't believe that I'm someone's fated mate any more than I believe I'm queen of the seven kingdoms and destined to marry Jon Snow." I loaded up my tray with more appetizers. "There's no scientific data to back up the theory of this…" I lowered my voice to little more than a stage whisper. "Bullshit."

Adam shook his head and laughed. "You mean you haven't read the Harvard studies?" His tone held such a note of scandal, I couldn't tell if he was serious. "Liza, there is a world of evidence—real science shit—that suggests fated mates exist. You just have to open your mind and look beyond the surface."

"Adam, the only surface I want to look beyond is the one that ends this evening with enough success that I don't have to worry about booking future jobs." Once again, I rolled my eyes. "All of this fated-mate malarkey is just what it is. I apologize if Harvard finds that offensive."

He laughed. "Yeah, your invitation to audit their results is gonna be rescinded with an attitude like that." He continued plating appetizers and shrugged a shoulder. "All I'm saying is, don't let fear keep you from finding true love." He hadn't really said that at all, but I appreciated the sentiment.

"Ah, true love. Another fairy tale we can debate later." I turned away and grabbed my tray. "And I very much appreciate your worldly advice, Adam. But right now, I'm focused on making sure everyone is happy with their meals tonight. That's all that matters to me at this moment."

"Got it, boss." He made to drag his gloved hand across the front of his mouth but stopped and looked back at the plate he hadn't quite finished yet. He didn't need me to tell him his job. He did it and could've probably done it while he match-made me with half the guests on the list. But he also knew how to read a room, and this wasn't the time for such conversation when I was as stressed as I'd ever been.

"All right, here we go." I carefully balanced the large tray on my left shoulder and moved into the dining hall. I'd done this a thousand times before. Carried trays. Walked. Nothing about it was abnormal.

As soon as the door swung closed behind me and I walked into the room, something shifted in the air. There was an electric charge I hadn't noticed before. It was a wave, or like a cable that reached from one side of the room to the other that I couldn't see. I stumbled forward, almost tripping, and I barely caught my tray before it crashed to the floor.

There was a gasp. It might've been mine or that of the room from the tables around me. When I looked up, a few guests were staring at me with wide eyes. I was either going to recover gracefully or make a fool of myself. At this point, it could go either way. I wasn't sure what to do.

So, I took a deep breath, shuffled my feet forward, and was struck again by that invisible wire. Then the wire shifted, and there was a pull in my chest so fierce it was impossible to ignore. My breath caught somewhere between my lungs and my throat, and I stood, frozen in place, as my head spun, and I struggled to stand upright.

Sabrina appeared at my side—I had no idea where she'd come from—and wrapped her arm around my waist. *Oh God*. This was a scene. The kind that ended careers. The kind that had every eye in the room pointed at me. Murmurs of worry, whispers of confusion passed from table to table, and I could see it like it was in slow motion.

Then a few more gasps filled the air, and Sabrina covered her mouth with her free hand. "No fucking way."

I had no clue what was happening, but the pull became stronger, leaving me no choice but to turn around and face the source of the energy. A man stood a few feet away. *The* man. I couldn't explain how I knew who he was, but there was no doubt in my mind that this was none other than Ty Keller, the future alpha.

Holy fuck.

He was everything Brina had said. Everything she had described. He stood there staring at me with wide eyes. His chest visibly heaved as his gaze raked over every inch of my body.

As hard as I tried, I couldn't stop looking at him. He was the kind of man who drew the eye. Well, mine, anyway. Because everything I'd ever heard about Ty was a hundred percent true. He was tall, dark, and so fucking gorgeous I could hardly breathe. And the pants definitely had a nice fit—nice was the most intensely grave understatement in the history of words.

The pull between us was almost visible, like an actual cord tugging me toward him. I tried to make sense of it and even looked down to make sure we weren't somehow tethered. When nothing was revealed, I was aware of what was happening between us. I just couldn't fucking believe it. For a moment, time seemed to stand still as we stared at each other. The room faded away, and it was just us.

Suddenly, the spell was broken. Persephone appeared beside her son, her eyes wide with what seemed like horror as she glanced between the two of us. "No." I could've done without the abject horror in her tone. The disbelief. It was disheartening. Moderately insulting. More so when she wrapped her arm around Ty's shoulders. "Come. Now." My mind went full bawdy, and I shared the sentiment, if not the meaning behind it.

She tugged his shoulders, and when he didn't move, she pulled at his arm. It would've been comical if I could've seen past him. She had both hands around his arm, and she was pulling, feet apart, ass sticking out. There was a desperation to this woman's moves.

To his credit, Ty didn't budge. His gaze remained locked with mine as if he were trying to send me a silent message I just couldn't get because I was mesmerized.

Persephone muttered something at Ty, but my mind was too clogged to make out her words. I could hear his every breath. I could hear my heartbeat. And his. Whatever she was saying to her son, he couldn't hear it, either.

Before anyone moved or said anything else, Dominic Keller, Ty's father, arrived. His face was a ghostly shade of white, and he looked at me as if I had two heads.

He leaned in to whisper to Ty, and after a few seconds, Ty nodded his head as if he understood, but his eyes continued to burn a hole into my soul.

I had no idea what was happening, but I couldn't move, and I certainly couldn't process the murmurs around me. But I didn't care about that. All I cared about was staying suspended in this moment.

Sabrina was still at my side, and someone must've taken my tray because I wasn't holding it any longer. My body gave an involuntary sway, and fainting in front of the entire dining hall became a very real possibility.

The gaze broke as Ty and his parents walked away slowly, his father still whispering in his ear. He'd only taken a few steps when he turned to watch me over his shoulder. I wanted to go to him.

Whispers spread like wildfire from table to table, but I ignored them even as I looked around. People were staring and pointing at me. I had just done the one thing, the *only* thing I'd set out *not* to do at the beginning of this event. I'd ruined my chances of being hired as a caterer by these rich sons of bitches.

Before I could fathom exactly what was happening, Sabrina pulled me into the kitchen. She gently pushed me into a chair and began pacing back and forth between our portable steam table and the refrigerator.

"Holy shit, holy shit, holy shit." She muttered the words over and over again. This was, indeed, a holy shit situation, and apparently, Sabrina had nothing else to say. I certainly couldn't form any words, so I didn't fault her for her repetition.

I sat there in a daze, trying to regain control over my breathing. My heart was throbbing, as if it was trying to beat a path out of my chest. The massive rush of adrenaline had left me shaky and weak. I needed food.

As I pushed my hands against the seat because I needed to stand, Sabrina blocked my way. "Oh, no. You're not going anywhere."

"What do you need, boss?" Adam asked. He was still plating food. With Sabrina and me both in the kitchen, we were falling behind. Although I supposed it didn't matter so much now since this was the last job I would ever cater, anyway.

"I don't know." I wasn't sure I needed anything. I'd just been a part of this spectacle, so the only thing I really needed was a time machine to go back and fix this mess before it ever started. I squeezed the bridge of my nose and closed my eyes, wishing the room to stop spinning.

"Here." Adam shoved a plate of food into my hands.

I looked up at him and smiled. This was a guy who was always good to me. A friend. Why, oh why, couldn't he have been my soulmate? My bond buddy.

My whatever-this-was-called. And if that sounded dramatic, I was only getting started. Plus, I had Sabrina nearby to keep me centered in my misery.

"Do you realize what just happened?" Sabrina knelt in front of me and gripped my knees. "Do you have a fucking clue?"

I had a clue. A pull, a tug. These were things I'd heard spoken about in the abstract. So, I was aware that some mating *thing* kind of happened. I shoved a bread roll into my mouth and sighed. My brain was fuzzy, and my hands wouldn't stop shaking.

All I could see was in my mind—all I wanted to see—was Ty's expression, the shock, the disbelief, and then behind that, the passion, the desire. It had been other-worldly, and I wanted to see it again. Closer. When there wasn't two hundred other people staring at us.

I was in a daze, mystified by what had just happened, but there was no mistaking it.

I'd just met my fated mate.

Chapter 4 - Ty

My heart continued to race as I paced the study at the Keller Estate. I wasn't paying much attention to the upholstered furniture or the marble tables or the mahogany desk. Not more than to notice that this room was exactly the same as it had been years ago. I'd spent many hours in here *thinking about what I'd done* as a child, then as a teenager. As an adult, this room now brought back the memories. Tonight, though, I wasn't interested.

I was anxious to speak with my parents, but I detected an even more severe urgency from my wolf. We fed off each other's stress until it felt like I was about to blow a fucking lung.

He continued to repeat the word *Mate!* in such a way inside my head that I couldn't ignore it. I didn't have to guess what my parents wanted to discuss with me. Obviously, the scene in the dining room had been... unexpected, to say the least. They'd wanted me to mate with someone like Chanel Blaidel or Jessica Mullens. Certainly not someone my mother had hired as a server. This, the study, was the scolding room.

When I'd needed a good talking-to as a child, this was where it had happened. I'd been scolded by my parents in this room more times than I could count, but it had been years since the last time. Certainly, at the age of forty, I'd thought those days were over.

Quite frankly, I didn't understand their issue. I'd played the game just as Mother had expected me to. I'd talked to all the Jessicas and the Ashleys and the ones named after purses and perfumes and designers. Year after year, I'd done my duty to find a mate. Nothing had happened. I had been prepared to give up on letting Fate decide, prepared to choose a mate based on preference and credentials. But tonight, everything had changed.

I honestly couldn't help it that everyone had seen the connection between the waitress and me. It had been as visual as it was undeniable. I hadn't been able to move or think or... breathe. The moment I saw her, all bets were off.

My parents, on the other hand, didn't seem all too enthralled with her. Of course, they really didn't have to be. In fact, they'd been fucking rude.

I glanced at my watch. It was nearing midnight. They'd dumped me here, far from the party at the country club, and had yet to return. The ceremony had to have ended by now.

Of course, I could leave and go to my house, but I didn't, even though there wasn't much reason to stick around. I was a grown man, but my alpha had told me to stay put, so I was staying put.

Every year I'd attended this thing, people couldn't leave fast enough once the ceremony ended. Including my parents. This year, since the party was on their turf, they had no choice but to stick around. Although, it wasn't like they had to supervise cleanup or any of the other things relative to tear down.

Somewhere in this house, they were having an in-depth conversation about the ceremony and my part in the evening's events. I would've bet money on that.

Their reactions had been so… unexpected. My mother's eyes had gone wild, and she tried to pull me away as soon as she spotted me and the waitress connecting. And oh, yeah… there had been connecting.

My dad, likewise, had gone pale, and then his mouth had pulled into a tight scowl. I couldn't make sense of it. I'd done the thing they'd been waiting for me to do my entire life. Granted, they hadn't counted on me mating with a woman my mother would likely forever call *the help*, but I didn't have the ultimate say about a fated mate. I was fate's victim—or benefactor, depending on how this turned out.

Every time I considered it or thought about her, a pulse of electricity shot through me.

In that moment, my heart could've exploded right there in the middle of the dining room. When my gaze locked on hers, I wanted to pull her to me, feel her body, and show her what it meant to be my mate. The yearning had been almost too strong to resist.

My parents, on the other hand, had acted like I'd chosen a human, which was worrisome. They'd spent years harping and fixing me up with every female shifter in a hundred-mile radius. All they'd ever wanted was for me to find a fated mate. At least, that was all they ever talked about. Especially Mother.

Again, at the merest thought of her, a full picture of the waitress popped into my head. I'd never met a woman more beautiful, and that wasn't only the mating bond talking. Had I met her on the street, I would've thought the same.

Normally, I wasn't a big fan of blondes. Some guys had a preference for blondes, especially that shade because it was so seldom natural and meant the woman specifically cared about her appearance. I didn't subscribe to that theory. I liked a natural woman.

Something about this woman, though, told me she was all natural. And her hair had smelled like strawberries. I'd breathed her in as we stood staring at one another. I'd noted every fleck of blue in her eyes, every strand of hair that had fallen loose from the bun on top of her head, which was adorably messy—*adorably messy?*—as if she'd been running around busily all day. It was easy to believe she'd been running her legs off since my mom was her boss.

She was shorter than me, but taller than average for a woman. But it was the eyes that did it for me. Ice blue. An unwavering gaze. When it met mine, I couldn't be certain that my heart wouldn't shatter into a million pieces.

Sure as fuck, she was different than any of the other girls in the pack. Most females were dark with tan skin, dark hair, and brown eyes. It was a signature trait of the members of the Keller pack. Everything about this girl was different, though. She was like a beacon of light. She was pale, light, smaller… it made her stand out in the crowd.

It astounded me that I'd never seen her before. I certainly would've known if we had crossed paths. And if we had, I wouldn't have been a forty-year-old bachelor, that was a hundred-fucking-percent for sure.

My wolf growled.

"I know. I want her, too." I stopped pacing and forced myself to sit in a leather armchair against the wall. We both needed a moment of calm.

I stared with a deep yearning at the wooded area behind the house. I'd spent many moonlit nights running through those woods. The longing ached in my gut, warring with the extra power surging through my blood. I needed to shift as soon as possible to get the pent-up energy out of my system.

Finally, after a time that seemed to stretch into an eternity, my parents calmly strolled into the study.

My dad led the way, which surprised me since Mom was the power figure in their personal relationship. At home, she was the authoritarian. She made the rules. Dad made sure the rules were followed. Not that we were still at that stage of my life, but something had gone down, and I was only here to find out what it was.

My mother followed close behind him with her hands clasped behind her back. She didn't look at me, didn't even acknowledge my existence with more than a nostril flare directed my way as if I smelled rancid.

This was not good.

I stood, looked at each of them for a second, then crossed my arms over my chest. "I've been here for a few hours now, and I want answers. I deserve answers." My teeth were clenched, but it was more to keep the growl from my wolf locked down than from fury at them keeping me waiting.

Dad raised his hands, his palms facing me. "I understand your frustration, son. Let's sit and talk it out."

I sighed. This wasn't a *let's talk it out* situation. We didn't have anything to talk out. I'd found my mate. Period.

"I just met the woman I'm fated to be with, and you dragged me in here, caged me up like I'm some kind of rabid fucking animal unfit to be in the company of your delicate guests." It was a barb aimed at my mother, but she stood unfazed. I glared at her. "How dare you treat me like that in front of the pack?"

Finally, she reacted. Mother stepped forward and lifted her gaze. "Ty, you have to trust us. You know that everything we do, we do for a reason. A calculated reason."

"Really? You acted like the woman—a woman whose name I didn't even get a chance to ask—was less than you are." Another barb aimed at Mom. This one hit. She frowned, but I wasn't about to be shut down. Their behavior was inexcusable. "Honest to fuck, tell me why you reacted the way you did."

I was a forty-year-old man with the weight of our businesses on my shoulders. I knew responsibility to the family and to the pack. I was next in line to be alpha. No way in hell would I let them get by with whatever they purported this to be. I'd found the woman I wanted to take as my mate, and I'd been led from the room like a fucking child.

It was unacceptable.

Embarrassing.

Mother sighed. "You can't mate with her."

"First, you can't tell me who the hell I can mate with, and second, why the fuck not?" My fury overwhelmed me, and I stormed over to the wall, punching it to get rid of some of my rage. A painted family portrait that hung opposite my father's desk shook, threatened to fall, but didn't.

My wolf would not stay quiet much longer. I *needed* to be with the girl.

Now.

"Ty, your mother's right." Dad took a seat behind his desk as if this was a casual business discussion.

No fucking way. He was taking her side, and still I had no idea why. "What the hell is wrong with you two? Fated mate. You know what that means better than anyone." Of course, they did. It was how they became husband and wife. How I came into existence.

No one moved, and they continued to stare at me. I sat in a chair and waited. There had to be an explanation. Something that would make their behavior seem reasonable.

Dad nodded and folded his arms so that his suit jacket tightened across his massive chest. I was tough, but he was the alpha. If he felt this strongly, there was nothing I could do, but I had to try. "Some things are non-negotiable, Ty. This is one of those issues."

"Why? What is it about that girl that scares you so much?" My gaze shifted back and forth between my parents. "I saw your reaction to her. As soon as you saw what was happening, you both looked as if you might pass out." I hadn't imagined it. It meant something. None of us were leaving this room until they told me.

They shared a look that said they were trying to decide how much information they could give me without letting me have it all.

It took every ounce of control I possessed not to tear the whole fucking house down. "What the fuck is going on?"

"She's not the right fit for you." Mother leaned against the desk and began unbraiding her hair. "You'll just have to trust us, Ty. We would never lead you down the wrong path." Softer, she added, "Your future is too important."

"You want me to trust *you*?" A piercing chuckle escaped my throat. "Trust the people who have been pushing... No, not just pushing, but poking and prodding and harping at me to find my fated mate? You've dragged me to every ceremony for the last twenty something years, and yet when I find her, you pull me away like we're about to infect one another with rabies." I popped my knuckles and stared out the window. I wanted to be anywhere in the fucking world except this house with these people. "Explain yourselves."

"It's a complicated situation," Dad began, and he stared at me like he was trying to use his mind to control mine. "But you have to understand that she's not the woman we've always envisioned for you."

I didn't know if other families dealt with this kind of thing, but I wasn't about to let them do this to me. I sent them both a scathing glare. I was a fucking adult with a life of my own.

"It doesn't matter what you want *or* what you envisioned. This isn't up to you or to me or to her. *Fate* decided this. The way it's always been meant to be." This was *their* sermon. *Wait for it to happen. Fate knows what she's doing. Maybe you aren't ready. When it's time, when you find her, you'll know.* Well, for God's sake, I knew.

Mother stepped closer to me and laid her hand on my arm. "Ty, you're older than she is. You have money and power, and she has... plates and spoons. It will be the only thing people can talk about." And there it was. "She doesn't fit into the life we've picked for you."

Whenever Mother lied—or *fibbed*, as she liked to call it—she fiddled with her earlobe. I watched as she tugged and rubbed her ear around her diamond earring. When I was young, I'd found it endearing because I had no idea what it signified. Now, it annoyed me because I knew exactly what it meant.

"Bullshit." She'd given the ear one too many pulls, and I had to call her out on it. "For fuck's sake, Mother." No one could say her name quite as angrily as I could. "You didn't come from a wealthy family. Your argument doesn't hold water because Dad chose you in spite of that." She had a lot of nerve acting like she was the high and mighty lady of the manor, and all others were beneath her.

I squinted in her direction and watched as she moved around the desk to stand by my father. I'd seen this move before. This was their moment of being a united front. Her face reddened because her *united front* was really nothing more than a sign that I had her backed into a corner. She was out of moves and needed Dad's support to battle.

I didn't have any choice but to move in for the kill while she was busy wiggling and twitching under my thumb. I stared hard at my mother as I spoke again. "Why can't you just be honest with me? Don't you think you owe me that much after the spectacle you made of me tonight?" Once the humiliation set in, and it would, pissed off would twist into enraged, and there wasn't anything that would protect them—mostly Mom—from my wrath.

My father stood, then started pacing from wall to wall behind his desk. My mother sank into his chair. They were beaten. They only needed to accept it and tell the fucking truth. My father's expression grew more distraught with every step, and my mother's cheeks flushed with color. A bead of sweat rolled from my father's temple to his jaw.

I'd never seen my parents so cagey.

"I don't understand what has you both wound up so tightly about this woman." The tone of my voice reached a pitch and volume not really suitable for a family discussion, but that was where we were. "Who the *fuck* is she?"

"Her name is Liza Mims." Mother stood and walked over to me. "She's a caterer. That's the only reason she was at the ceremony tonight."

There were worse things than being mated to someone who could cook. "And?"

Mother nodded. "Her parents are Scott and Rory Mims. Scott's a family lawyer, and Rory is a seamstress in town."

Things were becoming clearer. I knew those names. Mason and Michael Mims were Liza's older twin brothers. We'd attended several sports camps together, although they were several years younger than me. I still remembered them pulling pranks on the head coaches. They were a riot. "She doesn't look anything like her older brothers."

"Well, she wouldn't. She's adopted," Dad answered as he held the lighter to the end of his pipe before moving to the chair in the seating section in front of the fireplace. He was as anxious as I was, and if I smoked, I'd be lighting one now.

Instead, all I could do was sort through all the information, the scant bit I had. *Liza*—her name—was adopted. But it didn't explain why my parents were so adamant that I not mate with Liza. "How does that play into the fact that you're forbidding me to be with the woman *fate* decided I should be with?" They couldn't possibly believe they knew better than fate.

Mother turned her back to me and walked across the room. "Some things are just meant to stay buried, Ty."

Not when it affected my fucking future. "What the hell aren't you telling me?" It would have to be a fucking good reason for me to deny the pull I'd felt to that woman.

My mother stared at me for several long seconds. "Ty, I'm begging you. Please, forget about Liza. Reject her and find another mate."

My father took a long puff from his pipe. "There are swarms of girls ready to give you everything they have. You can choose a nice, respectable girl that's better suited for you. You have your pick of the litter, so to speak." He hadn't aimed for the obvious dad joke, it just happened naturally.

"You said yourself that having a fated mate is a blessing—an opportunity to live your life with the one person you were *designed* to be with." I stared at my mother, again using her own words to emphasize the ridiculousness of whatever point she was busy trying not to make. "You've been planting that into my head since I was a little kid. Now, fate gives me a mate, hands her to me at a time when we shouldn't have been together." Wouldn't have been if I'd listened to my gut and told my mother I didn't want to attend her soiree. "And you want me to completely reject this woman and the very idea of a fated mate that you've always told me reigned supreme?"

I leveled a glare at my mother. "And you're keeping secrets from me. If you can't tell me *exactly* why I shouldn't be with my mate"—and I wanted all the dirty details—"then I'll ignore your counsel and continue with my plans to pursue her."

"We don't want you to be with her." My father narrowed his eyes at me, and a low growl emanated from him. This was getting worse by the minute.

"That's not good enough. It doesn't matter, anyway." He wasn't the only wolf in the room. My growl was louder than his. "I'm not asking your permission."

The air in the room grew stale and heavy as my parents stared at me in shock. I wasn't a rebel. We'd never been a family of rebels, so this situation was unusual for all of us.

Mom looked at my father. She was nervous and needed consolation. In the absence of my father doing it, I wanted to console her. She was my mother, but I couldn't stop her wringing her hands as she paced between the door and the desk.

My father said nothing, only stared straight ahead with the resolve of a war general. He wouldn't budge. He was the alpha. He bent for no man.

When I was a boy, I'd seen him like this a few times when I'd screwed up. Once when I ruined one of Mother's houseplants with spray paint I'd found in the garage, then another time when I'd had a fistfight with one of my cousins. He'd simply stared at me until I admitted what I'd done and swore, on my honor—and he'd made a big deal of honor back then—that I would never do it again. I'd been weak, afraid of what he would do if I didn't tell the truth.

Finally, after what seemed another eternity, Mother spoke. "Ty, your father and I don't condone this, nor will we support your pursuit of *that* woman." She cleared her throat and looked away from me. She felt strongly enough to put off having grandchildren. That said something. "But if you feel strongly that this is the mate for you, and you choose to pursue her then... we can't stop you."

I nodded. That was all I needed to hear. But now, they needed to hear me. "I will expect you both to treat Liza with respect, regardless of whatever dumbass thing you have against her." I sliced my hands through the air. I owed it to all of us to give it one more try. "This imaginary issue needs to become a nonissue. Immediately." Neither of them moved or spoke, just averted their eyes.

I didn't want to stay in the study another second. Not waiting for a response, I turned and left, making my way to the wing of the house where I had a private residence.

My body was taut with tension with no way for it to escape. Even though this had been one of the longest days of my life, one of so many ups and downs that I'd lost count, I needed a run. Sleep would wait for me to shift and let the wolf out. As soon as I stripped out of my suit, my wolf took over. I raced out of the house and into the woods that surrounded our estate.

My wolf powered through the trees, joy and elation filling all the muscles and joints and sinew of my being. The cool, crisp air and the night sky beckoned me deeper into the woods.

I kept running, all the thoughts in my head silenced as the cool air rushed through my fur. The ground beneath the pads of my paws was cold, and it passed in a blur of color subdued by the darkness. Animals rustled in the brush around me, their scents mixing with the woodsy and pungent aroma of pine needles.

The stars twinkled above me, and I was connected to them like companions in the night. My wolf and I were in sync, not just with one another, but with the earth. There was nothing in the world quite like it.

Except… there was. I'd felt it tonight. When I'd found *her*—when I'd found Liza. She would be mine, my fated mate.

An electric current coursed through me, giving me strength as I ran. My heart raced with excitement and joy. For the first time in a long time, I felt truly alive. Nothing else mattered but this moment: me and nature intertwined in harmony.

I would have to court Liza, and that worried me. I wasn't what anyone would call a romantic. In fact, they'd call me whatever the extreme opposite of a romantic was. Here I was, the prince of the south, and I had no idea what I needed to do to convince her that we belonged together.

I was a good fuck—I'd been told that a couple of times—but I didn't excel at wooing women, and any woman I'd ever been involved with could attest to that.

I forced air into my lungs with long, deep breaths, trying to calm the fire raging inside me. I was desperate to be with her, so much so that I couldn't catch my breath. But I had to do this the right way. I had to take the time to get to know her and prove my intentions were genuine.

All I knew for sure was that she could either be my salvation or my downfall, depending on how she reacted to my pursuing her.

Time would tell whether I'd made the right decision by going against my parents' wishes and trusting my wolf.

***

The next morning, I rushed down the stairs, anxious to eat breakfast and plan how to woo Liza.

I wasn't surprised in the least to find my best friend, Bryce Fulton, lounging at the table in my dining room—it was much smaller than the one at the country club—with his feet crossed.

I could take a lot, but I would not be taking heat from Bryce. Not today. "Lose the cheesy grin or I'm kicking your ass." I rolled my eyes and pulled up a chair next to him.

"Touchy, touchy." He dropped his feet and sat forward, resting his elbows on the table. "I come bearing breakfast and many congratulations for finding your fated mate."

I stared at the platter of pastries and fruit. "Where's the meat?"

"I wasn't sure how long you'd be, so your cook stuck it in a warming drawer." Bryce, asshole that he was, snapped his fingers in the air to call for one of the kitchen staff. "My man's ready for his meat."

"Really?" I didn't treat anyone the way he did. "What are you really doing here, Bryce?"

"For the scoop, obviously." He put an appropriate amount of boredom in his tone, then popped a grape into his mouth. "What the hell was up with your parents last night?"

"They don't approve of fate's choice of mate for me." Softer, I added, "Liza." I took a sip of orange juice, then looked at him. He was wearing his dumb expression, with the arched eyebrows and pursed lips. "Liza's the waitress."

"Yeah, I got that. Saw it up close and personal. We all did." He cleared his throat. "You are all anyone's talking about."

"Damn it." I should've figured the rumor mill was churning. Nothing was sacred in this fucking town. By now, mouths were running and stories were being concocted. Truth would be a minor factor in this game. "Fuck." The last thing I needed was some tawdry story spreading through the community.

"You can't really blame them." Bryce's lips turned up into a sly grin. "They've all been anxiously awaiting the moment the prince of the south finds the one he's destined to be with. And if you didn't, there were about a thousand women ready to pounce on you as soon as you gave them the go-ahead." He shook his head and clicked his tongue. "You broke a lot of hearts last night, buddy."

"Whatever. Doesn't give anyone the right to discuss my relationship, or lack thereof, with Liza." I cracked my knuckles, then grabbed a pastry and bit into it. "It's no one's fucking business."

Bryce nodded. "Agreed, but you have to admit, this is a juicy piece of gossip. Especially since Liza is a waitress and you're…" He paused. "Royalty."

"Yeah. Such is life." I wasn't complaining as much as stating a fact. No matter what I did it would be newsworthy, simply because of who my parents were. "I hate that it fucking matters." I looked around for the bacon and sausage that still hadn't arrived. "To my parents and the rest of the pack."

Bryce nodded again. "Look, I don't presume to tell the great prince of the south what to do, but my advice is that if you want her, you have to prove her worth to them. Show them that you're serious about Liza and that she's worthy of being your mate."

I shouldn't have had to prove anything. I was their son, the future leader of our pack. This was a crock of shit and a whole lot of ridiculousness for no reason. No one else had ever had to prove the worth of the mate fate chose for them. It was decided and a done deal. It might sound like a poor little rich boy problem, and maybe it was, but as the poor little rich boy, it pissed me off. "Easier said than done."

He narrowed his eyes. "What did your parents say about her?"

I sighed. "That she isn't good enough. Not the woman they would've chosen." I shake my head. "It's bullshit. They're hiding something, but I told them I was moving forward, with or without their permission."

"Aww, my little Tyson is all grown up." He reached across the table and patted my hand.

I jerked away. "Don't be a condescending prick."

He laughed and tapped the table with his thumb. "What do your parents know that the rest of us don't?"

That was the million-dollar question.

"I'm not sure." I pushed the plate away, no longer hungry. "I've been thinking about it all night and I can't, for the life of me, understand why they're against me mating with Liza."

"You know, you have plenty of money and resources to do a background check. Why don't you do some digging on this girl?" Bryce shrugged. "Since your parents aren't talking, maybe you can get to the bottom of it."

"Yeah, maybe." I sat back in the chair and took a deep breath, then stared at the ceiling. I didn't have any better ideas. It couldn't hurt to do some digging and get a better understanding of my future mate's past. Especially since my parents felt so strongly about me not pursuing her.

"So, what's the plan? Are you going to let fate work its magic or do you have a grander plan to show her that you're the Romeo to her Juliet, the Jack to her Rose, the Jim to her Pam?" Bryce glanced at his phone, probably texting one of the handful of girls he dated casually.

"You watch way too much television." But I grinned. "Actually, I could use your help."

Chapter 5 - Liza

"Hold on a minute." I raised my finger, letting the driver of the red convertible know that I was almost done pumping gas. He'd already slammed his horn, but I couldn't make the pump spew faster.

The man threw his hands in the air as if I was making his bad day even worse, but I could've told him a thing or two about bad days. I had no control over the amount of traffic at the gas station, so he needed to lay off my ass and move along.

My parents had called me over to their house this morning, meaning I wasn't in the best of moods. A forced visit with the fam never boded well. They had, no doubt, heard the rumors about what happened at the country club last night. Based on the way my mom had stuttered into the phone, they were concerned. Not just the kind of concern you had when you worried about your child's grade in math class. This was a whole other level of stress.

I didn't blame them. Our family wasn't exactly high class, barely middle class, and the rumors that had circulated in a few short hours had solidified that fact.

"Miss, are you done?" The driver of the convertible tapped his fingers on his steering wheel and hung his head out the window.

"Does it look to you like I'm done?" The fucking nozzle was still in my tank, and I still had my hand on the trigger.

Asshole.

A small twinge of guilt washed over me. It wasn't fair for me to take my stress out on this guy, not any more than it was fair of him to be a prick, but I'd only managed a few hours of sleep the night before. I'd tossed and turned all night. Maybe if the impatient driver saw the dark circles under my eyes, he'd take pity on me and back his attitude the fuck up.

I finished pumping and replaced the gas cap before hopping in my car. I gave him a sarcastic wave as I drove off toward my childhood home. Going home was always annoying. I was on my own now. Last thing I wanted was to go backward.

Ty Keller's face popped into my mind, and I jerked the wheel to the right, almost driving off the road. Not because I was startled, but because the picture of him in my mind made me want to jerk something.

Why did he have to be so goddamn handsome? The reaction I'd had the night before was completely unlike me. Yes, I'd had little crushes as a teenager, and I knew the difference between a hot guy and one that had been hit with the ugly stick too many times, but Ty had attributes. So many fucking attributes. How was a girl supposed to remain immune?

He was on a completely different level. His jet-black hair was just a bit too long, too shiny, too *everything*. That alone was enough to cause any woman to stumble over her words. But when you combined that with his striking gray eyes and chiseled jawline, it was like any form of rational thought I'd ever had dissolved.

He'd cast a spell on me, or some other magic was in play, and that scared the absolute shit out of me. I didn't need any distractions in my life, especially not one as powerful as Ty Keller. I needed to focus on myself and make sure my catering business didn't suffer due to my inability to function like a normal person, thanks to my encounter with Ty last night.

Sabrina seemed to think everything would go smoothly from this point forward. "You've met your fated mate, the hardest part is over," she'd said as though she had firsthand knowledge of the process.

I didn't believe it; not for a second. Apparently, neither did my parents.

I pulled up to my childhood home. It was a small ranch-style house with white vinyl siding that Dad had upgraded years ago after a wind storm, and blue shutters at each of the windows. The front yard was full of memories where I had spent countless hours playing tag with my siblings, digging for worms, and chasing the neighborhood cats.

The memory that stood out the most was of me running around with a red bucket collecting tulips from my mom's garden. I could still picture how bright and yellow they were against the lush green grass and the warmth of the summer sun on my skin.

If only things were still that simple. Life had a way of kicking you in the ass. Just when you thought things were on the upswing, you had to meet your fated mate in front of the entire pack. I'd been wearing a waitress uniform, for fuck's sake.

"Hey!" I called from the front foyer. "I'm here."

The clicking of nails on the floor alerted me to an incoming attack from Chip, the family dog. He jumped up, balanced his front legs on my shin, and whined, pawing like he was trying to climb me, ready to be held.

"Hello, boy. How are you? I've missed you." I cuddled him and kissed the side of his face as he licked my chin. He seemed to have missed me. It was nice to be missed.

For a chihuahua, he was surprisingly calm. Well, compared to other chihuahuas I'd met. He wriggled and writhed until I set him down, allowing him to smell my shoes to try figure out where I'd been.

If he only knew what I'd been through the past twenty-four hours, he might've been more sympathetic instead of walking away—likely in search of his food bowl—once he'd tired of sniffing me.

"There she is." My mom walked out of the rounded doorway that led to the kitchen with a dish towel draped over her shoulder.

She was the one who taught me how to cook. I wouldn't have anything or be anything today without her. Seeing her made me feel at home again. A sense of relief washed over me, calming my frayed nerves.

This place and these people always had that effect on me.

"Hi, Mama." I wrapped her in as big a hug as I could without causing her worry and waited until she pulled away before I let go. She ushered me into the kitchen and began to tell me about all the home-improvement issues that still needed to be fixed and the ones that were no longer a concern. "Your dad finally fixed that leak in the back bedroom, though I didn't think he ever would. He's just so busy with his practice, it's hard to get him to commit to anything related to this old house."

She might've called it *this old house,* but she loved the place. She'd added touches of herself over the years and updated them as she changed. Thanks to that, there was no mistaking this was *her* place, no matter how much she complained about it.

"The house looks great, Mom." I gestured to the kitchen. "You keep it spotless, as always."

"It may look great on the surface but this house is a lot older than you. It's starting to fall apart from the center. Looks can be deceiving, you know." As she went to stir a pot of soup on the stove, I grabbed a piece of bread from the countertop.

"So, what's new with you? How's business?" She eyed me suspiciously, no doubt trying to figure out how to broach the subject of Ty or to entice me into bringing him up. There was no way she hadn't heard about last night's fiasco.

I took a deep breath, then huffed out an exasperated sigh. "It's been interesting. You already know I catered the lunar mating ceremony." Mom had been one of my first calls as soon as the contract was signed. I paused when Dad entered the kitchen, smiling as he walked straight toward me.

"What did I miss?" He hugged me and kissed me on the forehead, just as he'd done every day when he came home from work since I was a baby or when I came to visit.

Mom raised her eyebrows. "She was just starting to tell me about the catering job at the lunar mate ceremony last night." She gave him a look that I probably wasn't supposed to see of lifted eyebrows and wide eyes. It as much told him to be quiet as it did ask a question.

He didn't pay much heed. Instead, Dad's face fell. "Ah, yes. I'm sure that was quite the event. How did it go?" His tone had shifted from one of interest to one of concern. He'd probably been down at the barbershop or the hardware store or wherever men his age got their gossip. So, he'd probably heard enough already to know it wasn't good… if he didn't know the whole story. Chances were, he'd already been made aware that even if my fated mate had wanted me, his family did not.

"Well, you know. There's always room to improve, but it went all right," I said slowly, trying not to give too much away in case they'd not heard every shitty detail. "It started out like a usual event. Some of my staff called in sick, so I had to fill in as a waitress." That wasn't so unusual. It happened, and I dealt with it when it did. That was the mark of a good, solid business. "Everyone I spoke to had wonderful compliments about the food. But then …" I trailed off, my gaze shifting back and forth between them.

"We heard about your *encounter* with Ty Keller." Mom turned the stove off and turned to face me, giving me her full attention.

"Oh, I'm sure you did." I bit off a chunk of bread, thinking about the rumors that had been flying around town. "It was horrible. I was standing there, and then I could hear them all saying that I'm not worthy of Ty and his royal family." The absurdity of it wasn't lost on me. I wasn't in his social group or his economic class, but I wasn't anything to be feared, either. "For God's sake, they're all acting like I'm some kind of homeless criminal."

It was insulting and hurtful. Kind of ridiculous, too, since I had been raised by wonderful people who valued life and happiness, courtesy and kindness.

"Now, Liza." Dad placed his hand on my shoulder and squeezed gently. "Don't listen to the naysayers or focus on their immature gossiping. We know your worth and we raised you to recognize it, as well."

He was right, of course, because my father was always right. It begged the question of why I was allowing the words of others to influence the way I felt. But the public humiliation still stung.

Mom interrupted my thoughts. "We're worried about you, Liza. It seems you're being thrown into the middle of something you weren't particularly looking for."

My parents had always been overly protective of me. Especially as a teenager, when my body had started changing and boys became more... noticeable.

Through it all, though, I'd never had a boyfriend in high school. My parents kept me so busy with extracurricular activities that I didn't have time to even think about the opposite sex. Between ice skating, ballet, debate team, volunteering on the weekends at the local food bank, and more, I was lucky to have time to eat and sleep.

It wasn't until college that I actually started dating. Even then, though, I'd had my older twin brothers breathing down my neck, making sure I didn't get in trouble or date the wrong kind of guy. Whenever things started heating up, there they were, popping up out of nowhere to interrupt and cock block, so to speak.

But this situation with Ty was different, and Mom was right: it wasn't something I anticipated or could have controlled, and I sure as hell hadn't gone looking for it. I'd resigned myself to being mate free, to enjoying my time alone, and to a love 'em and leave 'em lifestyle. All I'd wanted was to grow my business and make my parents proud.

I was grateful for the love and concern of my family. Because of them, I was smart, self-sufficient, independent, a business owner, and a thirty-year-old virgin. Which had never really bothered me because I wasn't interested enough in anyone to surrender that particular attribute.

Until now.

Ty was definitely not inexperienced when it came to women and sex. He probably had a list of women on a rotating schedule who saw to his sexual needs. Poor bastard. And now, unfortunately for him, not only was he fated to someone who fell several rungs below him on the societal ladder, but he would also be dealing with an inexperienced virgin.

I sighed. I probably wasn't what he'd had in mind.

"I know you're worried," I said. "But don't be. We didn't even speak to each other, and his parents didn't seem too enthralled by the idea of him pursuing me." If I were honest, he hadn't seemed too enchanted, either.

Mom nodded in understanding, but they both still seemed uneasy at the idea of me finding a fated mate.

An alarm screamed through the speaker of my phone, reminding me that it was time to take my medicine. From the age of thirteen, when I first started my period, I had been plagued by horrible bouts of cramps and pain, not to mention sporadic, uncontrollable bleeding. Plus, there'd always been the weird reactions of men, the feelings I didn't understand. So, I'd been on hormone medication for the majority of my life. At the peak of all the worst times, my mother took me to the doctor to help regulate my cycles. Ever since, I'd taken strong pills that masked the scent of my pheromones making me less hormonal and less potent to men. A person could set their watch, hell the world clock, by the regularity with which I took them. In all the years I'd been on them, I'd never missed a single dose.

"Do you even *like* Ty?" Mom crossed her arms and leaned against the kitchen counter as I dug around in my bag for the little bottle of pills.

I shrugged. "Honestly, I've never really interacted with him. Yesterday was the first time I'd ever seen him, so I can't say whether I do or don't like him." Oh, he'd drawn a response all right, but I didn't want to say that to my mother.

She scowled, unable to hide her worry. "Maybe it's a blessing that the two of you found each other." She didn't sound convinced.

The pills weren't in my purse, so I gave up looking. "Why wouldn't it be?" I popped the rest of the bread into my mouth.

Dad smiled gently. "We're just concerned given your, err, *condition*."

We'd always called it my *condition*.

Mom held her hands up and came to stand beside me. "Don't worry, Liza. It shouldn't be a problem as long as you keep taking your medication." She wrapped her arms around me so tightly I thought my lungs would pop.

"You're probably right." I patted Mom on the back. She shouldn't have this kind of anxiety about an adult daughter. "You really shouldn't worry. Everything will work out the way it's meant to."

Mom pulled away and nodded, the worry still evident in her eyes. I hugged Dad, then grabbed my keys and headed out the door.

I had another event to work at the Presley Acres Country Club. Along with the lunar mating festival, I'd been contracted to cater an after-party for the ceremony to celebrate any matches that may have occurred. Never in a million years had I thought I would be included in that particular celebration.

As I backed out of the driveway, my thoughts drifted back to Ty.

Warmth spread through me at the thought of him, and I smiled. Maybe Mom was right. This could be a blessing, but only time would tell.

Walking into the country club, I tried to count how many plates we needed to prepare. While deep in thought, trying to remember the projected head count, Cecily Banks appeared at my side and tapped my shoulder. I jumped, gasped, and turned; Kung Fu Panda mode engaged.

Holy shit. Where'd she come from?

Cecily was young, beautiful, and an heiress. She was exactly the kind of woman that belonged with a Keller. That fact didn't go unnoticed. "I want to know, and I think everyone else does, too. How'd you do it?"

I had a thousand things on my mind, and deciphering one of Cecily's mystery questions would take more brain power than I had to spare. Instead, I pinched my face into a scowl. "I'm sorry. What?" For once, my tone wasn't pleasant or ingratiating. I was learning to use my annoyance to my benefit.

Kelis, another heiress with more money than good sense, stood next to her friend, a foul expression on her face.

"How'd you get Tyson to look at you like that?" Cecily crossed her arms and glared so deeply it seemed as if her anger had ventured into the depths of my soul. She was one of those people who called everyone by their given name. It irritated me.

Also, she was new in town, but she'd acted as if she owned it from the moment she'd arrived. Her family had only moved to Presley Acres a few months ago, then immediately made themselves well known by purchasing one of the most outlandish estates in the state of Texas. They had acres and acres of land, and a house that was long and wide with enough rooms to fit most of the town inside for a sleepover. It had once been a boarding house that had been converted to a mansion for some TV show and then put on the market for millions of dollars.

Cecily's family had money, and they weren't afraid to rub it in everyone's faces. On top of her wealth, Cecily had an unearthly level of pride and assumed privilege that made her a tyrant. She always seemed to be on the prowl for the next trinket, position, or man that would make her happy for that moment.

I took a step back. "I'm still not... What?"

She pointed a long, manicured finger at my face. "The mating ceremony was *my* chance to meet Ty and show him what he could have." She waved her hand down her skinny, model-like figure. "I want to know how you *tricked* him into thinking you are his mate."

I blinked at her. It seemed a few of her brain cells had gone on strike. There was no way to *trick* someone into a fated mate daze—at least none I knew of. The power that had taken over my body the previous night was uncontrollable, undeniable, and un-trickable.

I cleared my throat and smoothed the wrinkles out of my uniform. No matter what this bitch had to say, I refused to surrender my professionalism. Especially here at the country club in front of so many clients. Sighing, I forced a smile. "I'm sorry, Cecily, but I didn't trick anyone."

Kelis slapped the back of her hand against Cecily's shoulder and let out a sarcastic laugh, egging her friend on. "Did you hear that? She says *she* didn't do anything wrong. Are we supposed to believe that fate would be so cruel as to give Ty such a *common* mate?" She sneered at me. "You're expecting everyone to believe you didn't go to some witch doctor and poison him with a potion into wanting you?"

I rolled my eyes but kept my composure, though my brothers' voices rang in my head, telling me to *punch her in the tit.*

As tempting as that suggestion might have been—and boy, was it tempting—I refrained.

"Can you imagine? Tyson Keller being fated to *her?* A common servant girl." Cecily chortled and looped her arm through Kelis's. "Common trash."

I took a deep breath and allowed them to spew their bullshit. It was going to take a lot more than this to make me stoop to their level. We were in public, after all. Away from all the prying eyes, things might have been different, but it was easy to maintain my composure here.

They kept up their taunts and accusations, but I tuned them out, waiting for the perfect opportunity to walk toward the kitchen without them following me like hecklers on a dirty street corner. We hadn't drawn much of a crowd, but people were looking, and I definitely didn't need someone to take a video of this.

As I stood there occupied by my thoughts, I felt it again—that familiar and not wholly unpleasant tug in my chest. I couldn't fake it. There was no way I could trick anyone into feeling it. *My mate.*

I spotted Bryce over Cecily's shoulder—Sabrina had enjoyed a few rolls in the hay with him—and then I caught a glimpse of Ty coming in from the back entrance of the club. He wore a pair of khaki shorts that went almost to his knees and a blue polo shirt. His hair was windblown, and his face was red, probably because he'd just come off the golf course, but he still looked fine as hell.

He lifted his gaze, and it locked on me. A slow smile spread across his face. Without a doubt, he felt the pull, too. He froze.

Cecily and Kelis continued patronizing me, completely unaware that *my* fated mate had walked into the room. I didn't even bother trying to process their words as Ty strode in my direction.

His smooth and confident voice broke through their comments. He didn't glance away from me as he spoke to Cecily and her clone. "Need I remind you two that gossip and rumors aren't very ladylike. Chances are, you'll never find a mate that way. You should know better." He looked pointedly at Kelis. "You carry the Keller name and are an extension of my family. I expect you to behave as such."

His voice was deep and commanding, sending chills through my body. I stared at his full lips, imagining how they might part or pucker if I stepped closer to him. His presence had some sort of magical effect on me that warmed me and softened my anger. It was as alarming as it was pure and perfect.

Cecily and Kelis looked at each other, their faces turning red.

"I apologize, Ty." Kelis folded her hands behind her back and stared at the floor.

"Your apology should be directed at Liza." He stared deep into my eyes as I pushed my feet harder onto the floor, hoping to anchor my body so I didn't fall over.

He knew my name.

That was surprising, but I couldn't focus on it. My brain had turned to mush as I breathed in Ty's musky scent. This man was as intoxicating as anything I'd ever had to drink.

Desire surged. Feelings overpowered, primal and powerful.

Kelis sighed loudly and turned to face me. "I'm sorry." She spewed the words as if she might vomit on my shoes, but she had done as Ty asked.

She and Cecily bowed their heads in deference before heading in the opposite direction like two scolded puppies. I didn't mind seeing it. Didn't mind that he'd humiliated them. Didn't even mind that they were ugly on the inside. All I cared about was that he was standing here. With me.

Once Ty and I were alone, a long, awkward silence filled the air between us. I had no idea what to do or say and found myself moving my arms into different positions. I rubbed my hands up and down my apron, crossed and uncrossed my arms, wrung my hands. Nothing felt natural, except being near him.

Apparently, he didn't know the correct protocol, either. He shifted nervously from foot to foot, although he was grinning like a schoolboy.

Did I detect a red glow emanating from his cheeks?

Holy fuck. That only made him hotter.

Finally, he broke the silence. Clearing his throat, he placed his hand on his chest. "I'm Ty Keller." He smiled shyly and held out his hand.

"I know." I allowed him to take my hand in his and almost recoiled from the overwhelming sensation of his touch. Electricity zinged through my body.

It was then that I knew for certain Ty Keller was my fated mate. Everything felt right and complete, despite the onlookers and the harassment I'd just endured from Kelis and Cecily.

I could only hope he felt the same way.

He smiled sweetly, and I couldn't look away. I didn't want to. "So, it looks like fate has chosen us. Though this isn't exactly how I planned to approach you after such a surprising revelation." He looked me up and down, and there was nothing skeevy about it. "I have to agree with fate, though. It knew what it was doing."

My heart skipped a beat, took a break, then raced ahead. I had no idea what was happening on my face. I hoped I was smiling, but I couldn't be sure.

Damn nerves.

I was so flustered by this man, his voice, those eyes, and his handsome face, that I was almost certainly making a fool out of myself. It probably wasn't very wise to open my mouth and make matters worse, but I had to say something. Damned if I knew what, though.

I mustered up every ounce of confidence I possessed. "I'm Liza. Liza Mims." Clearing my throat, I tried to make a second coherent statement. "I'm supposed to be working right now, making lunch for the event. I was on my way to the kitchen when Cecily and Kelis stopped me. Wow, those two sure have a lot to say."

I nervously covered my mouth with my hand, pinching my lower lip with my fingers. When I wasn't sure what to say these days, I said everything. Babbled.

Damn it.

He chuckled. "Yeah, it's a party to celebrate the newly found couples. You should be celebrating with me, not serving like the help."

Ouch. "I am *the help*."

"Fuck. I'm sorry. That's not what I meant." He ran his hand through his hair and frowned. But he wasn't frowning *at* me.

He knew he'd screwed up and was back peddling, but the damage had already been done.

I sighed. This could only go from bad to worse since he'd already thrown his unfiltered observation of my work out into the open air.

Deciding to put him out of his misery, I held up a hand. "I have a job to do. Whether or not you approve, I *am* the help."

Chapter Six - Ty

"What did you say to her?" Bryce approached me almost carefully. "From where I was standing, it looked like things were going well. Her body language said she wanted you. She was leaning in, smiling, but then, just like that"—he snapped his fingers in my face—"she stormed off. What the hell, man?"

Things *had* been going well up until the point I'd let my big mouth get the best of me. I'd called her the fucking help, for fuck's sake. Now, I'd potentially ruined any chance I had with Liza. I'd be lucky if she ever talked to me again without me having to force it.

Being that close to her had been torture. Every muscle, every bone in my body ached to pull her into my arms and never let go. I wanted to kiss those full lips and caress every inch of her smooth, pale skin. But instead of swooping in and claiming what was mine, I'd insulted her. I wanted to kick myself for being so stupid and ruining the moment.

"I called her *the help*." I lowered my head and stared at the floor. Of all the dumb ass things I could've said, I picked *the help*.

Bryce's eyes widened. "Fuck, man. That was a low blow." He shook his head and clicked his tongue against his teeth.

"I'm such an idiot." I slapped my forehead. "She owns the company, for fuck's sake. Did I commend her for that?" I shook my head because I'd lived it, and I still couldn't believe I'd done something so stupid. "No, because I am my mother's fucking son. I insulted her job." It really didn't matter that it hadn't been my intention. "Now she thinks I'm an asshole."

When Bryce laughed, I wanted to kill him. "Yeah, dumbass move. As a bonus, you've turned her off with your very first real conversation." Bryce scoffed. "I thought you were smoother than that."

Bryce always called me out when I needed to hear the truth, though I was already fully aware of my blunder.

"I didn't mean for it to come out the way it did." I shoved my hands into my pockets. "You should've seen the look in her eyes. She went from staring at me with interest and intrigue to complete disgust within seconds."

Bryce patted my shoulder like I needed consolation or advice. I didn't. What I needed was a minute with her so I could fix this. "Look at it this way. It's not the worst thing you could've said, but it definitely didn't win you any brownie points."

"What do I do now?" Desperation seeped into my voice as I tried to figure out how to fix what I'd fucked up.

Bryce shrugged. "I suggest you make a genuine effort to apologize. Make it right with her first, then take it from there."

I stared at my best friend, wondering when he'd become a relationship therapist. This was the same guy who slept with anything that had breasts and refused to commit to anyone for more than twenty-four hours. Yet, here he was, explaining the best way for me to win back Liza's trust.

"She may never speak to me again." I scanned the room. Almost everyone had moved to the dining room. Fuck. I couldn't duck out yet, but I damn sure was going to as soon as possible. "We'd better take our seats."

Bryce nodded and followed me into the dining hall. Someone's sharp gaze was burning a hole into the back of my head, and I turned to see who it was.

Cecily watched me from a corner table, licking her lips like a hungry lioness.

She was the host of the event and had invited my family and me. No doubt she'd expected the ceremony to come and go without me finding my mate. It had happened so many times before. After all, that was what everyone had come to expect of me—a forty-year-old man who'd been to every ceremony over the past two decades and walked out as single as he'd walked in. Why would anyone expect anything different this time?

Cecily, though, was more than just an innocent bystander who watched as I consistently failed at finding a mate. She'd expected me to fail one last time and had spent weeks lobbying my mother to make my father agree to a *selected* mate instead of a *fated* one.

There Cecily would be, just waiting to sink her claws into me. I'm sure it had blown up her entire world when Liza and I spotted each other last night. No wonder she'd cornered Liza at the first opportunity. She wanted to stake her claim.

Cecily's family was new in town, but they'd quickly made a name for themselves. That tended to happen when you had more money than God.

Unfortunately for her, money couldn't buy everything. Sure as fuck couldn't buy me.

What she had in looks, she completely lacked in maturity and class. So, it wasn't the least bit surprising that she made sure I had no choice but to reprimand her over the way she'd spoken to Liza.

Unfortunately, Cecily had chosen Jacob's wife to be her best friend. That didn't win her any additional points with me since I considered Kelis to be a total diva and gossip, but it had probably been a calculated move once she learned I hadn't found a mate at one of those soirees. It was a way into the family, to get close. For me, seeing the two of them together was like watching a volcano's lava slowly bubble to the surface. Eventually, there'd be an explosion with several casualties, though I intended to protect Liza from their venomous words and intentions.

I spotted Mother, who'd already taken a seat at our assigned table at the front of the room. She glanced toward the kitchen doors, probably wondering why lunch wasn't being served the second her ass touched the velvet pad of her chair.

Anxiety had my heart pounding painfully against my ribcage. I wanted nothing more than to burst into the kitchen and apologize to Liza, but I had to be smart about it. She was working, and I didn't want to draw anyone's attention to the kitchen and my need to see Liza just as the luncheon began.

I could bide my time and plan what I wanted to say this time so I didn't fumble it. I'd wait for a more opportune moment. The idea was to protect Liza from the talk. The last thing she needed was more talk.

I squared my shoulders and approached the table. No matter what happened, I was determined to make things right with Liza. That woman had already burrowed deep inside me, and I wouldn't lose her, not now that I'd found her. It didn't matter one fucking bit that it was less than twenty-four hours ago.

"Oh, there you are, Ty." Mother stood, and for the sake of appearances tried to hug me as if we hadn't had a heated discussion about Liza the night before. And for the sake of appearances, I allowed it. "Have a seat, dear."

I turned to see Bryce make his way to a table with his family. He eyed me with a smirk. In true Bryce Fulton fashion—and I knew because he'd told me—he was counting down the minutes until the end of the luncheon so he could hunt down, assess, and maybe even coax one of the women who hadn't been matched the night before. He always said that the day after a mating ceremony was the perfect time to console the heartbroken. And by *console*, he meant *fuck*.

Dad took his seat across from Mother and avoided making eye contact with me.

All right, so that was how it was going to be. I wasn't surprised. My family didn't deal with situations unless it affected the pack. In our family, we ignored our own shit. So, of course, we'd be behaving like that whole conversation last night never took place.

Like hell we were. I had other plans.

"How'd the two of you sleep last night?" I smiled over my glass of water and glanced at my mother, then my father. They weren't going to avoid anything if I had my say. And by fucking hell, I was having my say.

They eyed one another, then Dad cleared his throat. "Slept like a baby. And you?"

"Oh, I got a full fucking two hours of sleep." I scoffed, my voice deep and low. I wasn't going to make a scene, but they were going to know exactly how I felt about what happened. "Having your parents tell you that you can't be with your fated mate will do that to you. Tossing and turning, trying to make sense of the whole mess. Kind of a shitty way to go to bed, don't you agree?"

Mother's cheeks flushed as she turned to me and lowered her voice. "Tyson, this is not the time or place to discuss the situation. I know you think you have everything figured out and that we're a couple of idiots, but you need to trust me on this one. Keep your mouth shut until we're in the privacy of our own home."

Shit. She wasn't backing down.

Well, neither was I.

Though, she had a point. It wasn't the time. I didn't want to cause a scene.

Nodding, I took another sip of water. I'd seen Mother's particular brand of tantrum, and she didn't discriminate over the situations that brought them out. At least half the people in this room were personally aware that she could cut through a person's soul with her icy stare, but it wasn't like her to speak to me in that way. But again, that was a fight for a later time.

I let it go. For now.

The waiters and waitresses made their way through the dining room, serving the guests their lunch of tea sandwiches, sliced vegetables, and potato salad.

I craned my neck, trying to catch a glimpse of Liza whenever the kitchen door swung open. She stayed hidden. My heart sank deeper into my chest. I needed to speak with her but it seemed she had no intention of making an appearance during the luncheon.

"Did you see how lovely Cecily looks today?" Mother raised her eyebrows and nodded in Cecily's direction, interrupting my thoughts of Liza.

"Are you really asking me that right now?" I nearly choked on my sandwich. I didn't know how she'd managed to miss the scene Cecily started, and although it was possible that she might've, I doubted it. "That woman is a total bitch. She cornered Liza earlier."

Mother waved her hand in the air as she swallowed her mouthful of pimento cheese. "I'm sure she was congratulating Liza. Cecily's family is top-notch, Ty. You know that."

"Oh, really?" I laughed loudly and dramatically. "She wasn't congratulating her, Mother. Cecily was tearing her to shreds."

She thought for a moment and then responded softly. "Liza must've said something to provoke Cecily. I simply can't imagine her being rude for no reason."

I opened my mouth to respond, but Dad stood and made his way to the podium. The room fell silent.

He leaned against the wooden stand and spoke into the microphone. "Good afternoon, everyone. Thank you so much for joining us today at the celebratory luncheon." He paused, allowing everyone to applaud. "Before I begin, I'd like to take a moment to thank the Banks family for hosting this event. We're always grateful for their generosity and commitment to our community."

On cue, Cecily and her family stood, waving to the crowd, flashing their bright white smiles.

I clapped softly, trying hard not to roll my eyes.

Once the applause died down, Dad continued. "As you all know, we're here today to celebrate the couples that were matched up last night at the mating ceremony." He gestured toward Mother. "Many years ago, I discovered my fated mate at a similar ceremony. Persephone and I have been living a fairy tale ending ever since, and we wish the same contentment on our newly paired couples."

Mother gushed, clutching her chest and blowing a kiss to Dad. The woman sitting near Mother patted her back and whispered encouraging words. The whole spectacle nauseated me.

"Now, I'd like to read off the list of couples that fate revealed to each other last night. If each couple would please stand, we'd like to congratulate you with a commemorative certificate."

Dad proceeded to read off a list of names. Each couple stood, and most were holding hands or, at the very least, standing extremely close to one another. The audience applauded wildly to show their approval of the matches.

With every name, I wondered if he'd read my and Liza's names. He didn't.

"We hope you'll all stay and visit with one another, and, of course, congratulate the couples personally. Now that they've found one another, we want to offer words of encouragement as they move toward mating. Thank you again for coming."

My entire body went rigid as my father returned to his seat. How dare he not mention the fact that Liza and I had been matched?

Mother grabbed my hand and shook her head. She didn't want me to say anything, at least not here in front of everyone.

I bit my tongue as Dad sat across from us, finishing his lunch as if nothing was amiss.

Was I living in the fucking twilight zone?

As the other guests stood and mingled, I leaned forward, unable to hold my tongue any longer. "Why the hell didn't you acknowledge that I'd found my mate?"

Sighing, my father leaned forward and rested his elbows on the table. "You and Liza haven't agreed to pursue a relationship like the other couples have. It usually moves quickly when fated mates find one another. They agree to date, and not long after, they're mated."

Date and mate. Simple. But not so much for the future alpha if his parents didn't approve of his mate. I suddenly felt like a teenager who had no say or freedom in his choices whatsoever. Now I was really pissed, and they were going to hear about it.

"Must I constantly remind the both of you that I'm forty goddamn years old? I don't need your fucking *permission* to pursue Liza." My hands balled into fists as my inner wolf stirred. Dangerously. Angrily.

I couldn't shift here, it wouldn't be appropriate, but if my parents kept pushing me, I wouldn't be able to hold back. The fury building inside me was not quite feral, but animalistic, and it could only be soothed by the touch of my mate or a very long run in the woods.

My dad gritted his teeth and held tightly to the edge of the table. "Let me remind you of your place, Ty." His voice was steel, as fearsome as he'd always been, but I could bend steel.

A low growl escaped my throat as I leaned over the table, staring my father directly in the eyes. "Let me remind you of *your* place, Dad. You have to step down because you're getting too old to be the alpha. Your strength is waning. Everyone knows that." I paused and studied his face. He wasn't happy, but I continued, including my mother this time. "You've both pushed me to find a mate for that very reason. It's time for me to take over, and fate has finally granted you what you've always wanted. So, why the fuck are you both so against it? Against her?"

Mother whipped her head around and gave me the look that typically sent her staff running for cover. I wasn't her staff. I'd been immune to that look since elementary school.

I raised my head, preparing myself for whatever shitty excuse she intended to spew in my direction. Instead, we were cut off by Cecily and her parents, who appeared so quietly, I wondered if they'd purposefully stayed back and heard some of our conversation.

"May we join you?" Tina, Cecily's mother, pulled out a chair across from my mother.

She was short for a shifter, but it was easy to see where Cecily had gotten her good looks. Tina's long, dark hair was braided over her left shoulder, and her red dress hugged her body in all the right places.

I had a sudden vision of her closet—not that I generally thought much of a woman's closet— as something as large as a master bedroom with racks and racks of shoes, and a personal wardrobe stylist that picked the perfect outfit from long bars of clothes for every occasion.

I sighed. I did not want to deal with this right now—or ever, honestly—but as the future alpha, I had to be courteous to all members of the pack, even if I thought they were shitty people.

"Absolutely." Mother beamed at the overtly wealthy family. "Please, join us."

Robert, Cecily's father, took a seat next to Dad and slapped him on the back. "Good to see you. Good to see all of you." He glanced at each of us like he was running for office and needed our votes.

He reminded me of a used car dealer. He knew just the right words to butter up a customer before he went in for the kill, so to speak. I'd never realized how much politicians and used car salesmen had in common.

"Great speech." Robert chortled at Dad, then clapped him on the back again, this time squeezing his shoulder, too. "I couldn't have said it better myself."

Dad chuckled in response. "I'm really not a public speaker but it's part of the job."

Cecily took the seat next to me, grinning from ear to ear. The girl was gorgeous, no doubt about it.

She had long, dark brown hair and curves in all the right places. Although, I assumed some of those were placed there surgically. Her fake eyelashes went on for days and slightly resembled a spider above each eye, and her straight, white teeth were so perfect they didn't seem real. Like the rest of her, they probably weren't.

Every man I knew wanted to be with her, but she did nothing for me. Being near her only made me want to get to Liza even sooner.

"Did you enjoy yourself last night, Ty?" Tina leaned over Mother and smiled warmly.

"Yes, I did. It was a nice ceremony." I didn't give her much, and I could tell she was disappointed with my answer. Her mouth turned down and her eyes narrowed.

She, no doubt, wanted to ask specifically about Liza, but even if she'd asked, I wouldn't give her the details of my experience with Liza. Truthfully, it was nobody's damn business.

Cecily was surprisingly quiet, which led me to believe her parents had instructed her to let them do the talking. Everything was a perfectly measured and precisely calculated move with this family.

Tina eyed Robert, and he spoke up, right on cue. "We hear you were mated last night. Is that something you plan on pursuing?"

Damn. The guy wasn't holding back.

Mother opened her mouth to speak, but I cut her off. "Yes, I very much plan to pursue my mate."

I glanced at Dad, whose face was flaming with anger. He balled his fists on the table. He was still holding on to the idea of me *choosing* a mate, possibly Cecily.

What my father wanted didn't matter. He could be as angry at me as he wanted, but I refused to entertain the thought of a chosen mate when my fated one was right in front of me.

Speaking of my fated mate, I suddenly spotted Liza leaving out the side door. She held her purse and apron in her hand as she quickly walked to the exit.

There was no time to waste, so I didn't. I stood. "Please excuse me."

I walked toward Liza as my parents and Cecily's family stared in confusion.

"Liza!" That might've been a little louder than intended.

Several guests turned to see what the commotion was and to watch the interaction between the two of us. Tongues would be wagging tomorrow... If they even waited that long.

Liza stutter-stepped, seemed to hesitate for a moment, then eventually came to a quick halt as she stepped outside into the warm sunshine.

I followed her and closed the door behind me. *Let the rumor mill figure out what to do with that.* She kept moving, and I had to jog to get to her side. I ran my hand through my hair; a nervous habit I'd had since childhood. "Liza, I want to apologize again for being such an idiot earlier. Would you please be willing to give me a chance to make it up to you over dinner?"

Liza glanced over my shoulder toward the club. I turned to see my parents standing in the doorway, watching us with absolutely no regard for how Liza might take it.

She pulled her lower lip between her teeth, which was sexy as hell. It made me want to kiss that lower lip.

I could see she was worried and unsure if she could trust me—or my parents, for that matter.

"Liza," I whispered. "Don't worry about them."

My instincts told me to reach for her hands, but her tight, rigid body language told me she wasn't ready for that.

"I can't explain the feelings coming over me, but there's a spark unlike anything I've ever experienced. Standing close to you is almost overwhelming." This wasn't an admission I would make to any other woman, but she was my *mate,* the one person who might understand this sensation.

Her breath hitched. She could feel it, too.

We stared into each other's eyes for what felt like an eternity but also wasn't long enough. There was something between us that was more than simply a sexual desire. For me, it was as if our souls were speaking to one another, like they didn't need words exchanged. I knew who she was. She was *mine.*

Finally, she took a step back. "I'll think about it."

A smile spread across my face. At least it wasn't a *no,* and there was still a chance she'd forgive me, meaning we could move past the stupidity that escaped my mouth.

I clung to that hope as I watched her drive away in her small, white hatchback. Part of me wanted to follow her to make sure she made it to her destination safely, but I wouldn't. I would apply pressure, but there was a difference between playing and chasing. I would do one, not the other. She would make the choice to be with me. My mind was already made up.

As I headed to my car across the parking lot, my dad barked out my name.

My wolf took offense to the commanding tone. He respected his alpha, and as positions of power went, Dad was still on top. But my wolf was stronger than Dad's and had been for a long time. He demanded respect.

"Now's not the time to make a stand," I instructed my wolf. "Let me handle my father."

My wolf agreed and settled as my father strode toward us. "Tyson, you're making a mistake with Liza."

Despite the firm tone and his hands fisted on his hips, I didn't believe that. Not at all. How could I when my attraction to Liza was more than physical?

My wolf claimed her as his mate, and my body and soul ached for her. How could it be a wrong choice?

Standing toe-to-toe with my father, I spoke firmly. "If it's a mistake, it's mine to make."

Chapter 7 - Liza

My day certainly hadn't turned out as I had hoped. I wasn't sure what I'd expected to come from my first conversation with Ty, but any preconceived notions I'd had certainly did not involve him insulting me. He was my mate, for fuck's sake. Of course, an insult had never occurred to me.

I was exhausted when I got home. I showered off the day, then changed into pajamas. By the time my head hit the pillow, I was asleep within seconds. For the past twenty-four hours, I'd been overstimulated, running on adrenaline and coffee. It had finally worn me down, so I drifted quickly into a deep sleep.

Suddenly, I was very small. Looking down, I noticed my hands and feet were small. In my mind, I was an adult, but my body was that of a child. I couldn't tell exactly how old I was, but there was a woman in front of me with hair just like mine. Her eyes were brimming with tears that made them all the more blue. "Hide," she said. "Don't let anyone find you."

I cried and pleaded with her. I didn't want to leave her side. I wanted to cling to her. Sadness and despair colored her face as she bent to kiss the top of my head.

Before I could cling to her waist, a little boy took my hand, and we ran into the trees. He stumbled over a fallen branch that I managed to hurtle over and hurt his leg. He waved me on. "Go. Go. Keep running. Don't turn around. Don't stop."

I had never known such fear and was scared to be alone, but I sprinted forward, anyway. I kept running until I thought I'd gone miles away and found a bush to hide in. When I turned to look, I could see the woman's face through the bushes, moving farther and farther away as she was dragged, fighting and struggling against whoever was taking her.

I woke up with tears streaming down my cheeks and a heartache I couldn't explain. I didn't recognize the woman, didn't know who she was, but losing her had felt like my heart was being ripped out of my chest. It didn't matter that I didn't know who she was. The pain was real.

I sat up and turned on my bedside lamp, then wiped my tearstained cheeks on my white comforter.

My wolf whined, and I tried to slow my breathing to calm us both.

The dream wasn't new, even though every time I awoke, the pain was as fresh as the first time I had dreamed it. I'd experienced it many times in my life ever since I was a young girl.

When I was a child, I would run to my parents' bedroom and climb between them, snuggling deep under their covers. Mom would smooth my hair and tell me everything would be all right while Dad tried to explain that it was only a bad dream, nothing to be scared of.

Yet, even after all these years, the dream felt different to a regular dream. This one was more like a memory, almost as if it had really happened.

There was no rhyme or reason to the dream. Although, I'd noticed I had the nightmare when I was more stressed or sleep deprived. Today had certainly caused a lot of stress, and I hadn't been getting a lot of sleep.

But what did it mean? Who was the woman? She could've been someone I knew back then. Maybe a relative, but I didn't know, and I'd never asked.

Now, though, my mind raced with unanswered questions.

After several moments of quiet contemplation, I shakily pushed off the bed and got dressed. There was no way I would be able to get back to sleep now. My wolf was too uneasy. The best option for me was to shift, so I left my small, stone, cottage-style house and went into the woods.

The night was still and quiet. The only sounds were the crickets chirping and the frogs croaking. There was little other movement, not even a slight breeze, which helped relieve some of my anxiety. I quickly stripped down and closed my eyes, allowing my wolf to take over. It only took a few seconds for me to shift. As soon as I was in my wolf form, my nerves settled.

My muscles stretched, coiled, contracted, expanded while my eyes adjusted to the night and the things I could see now that I couldn't see before. I swiped my front paws over the damp as I prepared to run. Moonlight glinted off my fur. I raised my head to stare at the starry night sky.

Taking a deep breath of the crisp night air, I tried to focus on the present instead of letting the past in and allowing it to consume me. But even with my surroundings providing me with some semblance of peace, I still had an uneasy tightness in my stomach.

    I ran, picking up speed as the worries weighing on me lightened. There was the constant rhythm of my paws hitting the ground, pushing off and flying between steps. The sensation of a cool breeze on my fur centered me, so much so that the fear and sadness had nowhere to go and no choice but to fade.

    There were no other wolves in the area, at least none that I could see as I sped through the dense forest, dodging thorn bushes and fallen trees. I was used to running alone. Even during pack shifts as a child, the other kids ignored me and left me behind. So, I tended to stick close to my brothers.

    I was different. An arctic wolf with a silvery blonde coat that matched my hair and blue eyes. Even women who paid a lot of money couldn't match this hair color. It set me apart.

    It wasn't often that I actually felt alone, but in moments like this I was reminded of how different I was from all the others. As I pushed harder and pumped my legs to run faster, I wondered where I had come from and how I got here. Why were there no other wolves like me in the pack?

I let the questions linger in my mind as I kept running, eventually coming to a stop when I reached the edge of a clear lake.

The moon illuminated the water and mirrored its light on me. I lay down on the bank of the lake and listened to the sound of the water's gentle ripples before closing my eyes and allowing sleep to take over.

Birds chirped above my head, gently waking me from my deep slumber. The sun would start to make its full ascent any minute, so I ran back home at a steady pace to prepare for my day.

By the time I returned to my house, my mood had changed from anxious and scared to calm and steady. I shifted back to human form and dressed quickly before making myself a cup of coffee and several strips of bacon.

Mom and I had hair appointments that morning, so I pulled my dirty hair into a high ponytail and covered my head with one of those new, fashionable black baseball caps that had a hole at the top for a ponytail. My mother had given it to me.

I pulled into the salon's parking lot a few minutes late, but Mom didn't seem concerned. I was late often enough that she was used to it by now. I found her sitting in the waiting area, reading the latest edition of a DIY home décor magazine. She loved being the caretaker of my childhood home. I found it to be quite endearing, though I never imagined myself becoming the mistress of a household. Well, except for the cooking. I had no problem making three home-cooked meals a day.

"Hi, honey." Mom stood and gave me a tight squeeze. "Ready to get all dolled up for your fated mate?" It had been a while since I'd seen her so excited.

My breath caught in my chest. I hadn't thought about Ty in a handful of hours. Since there was no positives to telling her about our exchange in the country club parking lot, and I didn't have the heart to tell Mom that Ty and I had gotten off to a rocky start, I kept it to myself.

"Absolutely." I laughed and pointed at my head. "This hair needs a lot of work."

We chatted while we waited for our stylists. I needed a distraction from my thoughts, which were mostly of Ty, despite how angry I was with him, so Mom filled me in on the latest gossip from her women's book club. I tried to focus on her, but thoughts of Ty came too often and were too powerful to be drowned out by anything else.

"How often do you find yourself thinking about him?" she asked between sips of coffee, taking me by surprise at the quick change of subject. That had probably been her plan.

I thought back to yesterday's interaction with Ty and frowned. There was no good way to tell my mother that my thoughts about him weren't all kind. "More than I should," I answered more honestly than I'd intended. But… it was my mom. Telling her didn't feel dangerous. It wasn't like she would run out and tell all her friends. "I still don't know why he's my fated mate, but I can't deny the attraction… the pull."

Mom smiled and nodded. "Maybe you should find out what his true intentions are. Maybe that's the key to understanding why he's the one fate chose for you."

I thought that over as we sat under the hairdryers. If I didn't give Ty a chance, even though he'd royally fucked up and hurt my feelings, demeaned my career, and acted like an entitled asshat, I would never be able to live with myself. I would always question what his intentions were and if I had prematurely ended the whole thing before it had even started. Plus, rejecting one's mate was a big deal, especially when he was about to become the alpha.

I glanced around the salon. Even after all these years, people in this town still stopped and stared when they saw me. It used to make me uncomfortable. There were no other arctic wolves in this town or near this pack. I used to be sure they were intrigued or repulsed by how different I looked from them because they didn't really socialize with me the way they did with my brothers. As I got older, it didn't bother me as much. Now, though, I was sure their stares were due to the mating business with Ty.

After our hair was newly coiffed and Mom's was colored, we met up with Sabrina at the local diner.

She waved to us from a corner booth. "Hey, guys!"

Mom slid in next to Sabrina, and I sat across from them. "Did you enjoy your day off yesterday?" I asked.

Sabrina grinned. "Of course I did. I slept a full twelve hours and binge-watched that new show about police detectives who hunt ghosts. But that's not what I want to talk about. I'm dying to know how the luncheon went." She tapped her long fingernails against her glass of soda. "Did you get a chance to talk with Ty?" Obviously, she hadn't heard the tale.

Mom patted Sabrina's arm like she was glad Sabrina had asked the question. "I've been anxious to know, as well."

"What can I get for you, ladies?" The waitress chomped on her gum and stood at the edge of the table; her pen poised over her pad of paper.

We all ordered our usual cheeseburgers and fries, then I turned my focus back to the eager faces sitting across from me. These were women who wanted details.

"To answer your question, yes, we talked." I bit my lip, unsure of what and how much I wanted to divulge. "He asked me out on an official date. Dinner."

Sabrina squealed and clapped, then rolled her hands in the universal motion of *tell me more*. "I am so stoked to hear that. I knew he wouldn't waste any time pursuing you, Liza."

Mom, on the other hand, seemed reserved over the idea of Ty and me pursuing a relationship. Sadness clouded her eyes. "I just don't want to see you hurt, baby girl. The Kellers live in a different world than we do. They run in a completely different social circle, and it's no secret that they are wealthy." She was trying to protect me, but there was nothing wrong with Ty's lifestyle—nothing I had to fear. I could hold my own.

I sighed. "I know all that, Mom. Besides, it shouldn't matter. Either Ty likes me for who I am or it just won't work out. It's as simple as that."

"It's not just their social standing that worries me." Mom took a sip of water. "Being an alpha's mate doesn't just give you a special title. You would have as many responsibilities to the pack as the alpha does. Do you think you're ready to take that on?" She sounded as if she didn't think I was.

Even though her doubts hurt, I shrugged as much to the question as to the uncertainty behind them. "I don't know. Honestly, I hadn't even thought about those things. I'm just focused on my potential relationship with Ty." Was it really called focus if I was *unable* to think of anything else? "If we're truly fated to be together then those responsibilities will come naturally to me. I hope."

Mom leaned forward, apparently not done airing her grievances or worries. I was having a problem discerning one from the other. "I'm worried the pack won't accept you."

"Oh, is that because I'm from a lower class than Ty, or is it because I'm not actually a member of the pack?" I wasn't part of his pack. Or any pack. Which begged the question: where did I belong? Would I know it when it happened? I also wondered with increasing regularity whether or not fate knew I needed a pack and chose this one for me by fating me to Ty. There were considerations to make, but right now, I was locked in a heated eye-exchange, watching their reactions to my accusation. Mom lowered her gaze to the table, and she and Sabrina fell silent. We all knew it was one or both of those things.

"Perhaps," Mom said quietly. "But you're just as much a member of this pack as anyone else." We both knew that wasn't true, but no one ever really mentioned it because the rules of propriety and our family forbade it.

I was tired of hiding behind the family tendency toward denial.

Her words floated on the air, and each of us might as well have had a bubble over our heads that said 'LIAR'. I was adopted. An outsider. It wasn't like it was a secret or that it ever could be. Anyone with eyes who could tell light hair from dark could see it without knowing my history. I didn't belong.

My dream came to mind. I wondered, not for the first time, if I should try to find out where I belonged. If I uncovered my past, perhaps it would explain why I was the way I was. One could hope, anyway. I'd never seriously considered it before, even though I thought about it regularly. Now, maybe it was time. Maybe knowing where I came from and how I'd ended up here would explain to me why fate had put me and Ty together.

I sighed, deflated. "Clearly it doesn't matter to any of these people that fate and Ty both chose me as his mate. All that matters to them, anyway, is what they think of us." And that was the word that spread from the one who thought it until everyone in town had an opinion they were more than happy to share.

Mom reached across the table and squeezed my hand gently. "No, Liza. What matters is what you think of yourself."

She was right. I had to believe in myself if I wanted this relationship to work out. If Ty and I were truly fated—and I had no reason to think we weren't—then we would make it through any obstacle the pack or society threw at us. We just needed to give it a chance.

Later that day, I tried to get Ty out of my head so I could concentrate on bookkeeping. It was my least favorite part of the job, and I looked forward to the day when I made enough profit to hire a professional accountant. Until then, though, I was stuck doing it, even if it made my eyes cross as I worked on inputting data.

A knock on the door interrupted my concentration. "Just a minute." I wasn't expecting anyone but assumed it was one of my employees stopping by to grab their paycheck.

"What the hell?"

Through the side window, I saw a huge bouquet floating midair. I flung open the door and was greeted with the largest flower arrangement I'd ever seen. The delivery person pushed the arrangement in my direction, and I took it, struggling to carry it through the door. The stems protruded out in every direction, making it almost impossible to maneuver myself and the bouquet past the doorframe. I gave up and stared at the door, wishing I'd never opened it. I certainly knew what was about to happen. I could feel the tingling in my nose.

Peeking over the roses, tulips, and lavender was none other than Ty, standing with his arms crossed and a huge grin on his face. He was proud of his ridiculous display, but didn't realize—couldn't have known, really—the error he had made.

Within seconds, the pollen invaded my nasal cavities, and I sneezed violently. The allergy attack was so severe that I couldn't hold onto the flowers. They began to tumble as I pushed them away.

"Oh, shit." Ty grabbed the flowers from my hands. "Are you okay?"

The sneezing fit continued, so I couldn't answer. Instead, I pointed to the flowers to indicate they were the cause.

"Damn it." He tossed the flowers over his shoulder and onto the lawn. "Here, step inside. Let me help you."

He followed me into the office where the fragrance of lavender lingered, causing my sneezing to continue. Ty ran to the bathroom and brought out an entire roll of toilet paper.

I nodded and blew my nose, turning away so Ty wouldn't see the watering eyes and runny nose that came with this particular allergy. It wasn't exactly the type of first impression I wanted to have on my fated mate.

When my allergic reaction finally abated, Ty moved closer and laid his hand on my shoulder. I didn't want to flinch away, but the electric current zinging my skin was almost more than I could bear.

As if he felt it too, he pulled his hand away, but his voice was soft, kind. "Liza, I'm so sorry. I had no idea you were allergic to flowers. Actually, I've never heard of a wolf being allergic to anything before."

I laughed nervously and wiped away the tears. "Yeah, well, that's just one of the many things that make me unique." My face warmed, and I covered my blushing cheeks with my hands. How embarrassing.

"Thank you for the gesture; it means a lot. For future reference, it's only lavender that gets to me. All other flowers are fine."

"Lavender. Noted." Ty smiled, and my stomach flip-flopped. This guy had the kind of smile that made a woman think of long nights and hot sex. Fuck. There wasn't much about him that didn't make me think of that.

A sudden flashback hit me, and I remembered being surrounded by lavender and sneezing. I tried to stop it as fear overwhelmed me, and I stumbled backward, almost into him. A hand appeared in front of me.

"Liza? Are you with me?" He waved his hand in front of my face, snapping me out of the memory or vision or whatever it was. Ty probably wasn't used to women spacing out when he spoke to them, but we were both on new and slightly unlevel ground. Anyway, the vision faded, but the snapshot lingered at the edge of my consciousness.

"I'm sorry." I pushed a strand of hair behind my ear. "All of that sneezing must have created some sort of brain fog."

I watched him, but not so closely that he would see. I hoped he'd accept my answer and not ask what I had been thinking about. I didn't know how to explain it or why it suddenly started happening, but I didn't want to dissect it with him.

Instead, he hung his head and chewed his lower lip before he looked up at me again. "I hate that you reacted so terribly to the flowers. But, hey! At least I learned something about you."

"Yeah, at least there's that." I smiled and motioned for him to take a seat as I made my way back to my office chair. "Are you here to inquire about a catering job?"

Ty's laughter had my body springing to life. The man had a laugh. It was melodic and deep, almost sensual. If I were to die right then, it would've been with a smile on my face. There was something about his voice, about the genuine tone in his laughter, that made me feel safe, protected, secure with him. "Actually, I came by to ask you out on a date." He paused, and as I was about to tell him he'd already done that, he added, "Again."

"Oh." I searched my brain for a more appropriate response, but something about him—be it the looks, the body, the sound of his voice or the smile—rendered me dumb.

He leaned forward, resting his elbows on his legs. Damn, he was fit. From that angle, I could see the muscles in his upper arms straining against the sleeves of his tight sweater. And I couldn't even look at his chest without getting the horny sweats.

He spoke, and I forced my gaze to move from his torso. "I wanted to ask you properly this time."

He cracked his knuckles and stared at the floor, seeming bashful over the whole flower debacle.

I sighed as my thoughts drifted back to the fact that I was so different from all the other wolves. I hated it. Being unique was one thing, odd was another, and I was the latter. Surely Ty had to have been somewhat uncomfortable with the idea of being seen with me. "Are you sure you really want to date me?"

He sat up straight and looked into my eyes as if he was trying to see how my brain was functioning. He scoffed, seeming surprised by my question. "Why would I *not* want you?"

I could've fallen hard for a guy who asked that question the way he did, as if he honestly couldn't see why I'd asked.

I sat back in my chair, crossing my arms. "You know…" I touched my hair. "There are going to be whispers, rumors, so much gossip." I could already imagine the conversations at the salon and the country club. "In case you missed it, I didn't see anyone applauding the fact that we're fated mates." I didn't mean to make it sound like I was blaming anyone. "I mean, I get it."

He cocked his head. "Really? Because I don't."

The words caused a ripple of goosebumps on my skin, but if he couldn't see what we would be in for, it was my duty to tell him. So, I plowed on. "I understand that image is important to the upper class, and I don't want to make you look bad, Ty. But people aren't going to be… kind."

He stared at me for a moment, considering my words, and I braced myself for him to tell me it would be better if we didn't start a relationship. I was surprised by how much it hurt to think of and how much his rejection was about to hurt me.

Instead, he stared into my eyes and said just what I needed to hear. "Liza, you're the most beautiful woman I've ever laid eyes on. I don't know enough about you to judge whether or not we fit, but I don't question fate. And, if you'll allow me, I'd like the chance to get to know you. Maybe we can discover whatever it is that fate saw that made her decide we were to be fated."

I sucked in a short, shallow breath because his words were as much a surprise as any others I'd ever heard. As grateful as I was for his understanding and acceptance of our situation, a small part of me was still hesitant. There was always a chance that once he got to know the real me, he would be disappointed.

Hell, I didn't even know the real me.

"Thank you, Ty." I smiled with relief. His intentions certainly seemed genuine. "I'm also curious to know what fate saw between the two of us."

He leaned back in his chair and grinned. "Good. So, what do you say? Will you go on a date with me?"

I returned his smile and reluctantly agreed. "Sure, why not."

We exchanged numbers, and I watched him walk to his car. I didn't know if this was the right thing. Didn't know if we would get along or have things in common. All I could do now was hope I'd made the right decision.

Chapter 8 - Ty

"Where the hell are you?" Bryce yelled from the base of the staircase.

"I'm up here." I'd spent most of the day in my office, searching online for the perfects spot to take Liza on our first date.

At first, I pictured us sitting at a corner table in a restaurant, having a nice conversation over drinks. Then I remembered she was worried about people watching us. A restaurant was out of the question. Too public. Too many eyes and ears.

I considered bringing her to our house and having Chef cook dinner for us, but there was no way she'd feel comfortable here. Not with my parents who would no doubt be lurking around every corner like damn creepers.

After hours of coming up with nothing, I'd sunk to the lowest point, possibly of my entire life, and invited Bryce over to assist me.

His heavy footfalls meant he was taking the stairs two at a time. He poked his head into my office with an expectant look on his face.

"All right. I'm here. I hope you know I'm missing a party to help you with whatever is so important you demanded I come right over."

I glanced at my watch, then eyed Bryce. He wasn't above embellishing for the sake of embellishment. Although, this time it was likely to guilt me into owing him a favor. "A party on a weekday afternoon?"

"Sorry." He waved a hand in dismissal as he plopped down in a leather wingback chair. "Let me clarify. It's a party in my pants."

"For fuck's sake." I rolled my eyes and threw a pencil at his head. "Can you be serious for one minute?"

He dodged the pencil and chuckled. "Doubtful." He sobered when he saw me scowling. "For you, I'll give it my best shot, though. What's up?"

Sighing, I leaned back in my seat. "It's Liza. I asked her out on a date." It sounded like I'd never been on a date before, I was the epitome of pitiful.

Bryce whistled. "Well, it's about time. What did she say?"

I didn't know why I was nervous to tell him, but my voice trembled. "She said yes." I'd been out with my fair share of women, and probably some extras who weren't my share, but none of them had been my mate. No woman had ever been so important.

Bryce rested his foot on his knee and tapped his fingers on his thigh. "So, what's the problem?"

"I've been looking for the perfect place to take her all day but nothing seems quite right." Obviously, nothing was right if I'd resorted to asking for his help. I didn't want to tell him about the lavender, but I didn't really have a choice. He needed to know it all before he suggested something like the botanical garden or more flowers. "Also, I might've sent her into a horrific allergic reaction with the flowers I surprised her with earlier today."

"Oh, shit." Bryce burst into a fit of laughter. After a couple seconds, he glanced up at me, held his hand in the air like he was a traffic cop telling me to stop. "Let me get this straight. So far, you've insulted her job, then you showed up with a bunch of flowers she's allergic to? Remind me again why this girl agreed to go on a date with a pathetic loser like you?"

I huffed because I wanted to punch him. "Yeah, yeah. Get it out of your system, Bryce." I could let him have his moment—his bit of glee at poking fun. There would come a time when I returned the favor.

I watched my best friend laugh until tears formed in his eyes and rolled down his cheeks. Asshole.

"Are you done?" I shot him a glare as he pulled himself together.

Finally, and just in time to save himself from an ass kicking, he clutched his stomach and took a deep breath. "Yes. I think I can keep a straight face now. You're usually so smooth with women. How did you manage to fuck this up so badly?"

I shrugged. I had no clue how things had gone so wrong for me. I hadn't been so far out of my element since high school. "I feel horrible about the flowers, but I've never known a wolf to have allergies." I fumbled with a pen on my desk. "Have you ever heard of that?"

Bryce cleared his throat and sat up straighter. "Now that you mention it, no. A shifter having allergies is odd."

"Yeah." I scratched my forehead. Shifters were immune to everything. Liza had definitely had a reaction, though. "I wonder what her story is."

"I thought you were going to dig into her background. You know, so there aren't any surprises." He stood and moved to the window to look out at the grounds. The lush green grass gave way to the dense woods that surrounded the estate. I'd told him I'd join him on a run if he helped me work this out. Bryce loved the woods here.

"Honestly, I want to get to know her without snooping around behind her back." I paused. Liza was so unlike any other shifter I'd met. The hair color, the eyes. "But I can't help being curious about her."

"Me, too." Bryce walked back over to the desk and leaned against it. "There's definitely something *different* about her."

"That's why I need help coming up with an idea for the date. I can't just treat her the way I would any other woman I've asked out." I turned my computer monitor around to show him the websites I'd been perusing.

"If you want to impress her, this is not the way to go." He paced from one side of the room to the other. After a few seconds of quiet contemplation, he nodded and grinned at me. "I think I know just the place." He paused for dramatic effect. Bryce always knew how to play to an audience. "What about a romantic picnic at the gazebo in the park? It's the perfect spot to get cozy and get to know each other better."

"Now that's what I'm talking about." I pushed out of my chair and walked around the desk. "When you use all your brain cells for good instead of evil, look how much you can get done. That's genius." I slapped him on the back and grinned. "Now, go forth and enjoy your pants party with my blessing." Not that he needed my permission for anything.

He laughed. At the door, he turned and saluted. "Thanks for releasing me, boss."

He'd really come up with the perfect date idea. The gazebo wasn't busy at night—the crowd who ate their lunch there would be long gone, and all the soccer moms would be at home making dinner. We would have the whole place to ourselves, and Liza and I could talk in private without all the staring and whispering she was worried about. I wanted her to be comfortable with me, so getting away from the prying eyes of the rest of the pack was perfect.

I pulled my phone from my pocket and texted Liza.

Picnic in the park tomorrow?

I watched the screen intently as the three dots flashed across it. Sweat formed on my brow. I hoped to God she wouldn't turn me down. It was too important for us as mates—for the pack. But things had gone terribly so far. I didn't like that I was so worried about her turning me down. Finally, she responded.

Sure, what time?

Thank God. Even when I first started dating, first tested the waters, even, I'd never been this nervous to ask a girl out before. This wasn't just any girl, though. Liza was my mate. The woman I was meant to be with. She was head and shoulders above all the other women I'd dated.

How about 6 at the gazebo?

Liza responded immediately.

See you then.

I stared at the screen, my heart pounding a happy little beat in my chest. I'd finally have time alone with Liza without my parents or anyone else breathing down my neck. Just the thought of being near her made my dick hard as a rock. I needed to clear my head and focus on impressing Liza. I wanted to sweep her off her feet with a dazzling date, not turn her off by acting like some kind of horny shifter who couldn't form a coherent sentence.

***

"Does your date like fried chicken?" our chef, Ramon, asked as he perused one of the three refrigerators in the kitchen. They were of the industrial type because my family did a lot of entertaining and we needed the capacity to hold food for a hundred. "I could do chicken or I could make chicken noodle soup with fresh bread."

I shrugged, thinking of the lavender debacle. Was she allergic to any food? "To be honest, I don't really know what she likes. Could you fix both so my bases will be covered?"

Ramon nodded, making a note of my request on his phone.

I didn't trust myself to prepare the picnic. Liza was a fucking chef, so there was no room for error. I didn't do a lot of my own cooking. The most I would be able to pull off was grilled cheese or some pre-packaged nonsense. I wanted to impress her, and I doubted a sandwich from the local deli would cut it. By hook or by crook, everything was going to be perfect.

The sound of my mother's house shoes padded across the floor of the dining room and into the kitchen. A second later, she appeared in the doorway wearing a housecoat and slippers. "What's going on in here?"

"Nothing exciting." I moved to the other side of the kitchen island, hoping she wouldn't pry any further.

"Is Ramon fixing you a snack?" She sounded once more like the mother of my childhood, but in there, in that woman, was a note of judgment I'd never noticed before. She filled her stainless-steel cup with filtered water from a pitcher in one of the refrigerators. "I wouldn't mind a little something myself. I had too much on my mind to enjoy dinner."

I suppressed a groan. She was not going to like the answer. "No, we're deciding what Ramon should cook for my picnic with Liza tomorrow." I glanced at her face, curious to see her reaction to my date with the woman she'd all but forbidden me to see.

To my surprise, she remained calm as Ramon and I finalized the meal plan.

Mother cleared her throat, unable to find it in herself to remain silent any longer. "Are you really serious about pursuing *that girl*?" Her tone was low but loud enough to convey her disdain.

Son of a bitch. *Here we go again.*

"Yes. I am." I didn't smile. Couldn't. I didn't enjoy arguing with my mother. Less, I disliked her questioning my judgment about Liza. Questioning *fate's* judgment.

She sighed. "I really wish you wouldn't, Tyson. Isn't there another woman you'd like to get to know? Cecily, maybe?"

I narrowed my eyes, attempting to keep my voice calm and level. "Why don't you tell me what, exactly, you have against Liza."

Mother shook her head. "I assure you, my issue isn't with the girl." She sniffed. "I *don't* have an issue with the girl."

What the hell? I was confused. I'd just spent the past few days attempting to convince my parents to support my match with Liza to no avail. They'd begged me not to pursue her, and now Mother dared to claim she had *no* issues with Liza? Ha.

"I don't understand." I leaned against the counter and stared at the ceiling. "If you don't have a problem with her, then why do you want me to ignore fate? Is it simply because you don't want me to be with her?"

She opened her mouth to say something just as Dad barked her name. He entered the kitchen with an air of dominance that we were used to. My father stared at my mother for a long minute without saying a word, but thoughts were exchanged between them. They, too, were fated mates. Where no one else might've understood what was happening between them, I'd grown up watching them exchange messages subliminally. This time, it would probably have been obvious to anyone and everyone that he didn't want Mother to speak another word about Liza.

Instead of quietly complying, Mother pinned him with a scathing glare. "Dominic, you need to remember that this is all on *you*." She spat her words as she pointed a shaky finger at him.

Whoa. My mother never talked back to my father. She didn't raise her voice at him. She might've treated everyone else as if they were beneath her, but she was always respectful to my father.

I glanced back and forth between my parents. "What the hell is going on here? What aren't you telling me?" Because sure as fuck, there was something.

Dad stared at me with ice cold indifference while Mother pivoted and stormed out of the room, leaving an almost visual trail of anger and disappointment behind her.

I glanced over my shoulder at Ramon, who tossed a hand in the air as he walked to the back door. "I'll see you tomorrow, Ty. And don't worry, I'll have your picnic ready to go."

Flashing an apologetic smile, I waved. Poor guy. How many times had he been caught in the crosshairs of our family's affairs? This time was different, though. This wasn't just a petty argument about a family get-together or social event. We were talking about my future, and emotions were running high.

I turned back to face my father, my hands on my hips. A fighting stance to show him that I refused to back down. "I'm sick of all the fucking secrets. If you're so adamant about me not being with Liza, you need to tell me whatever you're keeping from me. You owe me that much as your successor and son." It wasn't like they were keeping me from a school dance. This was my future. The future of the pack.

I watched as the ice cleared from my father's face, and he sighed. He looked worn out. As I studied his features, it hit me how old Dad was getting. It seemed like only yesterday he was young and full of life. His age was taking its toll on him. Deep wrinkles marred his forehead, and his eyes were dark and sunken.

My parents had me when they were in their twenties, so Dad was pushing seventy. Long gone was the youthful alpha who had more energy than anyone in the pack. Leading for so long had taken a toll on him and, for a moment, I felt sorry for him.

He should have stepped down years ago, but because I hadn't been able to find a mate and hadn't been willing to choose one for myself, he'd had no choice but to press forward and remain in his position of power. An alpha had to have sons to carry on the family name. It was a rule.

He stared at me, his lips moving as if he was forming his words carefully, but no sound came.

I couldn't wait all night. "Listen, if you let me pursue Liza, you'd get to step down and enjoy retirement with Mother. If it all works out, the sooner the better, right?" I had to reason with him and get him to see that finding and being matched to Liza wasn't a mistake but a blessing. "I just want to know what's causing you and Mother so much stress. I hate to see the two of you arguing like this." Maybe the way to get them to talk to me was to show some empathy, even if I had to fake it.

Dad turned and looked out the window into the woods along the edge of our property. He was lost in thought, so I stood, patiently waiting for him to answer.

Finally, he spoke softly. "Ty, there are some things that could bring the strongest man to his knees, and this is one of those things. It's better left alone." He paused, then turned to meet my eyes. "I'll stop interfering. You have my blessing to pursue Liza."

My mouth dropped open in shock. Dad's sudden shift stunned me. Not to be ungrateful, but I needed answers. I needed to know why he'd had such a change of heart. "Why?"

"You'll soon learn that as an alpha, you have to pick and choose your battles." He smiled weakly. "This is one I can't win. Fate made her decision, and it's out of my hands."

He walked away, leaving me to stare after him. Nothing had been resolved. But his blessing was enough for me. For now.

I tossed and turned all night, trying to make sense of Dad's sudden change of heart. He hadn't given me much of a reason except that some things weren't worth fighting over.

I slammed a pillow over my face and growled. All I'd wanted was for my parents to bless my match with Liza. And now that they had, I wanted to know why they'd questioned it in the first place and what led my father to rescind his refusal.

Of course, I wanted to go on my date with Liza and get to know her. Every time I allowed myself to think about her, the rest of the world went blank. But I also wanted to know what my parents knew about her. Once that thought was in my mind, I couldn't dispel or ignore it.

I didn't know her well enough to know whether she would be honest with me if I asked, and asking her about her past might scare her off.

Since I'd already fucked up twice, I didn't want to risk her walking away from me because I got too personal too fast. Maybe whatever was in her past that had my parents' backs up was painful—she might not want to talk about it. All the unanswered questions made my palms itch and my back sweat. My curiosity was beyond piqued.

Whatever information my parents were keeping from me wouldn't be easy to find. Luckily, I knew a guy who could find anything for the right price.

I hated to do it, knowing that I could potentially learn things about Liza that she might have preferred me not to know, but something was seriously wrong between my parents, and if they had some prior connection to Liza, I needed to know what it was.

I sat up in bed and switched on my bedside lamp. Unplugging my phone from the charger, I pulled up the number of a guy I'd used before for such a check. He was a hacker. Not just any hacker, but the best I'd ever seen.

"Hello?" He sounded wide awake, which didn't surprise me. The guy never seemed to sleep, and he did his best work under the cover of the night.

"Hey, Zephyr. It's Ty Keller. I have a job for you. One I need to keep on the DL." All the jobs he did for me were on the DL, but it needed to be said for clarity's sake. "Hope I'm not disturbing you."

"Hey, man." He sighed into the phone. "No, you're not disturbing me. You're giving me a welcome break from an investigation I'm working on. I haven't heard from you in ages. How've you been?"

"Good, good." I paused, still not sure whether I was making the right choice. "Like I said, I have a job for you, if you're up for it. Name your price and I'll send over the details."

"Name my price?" Zephyr laughed. I didn't make offers like that on a regular basis, but this was priority one. "Sounds pretty important. Your family in trouble?"

"No, it's nothing like that. I'd like you to look into a girl." I cleared my throat. "Her name's Liza Mims."

Zephyr was quiet, and I assumed he was taking notes. "Who is she?"

Word was out. No reason not to tell him. "Apparently, she's my fated mate."

Zephyr hooted. "I'll be damned. Are you serious? Fate finally took pity on you and matched you up. Nice."

"Don't sound so shocked." Although, I couldn't really blame him. Everyone had the same reaction. "It was bound to happen at some point." I ran a hand through my hair. "Listen, I don't know much except that she was adopted into the pack. I need to know where she came from." And like I needed to explain, I continued. "She looks... different from everyone else. Pale skin and bright, blonde hair. My parents aren't exactly happy about the match. I think they know something but refuse to tell me."

Zephyr blew out a low, long whistle. "And that's where I come in."

"Exactly. You want to give me a ballpark on the cost?" I'd told him to name his price, but he would be fair. He always was.

He sighed. "Let me finish this job tonight. I'll send you a quote in the morning."

"I need this process expedited." The desperation in my tone mirrored the desperation inside me. "I have to know what I'm dealing with here, and I need to know ASAP."

"Sure, man. No problem."

I'd known Zephyr since college. Everyone used him because he was a whiz with computers, but after graduation, he took it to the next level. The families with money knew he was the guy to hire if you needed a private investigator.

Not only did he have the skills to dig up even the deepest buried details about anyone, he also had the professionalism and discretion necessary for situations like this.

After we ended our call, I forced myself to fall asleep. I didn't want to look like hell for my date with Liza.

By the time the next evening rolled around, I'd already changed shirts twice from sweating so much. No girl had ever made me this nervous, but I was terrified I'd screw something up or say the wrong thing to Liza.

Yes, I was nervous, but I was also excited at the possibility of us getting to know one another better. It was a step in the right direction.

Ramon had prepared so much food that I had three full coolers to carry from the car to the gazebo. I laid out a huge blanket made of the softest cashmere. I set a bucket of champagne on ice on top of the blanket, then pulled out the food, napkins, and silverware. I lined the perimeter with several candles. When it was all put together, I stepped back to observe my handiwork. Not too damn bad for a forty-year-old bachelor. Hopefully, it didn't look like I did this too often or like it was my go-to for first dates, because it wasn't.

The gazebo was nestled in a lush, green garden in the center of town. Potted plants and trees surrounded it, providing a natural barrier from prying eyes. The evening sky was a kaleidoscope of golds and reds, purples and blues. The night would be clear and starlit. A cool breeze floated through the open sides of the gazebo.

I'd packed an extra blanket in case Liza wanted to cuddle up. My heart raced at the thought of our bodies touching. Just as my mind drifted to Liza's physique, my phone rang.

It was Mother. Shit.

I practically growled into the phone. "If this is another lame attempt at trying to stop my date with Liza at the last minute, you've got another think coming." She didn't speak. "Really, Mother, do you have nothing better to do with your time?"

She sighed heavily into the phone. When she finally spoke, it was evident that something was wrong. Her weak voice cracked on the first word. "Ty, it's your dad. He isn't doing well. You need to come home. Now."

Chapter 9 - Liza

Pink or red? Such a simple decision, yet all I could do was stare at the two bottles of nail polish as if they were cake and cookies … an impossible decision.

I didn't have much time before my date with Ty, and I wanted to look my best. Being a caterer, I always kept my nails trimmed short. They were neatly manicured but plain. Tonight, I wanted some color.

Scratching my head, I finally decided on pink. Red screamed *look at me, I want all of the attention*, and that was not the impression I wanted to make.

I was never the girl who wanted to be first picked for teams in PE, and I certainly wasn't the girl who wanted to stand on a stage and pretend to enjoy receiving praise for one talent or another. I was content to let everyone believe I was relatively talentless.

I'd also never considered myself to be beautiful, especially compared to high-society heiresses like Cecily Banks. Those women had more money than they knew what to do with, so they had the latest fashions, perfect makeup, and the most expensive perfumes.

    I had none of those things. I only had a few nice dresses and a single pair of black heels I'd had for years. Sometimes, especially recently, I borrowed Sabrina's clothes.

    My hair was usually pulled away from my face in some sort of a messy bun, and I deliberately kept my makeup minimal. Even the perfume I wore was something I'd received for Christmas from my parents, which had undoubtedly been purchased at a local department store. I wasn't a signature scent kind of gal.

    I didn't need any of that, though. Ty accepted me just as I was. So far, at least.

    My hands trembled as I tried to paint the pink polish carefully onto each nail. Between work and the whole fated-mate debacle, my nerves were frayed.

    I took a deep, cleansing breath to try clear my mind. I needed to relax and shake the anxiety, and not set any formal expectations about the date.

    Sure, I wanted everything to go smoothly. I wanted Ty and me to fall madly in love. But that type of idealistic, insta-love, cookie-cutter match might not be in the cards. Fated didn't necessarily mean it would be a one hundred percent done deal. In all my years and all the mating ceremonies I'd seen and heard about, I had only heard of a few instances of rejections, but it wasn't unheard of.

 A cold chill raced down my back as I imagined Ty deciding I wasn't the mate he'd always imagined. I teetered on the edge between being hopeful for the date to go well and praying that I didn't have to face the humiliation that came with that type of rejection.

 No. Don't think like that. I capped the nail polish and stepped back to admire my work. The pink hue seemed brighter than usual, but it was a good kind of bright. The sort that matched my mood for the night.

 Tonight was about possibilities, not endings. It was about taking a leap of faith and putting trust in something that went beyond the physical realm. Fate had matched us. Who was I to question our compatibility?

 I stepped into my small walk-in closet and perused my options, finally settling on one of my nicest sun dresses. I wasn't poor and didn't grow up poor. Granted, I didn't grow up with a lavish life like others in our corner of Texas, but my parents could afford nice things. I certainly wasn't a pauper or anyone who would embarrass the good Keller name.

My dad's position as an attorney afforded us the opportunity to take family vacations and for me to be involved in multiple activities growing up. I hated to think about how much money my parents had spent on costumes, art supplies, sports equipment, books, and other various items needed for my clubs and teams.

Now, with my career as a caterer, I made enough to provide myself with a happy life. I could splurge from time to time, pay my bills, and still put a little back into savings. I wasn't rich, but I was content.

Nice clothes and expensive makeup weren't top priority for me, though since fate decided to pair me with a guy who could've been a model, I'd been considering updating my wardrobe.

If Ty and I pursued one another, this would be the first of many dates, and I'd never wanted to impress someone as badly as I did Ty.

I took a final glance in the mirror. Not too shabby. My hair was braided across the front and curled at the back, and my makeup was a tad heavier than usual, but not so much that I looked fake, rather just enough to accentuate my wide eyes.

With my pale skin, it was so easy to overdo it with blush and bronzer. I'd learned that the hard way in high school when I first tried to wear makeup. The other kids had laughed me out of the cafeteria, calling me a clown and other nasty names.

I shook off the memories and grabbed my purse, keys, and phone.

The park was only a short drive from my cottage, so I arrived within five minutes.

My heart pounded about ten times harder than usual. My hands were sweaty and kind of gross, so I wiped them on the front of my skirt as I glanced around the parking lot. I didn't see any other cars in the area and assumed Ty must've been running late. Didn't that figure.

I rummaged through my purse and pulled out my phone. Maybe Ty had tried to call or text.

Nope. Nothing.

I looked back at our texts to confirm that I had the correct time. Then I told myself to calm down.

This didn't have to be a bad sign. Some people ran late.

I opened the door for some fresh air. Just because he was running behind didn't mean I had to stay in my stuffy car, so I slowly made my way to the gazebo.

As soon as I saw the setup, I smiled and slapped my hand to my mouth.

Ty had already been there. The perimeter of the gazebo was lined with candles. At the center, a large blanket was laid perfectly square on the wood floor. He had painstakingly thought of every detail, even cloth napkins folded like rosebuds.

I turned to see if he had arrived, but the parking lot was still empty.

Lowering myself onto the blanket, I took a closer look at the spread. A bottle of champagne was chilling in a silver bucket filled with ice. It was probably real silver too. A platter of chocolate-covered strawberries and an assortment of cheeses sat in the center of the blanket. Ty had spared no expense, ignored not a single detail. This was the whole nine yards of the promised picnic. Better than I could have imagined. Everything was perfect.

He had clearly gone above and beyond, maybe because he was used to above and beyond, or maybe he'd been trying to impress me. Not surprisingly. If it was about showing off and impressing me, it worked.

I waited a few minutes before I looked around again. As more time passed, my smile slowly faded. I checked my phone over and over again, but Ty hadn't called or texted.

What the hell was going on? Fuck. If this was his way of letting me down easily, it sucked, and if he'd suddenly changed his mind, the least he could fucking do was make a call. Why the fuck would he take the time to set everything up and then just vanish without a trace and leave me hanging without any form of communication? Bastard.

I was completely baffled. And pissed as hell.

By the time thirty minutes turned into forty, and forty into fifty, I no longer had even the most remote sense of excitement for the date. Now I was just embarrassed and more than a little irate. The jerk hadn't bothered to call or text, and he certainly hadn't shown up. He'd just left me out in the cold—might have been a slight exaggeration—dark park with a basket full of food.

My anger won the day as I texted Ty.

Where are you? I've been waiting for almost an hour.

I wanted to say more, but I kept a tight rein on my emotions.

The streetlights had kicked on, and I watched people walking the nearby trails, pointing and whispering behind their hands as if I wasn't a fucking wolf. I could hear every word they said.

One woman turned to her husband. "That's the waitress who matched with Ty Keller. He must've stood her up. Poor thing. She never stood a chance."

"Screw this." I stood and attempted to unwrap my foot from the blanket's edge. Snatching the champagne out of the ice bucket, I walked at full speed back to the safety of my car. I might as well get something out of this supposed *date*.

I glanced at my phone one last time as if Ty would magically decide to contact me. He probably never would at this point.

Instead of texting him again, I sent one to Sabrina.

Grab some orange juice and get your ass over to my place for some expensive mimosas.

Fifteen minutes later, Sabrina burst into my house carrying a gallon container of orange juice. "What the hell happened? Why aren't you on your date?"

I was upside down with my back against the seat of the sofa, my head hanging off the edge, and my feet dangling over the backrest.

I lifted my head from the edge of the couch where it had been since I got home. The blood rushed back to its rightful position, and I squinted to see Sabrina through the floating dots in my eyes. "He never showed."

"What?" She moved to the couch and plopped down next to me. "Did he call or text you?"

I sat upright and shook my head. "Nope. Not a single fucking peep. He had, however, set everything up. There were candles, chocolate strawberries, cheese, everything you could imagine. Except Ty. He was nowhere to be found."

I grabbed the bottle of champagne from my coffee table, and Sabrina followed me to the kitchen.

"Let me get this straight. He set everything up, left, and never contacted you." Sabrina stared at me with wide eyes. "That doesn't make sense."

"I agree, but he never replied to my text." I poured the orange juice into champagne flutes and added a hefty amount of champagne. "Guess today wasn't the day for me."

Sabrina clinked her glass against mine. "I wouldn't say that. You learned something at least."

If I did, I had no idea what it was. Maybe she had some insight. "Tell me the bright side to this fiasco." I felt like such a fool, like I'd put my trust in the wrong person. Like I'd let myself get my hopes up despite knowing I shouldn't. I took a sip of my drink.

"You're worth a hell of a lot more than a romantic picnic prepared by some guy who can't even show up for his own date."

Ty just didn't strike me as a guy who would go to all that trouble not to show up. I really didn't understand what had happened.

We both laughed and clinked our glasses again. Sabrina was always there to lend a sympathetic ear. I'd been stood up by the guy of my dreams and it sucked, but at least I had her.

And some really tasty mimosas.

We walked back into the living room and made ourselves comfortable on the couch. Not as comfortable as I'd been upside down, but I'd return to that position later.

Sabrina pulled the throw blanket off the back of the sofa and covered her legs. "I'm still shocked, though. Something doesn't feel right about the whole situation. Why would he go through all that effort to set up a romantic picnic if he was just going to bail on you at the last second?"

I shrugged. "Great question, and maybe if I ever speak to him again, I'll ask." I tucked my legs under my body. "Honestly, I have no clue what could've made him act like this when it seemed so important to him that we go out in the first place, but I feel like an absolute fool." I'd given one of us way too much credit. I just wasn't sure which one. "Why did I think for one second that he'd want to be with me?"

Sabrina turned to face me, reaching over to take my hands. "Don't say that, Liza. You're way out of his league. He should be thanking fate that you were matched with him, not acting this foolish."

"Thanks, Sabrina." I smiled. "I needed that pep talk more than you know."

She grinned back at me. "Any time. Now let's finish this bottle of champagne and move on with our lives—minus Ty Keller."

We finished off the champagne, toasting to a better tomorrow.

At some point, we turned the TV on to some over-dramatized cop show, which we found to be absolutely hilarious, thanks to the champagne. I couldn't understand why the lead detectives always missed the most obvious clues.

My mind drifted to my previous conversations with Ty. They'd been brief, and he'd insulted my job. He had apologized profusely, though. The effort he'd put in to show he regretted it made me think that he wanted to pursue me. Had I missed some kind of obvious sign?

Sabrina laughed at something on the TV and fell off the edge of the couch. Poor thing. She couldn't hold her alcohol, but it wasn't her fault. She was human, therefore well past tipsy after a few glasses.

Since I was a wolf, I barely felt a buzz, but it was lingering in the back of my mind. One more bottle and I'd probably be right there with Sabrina, and now I wished I could be drunk. Maybe then the sting of being stood up wouldn't be quite so damn bad.

But I knew that wasn't the case.

No matter how drunk I got or how many times Sabrina spoke encouraging words, it wouldn't dull the ache. Ty had broken my heart. Hopefully, it would only be a matter of time before another guy came around and made me forget all about him. If that was even what I wanted. Part of me didn't want to try again. I was content being on my own. I had been for years and I'd survived. Why change that pattern now?

I fumbled for my phone in the crevice between the cushion and the back of the couch. We needed food, and there was no way I had the energy or the inclination to cook. Chinese takeout fit the bill. I ordered two portions of chicken fried rice, egg rolls, and egg drop soup.

I'd hardly eaten anything all day in anticipation of some lavish picnic. Plus, my nerves probably wouldn't have tolerated food. I hadn't had much of an appetite leading up to the date, anyway.

"Food will be here soon." I squinted at Sabrina, who had decided to stay on the floor.

She was sprawled out like a seal sunbathing on a rock.

"Fantastic." She stretched her arms over her head and let out a loud yawn. "I'm starving."

"I know. All that drinking can really work up an appetite, huh?" I stood, and took our empty glasses and the equally dry champagne bottle to the kitchen.

"Why are hot men such pigs?" Sabrina called from the living room floor. She sat up and crossed her ankles. "Seriously, I'd like to know what makes a handsome man think he can do or say whatever he pleases with no regard to a woman's feelings?"

I shrugged and traipsed back to the couch. "The bigger the dick, the lower the IQ. That's a scientific fact."

Sabrina hooted and rolled on the floor. "Maybe that's what I should've focused on for my science project in high school. Think I would've gotten a better grade?"

I laughed as I imagined her trifold board with measurements and photos of her specimens. "I would've given you an A."

Our food arrived, and we devoured it as if we hadn't eaten in days. Neither of us cared that we spilled soup down our clothes or chewed with our mouths open. We were drunk and pissed. Nothing else mattered.

"Fuck Ty." I tossed my empty container onto the coffee table, then kicked my feet up next to it.

Sabrina pumped her fist in the air. "Right on, sister. Fuck him to the depths of hell. You don't need his shit."

Right on cue, my phone rang. I stared at Ty's name flashing across the screen. So *now* he wanted to call, hours after our planned date. Part of me wanted to answer, but the other, angrier part of me turned my phone off and tossed it onto the couch. I still had a few self-preservation instincts left.

***

Sabrina, being too drunk to drive, spent the night on my couch. I'd slept well enough considering my heart had been torn out of my chest the night before. I must've drunk just enough champagne to make me drowsy.

I took a quick shower and got ready for work. I would've much rather spent the day in bed, wallowing in my misery, but I had work to do. If I wanted to keep my company in the black, I couldn't take a personal day because some asshole stood me up on our first date.

My first client of the day was Dr. Cunningham, and elderly man for whom I prepped meals on a weekly basis. As soon as I knocked on his door, his cane tapped against the hardwood, moving toward the door.

"Hey there, Liza." He smiled warmly and stepped aside so I could carry the box of meals through to his kitchen. "How are you today?"

"I'm doing just dandy, Doc," I lied. "How are you?"

He followed me to the kitchen where I began unloading the meals into his fridge. He still had one from last week, so I put it on top. "You didn't eat all your food last week, Doc."

"I suppose I wasn't so hungry." He patted his stomach. "But don't worry about me. I'm ready for this week. Got my appetite raring to go."

I smiled as I closed the fridge and turned to him. "So, you didn't tell me what's new with you."

"Nothing new to report." He sank down onto one of the chairs around the kitchen table. "Do you have a little time for our weekly chat this morning?"

Dr. Cunningham always expected me to sit and talk with him for a few minutes. He was lonely. His wife had died a few years ago and his children were grown with families of their own. Honestly, I enjoyed his stories. His *chatter*, as he called it.

I pulled out the chair across from his and took a seat. "I always have time for my favorite client."

He grinned and reached across the table to pat my hand. "I hear congratulations are in order." He winked, which was kind of nice because he was absolutely sincere. Although it was also kind of bittersweet.

I didn't want his words to affect me, but they did and that wasn't his fault. He had no way of knowing how things had turned out between Ty and me, so I appreciated the thought behind his congratulations.

He continued. "Word on the street is that you and the future alpha are fated mates." I wondered how many streets said word had gone down, and how many people were chatting about it over their morning coffees and croissants.

For me, the sting of being stood up was still fresh, and I struggled to hide my disappointment. I lowered my eyes to stare at a nick in the wood. I traced it with my finger and shrugged the opposite shoulder. "I'm not really in the mood to discuss it."

Dr. Cunningham patted my hand again. "Can I give you a little bit of advice, dear?"

I nodded. His advice couldn't be worse than anything I'd come up with it.

"I was mated for sixty years. Sixty of the best years of my life." His voice trembled, and a tear rolled down his cheek. He swiped it away. "Relationships are never easy. They aren't perfect, either. But if two people care enough about each other, they'll always find a way to make it work. Not that you asked, but in my opinion, that's the recipe for a happy and healthy marriage."

I forced a smile. I didn't see a marriage in my future. I didn't even see a second date—or a first date that actually happened. "Thank you for the advice, but I guess I'll need to actually *start* a relationship before

I'll have the chance to put your recipe to use. I'll keep your words of wisdom in mind, though."

Dr. Cunningham rose. "I don't want to keep you from your other clients. Just know that if you ever need a shoulder to cry on or an ear to listen to you, I'm here."

I nodded. "Thank you. Have a good day."

He waited for me to grab my box and headed for the living room before he followed me to the door. "I'll see you next week, Doc."

I felt a little bit better than when I'd arrived. Even though things between Ty and me had not turned out how I'd hoped, Dr. Cunningham had made me hopeful that I'd someday have the type of love he'd experienced with his mate. The love he talked about with such reverence.

The rest of my day passed in a blur of activity, but at the damnedest time, no matter how hard I tried to focus on what I was doing, Ty's face popped into my mind. I didn't know him that well, had never kissed him or touched him for more than a second, and not in a way that was remotely sexual, but there was no denying the energy I'd experienced when I stood next to him. I truly thought we were fated mates. He obviously didn't agree. He'd given up on me.

  When I pulled into my driveway later that evening, Sabrina's car was gone, and Ty Keller was sitting on my front porch step as disheveled as a man so beautiful could look.

Chapter 10 - Ty

The past twenty-four hours had been absolute chaos. After the call with my mother, I'd hightailed it home, weaving through traffic, running through stop lights, and breaking the sound barrier with my car. I'd even left everything behind at the gazebo.

I hadn't thought to call Liza because I was in such a panic. Then, when it occurred to me later, it was too late. I had to see her in person. I had to look into her eyes while I explained everything.

The ten-minute drive to the estate was torture. In my mind, I was busy imagining every possible scenario, and none were good. The only information I had was my mother saying Dad was not doing well, and the odd tone of her voice. She spoke quietly, but with resolve. Something terrible must have happened.

As soon as I pulled into the drive, the staff met me at the door. They didn't speak, instead ushering me through the foyer and pointing up the stairs. Some of the women looked as if they'd been crying.

Fuck. This wasn't good.

My heart pounded against my sternum as I took the steps three at a time, reaching the second floor in a mere matter of seconds.

"Ty?" Mother poked her head out of their bedroom.

As soon as she saw me, her guard dropped, and she began to weep bitterly into her hands. Rushing over to her, I caught her just before she collapsed. I lowered her to the floor and held her close, allowing her to release the tears she'd obviously held back all evening.

Finally, she pulled away from my now-soaked chest and lifted her gaze to meet mine. "Your father took a fall in his study. We aren't exactly sure if he tripped or had a dizzy spell. Either way, he hit his head pretty hard."

My stomach clenched as I imagined my dad lying helpless on the floor. In my mind he was helpless, anyway. I didn't know the details—didn't care to ask. I needed to see him. "Is he okay?"

Mother shook her head. "I'm afraid not. He was unresponsive for a long time… much longer than the medical team would have preferred. The doctor came earlier and said we'd have to wait and see if he heals on his own. Medicine at this time could do more harm than good." Such was the way with wolves. "He's not supposed to get up for any reason."

"What does that mean?" Panic rose in my chest. No way in hell was the conversation I'd had with Dad the night before going to be the last. It simply couldn't. "Will he return to normal?" I couldn't imagine my father as an invalid. He would despise that.

"No one knows." Mother wiped her eyes and cleared her throat. "Come inside. You can speak with the doctor."

She led me into the dark bedroom where the curtains had been pulled, which told me Dad probably had a concussion. Even though it was already dark outside, the garden lights must've been too bright for him.

Dr. Anderson, our family physician, greeted me with a firm handshake. "Hello, Tyson. So sorry to meet under these circumstances."

I forced a smile. "What can you tell me about Dad's condition?"

He frowned. "Your father is getting weaker. As you know, wolves have a lifespan the same as humans, so we're not immortal. Though I think your dad likes to think that he is."

I hadn't wanted to say those things aloud, so I was grateful Dr. Anderson said them for me. It still hurt to hear, though. Dad wasn't the young, vibrant, strong alpha anymore. Instead, he was becoming frailer and weaker with each passing day.

Dr. Anderson gestured toward Dad, who shifted positions and moaned softly in his sleep. "The older shifters get, the weaker their wolves become. Your father's wolf is very weak."

This wasn't new information, either. Even the estate staff knew about Dad's declining health, though they knew better than to speak of it. Some packs prayed for the family's downfall. There was a lot of pack jealousy, not only of the pack but inside it as well, and the territory lines often bled at the chanting of an alpha. If anyone caught wind that Dad was vulnerable, they would use that against us in an attempt to take power from the pack.

"Is there anything we can do to strengthen him?" I asked, desperate for a miracle. We needed to transition publicly without Dad's accident being a factor.

The doctor shook his head sadly. "I'm afraid not."

Tears burned my eyes, and I gave a slight nod. I could hardly believe this was happening. No matter what, Dad would never be the same again. We had to accept it.

Just then, Dad cleared his throat. "Tyson, are you bothering the doctor?"

I forced a smile and knelt next to the bed. "Dr. Anderson was filling me in on your... situation. How are you feeling?"

His eyelids drooped as he attempted to make eye contact with me. "I'm only tired, son. You don't need to worry about me."

That was impossible.

"This probably goes without saying, but it's time for you to focus on mating more than ever before." He turned his face away from me. "There's nothing that can be done now because we don't have time to waste. You must become alpha soon, and I'd like to be alive to personally hand that honor down to you."

The truth was it wasn't about him being alive to see me become alpha. He could've just handed it down, given it to me right then if he wanted, and I would've been alpha for at least a year. But an unmated alpha could be challenged after a year, and they would come for me. All of them. I would be forced to fight every single wolf with a taste for blood or power. I needed to be mated.

Dad's voice cracked, and he covered his face with his hand. It was torture to watch him in that condition. He was broken, physically and mentally. I sat there, helpless, not knowing what to say to bring him comfort.

"Try not to worry about any of that right now." I patted his shoulder. "You just need to focus on regaining your strength. I'll do what's necessary to mate."

There was a long, awkward silence before Dad spoke up again. "What about Cecily? She's ready to take on the role of your bride immediately. You could skip all of the formal dating protocols. Her parents have assured me that she's ready to take the next step with you straightaway. There's no need for courting, Ty."

I stared in bewilderment at my dad, who'd just given me his blessing to pursue Liza the night before.

Was he so concerned about his health that he wanted me to settle for marrying a woman like Cecily?

"Let me stop you right there, Dad." I pushed to my feet and tried not to raise my voice. He did have a head injury, after all. Likely he wasn't thinking clearly. "There's no way in hell that's going to happen."

Dad sighed. "Fine, Ty. I'm not going to argue with you. If you're adamant on being with Liza, then all I'm asking is that you move quickly. I'm afraid time is not on our side."

The conversation had come full circle, back to the point where we'd started. I nodded and squeezed Dad's shoulder. "Don't worry. It'll all work out."

But I wasn't so sure of that. My thoughts returned to Liza.

Liza. Fuck!

I pulled my phone from my back pocket. I had been so panicked about Dad that I hadn't remembered to call her.

I dialed her number and held the phone to my ear. One ring turned into eight, then to voicemail.

"Shit."

"What's wrong?" Mother walked to my side as if to look over my shoulder to see who I was calling.

"It's nothing. I'll take care of it." I kissed Mother on the cheek. "Do me a favor. Get some rest and don't hover over him. That's what the staff is for. If they need you, they'll wake you up."

I leaned down and kissed Dad on the forehead. "Take it easy, old man. I'll be back to check on you first thing in the morning."

Dad smiled weakly and pulled the covers up to his chin.

As I made my way to my wing of the house, I tried calling Liza again, hoping she'd answer. This time, it didn't even ring, just went straight to voicemail.

I'd messed up. Again. But it hadn't been intentional. The thought of Liza searching for me at the park, wondering where I was, made me sick to my stomach. The poor woman probably assumed she'd been stood up.

I paced the floor of my bedroom and glanced at my watch. It was too late to show up unannounced at her house, so I forced myself to take a hot shower and get some sleep.

Tomorrow would be a big day, and I needed to prepare for it. Not only did I need to secure my mating with Liza, but I also had to ensure that no one in the pack caught wind of Dad's ailing health. For the time being, I'd need to take on more responsibilities to ensure nothing fell through the cracks.

***

The next morning, I woke up early and raced over to Liza's house. After ringing the doorbell and knocking multiple times, I concluded that she wasn't home. I was desperate to talk to her, so I called her office. The secretary said she had clients all day and wouldn't be returning to the office until later.

My phone rang, and I almost dropped it, scrambling to answer. My heart sank when a male voice came through on the other line instead of Liza's.

"Hey, Ty. It's Zephyr."

I'd forgotten about the job I'd given him. "Hey, man. What's up?"

"Can you meet me at the shop?"

The shop was a tech store Zephyr used as a front for his hacker business.

"Sure. What time?" I glanced at my watch, trying to decide the best time for me to return to Liza's house.

"Now, if that works for you."

Nervous energy coursed through me. Out of all the words he could've chosen, *now* was the one that stuck in my gut. When Zephyr wanted an immediate meeting, it never meant anything good. He must've unearthed something about Liza.

"Be right there."

When I arrived at his store, I walked to the back and through a door with a black and white metal plate that read *Stockroom*. His office was set up in a back corner behind several shelves of old computer monitors and various tech equipment. He apparently wanted to stay well hidden, probably due to some of his tactics. Sometimes what he did wasn't exactly legal.

Zephyr was sitting behind his enormous desk and multiple screens with a headset over his ears. I waved to get his attention.

"Hey. That was fast." He pulled the headset off and set it on the desk. "Take a seat."

I slid a metal chair closer to his desk, took a seat, and leaned forward, wringing my hands. "I assume you have some news. What did you find out about Liza?"

"Well...." Zephyr began. "It's what I didn't find that's more of the problem."

Of course, we had a *problem*. It was that kind of day.

"What *didn't* you find?"

Zephyr tapped a pen on the desk. "I didn't find anything. At all. Whatsoever. There's nothing on Liza anywhere."

I didn't get the sense that he was trying to gouge me for a pay rise, but how was it possible that he hadn't found anything? Zephyr was the best hacker around. How could there be nothing?

I stared at him in disbelief.

He held up a hand. "I know, it's shocking. I've had subjects with very little information, but never with nothing. Everybody leaves a trace somewhere, except this woman. Anything prior to registering her company with the state doesn't exist." He sighed. "This has never happened to me, not in all my years as a computer professional."

"She was adopted, though." I stood and rubbed my face. "Surely there would be records of that."

"Nope." He shook his head. "There's no record of Liza ever being in an orphanage or a foster home of any kind. No birth certificate for a baby with her birthdate in the country that is unexplained, either by adoption, death, or parental custody. I have no fucking clue how her parents got her, but I don't think it was done legally."

"An illegal adoption? What the hell?" I paced Zephyr's office, trying to make sense of what he was saying.

"The Mims did retain legal custody of Liza, but I have no idea where they got her. I did a search for missing persons, but nothing came up."

"What does that mean?" I stopped pacing and faced him. "What exactly are you trying to tell me?"

Zephyr sighed. "I don't believe Liza was kidnapped, but there's definitely something fishy about how she ended up here in Presley Acres."

"So, what now?" I had no idea why I was asking him. He'd done his part. I cracked my knuckles. "Is that it?"

"No." Zephyr stood and walked around his desk. "I'll keep digging. But I'll be honest with you, Ty, I have a bad feeling that somebody wants to keep her past hidden. They might not be too happy with me digging into it."

Nothing I could do about that. Now, more than before, I needed the information. We shook hands. "Let me know what you find. Send me a bill."

I trudged to my car; my mind heavy with thoughts of Liza's past. She was a mystery, and that didn't make me feel all warm and fuzzy inside.

How was I supposed to pursue a relationship with a woman whose past was a complete mystery? She might be mixed up in some nefarious conspiracy.

I drove straight to her house, resolved to wait on her porch until she got home. The minutes ticked off, one into the next, and I checked my watch a thousand times, reminding myself how important this was. I had to see her. A while later—one hell of a long while—she finally pulled into her driveway.

Liza got out of her car and stopped at the edge of the walk. She met my gaze, her eyes narrowing to slits. I held up my hand like it would do something to shift her anger into something else. She walked the rest of the way to the porch, then stopped and stared wordlessly. I didn't blame her. I'd royally screwed up and deserved to bear the brunt of whatever she had to say.

But I needed to say something first. "Liza, I'm so sorry."

She narrowed her eyes further, so narrow I thought they might have been closed. And then she looked away, refusing to meet my gaze.

"Liza." I kept my voice soft, but still, she didn't turn her head.

If she wasn't going to look at me, I was determined for her to hear me out. "I can explain. I promise it wasn't intentional. I would never stand you up that way."

Liza lifted her gaze and studied my face a moment. Finally, she cleared her throat. "I have some leftover food in the backseat. Can you grab it and bring it inside?"

I sighed in relief. At least she wasn't telling me to get the hell off her property.

After I grabbed the trays of food, I followed Liza into her small, yellow house.

"Have you eaten?" She toed off her shoes and tossed her keys onto a small table by the door. I was waiting for the anger, for the irritation and annoyance.

I shook my head. I hadn't eaten all day.

"Come on." She led me into her kitchen and pointed to a chair. "I'll warm up some food."

She moved gracefully from the cabinet to the oven, then over to the refrigerator. Every move was calculated for its efficiency, yet she did it all in a way that piqued my interest. I could've sat there and watched her forever without getting bored.

I wanted to know what was behind her walls. Who was the real Liza Mims, and why was there such a tight lid on all of her secrets? The questions only made me want to be closer to her, despite all the mystery surrounding her past.

"Here we go." She placed a plate full of grilled chicken with a creamy sauce, asparagus spears flavored with garlic, and potatoes seasoned with onions and chives on the table, then handed me a fork. "Dig in."

Liza sat across from me, and we ate in silence, though I found myself moaning because her food was so damn good.

Finally, Liza broke the silence. "Are you going to tell me what happened last night?"

I hesitated, unsure of whether I should share my family's business or not. Anyone knowing my father was ill was dangerous. Liza was meant to be my mate, though, so it was probably best that she knew the truth. "Right before our date, my mother called to tell me something had happened to my dad. When I got home, he'd been put on bed rest from an awful fall." I'd told her this much, so no reason not to go all in. "He's not doing too well."

Liza set her fork on the edge of her plate and blew out a breath. "I'm so sorry to hear about your dad. I understand how important family is." She laid her hand over mine, sending a bolt of electricity zinging up my arm.

My shoulders relaxed. Against all odds, she'd forgiven me. "Thank you for understanding. My family needs me right now, and I have to be there for them." I hoped that conveyed that I might not be as available as I'd planned. I didn't want to say the words.

"It's understandable." Liza nodded. "Family is always first. There's no reason you couldn't have contacted me, though. A quick text would have sufficed."

Damn. I should've known she wouldn't let me off that easily.

Liza stared at her plate, poking at her leftover chicken. "One of my clients shared something profound with me today. He said that communication is an important factor when you're building something new with someone. I get that something terrible happened to your father, but we won't have anything if we can't communicate from the start."

I mulled over her words. "You're right. There's no excuse. I should've contacted you immediately. I'm sorry."

The smile she gave me made my heart swell.

"I don't want you to ever feel like you're not a priority for me. I'll do better at communicating with you from this point forward." I was as sincere as I'd ever been. I'd never wanted anything to work out more in my life than I wanted things to work out with Liza.

She studied me for a moment, staring so deeply into my eyes that I assumed she could see my soul. Then she stood and cleared the table.

It was awkward sitting in her kitchen, watching as she cleaned up the dinner mess. "Can I help?"

She nodded and stepped to the side, allowing me to help wash off the dirty dishes.

As I handed her a clean plate, our hands touched, and we both paused. She could feel the sensation, too, I was sure of it.

A moment later, a slight smirk spread across her lips. "Thank you for coming over and explaining yourself."

I smiled back. "You're welcome. Since you've officially forgiven me, will you allow me to make up for our botched date?"

Liza dried the plate, then put it in the cabinet. "Yes, I'll give you another chance."

I couldn't contain my excitement as a grin spread across my face. "I promise I won't mess it up this time."

We finished cleaning up the kitchen and chatted about Liza's catering business and my family's business. Somehow, I managed to keep my hands off her, even though her scent was driving me wild. My wolf stirred, continuing to remind me that she was our mate. That we were meant to fuck.

Crude bastard.

I'd already fucked up with Liza multiple times. I couldn't afford to make a move too quickly and scare her off. We needed to take it slow and steady, but my cock had a mind of its own. On more than one occasion, I had to adjust myself while Liza was turned away from me.

The power she held over me was terrifying. I ached for her. It wasn't just her body I was interested in, though. She was intelligent, quick-witted, and kept me on my toes.

Even though my parents would've preferred me choosing Cecily, my mind was made up. I would focus all of my energy on Liza Mims and, hopefully, we would be mated. Based on Dad's condition, I hoped it would happen sooner rather than later.

After a few hours had passed, it was time for me to head home. Liza walked me to the door, and when I turned around, she squeezed my hand, sending electrical shocks up and down my arm.

"Thank you again," she whispered.

I jerked my hand back, afraid of what I might do if my skin remained in contact with hers a moment longer. "Thank you for the second chance."

My mood had lifted, but Zephyr's news sat in the back of my mind. My gut and my parents' reactions to her told me that the lack of information on Liza's past had something to do with them. Could Liza's undocumented arrival in Presley Acres have something to do with them not wanting me to mate with her?

Chapter 11 - Liza

The incessant beeping of my phone alarm jolted me awake from a deep sleep full of dreams and visions of my future—the future I wanted. Ty was a featured co-star, and I was sad to wake up. My dream world was much better than my reality, where an alarm continued to blare. I slapped at the screen, hoping to make the horrific sound disappear.

As I squinted against the morning sunlight, a stabbing pain shot across my forehead.

"Ugh. Not today."

Groaning, I unplugged my phone and propped myself up on one arm to scan my schedule. Last thing I needed on a day like today was a migraine. My schedule was booked solid, which wasn't out of the norm, and I didn't have time to nurse a headache.

I was shocked, and more than a little disheartened, to see that my assistant had neglected to inform me that I had a new client. Cecily fucking Banks.

Hell's fire. Not to say that she was my kryptonite, but if we were going with a superhero analogy, she was definitely at the top of the supervillain category. There was no reason in the world this woman would hire me to prepare several dinners for her. She had a live-in chef. This had to be a trick.

Even if I ignored the rumors—the shit she'd said about me that had made their way back to me thanks to everyone thinking I needed to know how she felt—she obviously hated me and cursed the ground I walked on.

I sighed. My head pounded, and my eyes only opened far enough to be two tiny slits, barely letting any light in at all.

This was not the way I wanted to interact with Cecily, with a pounding headache, and alternating which eye I kept closed to the light, but I couldn't cancel on a new client, especially one with Cecily Banks's money just because I had a migraine. Even if I would've preferred to cater for anyone other than that spoiled bitch.

Rolling my eyes, I scanned a spreadsheet with Cecily's many requests and requirements. She had more damn demands than anyone I'd ever worked for. What a delight this would be. Gluten-free, sugar-free, grade-A beef and pork. No chicken. No salt. No onion. Organic and free-range only.

I rolled out of bed, popped two aspirins, and showered. Feeling somewhat refreshed, I threw on my typical uniform of a black blouse and black chef pants.

There wasn't enough caffeine in the world to prepare me for a meeting with Cecily, but I decided to give the coffee a fair shot, anyway. I poured a large cup of black coffee, added enough sugar to power a team of toddlers, then sat down to review my account. Not surprisingly, Cecily's payment had already been posted. I didn't blink twice at the hefty amount.

I was used to collecting large sums thanks to the number of rich clients I served in Presley Acres and the surrounding area. They wanted the best, had demands, and to make sure they got what they wanted, they ponied up the cash, gladly handing over impressive amounts in the hopes that my food would impress their rich friends. It usually did. My return business as well as word-of-mouth made it difficult to take on new clients.

By the time I left to start my workday, I felt a bit more human and could open both eyes at the same time, although the headache lingered. My first stop for the day was the butcher. Cecily had requested several different cuts of steak. Luckily, I'd worked out a discount with Chad, the owner of the butcher shop. We supported each other's businesses, and in a town like Presley Acres, that was important.

"What'll it be today, Liza?" Chad greeted me when I walked in the door. He was used to my random visits, though I knew to come early in the morning before he sold out of the best cuts.

"Hey, Chad. Let me have ten filets, six ribeye, and three T-bones. A couple Porterhouse, a few sirloins, and a tenderloin each of pork and beef." I leaned over and peered into the glass case. "Go ahead and throw in some bones, as well. I need to simmer some more bone broth for an upcoming luncheon."

Chad quickly packaged my selections, handed me the invoice, and waved goodbye. The place was getting busy, and I had a lot to do.

I moved on to my next stop. The local bakery was owned by an older woman who'd been baking in Presley Acres since she was in her teens. It was a small shop, sitting in between much larger buildings that had been erected years after she opened her business. She was the best, hands down, so I refused to visit any of the newer and shinier bakeries in the surrounding area. No one dared open another bakery in this town because of her.

The enticing scent of freshly baked pastries lifted my spirits. Susan was known all over Texas for the lightness of her bread, and she had so many repeat customers from out of town who paid extra to have her bread shipped directly to them. I used to bake my own, but like the butcher, she'd given me a deal and hers was better. I stayed in my lane and bought hers.

After standing in a short line, I quickly scanned the case. "Can I get three loaves of white bread and two loaves of garlic bread, please? And an herb loaf, a cheese loaf, and a couple of bread bowls." I wanted to serve soup.

Susan smiled and looked at me over the rim of her thick glasses. "Nothing for yourself today, Liza?"

"Nah." I smiled in return. "No time for treats today." Although I wished there was when I spotted a mighty delicious looking eclair in the case covered in chocolate and stuffed with a smooth custard filling. If only.

She scoffed. "There's always time for a treat."

Susan stuffed a few sugar cookies into my bag and winked. "Don't forget to take a few moments for yourself today, dear."

"Thanks, Susan." My mouth watered. I'd probably eat the cookies the second I got in my car. I may have been working and focused on the job at hand, but one needed a specific sort of willpower to resist Susan's goodies, and I didn't have it.

Susan was just one of several local business owners who seemed to appreciate me and my catering business. When I'd first started out on my own, I cooked for a lot of middle-class families in the area. They continued to support me, and I loved giving back to the smaller businesses. Now that I'd made a name for myself, it was only right to return their support.

My last stop was the Presley Acres Farmers' Market. I grabbed my canvas shopping bag from the backseat and began perusing the tables. The market was filled with vendors in tents and booths who were selling homemade jams and jellies, pies and cheeses, homegrown produce from their gardens, and even a woman who created hand-selected bouquets based on each customer's request.

I made my way over to my favorite vendor: a local farmer with the best tomatoes and vegetables in town. While I inspected one of the cucumbers, a man appeared, seemingly out of nowhere, and stood a little closer than I would've liked.

Had he never heard of personal space before?

"Is it natural for tomatoes to be this big?" He held a tomato up to the light and twisted it slowly, as if he was trying to determine whether it was real.

I couldn't help but laugh. "You know, I thought the same thing when I discovered this booth a few months ago. Believe it or not, they're all natural and just as delicious as they are large."

When I glanced up at the guy, my breath nearly left my body. A very blond, light-skinned man stared down at me with icy blue eyes.

I hadn't seen another blond wolf in Presley Acres during my entire time living here.

I was shaken.

He held out his hand. "I'm Stone."

Reluctantly, I took his hand, trying to figure him out. "Hello." He didn't need my name.

Stone's gaze darkened as he looked me up and down. I glanced around the market, wondering if anyone else was surprised by this light-featured stranger, but everyone seemed to be going about their business as usual.

He drew his gaze back up my body and settled on my eyes. "Are you from here?"

I wasn't a share-my-life-story kind of gal, so if this guy expected me to tell him everything about myself, he would be sorely disappointing. I didn't know this pale wolf from Adam. Even people I knew pretty well didn't know everything about me.

He shrugged a shoulder. "Oh, I'm sorry." He pointed to my hair, which was piled loosely on top of my head in a messy bun. I still had an ache behind one eye so I wouldn't be tightening the bun. "You just don't seem to *fit*."

I recoiled. "Do you always speak so bluntly to strangers?" Who the fuck was this guy?

His eyes widened. "I'm so sorry. I didn't mean to offend you. I was just trying to point out that you're different." A slow smile spread across his face, and it wasn't wholly unattractive. Actually, it was quite the opposite. "I didn't mean it as a bad thing." He chuckled and pointed to his own hair. "Obviously."

I was suddenly more uncomfortable than I would have preferred, so I quickly selected tomatoes, cucumbers, and several heads of lettuce.

"Is this all for today?" Joe, the farmer, smiled as he looked at my selection and hit some keys on his calculator.

"Yep. That'll do." I eyed the strange man as Joe bagged my produce.

I handed him my card, then loaded everything into my canvas bag. Stone just stood there as if he was waiting for me to continue our ridiculously awkward and somewhat insulting conversation. All I wanted was to get out of there.

Joe handed my card back to me. "I'll see you next week, right?"

"You bet." I waved goodbye to Joe, then turned to Stone. "You should buy the tomatoes. You won't regret it."

I made my exit a little faster than usual, not stopping to peruse the other vendors' stalls. I could still feel Stone's eyes on me. Where had he come from?

As I drove to Cecily's, I pondered the questions milling around in my head. I wanted to know who that

Stone guy was and why he was in Presley Acres, but there were no answers. Brushing the questions aside, I dug into the bag of cookies Susan had given me.

There was nothing like a little sugar rush to calm my nerves after an odd and random encounter.

When I arrived at the address she'd put into her intake form, Cecily stood on the porch along with her entourage of assistants. She tapped her foot impatiently as she waited for me.

"Oh good," she said, and there was no missing the sarcasm when I stepped out of my car. "You made it."

Was I allowed to slap my clients? Probably not.

"It's great to see you, as well, Cecily." Her assistants met me at my car and helped carry in my supplies. "Care to show me to your kitchen?" It wasn't often that I cooked in a client's home, but sometimes, for the higher-dollar customers, I made adjustments as they wished. And this, apparently, was her wish.

I followed her through the enormous house, which was far too large for just one woman and looked more like a museum than a home. She had a Monet, the honest to goodness real deal and not a litho. I stared at it as I walked past.

Each room I passed was more luxurious and opulent than the last. Once I got past the thousand-dollar rugs and the priceless artwork and furnishings, I could see how she'd put it all together to create an elegant yet comfortable atmosphere. It was a shame that Cecily lived there. All the beauty was wasted on her, although it spoke to the professionalism and lack of prejudices against bitches her designer had.

The kitchen had smooth, cool marble countertops, and stainless-steel appliances, though I wouldn't have expected anything less.

As I unloaded the groceries, Cecily hovered over me, practically breathing down my neck. "Are you sure you picked up everything on my list?"

"Of course." I forced a smile. "Everything is from local vendors; nothing but the best quality."

I set the tomatoes on the counter and turned to grab the cucumbers, but Cecily had moved right behind me, which resulted in me slamming right into her shoulder when I turned.

"Watch it!" She huffed in irritation. "You'd think the *help* would have a better sense of direction in the kitchen."

Oh, so that was her plan. She'd brought me here to humiliate me. I shouldn't have been surprised. People seldom acted differently than I expected. Should've known she intended to treat me as *the help*. Some things would never change. I just kept reminding myself of what she'd paid. That money would cover a couple car payments.

I could take her comments. After all, I knew plenty of rich, entitled women like Cecily who had no regard for others unless they could help them climb the proverbial social ladder. This wasn't my first rodeo.

Not letting her get under my skin was the best recourse for such bad behavior, so I chose not to respond.

Instead, I ignored her snide remark. Cecily leaned against the kitchen counter and watched as I assembled her food per her dietary instructions.

Apparently, though, she didn't like being ignored. She amped up and doubled down on her insults. "You know, you're the wrong kind of woman to be with the alpha. If you end up being his mate"—which I would—"you'll make the pack look weak. The entire pack. You don't have status or upbringing.

You'll disgrace the pack. Aren't you concerned about that?"

Yeah. I'd known this was about Ty. Again, not surprising. There was a saying about leopards and spots that seemed apt.

I glanced in Cecily's direction. "No, I don't think that will be an issue."

Cecily threw her head back and cackled like an evil witch. "Oh? From where I'm standing, Ty couldn't have picked a weaker, more pathetic mate if he'd tried. It's sad, really. You're wearing polyester, for God's sake."

Okay. I'd had enough. I turned and placed all of the remaining food into the fridge, then grabbed my empty canvas bag and slung it over my shoulder. "May I have a piece of paper and a pen?"

Cecily looked at me with an odd expression, finally snapping for one of her assistants. "Get her a pad of paper and something to write with."

The young assistant jumped at Cecily's order, and I wrote down the heating instructions for the steaks, bread, and a detailed explanation of making a salad.

"What are you doing?" Cecily stared over my shoulder at the instructions.

"This will be our only business transaction. I'm dropping you as a client." I capped the pen and tossed it on the counter as Cecily's jaw dropped. "You're rude and entitled, and you make my working environment extremely uncomfortable. I have plenty of clients, and I don't have to work in those types of conditions."

Cecily took a step back, obviously stunned. "I'll make sure you never work in this town again, mark my words."

I shot Cecily a pointed look before responding. "I have a long-standing client list and they are extremely loyal to me and my business. They know me, the quality of my work, and the way I conduct business. So, if any of them want to drop me due to some baseless comments from a snobby little rich girl who didn't get the man she wanted, then I don't want to work for them, anyway."

It was rare for me to let my feisty side loose, but I wouldn't stand by and be treated like garbage.

I snatched up my purse and keys. "You should see a return in your account for the money left from the estimated budget by tomorrow."

Without giving her a chance to respond, I turned and walked out of her fucking nightmare of a house, and left Cecily fuming in the middle of the kitchen.

Just as I closed the car door, my phone rang. It was Ty.

"Hello?" I pushed the call to my car's Bluetooth, then pulled out of Cecily's long ass driveway.

"Hey, Liza. It's Ty." The sound of his voice provided a bit of comfort, and I breathed a quick little sigh. "Did I catch you at a bad time?"

Since leaving Cecily's, my time had gotten so much better. "Nope, I just finished up at a client's house." I shook my head. "Well, ex-client."

"Oh." Ty laughed. "That sounds interesting. Care to share?"

"Umm, no. I'd rather not give that person another second of my brain power today." I didn't want to talk about Cecily, and I preferred to not badmouth my clients, even if they were evil little shits.

"Gotcha. Well, I just wanted to tell you that you've been on my mind all day, so I thought I'd call and see how your day was going."

It was very sweet. My heart tingled. "Except for dropping a client, it's been fairly uneventful. I have a lot of other clients to visit, though. It's a full day. How about you?"

"I'm pretty busy myself. I plan on visiting most of our businesses to make sure everything's running smoothly."

"Sounds exciting." It absolutely did not.

Ty laughed. "No, not in the slightest. Let's not talk about work, though. Maybe we should talk about more important things."

Oh, crap. What was he referring to? "Like what?"

"How about you tell me your favorite sport?" I could tell in his voice that he was smiling. He thought he'd found a stumper of a question.

"My favorite sport?" I giggled. "I was expecting something much deeper."

"I'd really like to get to know you, and that means everything. Favorite color, favorite band, favorite everything. But if you'd prefer a deeper, more philosophical question, I can do that, too." He chuckled, and every cell in my body flared to life. That was a sound I wanted to hear again… And again. And again.

He was flirting, and I wasn't mad about it. On the contrary, I wanted the questions and the laughs to keep coming.

"No, that won't be necessary. We can do this. My favorite sport is baseball. Well, softball, really." Once upon a time, I was one of the great ones and could've had a future in the sport. I paused to check my blind spot before merging onto the highway. "My parents started me with tee-ball when I was four, then I graduated to coach pitch softball, then kid pitch, and I continued to play throughout high school."

"Really? I would've never imagined you playing softball." For a second, I wondered what he could imagine me doing, but I was too shy to ask.

I stayed on topic instead. "Why is that?"

"Well, you just seem like more of an indoor kind of person. You know, like cooking or baking. Maybe reading." His laugh sent flames of heat to my cheeks.

Why did the sound of his voice almost send me into convulsions?

"Maybe so," I admitted, my own smile sliding across my mouth, making my voice thinner and lighter. "I do love to cook, though that's not my only hobby."

"What else do you like to do?"

I thought for a moment. I didn't have a lot of time for other things since I started the catering business, but I had fond memories of hobbies I'd once enjoyed. "Well, I like hiking and camping, and I'm an avid reader. Oh, and I love to travel."

"Ah, that's all right up my alley. What kind of books do you read?" he asked, and I could have fallen right then for the amount of enthusiasm in his tone.

"Just about anything, but mostly non-fiction. I like reading about different cultures and exploring new places through books." I'd read about every continent and had a list of places I wanted to see, things I wanted to do. "Although, I do love a good edge-of-my-seat thriller."

"That's cool. I'm a fan of the classics myself, so you'll have to share some of your favorite reads with me sometime." As fated mates, I should've expected that we would talk about the future, but it still made my pulse quicken when he did, and right now, it was off to the races.

"I'd be happy to." Another surge of something, maybe contentment, shot through me. It was still hard to believe this was all happening. I didn't want it to end.

Was I really feeling a rush of adrenaline from the idea of recommending books to him?

I pulled into my next client's driveway and switched the call to my headset. These were clients who were at work and school, so I always let myself in and prepped their meals before they returned home in the afternoon. It was one of my easiest jobs.

Ty and I continued to talk for the next hour while I chopped vegetables and whipped up a large pot of stew.

Eventually, though, Ty sighed. "I wish I didn't have to go, but I have to pop into a business meeting. I'll call you later before you go to bed… if that's all right with you?" I had a feeling that a man like Ty wasn't used to asking permission, and that he was taking such care to make sure he didn't overstep the boundaries made me like him more.

"Sounds great. I'll talk to you then."

By the time we hung up, we had spoken for over two hours. I certainly wasn't used to that type of attention, but I didn't hate it. Ty was easy to talk to, and I suspected that was an important attribute for an alpha.

And a mate.

He had seemed so interested in learning the little nuances about my life that no one else had ever asked about. I hadn't experienced many relationships in my life, and the men I had dated were very surface level. Occasionally, they'd ask about my day, but I couldn't remember anyone who'd cared so deeply about what I thought. They certainly wouldn't spend two hours learning about my favorite hobbies, books, and what activities I'd been involved in at school.

Ty seemed different, which surprised me.

He didn't scare me, though. In fact, just the tone of his voice put me at ease. But someone potentially knowing me on an intimate level was new, and even the thought of allowing myself to open up was daunting.

That night, I crawled under my blanket and laid my head on the pillow on my 'side' of the bed, which was the middle.

I was exhausted. My thoughts drifted to Ty, and I wondered if anything would actually come of it. I didn't want to get my hopes up, even though I'd enjoyed our phone conversation more than I ever thought I would. Not to mention that he was sinfully, over-the-top sexy. I'd never dated a man like him before.

Sleep, despite my fatigue, didn't come easily. Instead, I lay in bed, wide awake, eyes open, brain churning with a thousand thoughts. Nothing substantial. Mostly shallow thoughts about Ty and me. I wondered whether he found me desirable. I certainly wasn't like all the other women in town.

Finally, with no other recourse and no way to fall asleep, I indulged in my thoughts. I closed my eyes and allowed myself to remember the contours and lines, the ridges and plains of Ty's body. He was built like a fucking rock.

There were times when thinking of him made my body vibrate with longing. He was a walking advertisement for lust. The kind of man who knew how to make my bones ache with need. This was one of those times.

I always felt a little bit wild, a little bit feral, when the first waves of desire washed over me, but no one had ever seen this side of me. I had never allowed it.

That didn't stop me from letting my desires have their way with me in the privacy of my own bedroom. I pulled my blanket up to my neck and turned off the light, imagining Ty next to me. He pulled me close, one arm at my waist, and the other hand tangled in my hair.

My breathing quickened as I imagined him stroking my face, his body hot and hard against mine, his hands gently caressing my body. My skin tingled with anticipation as I closed my eyes and gave in to the burning lust inside me.

The hands touching me might've been mine, but they were guided by his, gliding down my body, trailing heat over my skin, stopping for a caress, a moan, with every breath more desperate than the last.

I imagined the taste of his kiss, the sweetness of his tongue, and the power and demand behind it. My body ignited, and my breath caught somewhere between my lungs and my throat. My skin was tight, the only thing keeping me from blowing apart, and I ached. In that moment, I wanted nothing more, needed nothing more than Ty's body, his hands, his mouth. Oh, how I needed his mouth. To give, to take, to command, to ask. I needed all of it. All of him.

The kiss I wanted was hard and demanding, and I wanted it to go on, but I needed *more*. A touch. Something intimate that would bind us together.

I pushed my hands down, aching even more now with need, my body coiled tightly with desire. One hand tweaked a nipple, the other slid over the soft skin of my belly and down to brush against my clit. I sucked in a shaky breath, then puffed out over and over, panting with desire.

My fingers flicked and teased, circling the tight nub of my clit, rubbing as the other hand lowered and dipped a finger inside. I was sticky and wet, vibrating and aching.

I wanted his mouth, his body over mine, and his cock inside me. I wanted everything that was Tyson Keller. My hips bucked as the bolts of pleasure burst through every cell under my skin. When I cried out his name—"Oh, Ty! Oh, fuck, Ty!"—my entire being, heart, and soul succumbed to tremors.

I cried out because I couldn't help it, and I writhed because I couldn't be still as I pushed my fingers deeper, the walls of my pussy clenching around them.

I should've probably sent Ty a thank-you card for his part in what just happened. I fell asleep with sweet thoughts of him in my mind.

Chapter 12 - Ty

"Have a great weekend," I said to the security guard at the warehouse.

I'd spent most of the day working with the second shift manager on implementing a new inventory tracker. Glancing at my watch, I realized that it was well past dinner time. No wonder my stomach hadn't stopped growling for the last two hours.

On the drive home, I thought back over the busy week I'd had. I always kept a full schedule, but this week had just about done me in. On top of my normal agenda of business meetings and in-person spot-checking, I'd taken it upon myself to pick up Dad's slack. Being the alpha was a full-time job in itself. I would have to figure out a balance before the job became mine. This gave me the chance.

Luckily, Dad was no longer on bedrest, but Dr. Anderson insisted that he only work from home. He wasn't allowed to drive for at least another week—not like Mother would have allowed it even if he could somehow order the medical staff to give their blessing.

She'd spent every day since the accident fussing over Dad's every move, which was another reason I'd been as busy as possible all week. I was in no hurry to deal with my mother in her current take-charge state of being. It broke my heart to see the alpha of our pack being treated like a toddler, even though my mother only meant well. It didn't take away from the fact that Dad wanted to be seen as strong and fully capable. Their constant bickering these days were becoming unbearable.

My thoughts drifted to Liza, and a sudden spark of desire shot through my chest. I'd spent a lot of the day distracted because we had dinner plans tonight. I was looking forward to seeing her.

We'd spoken for several hours every day over the past week. Our conversations were mostly surface level, chatting about our days and making each other laugh with random anecdotes from our pasts. Honestly, she could've read from the dictionary and I would've been a puddle on the floor. I loved hearing her smooth, almost sultry voice.

No matter how hard I tried, I couldn't get her out of my head. Sure, she was attractive, but there was something else about her that drew me in so deeply. It felt like she understood me and penetrated layers of me no one else ever had before.

My heart raced with anticipation for our dinner tonight. I wanted to get to know her better in every way possible.

After parking my car in the garage, I made my way through the house. Just before I turned toward my wing, Dad hollered for me from his office. "Ty, get in here."

What a way to be greeted after multiple hours of keeping our businesses afloat. He sounded on edge, so I couldn't ignore him.

I rounded the corner and found Dad leaning against his desk, staring at his computer screen. "What's up?"

I'd figured he'd be refreshed and more on top of things after several days of bedrest, but I was wrong. Deep, dark circles still ringed his eyes. It was as if he'd aged ten years in the past week.

I nonchalantly eyed my watch. "I don't have long. I have a date with Liza."

Dad tore his eyes from the computer screen, and I half expected another lecture about dating Liza.

Tension filled the room while I leaned against the doorframe, waiting for him to tell me whatever had him in an anxious mood. I sighed, hoping my parents had moved past the grudge they had against Liza, whatever the hell it was.

"There's a man in town." Dad sat back in his chair and crossed his arms. "Apparently, he's been asking questions."

I was confused. "Questions about what?"

"He's been asking questions about us… our family and the pack. He seems particularly interested in the Keller pack's power."

Dad shifted in his seat and fiddled with a blank piece of paper. He seemed really on edge, to the point that I wasn't convinced he was completely in his right mind. Maybe he'd worked too hard today. Perhaps Mother was right about him needing to take more time off.

Regardless, I had reason to be concerned. A random stranger asking questions about the pack couldn't be good, and I hoped word hadn't gotten around that Dad wasn't in the best physical health.

Dad cleared his throat and continued. "I want you to find this man and get him out of town. Make sure he understands that he's not welcome in Presley Acres."

"Who is this guy?" I walked toward his desk. "Do you know him?"

Dad shook his head. "I have no clue who he is, and that's why I'm so concerned. I know everyone in town. It's my job to know who the members of our pack are in addition to those they associate with." He reached inside his desk drawer and retrieved a photo. Sliding it across the table, he shot me a worried glance. "Have a look for yourself."

I picked up the photo and stared in shock. My eyes widened as I tried to make sense of the man's features. He looked as if he could be related to Liza with his bright blond hair and pale features.

"Ty, this isn't something to sit on." Dad stood and shuffled to the door, leaving me to stare at the stranger. Just before he walked down the hallway, he turned back around and knocked on the wall to get my attention. "Make it a priority."

"Will do." My eyes drifted up from the photo just in time to see Dad disappear around the corner.

I was annoyed. Why did this have to be added to my plate just before my date with Liza? It was getting late, and I sure as hell wasn't going to keep her waiting—not after the whole gazebo snafu.

As I walked to my bedroom, I studied the photo closer. Who was this son of a bitch? He'd appeared out of nowhere without the good sense not to ask people in town about my family. Surely he knew that word would get back to us.

I tossed the photo on my bed, promising myself to deal with the issue in the morning. Tonight was about Liza and only Liza.

I walked into my closet and stripped out of my work attire to dress in something more appropriate for our date at an Italian restaurant in town. It wasn't super fancy by any means, but I still wanted to look nice for Liza. I decided on a blue button-up shirt and a pair of khakis. After brushing my teeth and dabbing some cologne on my neck, I hurried to the car.

With only a few minutes to spare, I pulled up in front of Liza's house. Still, I silently congratulated myself for not being late.

I knocked on the door and listened to Liza's approaching footsteps. She unlocked three separate locks, then opened the door.

My breath left me in a gush. She looked so damn hot. Up until now, I'd only seen her in her work clothes, but boy, did she clean up nice. Her black dress hugged her curves and stopped mid-thigh. It took everything in me to focus on her eyes and not rake my gaze over her body.

"Hi." Her eyes lit up as she smiled, and my heart skipped a beat.

I blinked to clear my head and pulled a bouquet from behind my back. "These are for you. You'll be happy to know I left out the lavender this time."

Liza laughed as she took the flowers, her fingers brushing against my hand. "Thank you. Do you mind if I put them in some water before we leave?"

"Sure, no problem." I followed her just inside and waited as she arranged the flowers in a glass vase and displayed them on her mantle.

"Shall we?" I extended my arm, and she took it without hesitation. We walked to the car in silence, an electricity sparking between us that made it difficult for me to think. Being this near to her was torture. *"Mate!"* my wolf growled in the back of my mind, but I ignored him and focused on opening the car door for her instead.

On the drive to the restaurant we talked about our day and what we'd been up to since we'd last seen each other. Liza laughed at some of my stories, and I found myself craving to know more about her.

I parked, got out and then opened the car door for Liza. My fingers grazed her waist and across her lower back as we were led to our table in the back corner. I was grateful that the place was pretty quiet—I didn't want any distractions tonight.

I studied her face in the candlelight. Liza was off-the-charts gorgeous. Her piercing blue eyes were like pools of crystal-clear water that seemed to shimmer and dance as the light shone on them. Her eyes held a depth that was both serene and alluring, drawing me closer to her with each passing moment. They were a reflection of her soul, revealing a beauty and purity I'd never encountered.

Her platinum blonde hair was board straight, cascading like a waterfall down to her full breasts. The sleeveless dress dipped low enough in the front to reveal a hint of cleavage, and even lower in the back, showing off acres of smooth, firm skin.

I shifted in my seat and glanced around the room, trying to focus on something, anything to keep me from sporting a massive boner in the middle of the restaurant.

"So, I've been wondering something, Ty." Liza cocked an eyebrow as though asking permission to ask the question, then leaned forward as if she were really interested. The idea that she cared about anything relating to me was as intoxicating as any alcohol I'd ever had to drink. "Do you enjoy your job? Every time you talk about it, you seem a little flustered."

That she'd paid attention when no one else ever really had caught me off guard. "I enjoy it well enough. This week has been a little more intense, though."

Liza propped her chin on her hand. "Why is that?"

"I'm picking up a lot of slack since Dad's accident, so I'm visiting most of our businesses daily. Gotta keep up appearances for the family, you know?"

She raised an eyebrow. "What do you mean?"

I sighed. "Everyone expects the alpha to be strong and on top of anything thrown in his direction." I never understood how many things were thrown at him in a day. "And with Dad becoming frailer, others will now see him in a negative light. I intend to keep that from happening." It was more than an intention. It was an obligation.

"That's got to be difficult. Sounds like you have the weight of your family on your shoulders." Liza took a sip of water, her lips parting ever so slightly. Every muscle I possessed tensed.

Shit. Her body was more distraction than I needed—than I could take.

I nodded. "It's been difficult, but I'm grateful I'm available to take care of things. What about you? Are you happily walking down the path of your chosen career?"

Liza's eyes danced with joy. "Yes, actually. I wouldn't trade it for any other job."

"What got you started? Did you always know you'd become a chef?"

Before she could answer, the waitress arrived for our orders. "Miss, what would you like?"

Liza smiled down at the menu. "I'll have the lasagna and a side of fried calamari." She lowered her menu and looked at me. "Ty, you have to try the lasagna. It's out of this world."

I closed my menu and handed it to the waitress. "I can't argue with a chef. I'll have what she's having."

The waitress took our menus, and Liza turned her attention back to me. "To answer your question, I wasn't always sure I'd be a chef. I enjoyed playing pretend when I was a child and *cooking* meals for my parents that were actually just random weeds I'd plucked from the garden. My parents made me take part in so many different activities, clubs, and sports in high school, I was exposed to a number of possible career paths."

"So, what was the deciding factor?" A sly grin spread across my face. "Were you hoping to become a professional softball player?" I wanted to know everything about her, every thought, and every desire. Of course, I wanted to know about the desires, but never before had I felt so strongly about knowing a woman's thoughts. On one hand, it worried me, but on the other, I was excited at the prospect.

Liza chuckled, her voice softening. "No. If you must know, I made a meal for the family who lived across the street when they were sick. I found so much satisfaction in making something from scratch that brought them comfort. That's when I knew it was my calling."

"If you want to speak of callings, I used to dream about becoming a professional football player. I played in high school with your brothers, and there's nothing in the world that will make a guy realize he's not good at something quite like lying on his back, gasping for air because he got tackled by a Mims man. Thanks to them, I figured out pretty quickly that I was shit at football." I watched as Liza tried to make the connection.

"You know my brothers?"

"Oh, yeah. We attended several sports camps together." I grinned, enjoying having a piece of new information for Liza. "They're good guys."

She nodded. "They're the best. A little overprotective, but they're the most fantastic brothers in the world. Which reminds me… they're coming home for summer break."

I found myself entranced by her smile, her laughter. She could've been saying the same words over and over again and I would've sat there like a fucking idiot, grinning from ear to ear. Her laughter was so contagious that I found more and more ways to bring it out of her. By the end of the date, I was pulling jokes out of my brain I hadn't told in years. Liza thought they were hilarious, which only made me want her more.

When we pulled up to her house later that night, I opened her car door and walked her to her front door. I was desperate to kiss her soft, full lips, but I refrained, not wanting to make her uncomfortable.

Instead, I stepped forward and wrapped my arms around her, pulling Liza flush against me. I could see every fleck of blue in her irises.

My wolf reacted to her scent in a way he'd never reacted before. Up close, I caught the real aroma—the perfume that was her. It confused my wolf because it seemed masked somehow. As I buried my face into her neck, I breathed her in deeply, taking a lungful of her. Her heady scent made my body thrum with need, and I had no choice but to step away before Liza felt the hard bulge of my cock against her hips. As I withdrew, my wolf snarled, wanting me to inhale more of her intoxicating essence.

"I had an amazing time with you, Liza." I took another step back into the shadows, hoping she didn't take my retreat the wrong way. I wanted to stay close to her, but all my years of careful control faded when I was near her. My cock strained against my pants.

"Thank you for dinner, Ty." If I wasn't mistaken, there was longing in her eyes.

I put my hands in my pockets and tugged on my khakis, attempting to adjust myself. "Lock up and sleep well."

Just before she turned to go inside, I noticed she looked a bit flushed. She waved, then closed the door behind.

I rushed back to my car, insanely turned on. The whole way home, I kept catching whiffs of her scent. What the fuck was wrong with me? I hadn't reacted like that to a woman since puberty when I couldn't control my erections. But this felt different. Stronger. Much stronger.

As soon as I was in the privacy of my bedroom, I shut the door behind me, yanked off my pants, and headed to the shower. My cock was so hard, I was afraid it would explode.

The water was blistering hot against my skin as my fingers curled around my shaft. I'd needed this from the first minute I looked at her, the first time I saw her, and since that moment when my wolf stirred and demanded I have her.

My head fell back against the tile; my strokes quickening. Thoughts of her body against mine, her hands tangled in my hair, her mouth hot and wet on my skin, spurred me on.

I wanted to press into her curves, bury my cock deep inside her and ride her until we were both exhausted and out of breath.

Eyes closed, I slid my hand along my dick. I craved her body, her mouth, her hands on me. I wanted to taste her skin, her mouth, her pussy. My balls tightened. My skin burned. For her. All for her.

Release came in a storm of passion. I stood trembling, my fist still clenched around my cock. Jerking off wasn't enough to appease my wolf, but it took the edge off until I could be with Liza. And I would be with her. I had no doubt about that.

***

As I drove into town the next morning, I pondered over my reaction to Liza the night before. Had I reacted to her that way because she was my fated mate? I'd been turned on by other women plenty of times before, but this was different. If I hadn't stepped away from her when I did, who knew what would've happened? My wolf was ready to take over, and my dick had a mind of its own.

I'd talk to my dad about it later. Being an alpha with a fated mate, he might have some insight into my strong reaction to Liza's scent.

After I spent most of the morning asking around about a blond shifter in a town, I finally narrowed down the location of the strange man who'd been asking about my family. Presley Acres was a town of about a hundred thousand people. While I didn't know everyone, I knew everyone in the pack, and this fucker had never attended a pack meeting. As far as I knew, he'd never even shown his face in town before, and this guy's features were light enough—the same pale skin and silvery white hair as Liza—that everyone knew who I was talking about. Plus, he wasn't exactly in hiding.

He was staying at the Blue Moon Motel on the outskirts of town. It only took a couple seconds for me to convince Marsh Walthrop—a local shifter we tolerated because of his family's friendship with my father—to give up the guy's room number. I settled in to wait outside his door.

After an hour of waiting, the guy walked out of his room. I didn't waste a second before I moved in. He turned just in time to see me approaching. He smiled, almost as if he had been expecting me.

"Well, well, well. If it isn't the first son of Presley Acres. How are you, Tyson?" I had no idea how he knew who I was. It didn't shock me, since a lot of people were familiar with me, but I sure as fuck wasn't answering this tool. I was here to ask questions and demand answers. Unfortunately, that didn't stop him from jabbering on. "I wondered how long it would take for one of the big bad wolves of Presley Acres to hunt me down, so to speak."

And there was no one bigger or badder, so this fucker had better watch it.

"Who the hell are you and what's your business in Presley Acres?" I snarled and took a step closer. He'd driven his fancy little sports car into the wrong pack's territory.

"My name's Stone Black." He held up a hand as if he was directing me to not come closer to him. I hadn't taken another step. I had no desire to invade his personal bubble... Unless he came at me, then I would match him. "And my business is with your father, not with you."

That condescending tone was going to get him killed.

"You don't have any business with anyone in Presley Acres. My father has no idea who the fuck you are." I crossed my arms and stood my ground. He'd have to go through me to get to my dad, and I would not be making that easy.

"Your father doesn't *know* he has business with me, but once we talk, he'll get the picture real quick."

I didn't like the sound of that. No way was I letting this fucker get anywhere near my dad, alpha or not.

Stone continued. "Run along on home, then mention Heather Falls to your old man." He handed me a business card. "Tell him to give me a call." His eyes were stone cold, icy blue as he lowered his voice. "Your father has things to answer for." His narrowed eyes and deep, steely voice spoke the one word he wasn't saying. *Crimes*. It was a big accusation—one I didn't intend to take lightly.

Stone calmly walked to his car and slid behind the wheel. I didn't know who he was or what he wanted, but I would damn well find out very soon.

Chapter 13 - Liza

My phone buzzed, and I glanced at the message when I stopped at a red light. The text was from my mom.

Dinner is in thirty minutes. Are you going to make it?

My brothers were in town, so I was heading over to my parents' place for family dinner. It was always exciting when my brothers made time to come visit, since each of them lived a few hours away, and their busy jobs didn't give them much time off.

I'm on my way! Be there in five.

I couldn't wait to see Mason and Michael. From the moment I became a member of the Mims family, way back before I could remember not being a member of the family, the twins had taken on the role of my protectors.

Mom liked telling a story about them immediately being overprotective of me as soon as I walked through the door for the first time. The twins had been about eight or nine at the time, and Mason had sniffed and circled me as if I was an enemy, but it didn't take long before he realized I was an innocent little girl in need of protection. Since then, they were the truest brothers a girl could ever have wished for.

    Some nights, when I'd had my recurring nightmare, the twins would be at my side, consoling me before I could even fling the covers off to rush to my parents' bedroom. One of the twins would tell me they'd kill whoever tried to hurt me, and the other stood guard at the door. Not because there was anything out there, but because it made me feel more secure knowing I had them to protect me. They'd never considered me to be anything other than their sister, even though I was adopted.

    Not that their protectiveness never went a little too far, like when they'd busted in on my movie night in the basement with Rex Wilson. He'd just put his arm around me during a scary scene when they practically broke the door down. They'd scared the poor guy so much that he never asked me out again. I had a lot of stories like that from my childhood. Times when their protection scared away a boy, took care of a bully, or made me mad until I calmed down enough to realize they were simply showing me their love like brothers did.

I pulled into the driveway and parked behind Mason's giant 4x4 truck. As soon as I walked through the door, my brothers rushed toward me and engulfed me in a brother-hug sandwich. Mason wrapped me in a big bear hug, then Michael did the same from behind.

"Oh, for heaven's sake," I said, finally breaking an arm free enough to push against one, then the other. "It's good to see you, too, but I can't breathe."

They both pulled away, laughing when I inhaled dramatically.

"Wow, let me get a look at the future queen of the south." Michael stood back with his hands on his hips, a grin spreading on his face. He was older by ten or eleven minutes, and he was the funny one… according to him. He was charming, never lacked companionship, and he was, one hundred percent, as quick-witted as he thought he was.

I groaned and rolled my eyes. If they knew half the things being said about me out in town, there would be a brawl, and the last thing I needed was to share that with them, but I didn't want them to get their hopes up, either. "Please. Spare me."

They both laughed as we moved toward the dining room.

The mouthwatering smell of baked chicken and roasted vegetables filled the house, and my stomach grumbled in response. I'd spent all day working and hadn't stopped to take a lunch break, unless the random vegetables and pieces of bread I'd popped into my mouth counted. My belly told me that did not count.

"Ahh. My heart is full." Mom walked out of the kitchen clutching her chest, a dish towel tucked into her apron. "All my babies under one roof again. It's been too long." Too long for my mother was a couple weeks. I was sure we'd had dinner less than a month ago, under her roof, all of us together.

I gave her a quick hug and peck on the cheek. "Thanks for making dinner. There's nothing in the world that beats Mom's home cooking." She didn't need the praise, but I adored the smile it gave her.

We all took the same seats we'd had our entire lives, as if we were still children. There was a certain comfort I'd never outgrown at seeing everyone in their usual spots.

Once we'd heaped our plates with food, the conversation flowed. Never a quiet moment in the Mims' house when the kids were all home. We were so excited to be together whenever we saw each other that we often talked over one another, and tonight was no exception.

"How's work going for you guys?" I took a bite of chicken and raised my eyebrows at Michael.

He quietly set his glass of water on the table and cleared his throat. He was the more reserved and introverted twin who preferred not to be in the spotlight. "Everything's going well in class. I had a great group of students this year. They were all extremely bright and full of conversation, which makes my job easier."

Michael was a history professor at a liberal arts college a few hours north of Presley Acres. His chosen profession never surprised us, given that he had been a very studious child and valedictorian of his high school graduating class.

"Are you still on the tenure track?" Dad piped up, though he was typically the family member who sat back and listened to the conversation, absorbing every word and taking the time to consider his response. A mid-dinner question was out of character.

Michael nodded, smiling like he'd won the lottery. "Yes. As a matter of fact, it was made official last week."

"What?" Mom jumped up and rushed around the table to Michael. She pulled him into a long, proud-Mom hug. "That's fantastic news! Why didn't you tell us before?"

Michael's cheeks went pink, and his forehead turned a deep shade of red. He was the kind of guy who didn't expect accolades and was surprised when he got them. "I didn't want to make a big deal out of it."

"It's a huge deal." Mason, who sat beside Michael, slapped him on the back. "You've proven yourself, and now they want to ensure no other universities steal you away."

Tenure was a career accomplishment. I was so proud of him.

Once the celebration died down, I turned my attention to Mason. "What about you? How's coaching coming along?"

Mason was the jock and had fallen into coaching football as his profession. He was damn good at it, too. The boys he coached at the high school had won the state championship title the past four years in a row. Mason had received tons of media attention, which he never fully appreciated but accepted with grace, anyway.

"It's been an amazing season." We'd all gone to the championship game and watched his team, after being down by seven, march down the field to tie the game to send it into overtime. Eventually, they won and brought home a championship cup. We were the kind of family who came out for support. "Next year's group of boys is looking good, too."

He'd always been like this—modest, yet one of the loudest and extroverted people I'd ever met.

"What about you, Liza?" Michael flipped the script on me. "Anything new in the wide world of catering? You still trying to give Gordon Ramsay a run for his money?" I'd kicked him out of the kitchen once when I was in college because he kept sticking his fingers in the sauce. I'd never managed to live it down.

I wiped my mouth with the fancy linen napkins Mom brought out for the very special occasions we called *family dinner*. "Really well, actually. Word of mouth is the only type of advertising I depend on, and most of the well-to-do families now depend on me for their events. Some of them even hire me to prepare dinner for their families during the week."

"That's wonderful." Michael clapped his hands together.

I smiled, feeling proud of my accomplishments. "It is."

We enjoyed the rest of the meal, the conversation, and each other's company. It was nice to be together, and I felt a sense of peace knowing that no matter how much time passed, our bond was unbreakable.

I sat back and observed the smiling faces as I listened to the warm conversation. It made me happy that we were all doing well in our lives and our professions, and judging by the glimmer of light in my parent's eyes, they were beyond proud of their children.

"All right, I have to mention the elephant in the room. Or the alpha, rather." Mason leaned on the table and squinted at me. "Are you going to fill us in or what?"

Before I could answer, Michael spoke up. "I remember playing football with your future husband." I was about to interrupt but he kept talking. "I wonder why we didn't know sooner that you two were fated mates."

"Maybe because she never came to any of our games." Michael shot me a smug smile.

I shook my head. "I doubt it, considering that I was still a minor and you're not supposed to have the ability to sense a bond until you're of legal age."

"Yeah, so even if they'd been around each other back then, they wouldn't have sensed anything." Mom folded her hands neatly on the table.

I could tell she was a little uncomfortable with the shift in topic. Mom was still trying to come to terms with the fact that I had been matched with the future alpha. All she wanted was for me to be happy, and she had her reservations about me mixing with pack royalty.

"How are things progressing?" Mason cocked his head to the side. "When's the big day?"

I rolled my eyes. Ty and I hadn't talked about our future yet. "We've only been on one official date, jackass."

He held his hands in the air. "Whoa. There's no need for name calling."

We all laughed until Dad spoke up. "Maybe it would be a good idea for us to formally meet Ty. We are his future in-laws, after all."

Oh no. I shook my head as my stomach dropped. I wasn't ready for that. "It's too soon."

"Are you blushing?" Mason pointed at my face with one hand and nudged Michael with the other. "You must really like Ty."

"Well, yes, I do like him. That's not the question." I like him too much to risk our relationship moving too quickly. "I promise I'll let you know when the time feels right for you all to meet him."

"We need to have a little chat with Ty." Mason postured, puffing his chest out and turning to Michael for backup.

"Yeah, we need to make sure his intentions are on the up and up." He sat up as tall as possible, his voice lowering an octave. "He'll have to go through us before he can marry you." They posed like bodybuilders, switching poses, energy bouncing off energy. It was so very much their way.

I groaned. "Both of you need to bug off."

"Listen, you could be forty and we're still going to interrogate your boyfriends." Mason smiled and slumped back down in his seat.

"Agreed." Michael crossed his arms. "You'll always be our little sister."

I shook my head, but a content warmth spread through my chest. They loved me so much.

After we'd helped Mom clear the table, Michael suggested we shift together. "Come on, Liza. It'll be fun. When was the last time we went for a run together?"

"It's been at least a year," Mason pointed out.

I tilted my head and tapped my chin with my finger as if thinking it over. Truth was, I didn't need to think about it. "All right, you've convinced me." I followed them into the woods where we quickly shifted and bolted through the dense trees.

I stayed back a bit as Mason and Michael eyed one another, deciding to take off in a race. They were the most competitive boys in all the land, at least out of the men I knew. We'd played this game hundreds of times as kids. They would split up and run off to some remote location, leaving me to hunt them down.

My instincts kicked in as I sniffed the ground, following their scent deeper and deeper into the forest. As soon as I lost track of one brother, I picked up on the scent of the other.

After about an hour of tracking them, I gave up and decided to go home. I was tired from a full day of work and didn't have the same energy I'd once had as a kid. They'd eventually figure out that they were on their own and they would come home, too.

Just as I turned to run back toward the house, I froze. In the distance, I spotted a white wolf. My wolf whimpered, and my heart careened into a gallop.

The white wolf didn't approach me, just watched from a distance. He seemed familiar to me but I couldn't understand why. Was it the fact that he was the same color as me? Or was there something more there? Some type of history?

I couldn't will my legs to move. It wasn't until I heard the sound of my brothers nearby that I finally lifted my paws. Turning to see them approach, I wondered if they'd seen the white wolf. When I twisted back around, he was gone. Had I imagined the whole thing?

Later that night, before I drove home, I pulled my brothers aside. "Did you see anyone else in the woods while we were out there?"

They both shook their heads.

I found it odd that they hadn't sensed the other wolf. And, even more concerning, why had he felt so familiar to me? Was it all in my head? Maybe I was more exhausted than I thought.

When I arrived home, I made a beeline to the bathroom, washing my face with hot water and brushing my teeth once I got there. I slipped my bra off and picked my comfiest pair of cotton pajamas to put on. After pulling my hair into a messy bun, I finally felt at ease.

Just as I climbed into bed and turned on the TV, a knock on the front door took me by complete surprise. I hurried to it and looked through the peephole to see Ty standing on my front porch.

Fuck! I didn't want him to see me like this, but there was no time to change.

Smiling, I opened the door. "What are you doing here?" I crossed my arms over my chest, hoping he didn't notice my tits enjoying their freedom beneath my T-shirt.

He laughed, the sound warm and rich. "It's nice to see you, too, Liza."

I blew out a sigh and shook my head. "I'm sorry. I didn't mean it like that." I glanced at my watch and realized it was only nine.

He held out a bag, and I caught a whiff of something sweet. "How do cherry turnovers sound?"

I couldn't help but giggle. He'd remembered our conversation from dinner when I'd shared my love for pastries. I was a great chef, but I wasn't the best baker. It's why I'd started to buy bread at the bakery.

"Yum! Want to come in?" I stepped aside and tried not to be too obvious about breathing him in as he walked past and made his way to the kitchen.

Holy hell. Could Ty be any hotter? He wore a sweatshirt with a college logo on the front, jeans that tapered at his waist and made his legs look long and lean, and a baseball cap that had his hair curling around the lower band in the back. He looked amazing.

Would it be inappropriate for me to grab his tight ass? It probably would. Keeping my hands to myself, I went to his side at the kitchen counter.

"How about I put on some tea?" I grabbed the kettle before he answered and filled it with water.

"Perfect." Ty opened the cabinet where I kept my plates, grabbing two. "Should I warm these up first?"

"Nah, I'm ready to tear into them now." Cherry turnovers were my weakness.

Ty chuckled and put the plates on the kitchen table. "How was your day with your brothers? They've always been competitive. I can only imagine them vying for attention around the family dinner table."

"We had a great visit and even went for a run after dinner."

I contemplated telling Ty about the other wolf I'd spotted in the forest. He might've decided I was crazy, but since he was the future alpha, he needed to know what was happening in his territory.

After pouring the tea, I sat down across from him. "Something happened in the woods."

Something in my tone had him sitting up straight. "What happened?"

"While I was in the woods, I spotted a white wolf, and it wasn't my reflection." Although I had tried more than once to convince myself that it could've been. I was the only arctic wolf in all the land. All this land, anyway, so seeing someone with the same fair coloring as myself in a place where everyone was dark and always had been had startled me. In all the years I'd been here, I'd never seen another arctic wolf.

Ty didn't question it. He clasped his hands together and leaned forward. "Did he approach you?"

I shook my head. He hadn't made a move toward me, only looked. "No, but he felt familiar to me."

Suddenly, I remembered the strange man I'd met at the farmers' market. "Actually, a guy approached me at the farmers' market the other day. He was blond and had light features like me. I'd never seen him before, but he seemed to be quite interested in me."

Ty didn't react to the new information, but I could sense the tension radiating off him. His knuckles had turned white, and fury blazed from his eyes.

I continued. "I don't want to assume that all blond shifters turn into white wolves"—they did—"but it just seems a little too coincidental to me."

Ty nodded in agreement. "I'll look into it, but if you're ever out somewhere and feeling unsafe, I want you to call me. Immediately. Whether it's a phone call or a howl, I'll always hear you." He took my hand and placed it over his heart. "We're connected, and the closer we become, the stronger our bond will be. Even when we're far apart, I'll still be able to feel you."

Not that I needed more incentive to want to be with him. My heart beat wildly as Ty stared deeply into my eyes. The moment was so intense that I didn't even blink when he leaned in to kiss me.

My eyelids fluttered closed as his lips gently brushed against mine. Passion flared inside of me, and Ty reacted with urgency and need.

Before I realized what was happening, Ty was pulling me to my feet, his tongue searching for mine. His breath came in sharp burst as he led me to the living room and lowered me to the couch.

He pinned me there with his body as his hands slid from my waist over my ribcage, stopping just short of my breasts. I'd never been kissed like that, and I never wanted it to end—never wanted to stop touching and being touched. I slid my fingertips down

Ty's back and grabbed his ass, then wrapped my legs around his waist.

I moaned into his mouth and ground my hips against his, which seemed to shake Ty out of his stupor. He rolled away, jumped to his feet, and backed into the wall on the opposite side of the living room. I lay on the sofa, panting, wondering what happened as he struggled to catch his breath and stared at me with a longing I'd never seen from anyone.

"Liza. I'm so sorry." When he spoke, I saw that his fangs were extended. His voice was gruff. "Your scent is driving me wild."

I couldn't think straight enough to make sense of what he was asking. I focused on his words, then shook my head.

It was the fucking pheromones.

I had taken my pills that morning, I was certain of it. Ty shouldn't have been able to pick up on my unique scent so strongly.

"No, Ty, I'm the one who should apologize." I pushed myself into the upright position and pulled my shirt back down over my stomach. "This shouldn't have happened."

Maybe I needed a higher dose of medication now that I'd found my fated mate.

Ty stared at me strangely. "Do you know anything about your birth family's history?" It wasn't like it was a secret that I was adopted, but I didn't often talk to others about it.

I didn't really know why that mattered or why he was asking, but I didn't know anything, anyway. No one had ever told me, and I hadn't ever been brave enough to ask.

"No. I don't know anything. I've always been curious, but I have no information on my past." Which was my own fault. My parents probably would have told me if I'd ever asked.

Ty shook his head. "I'm sorry I was too rough with you."

I bit my lip and wondered if now would be a good time to tell him I was a virgin. From the way I'd reacted to his body, I doubted he had a clue that was the case.

Tonight had already been much more intense than either of us had expected, so I decided to keep that tidbit to myself for the time being. I'd tell him eventually, but there was no rush.

He ran his hand over his face and turned away, then looked at me again. "I better head home and let you get to bed."

I walked Ty to the door. He turned and gave me an almost chaste but soft kiss on the lips. "Have a good night, Liza."

My lips tingled as I watched his car pull out of my driveway. I climbed into bed with a smile on my face. Ty thought he'd been too rough, but it was one of the most exhilarating moments of my life.

Before I allowed myself to fall asleep, I went online and requested an appointment with our family doctor. If the pills weren't working anymore, that would explain all the trouble with my scent and Ty's strong reaction. I couldn't fix it without help.

Chapter 14 - Ty

As I turned onto our street, I was still struggling to shake the feel of Liza's soft skin pressed against mine when I held her on the couch and explored her mouth with my tongue. What had possessed me to respond that way? I shook my head and tried to push her scent out of my memory. The main priority wasn't my lust for Liza, though it was so strong that I'd almost ripped her clothes off with my teeth.

    I glanced at the clock. It was later than I'd originally thought. As tired as I was, I couldn't sleep yet, and it wasn't in my nature to make something like this wait until morning. My brain worked on overdrive as I tried to process what Liza had said about her past.

    She didn't remember anything, and no one had ever told her about her life before Presley Acres.

    After my little chat with Stone earlier in the day, I'd had a few meetings before I went to Liza's place. I'd hoped she would be able to fill in the missing pieces that Zephyr couldn't locate, which was still a shock to me. The man was a computer whizz and knew the backdoor to every dark internet portal in existence. If he couldn't dig up someone's history, no matter how horrible it might be, no one in the world could.

Maybe there was a reason she didn't know where she had come from. Was she somehow connected to the place Stone mentioned? Heather Falls?

Walking into the house, I came to terms with the fact that several dots still needed connecting. But it wasn't the mystery itself that had me on edge. I was mostly worried that I wouldn't like the answers to my questions surrounding Liza and Stone. I wanted to be the kind of man that didn't care about history. I wanted to believe it wouldn't matter to me, but I couldn't say for certain.

I walked to my parents' room. I didn't spend a lot of time in this part of the house, but the memories were ripe here. Hide and seek from my bedroom to every room in the place. Though, I hadn't been here in years, except to see my father. Things looked different without the cover of worry. The light was softer, and I could smell my mother's perfume, the fresh flowers on the tables between the bedroom doors, and the clean linens in the unused rooms.

I continued down the hallway. Seeing the light still on in my parents' bedroom, I knocked.

"Come in." Mother's voice was soft, so I assumed Dad was already asleep.

I stood in the doorway and watched my father shuffling around the room. He was supposed to be resting after dinner. Doctor's orders. I shouldn't have been shocked, considering how damn stubborn the man was. He'd once sat in the car on a family vacation for two hours straight because we'd chosen a different restaurant to the one he'd suggested. Dad had refused to come in and had skipped the meal altogether.

When the alpha set his mind to something, he expected others to agree and follow his lead. In this case, he didn't want anyone telling him when to go to bed.

I understood Dad better than he realized, considering that I was so adamant to make Liza mine. There was no amount of nagging or elusive threats that would convince me otherwise.

Dad turned to face me, holding on to the dresser to prop himself up. "Did you do what you were supposed to do? Did you get rid of that bastard who's asking questions?"

"No." I crossed the room and sat on the edge of the four-post canopy bed. My father would see it as a failure, but I needed to know what I was up against before I could do anything about it.

"Why the hell not?" Dad crossed his arms and leaned his back against the dresser. "Fuck, Tyson. If you want to be the alpha, you have to learn how to assert dominance. If you can't follow a simple instruction like getting rid of a nosy son of a bitch who seems to be here with the intention of hurting the pack, then I don't see how it will ever be possible that you can *lead* an entire pack." Dad paused to catch his breath. "You're going to take the name of this family and drag it through the mud. They'll come out of the woodwork to challenge you, to turn you out and take everything we've worked so hard for. You have to protect the pack from all threats, no matter how big or how small. No matter what you have to do, Tyson." He coughed. "That's what being an alpha is."

Fury burned in my blood. He wasn't telling the truth about why he wanted the guy gone, and now he was using me as his whipping boy. I stood and held my hand up to stop him from saying something he might possibly regret later. "What do you know about Heather Falls?" I watched him as I spoke, looking for any indication of a lie.

Instead, he fell forward. It happened so fast that I couldn't tell if he'd tried to take a step forward or if his legs simply gave out on him. Thankfully, he caught himself on the bed before cracking his head on the floor again.

Mother's sharp gasp was filled with fear, and she ran to his side. I instinctively held out my arms and kept him from slipping onto the floor.

His face was as pale as a ghost's, which was saying something considering how tan our pack naturally was.

"Dad, you need to lie down." I wrapped my arms around his waist, trying to hold him upright while moving him toward the head of the bed.

"No." He struggled weakly against my grip. "I'm not a fucking invalid. Take me to my chair."

It took several minutes, but I finally got his shaky body into his leather armchair. He glared up at me, but it was my mother's whimper that filled me with apprehension. Whatever or wherever Heather Falls was, it scared the shit out of both of them.

"God, no," Mother whispered as she knelt next to Dad. "This can't be happening."

I wasn't sure if she was referring to the name of the town I'd just dropped into their laps or Dad's reaction to it. Either way, the churning in my stomach intensified. My father definitely knew what the Heather Falls business was about.

I'd spent a few minutes searching online for the name earlier, but all that came up was a couple personal profiles and an elderly human woman's obituary. There was nothing significant, and so few results—nothing red-flag worthy. I wasn't convinced it was an actual place. Perhaps it was code for something else, and something sinister based on their reactions.

So far, nothing about this day made sense, but I got the impression I was finally about to learn why my parents didn't want me to mate with Liza.

Before my father could start his tale, a knock on the bedroom door interrupted us. The mystery of Heather Falls, a white wolf, Liza, and my parents' connection to all of that had to wait another few minutes. I'd waited this long. A little longer wouldn't kill me.

"Yes?" Mother stood and smoothed the front of her gown. Nary a visitor nor maid would ever see my mother disheveled or crying. It just wasn't done. "Come in."

"Sorry to interrupt, ma'am." It was one of the housekeeping staff. "I'm leaving for the night, but I wanted to make sure everyone's okay. I heard a commotion a few minutes ago." She glanced in Dad's direction and lowered her voice. "Should I call Dr. Anderson?"

Mother looked at Dad, who shook his head. Her eyes stayed closed a second longer than normal on her next blink, but she turned back to the maid with a serene smile on her face. Dad didn't want a doctor, and Mother would honor his wishes. It was the way of things in our house.

"No, thank you." Mother forced a smile. "We're just fine. Thank you for checking on us. Have a lovely night. We'll see you tomorrow."

The housekeeper nodded, then closed the door gently.

I crossed my arms and stared at Dad, waiting for an explanation. Based on his expression, he knew he had no choice but to tell me. Stone had intel that my parents had desperately tried to keep a secret, and now they needed my help.

Dad didn't speak for a long time. Finally, he sighed deeply and raised his gaze to meet mine. "Sit."

Shit. Maybe this was worse than I had imagined.

My father glanced at my mother, then turned to me, this time sighing softly. "This is not a pretty story, but you need to know it. It will explain why we reacted the way we did when fate chose Liza Mims to be your mate."

Sweat slicked my palms, and I clenched my hands together. I wasn't the kind of man to get nervous or even mildly anxious about anything. My father taught me long ago that situations had solutions, and every problem was a priority until it wasn't—in business and in the pack. This seemed different, though. More.

Mother took a seat next to Dad, her shoulders rolling forward as if the stress of the moment had come crashing down on her.

I braced myself. Whatever he had to say wasn't going to be easy. The only question was: who would it be worse for?

"There's no easy way to put this, so I'm just going to come right out with it." Dad pinched the bridge of his nose and closed his eyes. "My father's father, your great-grandfather, had dealings with the Danish mafia. He wasn't the first. Our family's dealings with them went back for many generations." Dad sighed. I didn't see a problem. We weren't dealing with them anymore. Not as far as I knew, anyway. "And those *transactions* were passed down until I became alpha."

Okay. Dealings with the mafia. I let out a slow breath. Certainly, all this cloak-and-dagger and middle-of-the-night story time wasn't nearly as bad as he was making it out to be.

Dad cleared his throat. "Presley Acres was built on dirty money made off the sale of drugs and death. Blood money. Unfortunately, there was nothing honorable about the way our family came into its fortunes." He spoke softly but with finality.

I stared at him until I was sure this wasn't some warped bedtime story he was hauling out in dementia or some other affliction that came as a result of his head injury. It wasn't. This was our history, and it was real. Holy fuck.

"The good news is that we took that money and turned it into lucrative businesses designed to keep our family wealthy for many years to come."

My eyes widened. "That's the *good* news?" My family was built on a legacy of bullshit. It was all lies. All the stories I'd grown up hearing about my ancestors were made up.

Dad shifted his weight and shook his head. "I'm not done, Tyson."

I shut my mouth and glared at my father. To say I was stunned by his words would have been an understatement. In approximately one minute, he'd blown up my entire life. All this time, I'd thought our family to be pillars of the community. Now, that idealism had gone to hell.

"When your grandfather, my father, passed away, I became the alpha. I knew the truth. Not only did I want a better foundation for our pack, but I also wanted to cut our connections to the mafia." He raised his eyes to meet mine.

Mother stood and poured Dad a glass of water.. Maybe she needed a minute, too, but all of this sure as fuck wasn't a surprise to her. My parents didn't keep anything from each other.

My father gratefully accepted the water from my mother and took a few sips. "The alpha of the Heather Falls pack's name was Josef. They were our... associates." He took another sip of water, the glass shaking as he brought it to his mouth. "He was a drug-and-arms dealer, known for being smart and cunning. Josef made the money for all of us. Made us all filthy rich. But it was a dangerous game, and I wanted out. I wanted the pack out. We were finished." Shaking his head, he reached for my hand. "This isn't what I wanted for my son. You were only fourteen. I wanted better for you. I certainly didn't want you to inherit any of that shit."

I glanced at Mother, who wiped a tear from her cheek. She remained quiet, allowing her alpha to do the talking, but this was painful for her.

"What did you do?" I leaned forward, resting my elbows on my knees.

"I made it known to Josef that this pack was cutting ties with him." Dad scoffed. "He wasn't too happy about that. Josef knew the Keller reputation and knew we were seen as royalty. So, he played the hand he thought would win him the right to continue our dealings." I watched my dad, saw the tremble in his hand, and heard the crack in his voice, but I'd be damned if I was letting him wait for another day or another time to finish the story. "Josef threatened to reveal the truth behind our wealth. As if that wasn't enough, he promised to tell everyone how the king of the south was nothing more than a drug lord and weapon-distributing thug."

My muscles tensed. I didn't know how the story would end, but if I had been in Dad's shoes, I would have eliminated the threat.

"My council advised that I send a message by taking Josef out and taking over Heather Falls."

"That's what I would've done," I said.

"The council saw it as an opportunity to not only get Josef out of the picture, but also take control of the territory and halt all the illegal activity." The council obviously had an idea how to prevent those looking to keep Josef's business alive from taking over and coming for our pack. I hoped they hadn't blindly counseled my father into doing something that would hurt us now. "They thought this would, ultimately, unite the packs, which was a noble idea. Unfortunately, things didn't go as planned."

"They hardly ever do." That much I'd figured out on my own.

Wincing, Dad rubbed his forehead. "No. There was a mole somewhere among the council members, and Josef learned what we had planned down to the most minute detail. He knew when and where we were going to strike, how we planned to do it, and who would lead the charge."

Mom whimpered and pressed a handkerchief between her nose and her mouth.

Dad ignored her. "So, what was meant to be an execution of an alpha turned into an all-out brawl. Many great shifters died that day… on both sides." He looked at me. "A man who will follow his pack, who is loyal to his leaders, is a good man, even if he fights for the wrong side. Remember that." When I nodded, he took another drink, another pause. "After several hours of fighting, the attack ended in the demise of the Heather Falls pack."

"Do you need to take a break?" Mother rested her hand on Dad's arm. "You don't have to tell the whole story tonight."

He smiled weakly at her. "It's time. He needs to know it all."

She nodded and sat back in her chair, her hand remaining on his arm. It was a small gesture of support but kind and intimate. She loved my father, and I loved her more for it.

"The battle was brutal. Our wolves were taken by surprise when the Heather Falls pack descended upon them. Regardless, our pack was stronger and better organized." That was a credit to my father's analytical mind, his command that the pack be prepared for hunters and threats. "Josef may have been a good leader in terms of providing a solid monetary base for his pack, but his arrogance made him believe that his pack was untouchable. Their lack of organized training was their downfall. By the time the sun had set, the woods of Heather Falls were dripping with the blood of its pack."

I ran my hands through my hair, trying to imagine the death count. "You killed them *all*?"

Mother shot a worried glance at Dad.

He held his hand up and nodded. "Not all of them. I'd heard that there was a child; the only one in the pack at the time. She was the princess to the alpha, the mafia king and queen."

My heart beat so loudly in my chest I could barely think straight.

"I was the one who found Liza in the woods that day. She was only four years old." Dad's voice cracked. "I hate to admit it, but for a split second I considered ending her life and sending her to be with her parents. I just couldn't stomach murdering an innocent child. So, I brought her back with me to Presley Acres. I spent more money than I can count erasing any and all history of the Heather Falls pack, knowing that if I didn't, it would come back to haunt me. Or you."

My stomach clenched. God, Liza must have been terrified. She hadn't been much more than a baby. "What did you do with her? After you brought her back here?"

"I did what I felt was best. She was adopted by a local family that we weren't closely associated with. Even though I'd saved her life, I'd also killed everyone she'd ever known." Dad hung his head in shame. "I couldn't bear to live with the guilt of seeing her face, knowing all that I'd taken from her. She couldn't stay here, and I sure as hell couldn't have her in our social circles."

I stood and started to pace the room, trying to make sense of what I'd just heard. "What about Stone? How is he connected to all of this?"

Dad shrugged. "I don't know. I spared no expense erasing that pack's existence from any scroll or ledger that mentioned them. He shouldn't know a damn thing about Heather Falls because, as far as anyone is concerned, it doesn't exist. The fact that he knows anything at all is a very bad sign for our family and the pack."

Yeah. Of that, I was well aware.

***

Later that night, I lay in bed staring at the ceiling and forcing my muscles to relax. It was too much to process, and my body had gone into fight-or-flight mode.

I'd always considered our family to be upright and morally decent leaders. Now that Dad had shared the truth about our history, I was ashamed of who I was and of those who had come before me—of our entire lineage. We were a bunch of drug dealers. Not to mention we were murderers on top of all the lying and dirty money exchanged. Our *royalty* claims were bullshit, our high-society status nothing more than a facade.

The sins of my ancestors were a heavy weight on my heart. If the pack found out...

There was no way to know how Stone had uncovered whatever he knew or thought he knew about Heather Falls, but I suspected he had a plan to use that information against us.

How could I be expected to one day, probably sooner rather than later, stand in front of the pack as their alpha, their brave, and fearless leader, when I knew the truth? I wasn't the kind of sociopath I would need to be to pretend I didn't know, to hold my head up and be the man who led them. The pack would know. They would see right through me, and that would sway their confidence in me. Obliterate it. I would be useless.

My wolf whimpered, and I felt his pain. There wasn't a single part of me that wanted to reject Liza, but what other choice did I have? I couldn't mate with her or marry her knowing what my family had done to hers. Knowing who her family was.

Not only was it unfair to her but it was also unfair to my father. He'd said himself that he couldn't bear to look into her eyes. I didn't know if I would be able to either now that I knew the truth, knew what had been done. I couldn't risk the pack by being weak to her or for her out of guilt and shame. My father had taught me better.

It was best to break it off with her as soon as possible. I grabbed my phone from the nightstand and sent her a text even as my heart ached.

Can you meet me for breakfast tomorrow morning at Coffee and Chill? 8am?

It was late, so chances were, she was sleeping, but I needed to see her as soon as possible. There was no point in dragging this out. I had to do it. There was no other way.

I planned to reject her, but I braced myself for the pain that would cause both of us. It would eviscerate me. She was everything I wanted, and even the thought of ending what had barely gotten a chance to start had my heart cracking.

Yet, I had no other choice. Not with Stone sniffing around. If he knew about Heather Falls, it was only a matter of time before they would come for us. I couldn't sacrifice Liza's safety out of my own selfish needs. I couldn't give her back the family mine took from her, but I wouldn't risk her for the sake of my family, either. I would make sure she was protected. When the people who sent Stone came for us, they wouldn't get to her. She would be safe. Without me.

My wolf snarled and growled, desperately pleading for his mate.

I ignored him. It was for the best. Now that Dad had shared our family's history, I carried his burdens on my own back. I couldn't share the truth and ruin the pack's legacy. Not after everything Dad had done to ensure the Keller pack not only survived but thrived well into the future. I had no choice but to make my own personal sacrifice to save the family name.

It was the last thing I wanted to do, but I would end things with Liza. I suffered through the night thinking about it, understanding there was nothing else to be done. I didn't have any other choice.

***

When she walked into the coffee shop the next morning, the bond between us had changed. It was stronger. Fighting the pull toward her almost dropped me to my knees. My resolve weakened as she neared my table.

Liza looked wide-eyed as she glanced around the room nervously. I caught her scent and blinked hard. It was stronger than last night.

How was that possible?

Snarling, I dug my nails into the wooden tabletop with a need so deep in my bones that I couldn't stop myself if I tried.

Any thought of rejecting her vanished. I was desperate to keep her. So much so that all I could think was of claiming her and ripping the heads off of every wolf that got in my way.

Liza was mine.

Chapter 15 - Liza

Waking up when my body damn well pleased was exactly the therapy I had needed. I'd fallen asleep shortly after requesting an appointment with my doctor, leaving a note at the bottom of the email to explain my dire situation.

I'd come to the conclusion that my dosage needed to be increased, and I didn't want to wait a week or however long it would take to see the doctor. My pheromones were out of whack, as evidenced by the way Ty had all but ravaged me last night.

Groaning, I rolled over and snatched my phone from the nightstand. There was no response from the doctor's office, which wasn't surprising since it was a Sunday.

Still, I was anxious to get my body back under control. As much as I wanted Ty, I didn't want us to go from zero to one hundred like that until we knew each other better. He'd seemed out of control, and that's not how I wanted our physical intimacy to play out. Sure, I wanted him to *want* me, but not just because of my scent.

My phone alerted me to an unread text message. Ty asked if I'd like to meet him for breakfast at the local coffee shop. My heart skipped a beat at the thought of seeing him again. That was until I remembered how last night had ended. Would it be too soon for me to see him?

"Shit." It wasn't as if I could pretend it never happened. The memory of his hands on my body was a fresh reminder, and one I would want to remember for as long as I lived. It sent a shiver down my spine and a bolt of heat straight to my core.

At the very least, a conversation needed to be had. Ty had no idea I was a virgin, and I wanted him to know that before our relationship progressed. All other details about me could wait until another time, but not this one.

I quickly responded that I'd meet him for breakfast, then threw off the covers. I was already late, but I knew Ty wouldn't mind waiting a few extra minutes for me. He'd understand.

As I drove toward the coffee shop, I dug through my purse and found a light-pink lip gloss. There wasn't much pigment to it, but it gave my face a little extra oomph. I needed all the help I could get.

When I pulled onto the street on which the coffee shop was a few blocks down, heat flooded my body. I was hotter than usual, to the point that I cranked the air conditioner up full blast.

What the hell?

At a red light, I checked my cycle calendar app and discovered I was in my heat window. My hormone pills kept me from going into a full-blown heat, but I still had a lot of the same symptoms, just on a lesser scale.

I sighed. That explained the hot flash. This had happened multiple times over the years with no issues, so I didn't give it any further thought.

I popped my morning dose and took a swig of water just as I pulled into the parking lot of Coffee and Chill.

For a moment, I sat in the car and watched the shop door. I'd have to have the conversation with Ty, but I wasn't sure how to broach the subject. It wasn't the kind of thing I liked to blurt out. Just saying it made me think of the way he would rectify my situation. Another burst of heat flashed through me, and I took a few minutes to compose myself.

Taking a cleansing breath, I reminded myself that Ty was my fated mate. If fate wanted us to be together, nothing I told Ty would make him want to run in the other direction. That's what I assumed being fated meant.

He still had free will, and maybe the idea of being with someone so inexperienced would turn him off. It was a worry, though not one I'd ever had before. Prior to this, if someone was put off by the fact that I was innocent in that regard, then they weren't right for me.

Ty didn't seem like the kind of guy who would shut the whole relationship down because of my virginity. Then again, we were still getting to know one another. Stranger things had happened in my life.

I took a final glance at my reflection and fixed a rogue section of hair, pushing it back into my messy bun. The parking lot was full, but I spotted Ty's car and hoped he hadn't been waiting too long.

As soon as I opened the door to the coffee shop, I sensed that something was off. Snarls filled the room, and I froze.

The place was crowded, every table full and people were waiting at the counter, but the gaze of every male in the room was on me, and they looked ravenous. My eyes went wide as a few men got to their feet; their fangs exposed as they walked in my direction. My mind flashed to a scene from a zombie movie as I backed up a few steps and reached for the door handle behind me.

Just as more men stood to their feet, Ty was suddenly by my side. He stood in front of me and let out a loud growl of warning that stopped the other men in their tracks.

He turned to face me and lightly grabbed my arm, pulling me out the door toward his car. I was in such shock that I couldn't stop watching the men who continued to scan my body up and down as if I were a piece of meat, and they were ravenous. What the fuck was going on?

Ty put me in his car, then walked around the hood.

Were those men going to attack me?

I had never seen anything like this before. I didn't know what to do. I only knew for sure that I hadn't liked being ogled like that.

Ty slid behind the wheel and slammed his door shut, finally snapping me back to reality. He started the car and drove away from the coffee shop as if we were being chased, but when I checked the mirror, I didn't see anyone following us. He drove in silence, shaking his head and breathing erratically.

I was too stunned to ask if he was okay as he opened the window. Inhaling deeply, his shoulders curled in, then back out. He was relaxing in increments. One breath at a time. He let out a deep sigh.

After taking a few minutes to compose himself, he glanced over at me and spoke for the first time. "Are you aware of what you smell like, Liza?"

He was blaming me for their reaction. I bit my lip as a black hole formed in my stomach. I shifted in my seat nervously, staring down at my hands. "I take pills to mask it. They've never failed me before, so I don't understand what's happening."

Ty gripped the steering wheel so tightly his knuckles turned white. He glanced at me, confusion darkening his gaze. "How long have you been on them?"

This wasn't exactly the type of conversation I'd had in mind. Discussing the hormone pills was one thing. Talking about this was something else. It was bad enough I had to tell him I was a virgin, now I had to tell him about my first period, too?

But if Ty was going to trust me, I had to be vulnerable. He had just witnessed a whole room of men preparing to rip my clothes off. He deserved answers.

"I've been taking the pills ever since I started my period when I was thirteen." I stared straight ahead, too embarrassed to make eye contact.

He took a moment to digest my answer, then cleared his throat. "Have your doctors ever explained why your pheromones are so strong?"

I froze. I never wanted to lie to Ty, but I was afraid to tell him the truth. Though, since I was being vulnerable... I shook my head. "They assumed it was something genetic, but since I don't know who my biological parents were, they didn't even know what to test for."

I folded my hands together, hoping Ty wouldn't see them shaking.

He remained silent as he drove us down a road that led to the state park, then pulled into a parking area that didn't seem too crowded.

I watched him closely. His chest expanded and contracted, and deep lines furrowed his brow.

He was tense, and I couldn't blame him. What was meant to be a nice breakfast filled with good conversation had suddenly turned into a scenario where Ty had to rescue me from a room full of horny shifters.

I twisted my body to face him and spoke softly. "Ty, I'm sorry for what happened back there. I know that wasn't easy for you."

He stared into my eyes.

"I'm going to the doctor first thing in the morning to see if they should up the dosage of my medication." I sighed. Of all the ways I'd expected to start my Sunday morning, this wasn't it. "I'm fully aware of what my pheromones can do. I feel awful that I triggered those men back at the coffee shop. It wasn't my intention at all." I knew things were haywire right now, but I didn't know how haywire they had gotten. The last thing I needed was a repeat of what happened to me when I was younger. I pushed the thought away. Thinking about that now would do no one any good.

Ty rubbed his forehead. "You don't need to apologize for something that's beyond your control, Liza." His voice was calm and gentle, but still heated and harder than I'd heard it before.

"Are you upset with me?" I swallowed hard, trying not to cry. I didn't want him to see how weak I became when I thought of how my life had been upset by the pheromones and my being unable to control them. Crying served no purpose. Yet, I couldn't hold back the tears. It was just one more example of things I couldn't control.

The whole morning had been humiliating, but I couldn't stand the thought of Ty being mad at me. I was already feeling defeated enough without carrying the weight of his judgment.

"No, Liza." His smile was soft when he glanced at me. "My frustration isn't with you." He rested his arm on the steering wheel and shifted his weight so he could look at me. "Do your parents know anything about your biological parents?"

I shook my head. "As far as I know, they're just as in the dark as anyone else about my life before Presley Acres."

"Haven't you ever been curious?" Ty leaned forward, and I thought he might reach out to touch me, but he dropped his hand. "Sorry to pry, but if I had been adopted I know I would've had a ton of questions for my parents."

I laughed softly. A ton of questions wasn't the half of it. "Honestly, I spent most of my youth wondering who my biological parents were. It helped me cope by picturing them as horrible people who lived in poor conditions, unable to care for an infant. But as I get older, I find myself with even more questions than before." That I hadn't really worked up the nerve to ask didn't speak to how kind and open my parents had always been.

"Besides the obvious questions, what have you wondered about?"

There were too many to list, but I decided to tell him about my dreams. "Ever since I was a little girl, I've had this same recurring dream. Well, it's more like a nightmare."

Ty's eyebrows rose. "What happens in the dream?"

I sighed. "In the dream, I'm a little girl. I'm running from something or someone. A woman with hair like mine tells me to hide. I'm terrified because I don't want to leave the woman, but I hide, anyway. I watch from a distance as someone takes her, and still, I hide in the bushes."

"That sounds horrible."

"It is. Every time it happens, I wake up drenched in sweat with my heart threatening to tear out of my chest." I hesitated. Some of this was too hard to talk about, but I'd chosen to confide in him, so I wouldn't stop now. "Part of me doesn't think they're just dreams."

Ty crossed his arms. "Maybe you're right."

I studied his face. The muscles in his jaw were clenched. This subject was making him uncomfortable, too.

I shrugged. "My parents have always told me that I was only given to them temporarily. They were supposed to just foster me until I could be adopted."

"Did they ever mention your biological parents?"

I closed my eyes and tried to remember. "They said my biological parents had dumped me at the hospital, but they ended up falling in love with me and decided to keep me."

Ty stared directly ahead with his jaw clenched so tightly, I worried he'd hurt his teeth.

"Are you okay?"

His face was drawn when he looked at me. He was struggling with something other than what had transpired at the coffee shop.

He took my hand. "Will you take a walk with me?"

"Sure." Some fresh air and exercise would help, I was sure of it.

Ty moved to my door and opened it like a perfect gentleman. He held out his hand, and I twined my fingers with his.

We walked down the nearest path without talking.

The park was peaceful and serene with lush green grass sprawling across the landscape. The trees towering above us provided a canopy of shade, and wildflowers blossomed along the edges of the winding path. A gentle breeze brushed against our faces, carrying the scent of freshly mown grass, which I assumed Ty appreciated.

Maybe that's why he wanted to take a walk, so he could get out of the car. He probably felt trapped with my pheromones, and based on how he'd reacted last night, didn't want to have a repeat moment where he lost all control.

Ty squeezed my hand gently. "That was really tough for me back there at the coffee shop."

I grimaced. "I'm so sorry."

"No." Ty stopped walking. "Please, I don't want you to apologize. I just want to explain how difficult it was for me to see those other men wanting you. I could smell their lust. Knowing that it was directed at my mate was torture." He shook his head.

We started walking again, and I stayed quiet. Ty was opening up, and I wanted to hear every word he was willing to share.

"As an alpha, it took everything in me not to bite into their necks and demand submission."

Hearing that my fated mate wanted to murder other shifters shouldn't have filled me with warmth, but that was exactly what it did. Ty was protective of me, and that provided a sense of security I'd longed for from an early age.

My phone dinged in my purse, interrupting our walk. We stopped, and I scanned the email. "It's from my doctor. He's out of town and won't be back until the end of the week. He'll see me on Friday, but in the meantime, he'll call in a stronger prescription, doubling my dosage. He says there's no need to see another doctor until he can see me on Friday."

"Are you satisfied with his response?"

I liked that he'd asked that particular question, and hadn't insisted I see a different doctor. "Yeah." I dropped my phone back into my purse. "I assumed that's what he'd say. Maybe my body is becoming somewhat resistant to the medication so it needs to be upped."

Ty shrugged. "I have no clue how any of that works, but it makes sense."

"I'm just relieved there's a solution."

We continued to walk hand in hand, enjoying the peaceful setting.

Eventually, we drove back toward the coffee shop. We kept the conversation light since we were both still coming down from the rush of adrenaline of the heavy morning.

Ty parked next to my car and turned to face me.

I stared at the coffee shop, wondering if any of the men were still inside. And if they were, would they smell me and come after me?

Ty cupped my face. "Don't worry, Liza. Just go straight to the drugstore drive-thru and pick up your prescription."

I placed my hands over his. "Thank you for being so understanding. I'm still embarrassed about the whole thing."

"Don't be." Ty gently kissed me on the forehead. "You have nothing to be ashamed of."

I took a moment, allowing myself to be reassured by Ty. The warmth of his hands on my face and his soothing words brought me peace.

We said our goodbyes and I got into my own car. I needed to make one stop before I went to the pharmacy.

My parents had been steadfast in their support ever since I hit puberty and had to deal with the reaction of males when I was in heat. They'd gone out of their way to assure me that it wasn't my fault and had taken me to the doctor more times than I could count to adjust the dosage of my medicine or get answers to questions. Sometimes, they took me to the doctor just so he could console me and tell me that I wouldn't be suffering forever. I wanted them to know what had happened at the coffee shop, and I needed their encouragement.

They were both home, which I'd figured would be the case. Mom always cooked a big Sunday lunch, and with my brothers in town, I figured they'd show up to eat eventually. I was relieved to see only my parents' cars in the driveway. I sure as hell didn't want to discuss my pheromones in front of my brothers. Not that they hadn't heard it all before. In a house with two nosy boys and a mother with a voice that could bend steel, there weren't a lot of secrets.

Mom pulled the door open and smiled at me. "Hello, my beautiful daughter. We weren't expecting you. Are you joining us for lunch?"

"Maybe." I stepped inside. "I was hoping to talk with you and Dad before the guys get here."

Mom's smile faded. "Sure, honey. Let me get your dad."

She disappeared into the back of the house and returned a moment later, my dad following solemnly behind her. She'd clearly told him something was wrong.

They sat on the couch across from me, both staring at me expectantly.

I rolled my eyes. "Don't look so worried. I'm fine. Everything's fine."

Mom let out a puff of air. "You seem upset."

Dad furrowed his brows. "What happened?"

I took a deep breath, then proceeded to tell them what had transpired at the coffee shop that morning. They listened intently, their expressions turning from concern to disbelief, then finally to anger as they heard about the effect my pheromones had had on every single man in the building.

"I don't understand." Mom scooted to the edge of the couch, wringing the dish towel that was usually slung over her shoulder. "Is your medication no longer working? What did the doctor say? Do you need me to come with you to an appointment?"

She was always available to help me. It had been like that for as long as I could remember. And maybe I should've asked about the adoption, but perhaps I didn't need to know. This was my family. Not the ones who didn't take care of me and who had abandoned me.

"Mom, I'm fine." I smiled at her. "Need I remind you that I'm thirty years old? I don't think I'll require a chaperone to the doctor's office."

Mom nodded. She understood because she always understood. "Have you actually talked to Dr. Reynolds about this?"

"Yes, I emailed him. He's calling in a stronger dosage of pills. He's out of town, but I'm seeing him on Friday."

Dad cleared his throat. "Liza, you need to make sure Dr. Reynolds knows about your new... er, mating situation." *Mating situation.* This was my father trying to be delicate. Trying not to say something he probably didn't want to think about. I couldn't imagine how a father felt about this kind of thing—especially my father.

Dad blushed and averted his gaze. This wasn't exactly a conversation he wanted to be involved in, but he worried about me just as much as Mom. Maybe more. He just wasn't as vocal about it.

"I'll make sure he knows." I wasn't sure what that had to do with anything, but hopefully it would relieve their worries.

I studied their faces. They were anxious, which only put me on edge even more. I didn't know the kind of research my mother had done when this problem first arose. Maybe she didn't think the new medication would work, and what if she was right? I didn't know how I would be able to bear it if more symptoms popped up out of the blue. Other side effects.

Most concerning, I had no way of knowing whether Ty would still want me if he found out what I was and why my pheromones ruled my life. He was probably used to normal women with normal appetites and scent signals. And if he did want me, would it be for the right reasons?

Chapter 16 - Ty

I'd never been the kind of guy who found himself connected to a woman beyond the initial physical chemistry. Some ex-girlfriends had told me I was emotionally unavailable, and I didn't blame them. I was a workaholic who refused to settle down with a hot piece of ass, no matter how hot it was.

Now, I had suddenly been thrust into a relationship where I was connected to Liza in a way I couldn't even describe. I wanted to protect her, take care of her, and make sure she never had to worry about a room full of shifters looking at her like that ever again.

Being the next in line for the title of alpha was a cumbersome load to bear, but the weight of it had lifted the first time I stared into her eyes. I'd assumed I would move forward with my fated mate, taking my rightful position as alpha and relieving my father of a position he should've stepped down from years ago but remained in because I was yet unmated.

Now, my mind was laden with our family's dark secrets. My father's confession had sent my thoughts into a tailspin, ultimately leading me to break things off with Liza, which hadn't quite gone as planned.

After the coffee shop incident, I was conflicted. On the one hand, I needed to break things off with Liza to protect our family's future. Dad had made it perfectly clear to what lengths he'd gone to in erasing our family's past. No wonder he had looked like he'd seen a ghost when Liza and I spotted each other at the mating ceremony.

I'd been resolved to breaking things off with her—reject her as my mate—but her scent was irresistible. The need to claim her was overwhelming. Everything I had planned on saying to Liza had been forgotten. I couldn't reject her.

Watching the other shifters catch wind of her pheromones had been like a scene out of a movie. It was an immediate reaction as their cocks hardened and their breaths quickened. I shuddered at the thought of what might have happened if I hadn't gotten Liza to my car. It was something she'd need to protect herself against. Or I would.

Even more surprising than their reactions to Liza's presence was the shock and confusion that had marred her beautiful face. When I'd asked her about it, she claimed that her hormone pills should have kept that from happening. It must not have been the first time her pheromones had caused men to react in that way.

I shook my head as I started my convertible. It was a gorgeous day, so I put the top down and let the fresh air fill my lungs. Maybe a little sun on the drive into work would help clear my mind. The elements of nature often calmed me, and since I couldn't go for a run right now, this was going to have to do.

I pulled up in front of Bryce's house at the usual time. Since we were business partners, we carpooled when the morning was filled with meetings.

Once every quarter, we brought all of the branch managers under one roof to discuss the companies that were shielded under the umbrella of Keller Enterprises. Although each business was a separate entity, we wanted to ensure that they all complied with the Keller Enterprise mission statement.

The meetings were notoriously long and sometimes boring but necessary to keep our businesses operating at optimal levels.

I turned off the engine and got out of my car, inhaling deeply to clear my mind. I needed to focus on work, not Liza's pheromones or my family's secrets. But now that I knew what I knew, everything was connected—the businesses to the history and the history to the secrets and the secrets to Liza—there was no shield I could throw in place to make it easier to focus.

"Hey." Bryce was already waiting outside, staring at this phone. "Are you driving or am I?"

"Let's take the convertible." I stretched my arms high over my head and hopped back into the driver's seat. "I haven't driven it in months and figured it was about time to bring her out into the wild again."

Bryce buckled up—he was a nervous nelly and not a fan of open-air vehicles—as I pulled out of his driveway. "What's new? Any new developments with Liza?"

I sighed. Talking about it wouldn't help me clear it from my mind. "You wouldn't believe me if I told you."

Bryce shoved his sunglasses over his eyes. "Try me."

He had a myriad of crazy female stories from his many escapades. He was a known womanizer who didn't even try to deny it, and he'd made his way around the block more than once with multiple women in town. There was probably no better person to ask about pheromones.

"Have you ever gone through a rut?" I glanced at Bryce out of the corner of my eye, wondering if he'd laugh immediately or give me a chance to explain before he laughed in my face.

As if on cue, he chuckled. "That's something teenage boys experience when girls are going through heat. You know… when their hormones are raging and it's difficult to hide the scent." He explained it to me as though I was unfamiliar with the phenomenon. I, too, was a teenaged wolf once.

"Yeah. I know. Have you seen it happen in grown men?"

He shook his head. "I don't know many grown men who have experienced it. Actually, I don't know of any. Why?"

How much did I want to share with Bryce? Finally, I decided to tell him exactly what had happened at the coffee shop. Hopefully, he'd have some brilliant insight I hadn't already thought of.

I cleared my throat and shifted in my seat. "Yesterday, I met up with Liza for breakfast. As soon as she walked into the coffee shop, every guy in the place turned and stared at her." Fury heated my blood just thinking about it.

"Well, she is an attractive woman, Ty. You can't expect other men not to notice her, even if she *is* your fated mate." Bryce took a sip of water from his stainless-steel water bottle. If it had been just a couple guys, I could've bought that because she was pretty. "Really, Ty. I never took you to be so naive about attractive women and how men react to them."

I shook my head. I loved Bryce like a brother, but he had a tendency to be an asshole. "No. I don't mean they wanted to *look* at Liza. There was a vibe."

"A vibe?" He cocked an eyebrow like he was unfamiliar with a vibe as a concept.

"Yes, a fucking vibe. They wanted to fuck her."

Bryce scoffed. "I know you have an everybody-wants-what-I-have complex because you literally have everything, but I'm gonna need some more information before I can tell if you're right or if you're just being you. You start reading minds all of a sudden?" Yeah, he was an asshole.

"Her pheromones were so strong that every guy immediately reacted. Even I was caught off guard. In all my life, I've never smelled such a potent and blatantly sexual scent in my life." I paused, trying to think of a way to describe it in a way he'd understand. "It was like I didn't have any control over my own body. I was starving, and she was dinner. All I could think about was stripping her naked and fucking her brains out on the barista's countertop."

Bryce's eyes widened. He knew me and knew the control I exercised every minute of every day. "Sounds intense."

"Intense is the fucking understatement of understatements." I could still feel that… intensity. "And it wasn't just me, it was all of them. And I mean *all* of them."

"What did you do? Don't tell me your dad had to bail you out of jail for indecent exposure." Bryce laughed at his own joke.

I wasn't laughing.

I pulled into the parking lot of Keller Enterprises' headquarters and turned off the engine. "What else could I do? I got her the fuck out of there and into my car. I had to stick my head out the window like a fucking mutt while we drove so the fresh air could bring me back to my senses."

Bryce was contemplative for a few moments. "I've never heard of anything like that happening before. Sure, we're all physically attracted to a wolf in heat. Our dicks might perk up, but a primal reaction like that from a crowd... It's unheard of." Bryce went quiet again. He stared at the manicured lawn, obviously in deep thought since he wasn't glued to his phone. Finally, he spoke up again. "Unless..."

I loathed it when he left me hanging. "What? What were you going to say?" When he remained silent for longer than I could stand, I slapped him on the shoulder. "Say what's on your mind. I've probably already thought of it, anyway. I've been driving myself crazy thinking about it." And I had plenty of other things to worry and think about.

Bryce laughed it off. "I was just wondering if maybe Liza was an omega."

I snorted, immediately dismissing the idea. "Omegas aren't real. They're a myth. A legend at best." Weren't they? "And even if they were real, they existed a very long time ago."

It just wasn't possible.

Bryce shrugged. "It was just a thought. Don't get your panties in a wad."

"I'm just surprised you came up with that as an option. An omega. Hmph." It would explain a lot. It would also generate a shitload of new questions.

"From the stories I've heard, omegas have intoxicating scents that draws unmated wolves to them. Like moths to a flame."

I rolled my eyes. "What I experienced was more like steel to a magnet. I was powerless."

"Need I remind you that the Keller pack is rumored to have derived from an omega." Bryce cocked his head to one side. "Maybe it's not so far-fetched."

We had no time left to hash it out. We had to head into our first meeting, but I struggled to keep my mind on the matters at hand all throughout the day. I zoned in and out of meetings, the idea of Liza being an omega continually interrupting my thoughts. It made me look incompetent, and more than once, a manager had to ask the same question multiple times until I registered what they were saying.

It was clear I was having an off day, but I couldn't do anything about it.

Bryce's suggestion had blown my fucking mind.

I didn't know Liza well enough to know whether there were indicators that she might be an omega. My brain spent the entire day working overtime while I tried to recall the story I'd heard multiple times as a child.

It was believed that no one had witnessed the birth of an omega in centuries. Supposedly, the Keller pack had gained life from a goddess-like wolf believed to be an omega. She was the first to ever walk the earth.

Omegas were rumored to be the purest of wolves. They carried genes that could birth the *perfect* wolf, and had a high sex drive that pushed them to reproduce often.

It was also said that an omega had powers and strength that far exceeded that of a normal wolf.

I'd never actually seen Liza in wolf form, so I had no way to confirm or deny that she possessed special attributes. In her human form, though, she seemed so delicate; so gentle. I couldn't imagine her being a hypersexual, mythical creature.

I thought back to every encounter I'd had with Liza, starting with that night at the mating ceremony. I hadn't witnessed anything significant from her that I would deem special. She obviously had a strong power over me, but I assumed that was due to our being fated mates, not because she was an omega.

If the stories were true, the Keller bloodline was diluted from the original omega. Though my senses were more enhanced and finely tuned than most, and I was about five times stronger than the average wolf, there wasn't anything specific about our bloodline that made us stand out from other shifters.

I snapped out of my deep thoughts just in time to hear Bryce ending the meeting. I watched as the branch managers shuffled out of the room for their lunch break.

Sitting back in my chair, I replayed my conversation with Liza in the park. She'd mentioned her upcoming appointment with the doctor to discuss her hormone medication. I didn't specifically know if there were tests a doctor would run to determine if she was omega, or if there was a specific process to figure it out, but she had some of the signs.

After the managers had cleared the room, I turned to Bryce. "Have you ever heard of female wolves taking daily hormonal medications?"

Bryce clipped a stack of papers together and swiveled in his chair to face me. "I know plenty of wolves who take suppressors to stop their heat because they don't want to risk getting pregnant. But daily? Nope."

My curiosity had never been so piqued. "That's weird, isn't it? The way she explained it, she needs a certain dosage to keep her pheromones at a normal level to avoid incidents like the one I witnessed at the coffee shop."

Bryce nodded in agreement. "I don't know what to tell you other than that is really unusual. I've never heard of any shifter taking daily hormone medication before. Seems like it would be too much for the average female. Of course, I'm no doctor." He looked at me with a knowing expression. "Liza might be an omega. I'm serious."

I shook my head, still not sure it was safe to believe it. But the more I thought about it, the more sense it made. Nothing else could explain why she would need to take daily hormones.

"Maybe she has some medical condition that keeps her body from regulating her hormones?" I ran a hand through my hair, then smoothed it again. It was bad enough that I hadn't been able to pay attention to business. Last thing I needed was some disgruntled employee labeling me as disheveled and having that get back down the family pipeline of information. "Or maybe her parents passed on some gene that requires hormonal support."

Bryce shrugged and continued to lay out evidence that supported the idea of Liza being an omega.

My thoughts on the subject weren't very convincing, but I clung to them, nevertheless. A rare medical condition was more believable than a children's myth. Of course, it was a children's myth that provided the entire root system for my family tree.

We went back and forth for a few minutes until Bryce excused himself. He had another appointment across town.

I stood and looked out the window, feeling as if I might crawl out of my damn skin. My curiosity got the better of me as I devised a plan.

I pulled my phone out of my pocket and texted Liza.

Would you like to shift and run with me later today?

My heart raced as I waited for her response. If she agreed, it might answer the question that had plagued my mind all day.

I'd enjoy that.

She included a heart emoji at the end of her text. My stomach clenched. I wanted her, there was no doubt about it, but at the same time, I was so anxious to get to the bottom of her hormone issue that I tried to push my emotions aside.

If Liza was an omega, I wanted to know for sure, and the only way to find out was to shift with her and see if her power and strength exceeded that of a regular wolf.

 I quickly replied, letting her know when and where we could meet before ending the conversation. We'd meet on my family's estate when the sun set, since Liza didn't have wide open land at her backdoor. Also, I wanted her to be relaxed, without the danger of anyone else watching her.

 I stood outside, watching the sunset as I waited for her to arrive. The sky was a mixture of reds and blues and purples and golds. For a moment, I wished I'd suggested watching the sunset before we went for a run, but I was still knew at this romance thing.

 I cracked my knuckles. *I am not deceiving her.* If I repeated that to myself a few times, I might start believing myself.

 I needed answers, however, and being near her in wolf form would hopefully answer a few questions. I thought about the best route for us to run through my family's forest, then it hit me. I was going to see Liza naked tonight.

 My body reacted almost immediately, our heated night on her couch flashing through my mind. The moment had only lasted a few seconds, but it had been enough time for me to feel the curves of her body and the way she responded to my tongue exploring her mouth.

My cock hardened at exactly the moment I spotted Liza's car coming down our long driveway. I quickly willed my erection to soften. Unfortunately, my erection wasn't subject to my will.

Liza stepped out of her car with a wide smile on her beautiful face. She was gorgeous in the way most women wanted to be and paid good money for.

I walked down and hugged her when I reached her side,, careful not to press my erection against her. I tried not to breathe her in, but I couldn't resist. Just thinking of that tantalizing scent was enough to make my hard-on painful. She must have picked up her prescription because I wasn't so tempted to push her back to the hood of the car and take her in any way she would let me.

"Ready to shift together?"

She grabbed a duffel bag from the back seat, which I assumed held extra clothes. "Yes. After the day I had, a good run will do the trick."

I took the bag from her and carried it as we walked. "What happened?"

She sighed in a way that made the mental picture of her naked body pop back into my mind. I silently thanked the gods that we were outside in the fresh air to dilute the scent of her pheromones.

"It wasn't one thing in particular." Liza shot me a smile. "Just one of those days where you feel like you're chasing your tail and not accomplishing anything. I had three new clients to consult with on top of my repeat customers."

"Sounds like a full day." I grabbed her hand and led her to the backyard.

"Your text definitely brightened my mood." She stopped and looked around, letting out a low whistle that the forest swallowed. "Is all of this property yours?"

"Yes. Well, it belongs to my family." I pointed to the tree line. "We have hundreds of wooded acres to ourselves whenever we want to shift."

"Wow. I can't imagine having this much private space."

A gnawing feeling on my back told me someone was watching us. Glancing back toward the house, I caught my dad peering at us from his bedroom window. I couldn't read his expression, but I assumed he was curious and still disapproving, though he hardly had the right to throw stones. I picked up the pace and led Liza through the forest and into a clearing.

"This is where we usually shift. We run in that direction." I pointed toward a section of tall oak trees before turning to face Liza.

I could sense the anxiety building in her as she scowled and avoided eye contact. She had to be thinking the same thing as me. We had to undress before shifting unless we wanted our clothes to tear.

"I'll turn away while you undress." I jokingly bowed, but the color in her cheeks spoke to how seriously she was taking this matter. "I'm nothing if not a gentleman." Though, I wanted to look over my shoulder—wanted to see if she was as luscious as she was in my mind—my wolf didn't need the temptation any more than I did. We were already mid-struggle over whether or not he was going to take her for himself. Mate with her. My wolf didn't have the same measure of self-control I had, and even I was slipping some.

Of course, that didn't stop thoughts from running through my brain about what her body looked like beneath those clothes. I stared up at the sky, trying not to think about her exposed skin in the moonlight, even though I could hear the rustling of her pants as she pushed them down her long legs and stepped out.

"Thank you," she murmured.

My senses heightened as I listened for the sound of a shift. First, I had to live through the torture of hearing her bra unsnap and her panties gently gliding down her legs, then I had to breathe because my lungs were burning. Her scent wafted toward me, and my wolf lunged as if he was going to force the shift. I held him back. Pushed my will forward.

Finally, the tell-tale popping and growling that accompanied a shift occurred, so I slowly turned to look at her. When I did, my wolf whined to be free. I needed him to calm down and looking at her wasn't going to facilitate that. I glanced away and waited for him to gather himself before I looked again.

Liza stood majestically, her silky white fur reflecting the pale moonlight. Her piercing blue eyes gleamed with an inner fire that was undeniable.

It didn't surprise me that Liza was the most gorgeous wolf I'd ever seen. My wolf tore free, and as he did, so did my clothing.

Chapter 17 - Liza

Ty had turned his back to give me as much privacy as I could have in the open air of a beautiful night, but the sexual tension was overwhelming, like another entity between us as we prepared to shift. He was fully aware that I was stripping down to nothing, so I glanced up nervously as I slipped my panties down my legs. Still, he kept his back to me.

What if he turned around and caught a glimpse of my naked body before I shifted? Part of me would be embarrassed like the proper virgin I was. I would cover myself as best I could with a bent leg or an arm across my breasts, but there would be no covering the desire or the part of me that wished he would turn and take in every inch of my skin.

What would Ty think of my body? Would it live up to the expectations of a fated mate? Expectations that he'd probably been holding on to since he was a teenager. I was curvier than the average female shifter. Maybe he wouldn't like such a buxom body. Maybe that was why he'd dated Cecily… or thought about dating her. It wasn't often I compared my figure or my body traits to someone else, but Cecily was long and lean and beautiful. I was lesser, shorter, not so toned. It didn't bother me, but it was true.

He didn't turn around, so I shook off the idea of him seeing me naked for the first time and shifted as quickly as I could.

The familiar sensation of my wolf pressing forward washed over me as I embraced her. Every cell in my body tingled with electricity, and for a moment, I lost touch with the physical world. My vision blurred just before it intensified to a razor sharpness that made every color brighter, every edge finer, and amplified every scent.

Ty must have heard me shifting because he spun around to face me. To my surprise, he shifted abruptly, not even bothering to undress.

I supposed Keller money made it that much easier to replace clothing.

My eyes widened as I took in his strong stance. His wolf was the color of midnight, his brown eyes so deep and dark they were almost black. They sparkled with an enthusiasm that was, no doubt, aimed at my wolf.

His sudden shift confused me, but even more surprising was my wolf's reaction to him. She surged forward, ready to run with him in a way I hadn't known was possible. Her enthusiasm coursed through every vein of my being. She wanted to explore more than just the territory. There was an instant connection between us as our wolves communicated without words.

It was the first time our wolves had met since fate had brought us together. Instead of acting leery of the new and unfamiliar wolf, mine couldn't wait to sniff and explore her mate.

Our wolves were eager to meet one another, which shouldn't have been surprising. The magnetic energy between them was so intense that I didn't have much control as my instincts kicked in. My wolf yearned for him.

I circled Ty, sniffing the air around his strong body. My wolf stepped closer, nudging her snout into Ty's side. He didn't seem to mind as my wolf rubbed against him.

He rumbled with pleasure before finally rubbing against me. The wolves wanted each other, so they naturally exchanged scents, covering themselves in it.

Ty nuzzled my neck with his nose, causing the hairs on my wolf's back to stand to attention. My instinctive reaction was to bare my neck to him, so I turned my head to one side—a sign of submission.

Ty growled in response. He didn't bite me, though. It wasn't the time. Not yet. Instead, he buried his face in my neck and lightly nipped my skin before running off into the woods.

My wolf wanted him with an all-encompassing strength. There was something more than just physical attraction between us. It was as if we were two halves of the same being, meant to be together.

Even if I had wanted to stay still, my instinct to chase after him was too strong. My wolf shot through the forest, attempting to keep up with Ty's longer stride as he zoomed in and out of the overbrush that covered the majority of the forest floor.

Just when I caught up to him, I nipped at his heels. He turned to chase me. We ran at full speed under the light of the moon without ever running into another wolf. The Keller property was massive, allowing our wolves to spend quality time together with no interruptions.

I could get used to this.

We ran for what felt like hours, chasing and playing like we'd known each other our entire lives. It felt comfortable. It felt like home.

Although there were no other wolves, we did come across other forest animals. An owl hooted overhead while he kept a discerning eye on our shenanigans. A family of deer scattered and ran in the opposite direction when we disturbed their sleep along a creek.

As I turned a corner, my eyes homed in on an injured rabbit. I didn't typically feed in my wolf form—it had just never been my thing—so I had no desire to eat the poor creature. Its back legs were fanned out behind its body. I couldn't tell if it had broken its back or simply hurt its legs trying to escape from some predator.

Either way, the rabbit was suffering. It looked miserable and eyed me with complete terror. I could sense that it wanted to be put out of its misery.

For as long as I could remember, I'd always been sensitive towards animals. I would insist that my parents pull over on the side of the road if we came upon an injured creature that had unsuccessfully attempted to cross a busy highway.

In my human form, all I could do was offer the animal some comfort. Now and then we'd find an animal that had a chance of survival. The local vet was on a first-name basis with my family. We'd show up with some helpless animal in a shoebox or large plastic crate a few times a month; me with tears rolling down my cheeks and my parents patiently explaining that we'd found it on the side of the road.

As I stared at the rabbit, its breath becoming shallower and more erratic, a single teardrop fell from my eyes. I had to end its life, and that realization killed me inside.

Just as I stepped forward, prepared to do the right thing, the rabbit seemed to jolt, his heart beating faster as his breathing became steady and deep. Then, as if it had never been injured, it hopped off into the woods.

My legs refused to move. I stared in the direction the rabbit had disappeared. What had just happened?

A light rustle and whooshing sound brought me out of my stupor. I turned to find Ty staring at me in his human form. He was as naked as the day was long.

Shit. He was going to find out. There was no way left for me to hide it, and quite frankly, I was tired of trying. What I was, who I was… there was no going back now. Ty had seen whatever he'd seen, but looking at him now, there was no way I could honestly believe he didn't know.

My knee-jerk reaction on any other day with any other person would have been to panic, but there was no time for that. Ty Keller stood before me, a Greek god. Correction: a naked Greek god. And goddamn, he was glorious.

He was all muscle and sinew and chiseled chest and broad shoulders. His toned legs were tanned and powerful, his feet planted firmly on the ground as he eyed me curiously. His arms were strong and well-defined, lending themselves to the sculpted lines of his torso. A light sheen of perspiration glistened on his skin.

I allowed my eyes to drift down to his core, and my breath caught in my throat. His cock was thick and long, partially erect in the night air. Even him partially erect was impressive, maybe even a little bit daunting.

Seeing Ty completely exposed stirred something deep within me. Lust. It overtook all of my senses as I stared at him, drinking in the hard lines and the hard... everything. I breathed deeply, his scent on the air all around me.

His pheromones were so strong that my entire body clenched, and I trembled with need.

I didn't only want him—I needed him.

Ty's eyes widened as he followed my gaze down his body. I had been staring at his manhood. In one fell swoop, he was kneeling before me. "Shift, Liza."

Fuck. If I shifted, he would see me naked. There was no way around it. I was too shy for that, but my wolf would never disobey her mate. She forced me to shift by pushing me to the surface, and I was helpless to stop it.

Panting, I got to my feet, slowly raising my eyes to meet Ty's gaze. My body burned up as if I were standing next to open flames. There wasn't much that could hold me back as I imagined jumping Ty, pressing my naked body against his and urging him to have his way with me.

His eyes blazed. "You're in heat."

I shook my head. I couldn't be in heat. I had medicine... But he was right. My heat was supposed to come today. Even though I had done exactly what the doctor instructed and picked up the prescription that was twice the strength of my last one, there was no mistaking what was happening to my body.

Why was I in heat?

I inhaled and searched Ty's eyes. The longing between us increased as we stood in such close proximity to one another. The scent of Ty's lust filled the air, almost dropping me to my knees. I'd never wanted someone so much in my entire life.

I'd never even seen a naked man before; not in real life. Sure, I'd done my research when I pleasured myself, but this man was more exquisite than any in a magazine or video I'd found on the internet. Tyson Keller was the real deal. In living color.

A familiar sensation of my own juices moistened my inner thighs. Ty stepped closer as if he could see the lust dripping from my core. "You smell like the sweetest temptation. If I were a lesser man, I would back you against a tree, wrap my body around you and ravage you right here and now."

The growl behind his words only served to make my body react more strongly as my nipples puckered and the blood rushed to my pussy. I moaned.

Ty growled. "Fuck, Liza. I only have so much self-control."

His pupils dilated, and he stepped forward without warning. My breath left me in a rush as he pulled me close. My breasts pressed against his solid chest, and I felt his hard erection against my stomach.

He slid one hand around my back and pulled me closer, though I didn't think it was possible to be pressed any harder against his solid body. His mouth covered mine as he slipped his tongue between my lips.

He teased the tip of my tongue. I growled in the back of my throat, and he deepened the kiss. We searched each other's mouths with a desperation that made my knees almost buckle.

The kiss wasn't violent, but it was long, hard, and passionate. Desire made my instincts kick in, and I gently bit Ty's lower lip. He pulled back and pushed me away at arm's length.

I could see his heartbeat in the artery in his neck as he closed his eyes, attempting to regain control over his body. "We have to get a handle on your heat, Liza."

Panic set in when I realized he wanted to fuck me but I hadn't yet told him the truth. I stared at the ground, attempting to muster up the courage to admit that I was nowhere near as sexually experienced as Ty.

"What's wrong?" Ty placed a finger under my chin and tilted my head up, forcing me to make eye contact with him.

"I wanted to tell you this at the coffee shop the other day, but with everything that happened, I couldn't bring myself to drop another bomb on you." I leaned back to read his face.

He was scared. His cheeks flushed, and I wasn't sure if it was from his need to come or from his desire to make me come. Before this went any further, I had to confess.

"There's no easy way to say this." I picked at my fingernails, stalling.

Ty crossed his arms and stared at me as if I was about to tell him I moonlighted as a serial killer. "For fuck's sake, Liza, what is it?"

"I'm a virgin."

He took a step back, his arms falling to his side. His chest heaved as a stunned expression washed over his face. And then relief. He even smiled. "That's really not what I thought you were going to say."

I didn't ask because... serial killer. A giggle bubbled out of my throat, but then I saw the flicker in his eyes. They widened as I watched his cock grow longer and harder.

He wasn't upset over the new information. He was aroused.

How could it physically get any bigger? Gods, I needed him inside me.

Ty cleared his throat, but that didn't keep his voice from coming out hoarse. "Liza, are you saying that no man has ever pleased you?" He spoke softly, but the rasp was as hot as any growl or purr I'd heard so far.

I shook my head. "I trusted my doctor when he told me the hormones would suppress my pheromones, but I always had a fear that my scent would drive someone to harm me because they couldn't control themselves. So, whenever I dated someone, I always ended things before it became sexual."

Ty was quiet for a moment, seeming to compose himself. "I'm sorry you had to live with that fear. Just for the record, though, I would never hurt you. Do you know that?" He pulled his lower lip between his teeth. My answer mattered to him.

I nodded. "Of course. I trust you."

And I did. Everything that had happened so far, the incidents and moments that had brought us to this one here felt like a natural progression with Ty, and not something I was being forced into or that we were trying to force on ourselves. Fate wanted us together, and so did our bodies. There was no denying the powerful force pulling us together.

At that point, I would've allowed Ty to do whatever he pleased. My body was hot, my heart pounded as if it would beat out of my chest, and I was so wet that I clenched my thighs in hopes that Ty wouldn't see my juices dripping down my skin.

"How have you handled your past heats?" Ty cracked his knuckles, trying to keep his eyes on my face.

My cheeks reddened. "I've never experienced a real heat because the pills suppressed them. That is, until now. I doubled my dosage, yet here we are."

"Yes. Here we are." Ty narrowed his eyes on me. "Do you want me to handle it for you?"

Before I could respond, my body answered for me. My chest rose, thrusting my breasts in Ty's direction. My hands drifted down my stomach, though I caught myself before I allowed my hands to rub over my throbbing clit.

My body wanted Ty and only Ty.

He'd watched my hands skim along my skin, and he reacted immediately, stepping forward and closing the gap between us.

Our lips locked as Ty's hands ran up and down my back, eventually landing on my ass, cupping both cheeks and squeezing tightly.

Arching my back, I grabbed the back of his head and pulled him to me, running my tongue along his top lip.

Ty let out a groan and pulled his mouth away, nudging my face with his and nipping at my ear. His tongue traced my jaw, then trailed down my neck, where he stopped and gave special attention to the exposed skin at the side of my throat, nipping gently with his teeth. I moved my hands down his chest and across his stomach. My fingers danced along the ripples of muscle and sinew and skin. It was so smooth, so supple. Holy fuck, he had good skin.

Ty breathed into my ear, his hot breath sending a chill down my spine. "Shift and follow me back to the estate."

I pulled back and studied his face. Ty wanted to please me as much as I wanted to be pleased, and he didn't want it to be on the forest floor, so I gladly shifted.

Ty followed suit and ran at full speed. I struggled to keep up with him as his strong legs followed a path he was familiar with. Within minutes, we were back at the estate. Ty led me to a lower patio area, where he shifted and grabbed a blanket from an outdoor storage container near a fire pit. "You're safe to shift. My parents will be asleep by now and the staff will have gone home for the evening."

I took him at his word and shifted back to human form. Ty quickly wrapped me in a warm, fleece blanket, then led me through the backdoor.

We scurried through the house, but I still caught glimpses of the elaborate décor, one-of-a-kind art pieces, and furniture that was, no doubt, custom made for the Kellers.

I knew Ty came from a wealthy family—I'd even been to the estate before—but I was shocked as he led me to his own wing of the house. They were loaded.

Once we were safely inside his bedroom, Ty shut the door and dropped my hand.

His room was extremely clean, though I reminded myself that his family had staff who saw to all the cooking and cleaning.

"Nice room."

Ty scoffed. "What do you think about the bed?"

My cheeks flushed as I eyed the king-sized bed. The mattress was covered in a gray comforter that I couldn't have afforded with the profit from my business, and I imagined how it would feel against my exposed skin.

Ty sighed. "I'm not going to take your virginity. Not yet." He took a step toward me, gently nudging me to sit on the bed. He traced a line from my neck to the top of my breast where the blanket was dipping lazily. "If you'll consent to me making you come as many times as your body can handle, then I'll give that to you."

My skin and every cell in my body heated, overheated, was so overheated with lust and desire and need that I would've been a fool to turn down his offer.

So, I didn't.

Pushing my shoulders back, I allowed the blanket to drop, exposing my breasts. My nipples hardened immediately from the cool air and the need in Ty's hot gaze.

His eyes narrowed, his breathing quickening. "You are gorgeous, Liza."

My own breath caught in my throat. Unable to respond, I stood and dropped the blanket to the floor. Ty stepped in close and wrapped his arms around me, bringing his lips to mine once more.

This time was different, though. He was bold, running his hands down my sides and back up to my breasts, letting his thumbs graze my nipples for a second and only a second. He gently cupped them, taking in the heaviness of each one. He pulled his mouth from mine and stared at my nipples as he slid his thumbs over the peaks until I was mindless and breathless and weak-kneed.

"Ty." My voice was no more than a rasp. "Please."

He dropped his hands, misunderstanding exactly what I was asking of him. "Am I moving too fast? Is it too much?"

I shook my head. Too much? I'd come back with him. I knew exactly what was going to happen, what he wanted, what I needed, and I wasn't too ashamed to tell him. "I need you. Please."

The corner of his mouth lifted in a smile as he moved me back toward the bed. "Lie down, Liza." His voice sent a purr of pure pleasure through me.

He slid onto the bed beside me, his breath hot on my skin as he kissed his way down from my shoulder. I was one soft touch away from imploding.

His tongue flicked across one taut nipple, the sensation of it against the sensitive nub stealing my breath. I whimpered. I wanted more. Was desperate for more.

His hand slid down my belly in a diagonal line toward my hip, and he pulled me closer so my other hip was pressed against the length of his impressive erection.

I wanted to touch him, taste him, put him in my mouth and lick, but he brushed my hand away and lifted his head. "Tonight is about you, sweetheart."

He raised my hand to his lips and kissed my knuckles, then turned it over and licked my palm. The quick flick of his tongue over my skin made my insides clench.

Ty moved my arms up over my head and hissed out a breath. His gaze caressed me, moving over every inch of my naked body.

I wanted to kiss and be kissed, but he'd already started kissing his way down my body. He paid equal attention to each nipple, laved them, blew on each one, then sucked hard on the left then the right. My breath trembled because nothing in my life had ever felt so perfect.

His stubble grazed my skin as he trailed kisses down my stomach, circling my belly button with his tongue, then lower still before he stopped. He inched away, just enough to spread my thighs.

He settled himself on his knees between legs, fisting his cock as he looked at me. "Fuck, you're beautiful, Liza."

My skin flushed with pleasure. I loved that he said things like that. Beautiful. I savored the word as he continued to stare and continued to stroke his beautiful cock.

Then he leaned down, braced himself on his free hand, and dragged his tongue along my tender folds. Without warning, he pushed his tongue inside me. I gasped and arched and whimpered, pleasure unlike anything I'd ever known bursting through my blood. I lowered my hand and tangled it in his hair.

He lifted his head. "Put your hand over your head. Don't move it again."

Sweet fuck. This was the most erotic moment of my life. Ty licked and sucked and teased me until I was a writhing blob of sensation, of frayed nerve endings and raw need.

I cried out when he slid a finger, then two inside me. The pleasure within me built and built until I was quivering.

"Oh, Ty!"

He sucked my clit into his mouth, his tongue teasing me until I couldn't hold still, until my body shattered. His fingers thrust in and out of me while my pussy convulsed, and I rocked against him, threading my hands into his hair, holding him to me because if he stopped, I would die.

When the convulsions stopped, and when my body and mind were, once again, in sync, I breathed out slowly, stretching languidly in his bed. The warmth of him vanished as he got up and went to the bathroom, but after a few minutes, he came back and lay beside me.

"God, Ty." I could hardly speak, had no words, and didn't really need any.

"You need a few minutes?" he asked as he brushed my hair away from my face.

"Maybe a couple." I smiled. I imagined there would come a point where my body couldn't take anymore, but we'd find out exactly how long that took.

Chapter 18 - Ty

  I stifled a yawn and stretched carefully, doing my best not to wake Liza. She'd stirred a few times but had fallen right back into a deep sleep. Meanwhile, I'd been awake for at least an hour. I had to piss so badly I wasn't sure I was going to make it to the bathroom even if I somehow managed to fly there, but I couldn't stand the thought of waking her up.

  As excited as I'd been to shift with her, my wolf was even more so. Had I been one of those horny high school shifters, there would've been no stopping my wolf. It took every ounce of control I possessed to keep him from mating with her right there in the yard, though I'd managed. Somehow.

  Because of that, I was now able to enjoy watching her sleep. As much as I enjoyed watching her sleep, there was also something to be said for sleeping next to her, her body curled into mine, her hand laid over my heart, and her head on my chest.

  Waking up with her was almost as good. She was gorgeous, and my sheets smelled like her perfume. There was no way I would be able to go back to sleeping alone. Not even if I wanted to. God, what was this woman doing to me?

Last night had been an adventure, so I wasn't surprised Liza was sleeping in. I'd lost count of how many times I'd brought her to orgasm, but the final one made her blackout. Since she was sexually fulfilled, her heat passed, and we both slept like rocks.

After waiting as long as I possibly could, I slipped out from under the covers and relieved myself in the bathroom. After a glance at her to make sure she was still asleep, I went down to the kitchen. She'd burned about three billion calories last night. She'd be ravenous when she woke up. No person could withstand that much pleasure and not have a complete blood-sugar crash or end up partially dehydrated.

I sliced a few bananas into a bowl and added fresh strawberries, blueberries, sliced mango, and peaches from the fridge. Ramon wasn't in it, and it was no secret that I couldn't cook for shit. Fruit was going to have to do for now.

After filling a few stainless-steel water bottles to the brim and closing the lids tightly, I walked back up the stairs with my arms full. Now that the sex fog had cleared, the concern I'd had that stemmed from our run in the forest crept back to the forefront of my mind.

Our wolves had taken to one another immediately, which wasn't a surprise since Fate was the one dealing the cards here. They had gotten along so well and bonded immediately, but that was not the concern.

The concern was the injured rabbit she'd somehow brought back from the brink of death.

We needed to have an open and honest conversation about that damn rabbit. Either my eyes had played tricks on me or something miraculous had occurred, and there was no way I could deny she was the source of said miracle. Although, I couldn't imagine bringing this topic up would make either of us very happy.

I retraced the timeline of our evening. We had chased each other for hours, but then she'd suddenly dropped out of sight. I'd followed her scent until I found her staring down at a dying rabbit. Even from where I'd stood, I could hear the labored breathing and the decreasing heartbeat. My wolf had wanted that rabbit.

Then, out of nowhere, that little fucker had jolted as if shocked by electric paddles. The rabbit hopped out of sight as if it had never been hurt.

I'd stared in disbelief and even glanced around to make sure no one else had been around, because if anyone else had seen, it would be damaging to her. She was an anomaly. Thankfully, we were alone.

Liza must have healed that rabbit somehow; there was no other explanation. Nature didn't work that way.

"Good morning, Tyson." Mother's voice pulled me out of my head.

She was dressed to the nines in a Prada pants suit and Gucci heels.

In all of my life, I'd never been able to figure out how a woman like my mother, who required so much maintenance, was such a morning person. Most people would take some time to wake up, maybe read the paper and drink a cup of coffee. Not my mother. The moment her feet hit the floor, she was raring to go and ready to conquer the world.

"Good morning." I set the water bottles on the step and gave her my attention. "Did I wake you?"

"Don't be silly." She waved her hand in the air. "I've been up for a while, although I can't say the same for your father. He needs his sleep, though, so do try to be as quiet as possible."

"Of course." I glanced up the stair in the direction of my wing, wondering if Liza was still sleeping.

The last thing I needed was for her to come down the stairs and have yet another confrontation with my mother. Who could ever predict how my mother would treat Liza?

She followed my gaze. "Please, tell Liza I had her car moved to the garage because rain is coming."

Shit. So, she knew Liza had spent the night. I was an adult who'd had a number of overnight visitors, but this was the one who might kill my mother.

"Thanks," I mumbled. I shifted the bowl of fruit to my other hand.

"Tyson, look at me." Mother pinned me with her gaze. "Do you really feel that there's a chance for the two of you? Even now that you know about the sins of your father's past?"

I stared at her, wondering where she was going with her questioning. I hadn't decided how to tell Liza what I knew about her past, but I also didn't want to wait too long and risk my mother doing it for me.

She smiled weakly and continued. "I promise that it was never about Liza. I'm sure it seemed that your father and I disliked her because of her social standing or whatever other nonsense is being spread right now. But the truth of the matter is that I couldn't stand to think about what our family had done to that poor baby."

I wrapped my free arm around her. She hugged me back tightly, her arms snug around my waist, her head over my heart. My understanding was much clearer now than when Liza and I had first spotted each other.

"Honestly, I don't know what I'm going to do with the information about our family, but I'll figure it out. And, yes, I hope Liza and I have a chance. She means a lot to me." I pulled away from her embrace and bent to pick up the water bottles. "I should get back to her."

"Of course." Mother patted me on the chest and smiled, her eyes a little misty. "We'll talk more later. You need to tend to your mate."

I returned to my room just as Liza rolled over and groaned softly. She sat up, her delicate, pale skin covered in love bites.

My natural instincts leaped to life, and I let out a low growl of pleasure at the sight of the red marks and her full breasts.

"Don't be such a caveman." Liza yawned and stretched her arms over her head. Her full, luscious breasts pushed forward, which had me growling again.

"You don't seem so shy anymore." I smirked.

"I suppose I'm not." Although, she did blush and pull the sheet around her. "You saw and did things to me that would make it a little silly for me to be shy around you now."

"Yes, I sure did." My cock stirred at the memory of Liza's legs spread wide, her back arched as she moaned with pleasure.

I moved to her side of the bed and leaned down to kiss her gently on the forehead. There was no way I would be able to kiss her while she was naked without acting on it. Instead, I gave her a chaste kiss and kept it G-rated.

"I brought you some fruit and water."

She took the bowl from me and one of the bottles. "Thank you, you're so thoughtful."

Thoughtful. I couldn't think of one woman who had ever described me as being thoughtful. Not that I was an asshole. Far from it, actually. I was known for being level-headed and kind, just aloof. Most of the women I dated didn't get to see the romantic side of me because I was out the door too quickly. Plus, no other woman had left me so badly wanting more of her body and mind as Liza had.

"What do you have planned today?" Liza eyed me as she popped a few blueberries in her mouth. "I have all day free thanks to Cecily running her mouth. Two of my clients dropped me because of her."

"What?"

Cecily Banks. The world was full of women like her; jealous women who had no conscience about hurting others when things didn't go their way. That she'd done it to Liza didn't bode well for Cecily.

Liza sighed. "She hired me to cook some meals for her, then belittled me from the moment I pulled into her driveway. She was flat-out rude, so I fired her as a client and told her I would no longer cook for her."

"What the hell?" I jumped up from the bed and dragged my hand over my face. "So, she's been gossiping to anyone who will listen, I'm sure. Cecily is such a bitch." I blamed her entitled, rich girl upbringing. Not that I planned to allow such behavior to stand.

"You said it, not me." Giggling, Liza rolled her eyes as she took a sip of water.

I didn't laugh. "This kind of thing pisses me off. The only reason she's treating you this way is because I didn't fall into her family's trap of matching the two of us together." I was certain her family had had their eye on making her royal since she was a child. "She's acting like a toddler who didn't get a toy from the grocery store, pitching a fit to anyone and everyone. I'm so sorry she's letting her disappointment out on you."

Liza patted the bed. "Come, sit down. It's fine. I have plenty of clients. I'm not concerned about my business, finances, or the opinions of women like Cecily Banks."

This woman awed me. Never in my life had I met a woman who handled this type of situation with such maturity and grace. Her positivity only made me like her more.

"Well, it turns out, I have the day off." I snatched a strawberry out of Liza's hand before she took a bite.

"Hey!" She crossed her arms and stuck her bottom lip out, pretending to be mad.

Fuck, I wanted to bite that lip.

I turned my head, forcing the lustful thoughts to the farthest corner of my mind. While I wouldn't have minded spending a day in bed with Liza, I wanted to get to know more about her, too, beyond how well we fit together physically.

"Would you like to spend the day together? Mother said it's going to rain, but there's a lot we can do to kill some time here at the estate." Although, right now, my mind wasn't thinking much beyond spending the day in bed with her.

"I'd love a tour, actually." Liza grinned. "I didn't see much of the house except for your bedroom last night."

"Well, then. Follow me, ma'am."

Liza stood, completely naked. "Hmm, I might want to get dressed first."

I gestured to the bathroom. "I'll give you the grand tour in a few minutes."

"Perfect."

I watched her flawless, bare ass as she scooped her clothes off the floor and walked into the bathroom. The woman was a goddess, and I was completely defenseless against her beauty.

She glanced over her shoulder. "What about you?"

"I'll throw some clothes on and use the bathroom down the hall. There are a few new toothbrushes in the bottom drawer. Feel free to use my soap and shampoo. Sorry that it's not super girly." I'd stopped keeping flowery-scented things in my room. For whatever reason, women found it offensive, like instead of being thoughtful, I was being presumptuous or trying to pick how they smelled. It was ridiculous since I'd only been trying to be kind, but they took it wrong.

Liza laughed. "First of all, why do you have extra toothbrushes? Do you do this often with your dates?"

Oh, for fuck's sake.

"No way." I held both hands up in defense. "I'm just a man who likes to be prepared. That's all."

"Okay, I'll accept that answer." A sly smile spread across her face.

She started to close the door, but I stretched out my leg and blocked it with my foot. "Wait. What was the second thing?"

"Oh." She held onto the edge of the door and stared at me with doe eyes. "Don't apologize about not having girly-smelling toiletries. I won't mind smelling like you all day."

With that, she closed the door and turned on the shower.

I gritted my teeth as I rushed to the hallway bathroom. I needed a cold shower.

After we'd both dressed, I led Liza through the house, showing her the conference room, the library, and the conservatory off to the side of the house.

Liza was in awe of everything she saw, often stopping to study an intricate painting or to sit on an antique sofa.

"What's in this room?" She eyed the double doors like a kid in a candy shop.

"Oh, that's the theater room."

"Theater? As in a movie theater?" She pushed the doors open and clapped her hands. "We *have* to watch a movie. What do you say?"

I laughed and followed her in. Her enthusiasm was contagious. I couldn't remember the last time I'd sat in here without a care and watched anything. "It's your call. What do you want to watch?"

Liza scanned the shelves of movies and then looked up, biting her lip with a mischievous grin. "Do you like horror movies?"

I shook my head. "No way. I'm not a fan of horror."

"Oh, come on, it'll be fun!" She grabbed a movie off the shelf, walked to the projection set up, and popped it in.

"Well, if you insist." I pretended to be annoyed as I followed her to the second level of movie seats and sat down.

As Liza snuggled in, I used the remote to lower the lights in the room and start the movie.

"How about brunch while we watch?" I asked.

"Perfect."

I pulled my phone out of my pocket and texted our cook, asking him to bring a full spread of brunch food and drinks to the theater room.

Within thirty minutes, trays laden with fresh pastries, bacon, omelets, and orange juice sat on our laps.

"I could get used to this." Liza crossed her ankles and took a bite of her buttered croissant. Her almost-silent moan as she took a bite wasn't silent enough, and my cock twitched.

I smiled, ignoring the urgency in my jeans. "Considering I botched the first picnic, this is the least I could do on a rainy day."

"Your house is like a strip mall." She chuckled. "I wouldn't be surprised if there was a bowling alley."

"Umm." Stifling my laugh, I grimaced. I hadn't built the house, but I did enjoy the privacy and benefits it afforded to me. Especially right now.

"You're shitting me, right?" Liza turned to face me and dropped her croissant on the tray. "You have your own bowling alley?"

My cheeks reddened. I had never been one for showing off my family's wealth. It was especially difficult and disheartening since I'd been made aware of how we'd come into the money. Of course, Liza didn't need to know that. Not yet. At some point, however, I would have to tell her that my wealth was directly linked to the life she'd been forced into. First, I had to figure out the exact right way and the exact right time. I couldn't rush it.

"Your family does have an excessive amount of money. It's honestly hard to comprehend someone living this extravagantly." She shrugged. "I guess it's okay if you like to bowl, though."

"Do you? Like to bowl, I mean?" It didn't matter to me one way or the other, but I was curious.

"I know how, and I do okay." She smiled, and her eyes sparkled.

Her humor amused me. Just when I thought I did or said something to turn her off, she spun the situation to focus on the bright side. Apparently, a bowling alley was a bright side.

There were women who would hold it against me that I had so much generational wealth, much the same as there would be women out there who only wanted me because of the wealth, but Liza was her own brand of female. She rolled with the punches, seeming unfazed by most of the curveballs that life threw her way.

With each passing moment, I liked her more and more. I didn't want to ruin the mood, but my brain wouldn't turn off. Not wanting to wait a moment longer, I paused the movie and turned the lights up.

"Hey!" Liza eyed me. "We were almost to the best part. He was just about to pop up out of the woman's shower as she rinses her makeup off at the sink. It's an iconic scene." I knew the scene. Everyone knew the scene. It could wait.

"I'm sorry, I just need to ask you something." I studied Liza's face, which seemed to pale a little. "What happened to that injured rabbit in the forest last night?"

She opened her mouth to answer, but snapped it shut and pursed her lips, hesitating. Liza clearly didn't want to talk about the rabbit, though I wasn't sure what she was conflicted about.

Finally, Liza answered my question. "I have no idea what happened."

I had no reason not to trust her, so I kept my mouth shut and waited for her to go on. Maybe she'd say something to ease my mind and lay to rest any thoughts I had of her being an omega.

"I was just standing there, staring at the poor little thing. My heart hurt. The whole situation was pitiful, so I decided to put it out of its misery." She looked down at her hands, then clasped them together and directed her gaze toward me. "It was dying one minute and then it jolted like it had been struck by lightning or some other electric charge." She shrugged as if she had no idea how it had happened or what—or in this case, *who*—was responsible.

"Did you touch it at all?" I asked. *Something* had happened.

"No. I never laid a paw on it." Liza paused, her nose scrunching as she thought. "I did cry a little. A tear or two might have fallen from my eye, but I don't see how that would be significant."

My mind spun with multiple thoughts, the main one being Bryce's suggestion that maybe Liza was an omega. All the legends said they had special powers. I didn't know the depths of those powers, but I couldn't quite believe that Liza had the ability to bring a creature back from the brink of death to restore its life force.

"Has anything like that ever happened to you before?" I hoped my question wouldn't be too obvious, considering that I wasn't just dropping the subject. There was no easy way to ask these questions. No way that wouldn't reveal my suspicions.

Liza shook her head, then stopped and stared at the screen as if in deep thought. "Michael, my brother, scraped his arm up really badly one time when he was trying to save me from falling off my bike. I cried all over him because I felt so bad that his arm was so black and blue and swollen. The next day, it was healed." Her mouth twisted to the side as if she'd only just now considered that she'd had a hand in her brother's healing.

I cocked my head to one side. "Completely?"

"Yeah. My parents said it was because Michael healed so quickly." She scoffed. "I remember them giving me a few examples of him overcoming viruses within a day and only needing a quick nap to overcome a headache."

"Did you believe them?"

"I did." Liza shook her head as if she was only now considering that there might have been another explanation. "That is, until Michael scraped his knee a week later. It took three days for it to heal, and it wasn't nearly as bad as his arm had been. I never really questioned it, though. I just figured it was a fluke. I didn't give it much thought. I moved on with my life."

We sat in silence for a few minutes until Liza spoke up again. She cleared her throat and lifted her gaze to meet mine. "Do you think I had something to do with healing that rabbit?"

Of course I did, but how could I tell her without suggesting that I thought she might be an omega? Instead, I lied. It wasn't a great precedent to set, but I didn't think I had another choice. "No. I was just wondering if you saw something I didn't since you were closer to the rabbit."

Liza studied me for a few long seconds before finally nodding. There was nothing more to say, so I turned the movie back on and lowered the lights. We finished eating in silence, the movie only serving as background noise to our thoughts.

Liza placed her empty tray on the floor and tucked her legs under her body. "You'd tell me if you knew something I didn't. Right?"

Her question surprised me. It made me wonder if she had an inkling she was different. If she hadn't before, my questions might've stirred some realization in her. Damn it.

Somehow, I managed to keep my composure, though I completely understood the concept of being a damn deer stuck motionless in headlights. I didn't let my heart skip a beat before answering her. "Of course, I would. We're going to be mated, and the worst thing we could do is keep things from one another." I meant that, and I would tell her everything. Just not yet.

My answer seemed to satisfy Liza. She cuddled up next to me, resting her head on my shoulder. I wrapped my arm around her and turned my attention back to the screen.

I paid no mind to the psychotic killer loose on the screen, or to the innocent people running and screaming through the night, trying to escape the slash of his bloodied knife. The only thing that mattered to me was the fact that I'd just lied to Liza.

I was a fucking tool for not being honest with her, but I needed more proof before I said anything about her possibly being an omega.

After several more minutes of thought and contemplation, I decided it might be time for me to meet my future in-laws.

Chapter 19 - Liza

"Spell that last name for me." I typed a new client's information, careful to get their last name correct.

"It's Boling: B-O-L-I-N-G, no W." The woman laughed. "I can't tell you how many people think our name is spelled with a W."

"And Wednesdays work for your family?" I pulled up my calendar, double-checking that I wasn't overbooking and spreading myself too thin.

"Definitely. Our kids have baseball practice on Wednesdays, so we can leave a key for you, and you can work uninterrupted."

Perfect.

"Let me reiterate, Mrs. Boling, that it won't bother me if the kids are running around." I typed a note to myself. "It's your house, and I don't want to disrupt your flow. If baseball practice is ever canceled, don't worry about it."

After I'd lost a few clients due to Cecily's temper tantrum, I was happy to add a new family to my weekly dinner rotation.

My phone vibrated on my desk, and I glanced at the message that popped onto the screen. It was from Ty.

Hello, beautiful. I hope you're having a fantastic day.

My heart fluttered. No matter how many times Ty texted or called, I couldn't quite get used to someone checking in on me so frequently.

My parents had always kept close tabs on me, sent me regular messages just to make sure I was doing well, but this was different. Ty cared for me in a way a parent didn't. He cared like a lover. He'd proven that in the way he'd taken care of my heat a few nights ago. Just the thought of that night sent delicious shivers through my body.

I ended the call with Mrs. Boling, then sat back, letting my mind wander as I looked out the window. Ty's tongue was magical. I hadn't known oral sex could be so satisfying, but his warm tongue had sent me into convulsions.

I sighed and forced myself to focus on something else—anything else. I switched off my computer and gathered my paperwork.

After I tapped out a quick response to Ty, I locked my office door and hopped into the car.

My week had been busy with multiple client meetings and a few catered events, so the time had sailed past. Through all of it, Ty had touched base with me every day, sometimes multiple times a day. It was strange at first, but I liked it. Having someone who cared enough to check in left my heart racing.

Whenever I saw his name pop onto my phone's screen, I couldn't help but smile. Something about him guy made me giddy. Yet, there was a nagging feeling in the pit of my stomach that just wouldn't subside. I was missing something, though I couldn't exactly put my finger on it.

Whenever we had a conversation, whether in person or on the phone, I played it out over and over again in my mind, picking it apart and analyzing every word spoken because I couldn't shake my feelings.

I was worried. He hadn't said anything specific, nothing that gave me pause, but it was what he hadn't said. Also, there had been those lingering looks, as if he were trying to figure me out or wondering whether I was being honest with him.

It had all started with our conversation in the theater room. He'd asked me about the rabbit and how it had healed. I couldn't imagine how I must have looked to him at that moment because I wasn't sure how to answer him. I hadn't wanted to lie—no relationship that started on a lie ever lasted—but I couldn't just blurt out that the rabbit had, indeed, been brought back to life by my mystical, magical teardrops. Who would believe such nonsense? I'd done the research. This kind of thing didn't happen except in fairy tales.

Ty's eyes had narrowed, and I could practically see the wheels starting to turn in his head. I couldn't tell one way or the other if he believed me. There was no way for me to be certain.

Something told me that he might have figured out the truth about my status. Undoubtedly, he'd heard the legends before. Maybe he did the math and figured it out. Who knew?

Whether I was right or wrong, I'd contemplated coming clean with him all week. Perhaps I needed to step way outside of my comfort zone, since this was the man I hoped to mate with. He needed to know what I was. It was only fair given that

I knew exactly *who* and *what* he was, and the more I thought about it, the more the word *perfect* came to mind.

Those thoughts stayed with me all week as I worked my various catering jobs. My mind always circled back to my relationship with Ty. I had to be honest. The more I got to know him, the closer I felt to him. Being intimate certainly hadn't hurt our relationship. There was another side to me that he'd discovered, and he'd shown me how strong an orgasm could truly be.

By the time Friday rolled around, I'd thought of every aspect of our relationship: our conversations, texts, and even our lust for one another. I wanted to be with him. There was nothing that detracted from my desire for him.

When I pulled into the parking lot at my doctor's office, I made a silent vow. I would be open and honest with Dr. Reynolds and explain my relationship as well as my concerns moving forward with Ty as my fated mate. I had nothing to lose at this point and was confident that Dr. Reynolds would be candid with me. There might have been another option I hadn't thought of, but I'd tried to consider them all. Everything from changing my diet to a rigorous exercise routine, even though those would help me, not the ones suffering the effects of my scent. Maybe he could give me another type of pill that would suppress my urges and powers.

I smiled at the front desk receptionist when she glared at me over her glasses. "Hello, dear."

"Hi, Susan." I picked up a pen to sign the usual forms and permissions.

Susan held up a hand. "No need for that, Liza. Dr. Reynolds is expecting you and has been anxious to follow up with you. He said you emailed him last week." She smiled, and stood to point to the door marked: *Employees only.* "He explicitly instructed me to send you straight back. He's waiting for you in his office. Third door on the right."

Shit. That was either a very good sign or a very bad one. My doctor wanted me to bypass the waiting room. In this office, which was always busy, that kind of special treatment was unheard of.

I wrung my hands and nodded, walking through the ever-mysterious employee door that led to another hallway. Pausing, I took a deep breath before knocking on Dr. Reynold's office door, rapping my knuckles on the wood just below his name plate.

"Come in," he instructed, his voice gruff and raspy.

Dr. Reynolds had been my doctor ever since my parents adopted me. He knew everything there was to know about my medical history, and it went without saying that I truly trusted him with my life. He'd always been the final authority on my health, and today was no different. I needed his advice.

"Well, hello, Liza." Dr. Reynolds stood from his large desk and pulled his glasses from his face with one hand, holding the other out for me to shake. "So good to see you, dear. Please, have a seat."

I pulled out a burgundy leather chair—one I'd sat in on multiple occasions. A few years ago, he'd gotten new ones, but this one was a relic from his former office.

"Thank you so much for fitting me in so soon. I appreciate it." That, too, could've gone without saying, but he had fit me in between other patients, and I was grateful enough to mention it.

"Of course. I wouldn't miss a meeting with my favorite patient for anything in the world." He returned to his chair and slid his glasses back on. "Now, tell me how you're doing with the double dosages I prescribed. Have they been working out for you?"

I put my purse on the floor and folded my hands in my lap. "I feel like they've been working fine as far as keeping my pheromone levels down, but I experienced a full-blown heat this past week."

He sat back and steepled his fingers on his desk. "Really? What happened?"

There were things a woman did that she didn't necessarily like to speak about with anyone. This was that kind of thing. The hard part.

I reminded myself that he was a doctor, and this was a safe place to open up about my experience. "I walked into a coffee shop and my scent caused every man in the room to turn their attention toward me. As a matter of fact, if it wasn't for Ty, I'm not sure how that would've turned out."

"Ah, yes. Tyson Keller." Dr. Reynolds smiled like he was taking some credit for my having snagged a Keller. "I heard about the two of you being matched. How is that working out, with the pheromones?"

"Well, like I said, he saved me from the coffee shop before anything bad happened ... but he had to roll the window down and get some fresh air before he could think straight." I pushed a strand of hair from my face and tucked it behind my ear. "I don't like that my scent makes him feel out of control."

"I see." Dr. Reynolds typed some notes in what I presumed was my chart. He did the hunt-and-peck method of typing, so I waited patiently for him to look back at me. "And what about the heat? How did you handle that?"

The blood rushed from every cell in my body and pooled in my cheeks. My face flamed. "Ty and I shifted together. I assumed the pills would stop my heat cycle, but that wasn't the case." I shook my head. Someone should have warned me the heat was this potent. "I felt out of control in my desire for Ty. Ultimately, he..." I cleared my throat and look down at my feet. "Took care of things for me until the sensation passed."

I didn't dare look Dr. Reynolds in the eye.

He must've picked up on my discomfort because he simply continued to speak as if I'd just recited a nursery rhyme. He was completely unfazed. At least as far as I could tell.

"Liza, these feelings you've been experiencing, they're completely normal, so let me get that out of the way first. No need to feel ashamed or embarrassed in the slightest." He pushed his chair back and crossed his legs, looking at the screen for a moment before glancing at me. "Have you told your parents about these experiences?"

Hell no, I hadn't! I was a thirty-year-old woman. My days of sharing things like that with them were long past.

I frowned. "Doc, I love my parents, and I appreciate all the years of care they've provided, but I don't think I need or want to consult with my parents about my sexual health."

He chuckled. "Of course." He blushed slightly, and I doubted it was from the subject matter as much as the faux pas about my age. "You're right. However, your pheromones tend to be on the very high-end of the spectrum, and from what you've been telling me, they continue to rise and emit at a level that renders men helpless. That's certainly not to say it's your fault."

I nodded. I did tell my parents that I'd upped my dosage, but I didn't see why changing medications had anything to do with them. The problem with having the same doctor since childhood was that in his eyes, I still hadn't grown up. "Fair enough, I see what you're saying. They've been made aware."

"Good." Dr. Reynolds picked up a long, silver pen from the holder attached to the blotter on his desk. "I'm going to prescribe you a different medication with a higher dosage. Please keep in mind how important it is to take these every day. Don't think you can skip a day and not be affected in some way. Try to take them at the same time every day, too. Even the difference of a few hours can have an effect on your pheromone levels."

My heart thumped loudly as I tried to muster up the courage to ask the question that had been weighing on me since this whole thing with Ty started. "What will I tell Ty if he wants to have kids? I understand that the pills I've taken for years stop me from having a heat cycle—I'm assuming these will do the same—but if I stop taking them long enough to conceive, I'll be putting myself at risk. Correct?"

Obviously, he knew about my condition. He was the one who diagnosed it.

Dr. Reynolds was silent, no doubt choosing his words carefully. He was a good man and often had to walk a fine line with me as doctor and mentor. "Honestly, Liza, I'm not sure. I know the risk you'd be taking if you're honest with Ty about what you are. That is something the two of you, as mates, will have to overcome together. You shouldn't have to do this alone. Isn't that the whole point of having a fated mate?"

I bit the inside of my cheek.

He continued. "Do you trust Ty enough to tell him?"

I opened my mouth to answer but hesitated. Did I trust Ty? I'd certainly trusted him enough to let him put his head between my legs and keep it there for what had seemed like hours. But just because we'd been intimate, that didn't mean Ty had truly earned my trust. On the other hand... "Yes, I believe I do trust Ty."

"You know I've always leveled with you... told you the truth because it's your body and you're the one who has to deal with it." Doc leaned forward. "It's a risk for you to stop taking your medication because we don't know what will happen now that you're an adult and the pheromones are at adult strength." That wasn't quite the reassurance I was hoping for. "The incident at the coffee shop is concerning, to be sure, and I think you have to be very careful in whatever you decide."

I nodded. He was right.

"The way you described those men turning their full attention on you reminds me of when you were much younger and your brothers almost beat the neighbor kid half to death." He raised an eyebrow. "Do you remember that incident? How quickly the boy reacted?"

Of course I remembered it. That wasn't the kind of thing a girl forgot. I'd just started my period for the first time and was riding my bike. I'd stopped in front of my neighbor's house to drink some water, and before I knew what was happening, Tommy, a fifteen-year-old, had run out of his house and tackled me off my bike. If not for my brothers tossing a football back and forth in the front yard and witnessing the whole thing, there was no telling what Tommy would've done.

Tommy told his parents he had no idea why he'd had such a strong reaction toward me. He wasn't the kind of boy who would do that. His black eyes and busted lip, however, said otherwise. But he'd sworn to my father and his that he'd been watching TV innocently when he'd scented me, and his desire to mate with me had been way too strong for him to control. He'd been fifteen, and I was only twelve. I'd sworn never to mate—with a boy, ew—ever.

I'd never been more grateful to my brothers for pulling him off me and beating him to a pulp. My parents had called the police and filed a report.

I met Dr. Reynolds' gaze. "Not one of my fondest memories, Doc."

"I would certainly think not." He tapped the pen against the side of his leg. "I'm not saying something similar would happen, but based on what you've told me, your pheromones are now attracting multiple men at once. It's simply too dangerous, Liza." *Too dangerous* sounded so ominous.

I studied the floor again, my body deflating.

"Liza, look at me." Dr. Reynolds' voice softened. "None of this is your fault. Tommy and the men at the coffee shop were just reacting to the scent of an omega."

There it was. The word that no one ever spoke. *Omega*. My life would never be normal, and the past week or so had just been further proof of that.

I thanked the doctor and took the prescription from him.

As soon as I was in the parking lot and some of the embarrassment had faded, I checked my phone. Sure enough, Ty had texted to see how my appointment went.

It's all good.

I couldn't summon up a more detailed response. I was spent.

Before I could slide in behind the steering wheel and buckle up, Ty responded.

Let's meet at What's the Scoop for an ice cream. My treat.

Ice cream sounded wonderful.

I'll be there in five.

It was only around the corner and down the block, so when I pulled up, Ty was already waiting on the sidewalk in front of our town's oldest ice cream parlor. It was one of those old-style hand-dipped places with red leather booths, a Formica bar trimmed in chrome, and black-and-white checkered floors. Straight out of an Archie comic.

Ty opened my door, then offered his hand to help me out.

I couldn't help but smile. He was a sight for sore eyes in his button-down, collared shirt and fitted khakis with the skinny legs.

Ty smiled as he pulled me into his arms and kissed me lightly. I breathed deeply, taking in the scent of his cologne. "I needed that after the day I've had."

"Let's go inside and you can tell me all about it." He held my hand and opened the door for me. "Hmm. What should we order?" Ty stared up at the menu hanging above the counter like a little kid.

"Strawberry cheesecake is always a winner," I pointed out, and the picture on the little A-frame board sitting atop the glass case was enough to seal the deal for me.

"True, but I think I'm in the mood for some chocolate." Ty tapped his chin and glanced down into the glass case at the open containers of ice cream.

The woman working behind the counter overheard his comment. "If you're in the mood for chocolate, we have mint chocolate chip, caramel turtle surprise, triple chocolate, and there's always the option to add a brownie to any bowl or cone."

We both shared a look and smiled.

"Perfect." Ty held up two fingers. "Two scoops of mint chocolate chip with a brownie on a sugar cone, please."

I ordered the same. When she handed us our cones, we went to sit at a table outside.

"So, what did your doctor have to say?" Ty licked his ice cream, and I tried not to imagine him licking something else.

I frowned as I bit into my brownie. Maybe it would cool me off.

"You look upset." He reached across the table, twining his fingers with mine. "What happened?"

For the smallest fraction of a moment, I contemplated telling him everything. I was strangely comfortable with Ty, and I was confident that the feelings were more than just our mating bond. He was a natural at being an alpha—everyone could see that in his day-to-day interactions with the pack. His presence was a comfort to those around him, which made it easy for people to talk to him.

We were fated mates, and I wanted to tell him the whole truth of who and what I was.

Before I could stop it, a lump rose in my throat and tears pooled in my eyes. The very last thing I wanted was to get emotional in front of Ty. "I just hate that I'm so different."

Ty's eyes softened with concern. He was completely unaware of the actual extent of how different I truly was, and the guilt of keeping it to myself caused a physical pain in my head. Or maybe the ice cream was to blame. I couldn't say for sure. I only knew I hated lying.

"I just wish I knew the truth about where I came from." I wiped a tear before it made its way down my cheek. "Maybe if I had that information, it would make dealing with my *quirks* a little easier."

Ty stood, tossed the rest of his ice cream in the trash, then knelt next to my chair. He cupped my face with both hands and stared so deeply into my eyes, I felt it in my soul. "There's nothing wrong with you. You are perfect just the way you are, Liza."

His eyes darkened, and something akin to pain flashed in those depths. I was surprised to see honest emotion there. I'd expected sympathy, but he looked sad, almost guilty.

His brow furrowed. "I'm sorry, Liza."

Just as I opened my mouth to ask Ty what he was sorry about, our moment was interrupted by a tall figure who cast a shadow over our table.

The man cleared his throat, and I tore my gaze from Ty long enough to look up to see Stone glancing between the two of us.

He looked pissed.

Chapter 20 - Ty

I wanted to tell Liza what I knew so badly, it was killing me. Ever since Dad had filled me in on our family's history the other night, I'd thought about how Liza might react if she knew that we were the reason she had so many questions. The reason she didn't know who she was or why she'd been brought here.

Liza swiped a tear from her face and looked down at her rapidly melting ice cream. She looked so beaten down, and there I sat, like it wasn't a total asshole move not to tell her the truth. All she wanted was answers about where she had come from in order to better understand who she was today. The word 'omega' bounced around my mind, pinging off the edges like a pinball. If she didn't know what she was—but she *had* to know—it would be the biggest of all the surprises, and there were a plenty.

She hadn't gone into detail, but she considered herself to be different from others. Liza needed reassurance, but more importantly, she needed to resolve the mystery surrounding her birth family.

Yet, there I sat, keeping the information to myself, not even hinting that I knew all the answers.

I was a dick.

If I shared what I knew with Liza, there was no way in hell she would want to be mated to me. My family had wiped out her entire family; her entire pack. She was an orphan because of us, and no one who knew the truth had bothered to step forward and tell her about the massacre or explain why it had happened.

As soon as she found out, I was going to lose her, no doubt about it. That alone would destroy me and probably my entire family, and my place as the next alpha would be in jeopardy. If Liza walked away from me and refused to be my mate, I would backslide and have to start over again at square one.

The thought of mating with someone else for the sake of keeping my family's legacy intact made me sick to my stomach.

I couldn't lose her. So, no, I wouldn't tell Liza the truth. I was not taking that chance.

Not an option.

I cradled Liza's face in my hands and pointed my gaze at hers. I wanted her to see how much she meant to me. It was my feeble attempt to reassure her. She was perfect in my eyes, even if she was shrouded in a mystery she didn't understand, and I couldn't tell her. I wanted her. All of her.

She stared into my eyes with a recognition that knocked the air out of me. I opened my mouth to tell her what she had come to mean to me, even within such a small span of time, but something in the air shifted.

I sensed his presence before he reached our table. It was a stench in the air, a sickening kind of haze. Doing my best to keep my composure, I slowly looked up and stared into Stone's eyes. He glanced back and forth between Liza and me, his nose wrinkled in disgust, his lips pulled in a sneer. His scowl deepened with every silent second that passed.

The way he studied us put my back up. What the hell did he want? And how did he find us?

Stone let out a dry chuckle. "Fate sure is one sick bitch."

Liza jolted at his brash words, accidentally dropping her ice cream cone on the Formica table. As Stone glared at her, she bit her lip and turned her terror-stricken eyes on me.

He lowered his voice and pointed his finger in her direction. "Do you have any idea of the mockery you're making of yourself?" His tone was little more than a growl, but he might as well have struck Liza across her face.

She reached for my hand, her face a picture of confusion.

I didn't know who this motherfucker thought he was, but damned if I was going to stand by and let him harass Liza. Rising, I dropped Liza's hand and crossed my arms, planting my feet firmly in front of Stone. There was nothing he could say that I wanted to fucking hear. Not that I was going to give him a chance to say anything, anyway.

I towered over him, pushing my chest forward and shoulders back. This fucker needed to be made aware of just who he was messing with. "If you have something to say, then say it directly to me. Leave Liza out of it."

Stone's eyes narrowed to slits, and he let out a low growl. He wasn't backing down, and it didn't take a genius to realize he was going to ignore my warning.

I glanced around the outdoor patio of the ice cream shop, taking inventory of the multiple families and couples enjoying their treats and conversation. I couldn't very well beat Stone's ass in front of them, but he didn't have to know that. Better he think of me as a wild card; a rogue who obeyed no rules and followed no code. It would suit my purposes.

Without warning, his face softened, and he turned to Liza. "I'm sorry for speaking that way to you. Of all people, you deserve much more from me."

Of all people. What the hell did he mean by that?

Liza looked even more confused as she stood and shoved her hands into her pants pockets, taking a step closer to me. She wasn't trembling. Wasn't scared. I liked her courage. I liked it even more that she leaned into me.

Stone looked as if he might say something else about the two of us, but I held up a hand and stopped him.

"Meet me in the back parking lot," I growled, my jaws clenching so hard that they ached.

"You bet." Stone forced a smile and looked at her. I wanted to gouge his eyes out so he could never look at her again. "I'll see you around, Liza."

The fuck he would.

He walked around the side of the building. Once he was out of sight, I grabbed Liza's hands. "I'm sorry for the interruption. Stay put." I kissed her gently on the lips.

"Maybe you shouldn't… here." Her voice was soft, tentative almost, and I wanted to reassure her as much as I wanted to kill Stone.

"Don't worry. I promise, everything will be okay. I'm just going to have a chat with Stone. Don't leave without me."

She pulled her lip between her teeth and nodded, then sat down again. Liza quickly grabbed several napkins to clean up her melted ice cream mess. Bewildered as she was, she didn't hesitate to heed my wishes.

Liza trusted me, which only increased my guilt at hiding the truth from her.

I thought of her as I walked, thought of the man she thought I was: honest, honorable, decent. I was none of those things, and I was about to prove it.

I tried to keep a level head, but by the time I reached him, I couldn't rein in my rage.

I shoved him into the SUV parked behind him, satisfied when the metal dented in the shape of his back. I grabbed the collar of his shirt and brought his face close to mine. "Stay the fuck away from Liza."

Stone's eyes were ablaze with fury. "You're a bastard! If you had any decency, you'd end your mating bond with Liza immediately."

What the hell? How did he know that Liza and I were fated mates?

I released his collar and took a step backward. "What the fuck do you know about the two of us? Have you been following Liza? Following me, you piece of shit?"

Stone scoffed and rolled his eyes. "Seriously? I don't have to follow you to know what I know. Any fool can see it. Your scents are all over each other, and your auras are starting to intertwine. It's obvious you're trying to mate with her."

This motherfucker could sense our auras? As an alpha, I could pick up on bonds once a couple was fully mated, but not before. I'd never heard of any shifters with that ability.

"How the fuck do you know about our auras? That's impossible."

Stone smirked and leaned back against the black SUV, nonchalantly hooking his thumbs through the belt loops of his jeans. "I suppose old Daddy dearest didn't tell you everything after all. I guess he wanted to keep some of the delicious details to himself. Figures. He's a shady prick who twists the truth to serve himself." He paused and looked around, seeing if anyone else was in the parking lot. "The Wylde pack was known for their special *gifts*. Legends say that the elders made a deal with the Devil, certainly with a demon for the powers they had. Who knows? Maybe they were on to something."

I had no clue what Stone was referring to, but I glanced at my watch. If we were going to fuck each other up, I wanted to get it over with because I didn't want to leave Liza alone for too long. I twirled my finger in the air. "And?"

"The gifts were revered and celebrated, but for every gift there was a price to be paid. The pack had very low fertility rates."

I really hoped my dad hadn't kept this from me on purpose. I had to hold on to the hope that he knew nothing about this, otherwise, the motive for decimating the pack was very different from what he'd told me. Of course, I couldn't think of why I would believe this fucker over my dad, but it was a lot to sort through.

"I was the first to be born in almost twenty years, and I came out of the womb with the gift of sight. I can sense things others can't. Things that are invisible to the commoner's eye."

Interesting. He had my attention now. "What other gifts did your people have?"

"They had other similar gifts, but when it was obvious no other children were being born, we all felt that the gifts would die with me." He paused and shot me a pointed look. "That's why Liza's birth was celebrated the way it was. Her parents were the most gifted of all and, considering what they gave birth to, Liza was seen as the golden child." Now I understood his anger. I was stealing from him. A birthright.

Before I could ask or accuse, a man burst out of the ice cream parlor, his hands flailing in the air. "Hey! Get off my car, you asshole."

We both turned to face the man who was ready to punch Stone in the face. If I didn't step in to defuse the situation, the police would be called, and I would miss out on the opportunity to get some real fucking answers.

"Whoa." I held up both hands and stepped in front of Stone. "He didn't mean any harm. We're just having a conversation."

"Oh." The guy looked at me and blinked, his eyes opening wide with recognition. "Sorry, Ty. I didn't recognize you from the window."

"No harm done, man." I reached out and shook his hand. "Send me the bill for getting that dent pulled out. Sorry about that. And no worries. My friend here will rest his ass against something else."

"Thanks, Ty, but it's not so bad." He chuckled. "I can probably pop it out."

Our ideas of bad were obviously different, but the man smiled at me, then shot one last glare over his shoulder in Stone's direction. Stone had already stepped away from the vehicle, also not wanting to cause more of a scene.

"Thanks." Stone shot me a glare of his own, apparently blaming me for the interruption. "Where was I?"

"You said that Liza was considered special. Why was that?" Maybe if I knew it all, we could figure out a way to work through it together once I told her.

The look he gave me told me he thought he was talking to the stupidest human on the planet. I, on the other hand, thought I was the one talking to king dumbass. "Her birth was looked at as the beginning of a new era. She was the mother of the next generation of Wyldes."

"Hmm." My heart raced, and a lump rose in my throat. I had an inkling I knew exactly what Stone was trying to tell me. Even though it scared the shit out of me, I forced myself to focus on what he was saying.

Stone rubbed his chin. "Liza's parents sought protection for her. She was special, and they didn't want anything to happen to her. They were willing to pay everything they had and everything they could beg, borrow, or steal to keep her protected because, as you already know, omegas are revered and meant to be protected at all costs."

Yeah. I knew that.

Fuck.

My face paled as my breath almost left my body. There wasn't going to be any talking to him once I told Bryce he had been right all along. Liza *was* an omega. The thought was staggering.

Somehow, I kept my composure in front of Stone. The last thing I needed was for this tool to sense a weakness within me. He would pounce at the first chance he got.

Stone continued. "Liza was promised to me. The plan involved the two of us bringing forth the new generation."

His voice turned so hard it could have broken through steel. "The Keller pack was supposed to help *protect* her. Instead, they slaughtered the entire pack." He quirked an eyebrow, wanting to hear my response, daring me to deny it. His fists were clenched at his sides, and it wouldn't take much to provoke him into a fight.

"Stone, I don't know what to say. The sins of my family have nothing to do with me. I just learned about all this shit from my father." I hadn't even managed to sort through all the dirty details yet.

"Your father is a fucking coward," Stone growled, and there was real hatred in his tone, as well as a searing need for vengeance. "I saw him that day. His claws were out, and he was ready to pierce them into Liza." He shook his head, and his eyes glowed with rage, fists still clenched at his side. "She was just a child, for fuck's sake." His nostrils flared. "I suppose his conscience finally kicked in and he decided not to kill her, but I saw the blood in his eyes. He knew it would be easier to have her out of the picture completely."

I raked my hand through my hair. According to my father, the entire pack had been killed. Seems he'd had it wrong. Stone had seen it all. No wonder he was so enraged. His fury was an entire third entity in this discussion.

"I never knew the names of the monsters who destroyed my home and took my queen, but I vowed to find her again and restore our pack to its former glory." His eyes were as black as his soul when he looked at me. "Reject Liza. She shouldn't be tainted by the bloody hands of the family who kidnapped her. She deserves better than a Keller."

He turned to leave without giving me a chance to respond, although I couldn't have even if I tried. I was at a complete loss for words.

Just before he turned the corner, Stone stopped and spun on his heels. "Liza was promised to *me*. Keep that in mind. If you don't fucking walk away, and soon, I'm going to start letting secrets slip to anyone who will fucking listen. I'm sure your pack would be eager to learn the truth." That was a threat I couldn't take lightly.

The truth always had power. Stone's final words rang in my head as I stood, unmoving, shocked to my core. Liza was an omega. What would that mean for our relationship?

I trudged back to the front of the ice cream shop, my mind reeling. Most of the other patrons had left, so Liza had the patio almost completely to herself.

She was shaded under the patio awning, scrolling on her phone when I sat down in the seat across from her. Putting her phone down, she watched me expectantly.

Of course, she wanted answers. I'd just left her alone on our date for a good thirty minutes to have a conversation with a mysterious man who shared her light features. To top it all off, we had been in the middle of a discussion about her past when he'd conveniently strolled up to our table. The timing couldn't have been worse.

I couldn't tell Liza what Stone and I had discussed, so I reached out and grabbed her hand instead. "I'm so sorry, Liza. I've got to get home."

If I wasn't near her, I wouldn't be tempted to blurt out the facts that were now stored deep in my mind. I needed to sort through them first and decipher the truth from whatever else I'd been told. Fiction. Lies. Embellished legends. I wouldn't be able to tell until I had some time alone with my thoughts.

She laid her hand over mine, her brow creased, eyes bright with worry. "Are you okay?"

Her touch against my skin brought me crashing back to reality. I studied her face, agony twisting my intestines. I had to tell her everything. I knew that, but I couldn't do it in the middle of town at an ice cream shop, and I couldn't do it right now.

Right now, I had to be an alpha and put the pack first. If the pack no longer existed, there would be no future for Liza and me. We'd lose everything.

That didn't stop me from standing and pulling her against my chest. I kissed her long and hard for all the world to see. Her scent wrapped around us as she relaxed in my arms. She was special. No, she was *beyond* special. She was an omega.

Stone's words rang in my ears. *Omegas are revered and meant to be protected at all costs.*

Everything Stone had told me should've made me push her away, but fate chose us for a reason. I had to trust in that. I didn't know what the outcome would be, but I wasn't giving Liza up.

Not for anyone.

Especially not for a piece of shit like Stone.

Chapter 21 - Ty

The short drive home seemed to take a lot longer than usual. My parents had always frowned upon speeding, since our family was the upholders of the law, but I was in a hurry. There was a discussion to be had, lies to correct, and a history I needed to understand.

Knowing my father had left out vitally important information about Liza in his confession, I had to confront him. And now.

I slammed the front door behind me, yelling as I rushed into the foyer, "Dad? Are you up there?"

"What's all the ruckus about?" Mother appeared at the top of the stairs, staring down at me with her usual amount of disapproval. "Tyson? What's wrong?"

"Oh, I'll tell you what's wrong." I took the steps two at a time, shrugging off my mother's hand when she reached for me. "Is Dad in his office?"

She scurried after me. "He's on a phone call, Ty. Lower your voice!"

"Nope. Not happening." I barged into the office, and my father's wide eyes landed on me. It seemed he had some inkling of what was coming.

"Tommy, I'll call you back." He set the corded receiver back into its cradle and stood, using the backs of his legs to shove his leather chair away. "What is so damn important to have you barging in here like a maniac, Tyson?"

I strode forward and slammed my fist onto the mahogany desk. A lesser piece of furniture would have folded under the pressure, but my father spared no expense on his furnishings. Or his lies. "Why the hell did you keep information about Liza to yourself? I thought you were being open and honest with me the other night." I shook my head. "But I guess I should have fucking known, huh?"

"Excuse me?" Dad folded his arms beneath his massive chest and huffed. "What exactly are you accusing me of, son?"

I fell down into a wingback chair across from him and leaned forward, resting my elbows on my knees. "Based on the conversation I just had with Stone Black, you seem to have omitted some pretty important facts from the story you told me about Liza."

"I don't know what you're talking about. I told you everything." As my father sat down again, he challenged me with a glare.

He needed to know that he'd fucked up royally—no fucking pun intended—by keeping everything to himself. There was, however, a very slim chance, and I was willing to give him the benefit of the doubt, that he didn't know Liza was an omega. I couldn't blurt it out, but I could wait to see if my old man manned up and told me the truth. For the time being, I chose to keep that bit of information to myself.

I sighed. "Stone confronted me while I was on a date with Liza tonight. We had a conversation about the Wylde pack. You said you'd killed everyone!" My father didn't react. "Stone said he witnessed you almost murdering Liza but, for whatever reason, you changed your mind at the last second."

"Damn it." Dad cursed under his breath and rubbed a hand across his forehead. "What else did he say?" He was more than curious. He was wary.

"Stone told me he was supposed to be Liza's mate and that she was promised to him many years ago." The words were bitter in my mouth. "He also said that if we don't allow him to pursue her, he'll start telling everyone the Keller family's secrets. Call me crazy but I'm assuming that would include the fact that we *slaughtered* the Wylde pack." I would be screaming that from the rooftops if I were Stone.

Dad shook his head, sighed, and paced the room. "All right. This is fixable. We need to come up with a plan to eliminate him … immediately."

It didn't surprise me that he wanted to silence Stone, that he wanted to kill him. My father didn't like tedious details, and if there was one word that described Stone, it was *tedious*.

I sat back, tapping my fingers on my knee. "Dad, do I really need to remind you that slaughtering an entire pack is what got us into this situation in the first place? Do you think it's wise to put even more blood on our hands?"

He stopped pacing and spun around to face me. "Yes, I'm fully aware of the absolute shit show I created, Tyson. I don't need you to point it out for me." Someone should've counseled him before the slaughter. His advisors had failed him miserably.

Mother sighed, and I turned in time to see her wiping tears from her face. Honestly, I'd forgotten about her.

Dad made his way across the room and put his arms around her, kissing her forehead lightly. "My love, you don't need to listen to all of this. Why don't you go read your book. I'll work this out. There's nothing to worry about. I promise."

She nodded. I could've told her a thing or two about believing his brand of BS, but I kept my mouth shut. My mother forced a weak smile. Before turning to leave, she peered at me over Dad's shoulders. Her eyes pleaded with me, perhaps hoping I'd talk some sense into Dad or wishing I didn't goad him into a medical emergency.

Dad closed the door behind him, then came to sit down on the chair next to mine. "Ty, I'm going to be straightforward with you because you're no longer a child." He breathed in deep so that his nostrils flared. "As the next alpha, you're going to need to learn to step back from the situation and try to remove all personal feelings from the equation." He waited, as if he thought he would be able to see me do so right now.

There was no way I could see myself stepping back from a mass murder that didn't have to happen, and no way was I committing murder just because he was asking me to, but I didn't say that.

Dad continued. "The only other alternative to killing Stone is handing over Liza." I sure as fuck wasn't going to do that. "Even then, Stone being alive is a risk I'm not willing to take. The information he has is too dangerous for our pack."

I sighed.

"He holds a secret that, if it gets out, would ruin us. Who's to say he won't come back and make more demands? When would the blackmail end?"

Fuck. He was right.

I lowered my voice. "I see your point, but I'm not killing anyone. I don't want to start off as alpha with blood on my hands." Secrets or not. "As someone who's living with the guilt of murdering an entire pack, surely you can understand?"

Dad covered his mouth with his hand but remained silent. He was deep in thought. I probably only had one chance to convince him to choose another route to keep the pack safe. Although, for the life of me, I didn't have a clue what that route would be.

"According to you, you'd supposedly put all of this behind us after you massacred the Wylde pack, yet here it is rearing its ugly head into our lives again. Murder isn't the answer."

"You're right." Dad cleared his throat. "This is all on me. I never knew there was another kid hiding and watching from afar. I should have checked. If I had, maybe I would've been able to bring him into the fold the same way I did with Liza."

Could have. Would have. Should have. His regrets didn't help us at all.

"That misstep is on me and no one else. I want to meet with Stone."

"Absolutely not!" I responded louder than I intended, and my father twisted his head to look at me. More accurately, to glare at me. This wasn't a man who was used to having his word questioned. "That's a very bad idea. Stone will know it's a setup and expect you to kill him. What do you think he'll do? He'll come prepared to defend himself. If he even smells a setup, I guarantee you he'll strike first."

My father chuckled. "Let me assure you, I can handle myself, Ty. You seem to forget who I am." Dad stood and puffed out his chest, which though massive, wasn't nearly as impressive as it used to be. "I'll try to bargain with him before I make a final decision on whether his life can be spared or if he's too dangerous to the pack to live."

"If that's what you choose to do then I can't stop you, but I am asking you to give it more thought." I stood, my blood singing in my veins. There was nothing I could do about my anger, and I couldn't argue with my father anymore. Every word against him planted his idea deeper in his mind. I walked to the door. As I turned the doorknob, I turned to look at him. "Mother's worried enough without her catching wind that you're inviting Stone to a private meeting."

"Don't worry about your mother, I've got it all under control." He scoffed. "Liza has proven to be more trouble than I thought." He was having a bad case of *if he knew then what he knew now*, and I didn't like it one fucking bit.

I spun to face him, my body tense, poised to fight for her. "Choose your next words carefully because Liza is still my mate, and I won't tolerate *anyone* speaking of her in that way." It was a good thing I hadn't told him Liza was an omega.

Dad, weak as he was, was at my side in a flash. He grabbed me by the shirt. "Don't forget that I'm still the alpha, Tyson. I'll say whatever I damn well please. Your little girlfriend is causing our family more grief than we deserve."

Deserve? He had no fucking idea what we deserved.

Letting go of my shirt, he shoved me back.

I stepped toward him until our chests nearly touched, and I glared down into my father's eyes. "She is my fated mate, whether you like it or not, and any grief this family receives is *well deserved*." I couldn't believe he had the nerve to defend his behavior. "You killed an entire pack: her family, his family, all of them instead of finding another way to handle a situation you should have stepped back to assess before you did something so reckless and ridiculous. Leave Liza the fuck out of it!"

"It's obvious your priorities are screwed up, Ty. Listen to yourself!"

My hands balled into fists, and I growled. I fully understood my role and responsibilities as future alpha, but I could be a good alpha, keep the pack safe, and still find a way to be a good mate to Liza. She was *mine,* and I would protect her at all costs, even if that meant going against my own father.

"Dad, I'll warn you one last time. Think wisely about the moves you take with Stone. He owes you no allegiance, and he has plenty of reason to want vengeance." I stormed out of the office before he could respond.

I had some moves of my own to make. Liza wasn't safe, and that was unacceptable.

Once inside my bedroom, I shut the door and pulled out my phone to call Zephyr.

When he answered, he started talking right away. "Hey, Ty. Sorry, man. I don't have anything else on Liza."

"That's not why I'm calling, Zephyr." I sighed. "I need you to see what you can find on Stone Black, if that's even his real name. I need any dirt you can dig up." Maybe there was a way to fight him without involving weapons and bloodshed.

Zephyr was silent for a moment. "All right, I'll see what I can do. How fast do you need it?"

"Yesterday." The sooner I had the information, the easier it would be to keep my dad from getting himself killed.

I ended the call and tossed my phone on my bed. There was nothing to keep me from using anything I could find against Stone, and no reason not to. I needed him far away from Liza, and fast.

My phone vibrated, and if it was Zephyr, he'd worked fast this time, and safe to say I hoped he had some good news. Instead, it was a text from Liza.

Are you okay?

Instead of texting back, I dialed her number.

"Hey, Ty. Is everything okay? I thought I'd have heard from you by now."

I could tell by her tone that she was worried about me. The desire to tell her everything overwhelmed me, but I couldn't fill her in until I knew for certain that Stone wasn't going to be a problem anymore. Then I'd figure out a way to break all of this to her. There was no fucking way her parents had been in the dark about it all.

"I was just thinking about how I'd like to meet your parents. It would be nice to have a man-to-man chat with your dad about becoming your mate." *Liar, liar, pants on fire.*

"I'm sure Dad would like that. I'll call them and get back to you." I heard the smile in her voice as she spoke, and that nagging guilt whooshed through my body again.

I put as much enthusiasm as I could in my tone. "Perfect. Let me know. Bye, Liza."

I fell back onto my bed, holding my phone up and staring at it, willing the goddamned thing to ping or ting or chime with information from Zephyr.

It didn't.

Fuck.

Depending on someone else to do the things I should've been doing myself but couldn't without garnering some attention and provoking questions was pure torture. I needed to make a move, not idly stand by while Stone ironed out his plan to mate with Liza and ruin my family along the way.

My phone buzzed in my hand. It was Liza again.

Damn, that was fast.

Dinner with my parents tomorrow night at six? Does that work?

I smiled, sensing her excitement, even via text.

Yep. I'll pick you up. Sweet dreams, beautiful.

***

I was on edge when I went to pick Liza up for the dinner with her family that I'd instigated. Zephyr still hadn't responded, and I hadn't quite worked out the best way to broach the subject with Liza's parents.

Each hour that passed was another hour Stone had to devise a plan to take our family down. There was no way in hell I was going to allow Liza to leave Presley Acres with him, but I didn't take Stone for the kind of guy who played by the rules. I could see him going full kidnapper to prove his point and get his way.

Liza's safety was in jeopardy, so seeing her safe and smiling as she walked to my car was a massive relief.

Honestly, I was surprised she still wanted to spend time with me. I'd been so keyed up, I'd called and texted almost every thirty minutes throughout the day, checking to make sure she was safe. If she took longer than a couple seconds to answer, my heart throbbed, and blood rushed to my ears until I got a text from her.

"You look amazing." I walked around the front of the car and opened the door for her.

The smell of her perfume combined with the sensory overload of her tight jeans gave my brain a moment of respite from thoughts about Stone.

"Thank you." She grinned as she kissed me on the cheek. "You don't look so bad yourself."

As she directed me to her parents' home, she smiled and chattered like she was nervous, but that was on me. I could hardly speak at all. The relief and happiness at seeing her overwhelmed my very being.

When I turned onto her street, Liza pointed out her parents' home. We pulled in behind several vehicles. "How many people am I meeting tonight? Looks like a whole basketball team is joining us for dinner."

Liza laughed, "My brothers are here."

Oh, good. Nothing like a pair of brothers to take the pressure off.

Her parents met us at the door. Her mom's smiled reached from ear to ear, and her dad stood behind his wife, his gaze unwavering. This was a man who was keeping a close eye on the suitor for his daughter. I didn't blame him. I only hoped he couldn't read the thoughts I had about his daughter and the outline of her ass in those jeans.

"Welcome, Ty." Mrs. Mims embraced me. "I haven't seen you since the boys played baseball at the summer league downtown. You've grown quite a bit since then."

I chuckled. "So nice to see you again, Mrs. Mims." I reached to shake hands with Liza's dad. "Nice to see you, as well, Mr. Mims."

Mrs. Mims giggled nervously. "Oh, please call us Rory and Scott."

Scott took my hand and shook it firmly but didn't say a word.

When we entered the dining room, Liza's brothers rose from their chairs.

"Holy crap. If it isn't Tyson the bison," Mason said with a laugh.

Shit. I hadn't heard that nickname in years.

Michael and Mason each slapped me on the back and shook my hand.

We reminisced about our days in sports camp together while Liza listened and laughed at our antics. I'd been a junior coach at the time. Even though the twins were several years younger than me, it was easy to pick up on their dedication and drive to be winners.

Dinner went well and the conversation flowed easily, even though Liza's father barely spoke. Once we finished our dessert, I caught Michael giving Mason a look.

I suppressed a groan. I knew that look. It was time for the interrogation to begin.

Mason cracked his knuckles. "So, Ty, what are your intentions with our sister?"

His demeanor morphed to protective big brother. It happened so quickly it took me by surprise. I considered and reconsidered my words as I tried to think of the best response.

"Your sister is unlike anyone I've ever met. Fate wants us to be together, and the more I get to know her, I can see why. She's kind, compassionate, strong-willed, and intelligent... not to mention she's an amazing cook."

There were chuckles and laughter all around. I wasn't the only fan of her food.

"In all seriousness, I care so much for Liza that I would do anything in my power to keep her safe and happy." That was the God's honest truth.

Liza reached for my hand under the table and squeezed tightly.

Rory wiped a tear from her eye. "That was beautiful, Ty. I love seeing the two of you together. The connection between you both is undeniable."

Michael and Mason grinned, so I assumed I had their approval. That small relief did nothing to unclench my stomach. I still needed to have a conversation with Liza's parents.

Once we'd cleared the table, I turned to Scott. "Could I speak with you and Rory privately?"

"Sure, we can speak in my office." These were the first words I'd heard him say all night.

I turned and kissed Liza on the cheek. "Don't have too much fun without me."

She blushed, then went to join her brothers in the living room.

Scott led us into his office upstairs and closed the door behind him. "This room is soundproof, so they won't be able to hear from downstairs."

I nodded and took a seat in an office chair while Rory and Scott sat on the couch across from me. "I'm going to cut right to the chase. I know how Liza was brought to you from the Wylde pack after the members were slaughtered."

Scott's eyes went wide, and Rory's face paled.

I continued. "There was a survivor from that pack, Stone Black, and he says that he was promised Liza many years ago. I'm assuming before the pack... ended. He's shown up in town, ready to claim her. Stone is a very dangerous man, so I'm working on getting him out of the picture, and I intend to protect Liza at all costs."

"Fuck." Scott stood, and rubbed his temples. "How could this be happening?"

Rory choked back a sob. "We always worried that Liza would find out the truth about her past, but our biggest concern was how she'd react to that truth."

Scott walked to the window and stared outside. "We wanted to protect her. She didn't talk for six months when we got her. We figured she was dealing with her trauma. The poor little girl was only four. She had to be terrified after witnessing everyone she knew and loved being slaughtered."

"Did she not remember?" I asked. It was conceivable. She'd been young. I didn't have any memories from back then. Of course, I hadn't been through that kind of trauma.

Rory wiped away a couple of errant tears. "When she finally did start talking, it was like she didn't remember a thing, so we never brought it up." She clasped her shaking hands in her lap.

They were both scared, and with good reason. Stone wanted Liza to know the truth, and they didn't want her to know at all. Since they hadn't told her, it could have been that she wouldn't take it well and that she would be angry they'd kept it from her. I wondered how many things would have been different if she'd known. Liza would be wondering the same when she found out.

I couldn't see a way that I could keep it from her. She deserved to know the truth.

Did her parents know the whole truth? I shifted in my seat and looked up to meet Rory's eyes. "Do you know what she is?"

Rory covered her mouth, and Scott went to sit next to his wife again. Their reactions and lack of response told me everything I needed to know.

"I promise you both that I will never expose her secrets to anyone."

They shared a look like they wanted to say something but must have decided against it.

After giving Rory a few minutes to compose herself, we opened the office door and walked downstairs. We spent the rest of the night playing card games and laughing as if the conversation had never happened and nothing was wrong.

Liza finally yawned and glanced at her watch. "We'd better go. I have an early meeting with a client."

We said our goodbyes. As I shook Scott's hand, he gave me a knowing look. He was entrusting me with his daughter, and the news I'd shared had put him on high alert. I squeezed his hand, hoping that would convey how I intended to protect Liza.

On the drive back to Liza's house, she reached over and held my hand. "That went better than I thought it would."

"Hey," I laughed. "Are you saying you thought I'd screw it up royally? I think your family liked me, Liza Mims."

"Honestly, I'm a little disappointed."

I tilted my head and looked at her.

"I figured they'd spend more time grilling you to determine if you were worthy of my time." She shrugged and pouted. "You must've won them over with your charm."

"Don't forget my blinding good looks. My wit. The muscular body." I raised my eyebrows and flexed my biceps. "I'm the full package." True enough, but I said it with some measure of humility.

Liza rolled her eyes. "All right, Hercules. Are you going to walk me to my door?"

"Naturally. I wouldn't miss an opportunity for a proper goodnight kiss."

Liza giggled, and I opened her car door. With our hands clasped, we walked to her house. She unlocked the door, then turned to me. Just before she went inside, I tugged her close, brushing my lips over hers. It wasn't enough. It would never be enough.

I moved in again, pulling her into a deep kiss with sweeping tongues and half-whimpering moans. I wanted the kiss to convey how much she meant to me. How much I needed to be with her.

She returned the kiss with the same fervor, clinging to me, the fabric of my shirt fisted in her hands. We stayed in that tight embrace for several minutes.

I finally pulled away and took a deep breath. "I promise I'll make up for our ice cream date."

Liza waved her hand in the air. "You already have. Thank you for being so kind to my family."

I grabbed her hand and pulled her body close to mine. I needed one more kiss before I walked away.

Chapter 22 - Liza

"Are you hungry?" I wiped a smudge of lipstick from my chin. I was real glad I hadn't gone with the lip stain for tonight.

Putting makeup on in the back of an Uber while we hit multiple potholes wasn't exactly the best idea I'd ever had. Sabrina had called earlier in the day and asked if we could please have a ladies' night out.

It had been so long since we'd done more than speak on the phone, and the brunt of it was my fault. I'd been so busy between work and trying to figure out my relationship with Ty, I'd completely neglected my best friend. A night out on the town and a distraction from work and everything that was going on was exactly what I needed to set my head straight.

Sabrina harrumphed. "Nah, I'll just eat some pretzels at the bar. I want to save room for the alcohol."

I chuckled. On her best day, Sabrina couldn't hold her liquor, and I worried that her stomach would be too empty when she started throwing back beers.

Who was I kidding? She'd be sloshed within minutes, pretzels or not.

"If you say so." I zipped my purse and stared out the window at the old brick buildings that lined the streets of downtown. "What's the name of this bar again?"

Sabrina had convinced me to go to a new bar that had opened a few weeks ago. It was country-and-western themed with live music and a mechanical bull. It wasn't exactly what I would have called my style, but it was the perfect spot to go dancing with my friend. I'd even pulled out an old pair of pink cowboy boots and a matching hat I'd bought during college.

"It's called The Boot Scootin' Bar," Sabrina answered, as if she were one of their national spokespersons. "And I heard they have the best margaritas in *town*."

The Uber driver pulled up to the entrance of the bar and we handed him a cash tip before hopping out. The neon lights around the perimeter of the sign of a giant cowboy boot outside the entrance were a bit garish, but men and women dressed in their finest western boots and hats funneled through the entrance as fast as the bouncers could open the stanchions. It seemed Sabrina had been right about it being the latest hot spot in town.

As we made our way inside, my heart raced with anticipation. The bar would, no doubt, be full of single men. I said a quick and silent prayer that the new medication would do what Doc had promised, and I wouldn't have to live through another nightmare. I should have considered that before I left, and if Ty asked, I would assure him I had thought of it.

The smell of stale beer and whiskey hit me as soon as we stepped through the entrance. The country music was loud, and I couldn't help but smile. This was exactly the kind of place I needed. I'd been so focused on Ty and my business that I couldn't wait to let loose.

Sabrina grabbed my arm and pulled me toward the bar. She shouted her order over the noise, and within seconds she had a beer in her hand. I was more of a margarita kind of gal, so I ordered one and sipped it slowly as we made our way to the dance floor.

As soon as we stepped onto the wooden planks, Sabrina twirled around and squealed with excitement. We put our empty drinks on a nearby table, then she grabbed my hands and pulled me into the fast-paced line dance. There was kicking, thigh-slapping, toe-tapping, hip-gyrating, and spinning. I laughed and followed her as best I could, trying not to trip over my own feet. I wasn't exactly the most coordinated shifter in town, but no one pointed or laughed. It didn't seem to matter to anyone that I was a stumbling, bumbling, trainwreck of a dancer.

The music was intoxicating, and in this place, with all these random, unassociated people, I finally felt free from all of my worries. The night had just begun, but I already knew that it would be one for the books.

After the song stopped, we went back to the bar and pulled out a couple of stools.

"I think I'm ready for those pretzels." Sabrina signaled the bartended for another round.

As we snacked on pretzels and sipped our drinks, I noticed a couple of guys over Sabrina's shoulder. They were eyeing us pretty intently, so I wasn't surprised when they got up the nerve to walk in our direction.

It was nothing new for us. We were used to men hitting on us in bars. The only difference now was that Ty and I were together, so I had no interest in their attention.

"Hello, ladies." A man with a slight southern drawl stepped in front of Sabrina when she turned on her stool to look at them. His black hair was slicked back, and he wore jeans with a nice blue dress shirt that had pearl button covers.

Sabrina looked from him to me and back, then flashed her sexiest smile. "Hey there, cowboy." She had a tone, a way of being that conveyed everything she wanted to say without actually saying it.

She oozed sexiness. It came naturally to her, and I had yet to see a man who wasn't drawn to her flirtatiousness like a moth to a flame. I sipped my drink, trying to stay in the background as Sabrina soaked up the attention, but my presence was a safety net in case anyone got too aggressive.

The man smiled broadly, flashing a set of perfect white teeth. He extended his hand to Sabrina. "Hi." He gave her another smile. "I'm Jack."

"Very nice to meet you, Jack. I'm Sabrina."

Jack's friend eyed me. I flashed him a smile, but shook my head. Ty would kill these guys.

"She's in a happy relationship," Sabrina said. "Don't mind her." She gave the other guy a once-over. He was blondish with stormy gray eyes, an equally gray shirt, and pointy boots. "What's your name?"

He cleared his throat. "Jason."

Sabrina continued to flirt with Jack and Jason while I stayed distantly friendly.

"Want to dance?" From the other side, a blond-haired, blue-eyed man placed a hand on my shoulder.

I didn't like being randomly pawed, and I wriggled out from under his grasp. "No, I'm sorry. I'm taken."

He shrugged, then went to the other end of the bar where a group of scantily clad women were giggling loudly. They might as well have had a blinking LED sign that announced they were there to get laid.

Jack must've overheard my comment about me being taken. He leaned down and whispered in my ear, "Oh, come on." I shook my head, but again, he moved in closer. "He isn't here, and no one but you and I would ever have to know."

"I said I'm taken." My voice was firm and brooked no room for further conversation. I turned and faced the bar, slurping down the last of my margarita, hoping I'd seen the last of Jack.

I overheard him asking Sabrina to dance, but she took my cue and turned him down.

"Hey, are you going to be like this all night?" she asked me.

"What do you mean?" I popped another mini pretzel into my mouth. "Like what?"

"Like a stick in the mud, that's what." Sabrina laughed and rolled her eyes. "Just because you and Ty are dating doesn't mean you can't have a little fun."

I grimaced. "Do I need to remind you that it's girls' night? Not 'pick up random strangers for a quickie in the bathroom' night." Tonight was our night. Besides, I had Ty. I simply had no desire to flirt, dance, or otherwise associate with another male tonight, or likely, any night. Ty was the only one for me, and I wanted it to stay that way.

Sabrina snapped her fingers in my face. "Liza, I asked you a question."

"Oh, sorry. I was thinking about something."

"Uh-huh." Sabrina took a swig of beer. "You weren't thinking about something, you were thinking about *someone*. I asked if you're still a card-carrying member of the V-club."

Oh, for the love of fuck. Was she really going to ask me about my virginity at a bar?

"I am, as a matter of fact, and maybe we could talk about this another time," I whispered the last part, causing Sabrina to burst into a fit of laughter.

She wasn't even two beers in, and she was already losing control. It was going to be a long night.

"Let me get this straight. You're dating the future alpha, who also just happens to be the hottest man in Texas, and he hasn't managed to talk you out of your panties yet?" She laughed even harder. "Can he not... perform?" She puffed out her lower lip in a pout.

"He can perform. Absolutely, he can." And now I sounded like the lady that doth protest too much. I shook my head. "You have no faith in my self-control, do you?"

"Liza, sweetie, you do realize that the process of him claiming you involves sex, right?"

Sometimes I didn't know why we were friends because she said the most horrendous things, and she said them when other people could hear. My cheeks burned. "Yes, I'm aware," I hissed at her in a low, semi-angry whisper.

I didn't tell Sabrina about Ty's magic tongue or his ability to make me see stars multiple times. She was already tipsy, and I wasn't sure how she'd handle that information. She'd probably fall off her barstool.

The night went on as usual and, just as I expected, Sabrina ended up wasted. I, of course, remained sober so I could look after my friend. It helped that my alcohol tolerance as a shifter was pretty high. Poor human. If only she could hold her liquor like she did the attention of random men.

Jack and his friends circled back around to us. He leaned in and tucked a stray hair behind Sabrina's ear.

My asshole radar went off. Surely this guy could see that Sabrina was drunk.

"Why don't you ladies come back to my place? We can have some fun." Jack leered at me and Sabrina, his gaze tracking lasciviously down our bodies. Every hair on the back of my neck stood on end. I didn't trust this guy, and the more he spoke, the worse it got. "I've never been with a shifter before, not to mention two at the same time."

Gross. I shuddered, my body tensing as my wolf's hackles rose.

"What's the matter with you, honey? You look like you've seen a ghost." Jack's sour breath invaded my nose.

My wolf snarled at Jack, warning him to stay the fuck back.

Jack chuckled and looked around at his friends. They laughed, too, which only encouraged him.

"You're such a sweet, fair little thing. If I was your mate, I wouldn't let you around us bad boys." He reached for my face, but I leaned away.

I'd never been one to really show aggression, but my wolf was pissed. She growled again to show Jack that I wasn't fucking around.

Any sober man would've backed away, not willing to risk getting caught in the crosshairs of a shifter. Not this asshole, though. He had whiskey judgment going on, which led many a man to act foolish. And here he was—living proof. He stopped closer, ignoring my warning.

"I'll make you a deal." Jack smirked. "If you come back to my place, I'll let your friend go first while you watch. That should get you in the mood to join in, don't you think?" Obviously, this tool had no idea how women worked. Probably why he was coming off as such an asshole.

I shifted in my seat, trying to ignore the rage building inside me.

He must've taken my movement as an open invitation to molest me because within seconds, the fucker reached for my left breast.

That was enough. My wolf roared, and I jumped to my feet.

Jack tried to step back out of my grasp, but he was too slow. Within seconds, I had him face-down against the bar, his arm twisted behind his back. Petite as I was, I was a shifter, which meant I was stronger than most human men. Especially the drunk-off-their-ass variety.

"First of all, you jackass, no woman likes sloppy drunk boys. Second, sloppy drunk boys can't keep it up long enough to satisfy one woman, definitely not two. And you never had a chance with either of us, so keep your hands to yourself, you piece of shit."

"You fucking bitch!" Jack howled and tried to twist and writhe out from under my grip.

I leaned down and calmly spoke into Jack's ear. "If you ever try to touch me without my consent, I will rip your fucking arm off your body and beat you to death with it. Do you understand me?"

Jack whimpered and nodded.

I should've let him go, but I didn't. My whole body burned like fire, just as it had when I was in heat. This time, though, it was something different. It was aggression.

I frowned down at Jack as he stopped struggling. I had never been this out of control before. Sure, I'd been frustrated or mad, but this was a whole other level of anger.

Sabrina shook her head, suddenly as sober as if we'd only just arrived. She stood, clutching her beer, eyes wide and mouth gaping. Her gaze shifted quickly between Jack and me. "What's your next move, Liza?"

Hell if I knew.

The bouncers would come soon, and if not the bouncers, certainly Jack's friends who were gathered around, shouting and threatening to pull me off him, would jump into the fray. They wanted to stir up trouble, but they were keeping a safe distance from me. None of them seemed eager to partake in this kind of humiliation.

My wolf readied for an attack just as a familiar aura filled the air. My wolf immediately calmed, craved, and yearned.

I didn't ease my grip on Jack's arm, though.

I breathed a sigh of relief when I caught sight of Ty walking toward us. His aura was so strong that even the humans could feel it. They parted like the Red Sea as he came through, creating a path that led straight to me.

Beside me, Sabrina shrugged. "Did I forget to mention that I might have texted Bryce and asked him to grab Ty and meet us at the bar?" She shot me a toothy smile. It was her *I'm sorry* smile, and it meant she didn't want me to be mad. Like I would be mad that she had Ty come out with us. "I told him you didn't seem like you were having fun and that I thought you might enjoy having Ty by your side." Sabrina fake grimaced. "Was I wrong?"

I shook my head, smiled, and kept my eyes on Ty.

His voice was gruff as he surveyed the scene. "What's going on here?"

Sabrina was happy to replay the last few moments for Ty. "This guy was hitting on us and asking us to come back to his place. He tried to grab Liza's boob, and this is how she responded."

Ty's eyes narrowed on Jack, then they slowly met mine. "You can let go of him now, baby."

The endearment unleashed a swarm of butterflies in my stomach. My heart fluttered, but it usually did when I was around Ty. He would take care of it now. I released Jack and took a step back to stand next to Sabrina. It wasn't my burden to carry anymore.

Jack stumbled to his feet, sweat dripping down his face. "You're a fucking bitch!"

Ty wasn't too happy with Jack's choice of words. Within seconds, he had him by his collar, lifting him up, his feet dangling a foot above the wooden floor. His eyes blazed as he growled, "Someone should teach you some manners about how to treat a lady. Maybe you don't need your hands, considering you don't know how to keep them to yourself." Ty's eyes glowed.

"Holy hell, man. Please!" Jack grabbed Ty's hands as though he was about to rip them off. "Don't hurt me. I'm sorry. It was a mistake."

"This is the only warning you'll ever receive from me." Ty lowered Jack to the floor but still gripped his collar. "Learn how to treat women with respect."

Ty shoved Jack to the floor, then stood back and watched as Jack and his friends scrambled for the exit, shoving people out of the way to escape Ty's fury. If Ty had wanted to catch up, there wouldn't have been anything they could have done to get away.

The smell of fear drifted behind them, which only increased as Bryce jumped at them. He'd been guarding the door and decided to give them one last scare.

Ty moved quickly to my side and cupped my face with both hands. "Are you okay? Did he hurt you?"

A dull pain throbbed in my head. Maybe it had been hurting all along and I was just now noticing it. I was overheated, fighting to inhale enough oxygen.

Ty looked concerned. "Bryce! Get over here."

Bryce jogged over and joined us. "Is everything all right?"

"No, something's wrong with Liza." He pointed to Sabrina. "Make sure she gets home safely, all right?"

Bryce nodded.

The loud music became muffled as the world turned on its axis. "I'm dizzy."

Ty scooped me off my feet and into his arms. He carried me out of the bar and into the fresh night air.

I groaned, clutching my stomach as the world continued its slow spinning. Was it just me, or was the spinning getting faster? "I haven't been this sick in a long time."

Ty gently set me on the curb and sank down beside me. "Has this happened before?"

"Yes. I used to get really bad headaches as a kid, which led to terrible temper tantrums." I rested my arms on my knees and sighed. "My parents thought it was just me going through puberty."

Ty wrapped his arm around me and kissed my temple. "Did anything help when you felt that way?"

I nodded. "Those angry sensations seemed to calm down when I started taking the hormone medications."

Shit. The medication!

"Maybe the new medicine I'm on is causing this."

Ty was quiet for a bit. "Long-term use of medications can cause a lot of complications, not to mention high doses of hormones. Once we've mated, I don't think you should take your medication anymore."

I turned to face him. "Really? Don't you think that would be too risky?" It was certainly something I'd have to discuss with Doctor Reynolds again before I made that decision.

"You'll have a mate, and our scents will mingle once I claim you. There'll be no need to mask your scent anymore." He grabbed my hand. "Isn't that the whole point of taking the medication?"

He was right. I hadn't thought about our scents mingling and possibly toning down my intense pheromones.

"Honestly, I would be happy to not take them anymore. They stifle me," I admitted.

"In what way?" He cocked an eyebrow.

Before I could answer Ty, Sabrina hollered from the front steps of the bar. "Liza? Are you okay? Should I call an ambulance?"

So much for her sobering up and gaining some volume control.

"No, that won't be necessary." I smiled weakly in her direction. "Let Bryce take you home. Ty's taking care of me."

"Oh, I bet he *is* taking care of you." She stumbled over her own feet as a chuckling Bryce caught her before she fell on her face.

My face flamed when I met Ty's gaze. So much for having a serious conversation without us thinking about banging one another.

We watched as Bryce walked Sabrina to his car before Ty turned his attention back to me. "You were just about to tell me how your hormone pills stifle you," he reminded me.

"My wolf always seems lethargic. Not just that, but I no longer feel the pull of the moon like I did as a child." I stared straight ahead, a little embarrassed to admit how different I was from other shifters. "I don't even feel the need to shift often. And, if I'm being honest, I don't have a strong sense of connection to other wolves." I hated being this way. I just wanted to be like he was. I wanted to be enough to deserve him.

Sympathy radiated from Ty as he squeezed my hand. "I can tell you want to say more. Go on."

A lump rose in my throat. "I've often wondered if my lack of connection was due to the fact that I was depressed because I'd been displaced. My wolf knows this isn't her pack. Or, maybe the pills affect more than just pheromones. Either way, I stick out like a sore thumb." I touched my hair and pushed it back from my face as if I wasn't touching it to point out how out of place I was in a sea of dark-haired shifters.

Ty looked away and didn't say anything. Had I said something to make him rethink mating with me? He would soon be an alpha. Perhaps he needed a woman by his side who had a much stronger sense of belonging to the pack. Instead, fate had stuck him with a depressed, hormonal, light-colored shifter who didn't even know who her real parents were. Lucky guy.

He turned back to me, stroking the back of my hand with his thumb as he curled his fingers into my palm. "I'm sorry you've felt so out of place all these years. I can't imagine feeling the way you've felt for so long." He paused, and I sensed the emotion emanating from him. "I promise that from now on, I'll make sure you know you belong to the pack. You're mine, and you'll always belong by my side."

Who wouldn't fall for a guy who said stuff like that?

Chapter 23 - Ty

Liza remained silent as I drove her home. She was concerned about her health, and I could understand that. With her pheromones being out of whack, and now this sudden onslaught of rage and uncontrolled aggression, my girl had had a rough week. Not that she was wrong for putting that son of a whore on the floor, but the rage had rolled off her like waves. I felt bad for her, even though I was sure pity was the last thing she would want.

There was so much running through my head that I didn't remember why I was driving to her place instead of to mine. I wanted to tell Liza she was right. Those fucking hormone pills were affecting her wolf. The way she'd responded tonight was a sign that her wolf was over it. She wanted to be free. A wolf wasn't meant to be suppressed like that for even a short period of time, not to mention for years.

Of course, I didn't know a lot about her wolf or the special attributes of an omega. It was crucial to remember that I wasn't dealing with a typical wolf. She was an omega. They were powerful beings capable of so much, yet Liza had the distinct impression that the pills were stifling her wolf. And only she would know.

I glanced over at her. She was so beautiful, even with her brow furrowed and her hands clasped tightly together in her lap. Her eyes had had a fiery determination to them earlier, and I didn't think that fire would have faded just because she'd climbed into my car. She was staring out the window at the night sky, though, so I couldn't be sure.

Liza was so brave, but the closer we became, the more I realized that her internal struggle was a constant battle I would never fully understand.

I was unsure of my next move, but one thing was becoming increasingly clear: Liza and her wolf needed to be free. She deserved it.

I pulled up to her house and put the car in park. "Do you want me to stay?" I asked gently, brushing my thumb across her cheekbone. I wanted her to say yes, but I didn't want to pressure her.

She covered my hand with hers and turned to face me. "Would you mind coming in for a while? I don't want to be alone right now. Not until I'm completely calm."

"Absolutely." I had a few ideas on how to calm her, too. And damn, I wanted to. "Let's get you inside."

I'd stay all night if she wanted me to.

While Liza changed into her pajamas and washed the makeup off her face, I brewed some chamomile tea, hoping it would ease her raging wolf.

She snuck up behind me and wrapped her arms around my waist. "Thank you for saving me tonight." She pressed a soft kiss against the side of my throat, and her body slid along mine—even this way, it was fucking hot—and I felt the softness of her curves. It was too much to resist. *She* was too much to resist.

I turned into her and put my hand at the back of her neck, pulling her in close. Her hair smelled like wildflowers, and her skin was so soft. "No need to thank me, baby. I'm just happy to be here for you."

We stayed like that for a few moments, neither of us willing to let go. Suddenly, she backed away and looked up into my eyes. "I'm sorry for the scene at the bar. I can't imagine what must have been going through your mind when you walked in and saw me manhandling that prick."

I couldn't help but laugh. She hadn't just manhandled him, she'd humiliated him, and it had been glorious. Now that it was over, I found the whole situation hilarious. "That poor guy had no clue who he was messing with, huh?" I didn't want her to think that she'd done anything wrong. She should never have to apologize for taking care of such a fucked-up situation.

Liza smiled and crossed her arms under her breasts. The move pushed her breasts up, and I struggled to keep my eyes off the enticing swells. "I was afraid you'd be embarrassed that your future mate caused such a scene." She frowned, and her skin turned an adorable shade of pink. Or maybe it was only adorable because she was the one wearing it. I didn't know.

"No way." I handed her a cup of tea. "Honestly, it took a lot of my willpower to get my dick to calm down after seeing you handle yourself so well." I grinned at her. "It was pretty fucking hot."

Liza's eyes widened, and the pink darkened to a deeper red. "Oh. That's not really the response I expected." But she was smiling.

"I find it extremely attractive that you can take care of yourself." I would've said fucking hot. I really needed to find a better descriptor so I didn't sound full Neanderthal. "Also, that's a sign of a strong leader. You didn't have to wait for someone else to step in or give you instructions." I didn't think she needed her ego blown up, but support didn't hurt. "Instead, you went with your gut and protected yourself. Who knows what that son of a bitch would've pulled if you hadn't taken matters into your own hands."

She sipped at her tea and leaned back against the kitchen counter. "I never considered myself to be a leader." She shook her head and looked down. There was something seriously seductive about her humility. Or maybe it was just her. "I mean, I can dole out instructions and manage a kitchen, but that's not exactly the same, is it?"

"Well, no, but it's also nothing to downplay." I wrapped my hands around the hot mug. "Either way, I'm happy you can handle yourself in different situations. Being the mate of an alpha isn't some cushiony role. Especially with my family." I could tell her stories, but I didn't think now was a good time to share all that with her. I didn't want to scare her away, and any story with my mother as a character had the potential to send Liza running for the hills.

Liza sighed. "That's something I've been thinking about."

"What's that?"

"I'm not sure if I'm worthy enough to carry on your family name." She tucked a lock of hair behind her ear. "Your mom scares the shit out of me. Our personalities are complete opposites, and I get the feeling she isn't my biggest fan." I didn't deny it, but I also didn't explain. "Do you really think I can live up to her expectations?"

I wanted to scream—to tell her that she was fucking royalty herself so she would stop doubting herself. To top it off, if people knew what family she came from, they would kiss the very ground she walked upon.

I set my mug on the counter and cracked my knuckles as Liza eyed me suspiciously. I wanted to hold her, to kiss her, to celebrate her in a way that let her know she was valuable. Knowing I couldn't tell her just how special she really was burned a hole straight through my soul.

My emotions drowned out all reason, all decorum, as I took Liza's mug and put it on the counter next to mine. I pulled her into my arms and kissed her, unable to hide what I felt toward her.

I needed her to feel wanted and to know beyond a shadow of a doubt that she belonged with me. At that moment, I couldn't have cared less what my parents thought. Liza and I would create our own family. Those who didn't want to be a part of it could be damned. She was exactly what I needed, and she was exactly where she was meant to be. Fate didn't make mistakes.

I pressed my body against hers, pinning her between me and the counter as I tasted her mouth and worked hard to control the desire to grind my hips against hers. Liza moaned in response. She kissed me back with just as much passion, her fingers tightening into a ball at the back of my shirt.

As my hands roamed down her back, Liza lifted her head suddenly and pulled away. "I'm tired of holding back."

I knew she had spoken, and I took a deep breath, giving myself a second to let the words sink through the fog in my mind. "I don't know what that means, Liza." But I sure as fuck hoped it meant she was saying *green light*.

She shook her head and clung tighter when I made a move to step back. "I've always feared what would happen if I gave in to my deepest desires." I thought I had an idea what she was talking about, but I needed to make sure before this went any further. "They spring up from time to time and I take care of myself."

Oh fuck. The picture in my head—Liza in the throes of passion with her fingers working in and out of her pussy while she fondled her own breast—drove me wild, and my cock hardened in response.

"What kind of desires?" Desire was so thick in my throat that I sounded like a teenager whose balls hadn't dropped yet, but I couldn't help but prod for more details.

"My body craves to be touched, and it creates an inherent instinct to let go of my inhibitions." An exquisite shade of pink crept up from her throat to her cheeks, and her eyes went dark with lust. She pushed her hand between us, fumbling with my belt. "When I'm with you, every nerve in my body is alive and on fire." She pulled the belt free. "Just this once…" She paused and smiled, pulling her lower lip between her teeth. "I want to let go and not think about my actions. To act on my instincts and let them take over."

Hell yeah. I was all for it.

"But I've always feared the reactions of others, worried that I might do something or, hell, smell a certain way that would make them lose control." She shook her head. "I was afraid, but I'm not afraid with you." The strength in her voice was such a fucking turn on. "I don't want to hold back, Ty. Not anymore."

She trusted me, and I wasn't going to do anything to fuck that up. I pulled her flush against me, her breasts flattening against my chest, our bond only growing stronger. We were fated mates, and the attraction wasn't the kind of thing either of us would survive if we tried to deny it. I leaned in and captured her mouth with mine, molded her against me, and she responded, pushing her tongue into my mouth. And so, the duel began. It was eager, sensual... a mating all on its own.

As our mouths warred, each of us fighting for control and moving in sync, the most primal of urges stirred within me. I didn't bother trying to resist the need to explore her body. I slid my hands along her rib cage, down to the curves of her hips as I pulled her closer. She wore only a T-shirt and sweatpants, and as I continued kissing her and being kissed by her, I drew one hand up her body. The little minx wasn't wearing a bra.

The kiss intensified and became rough as I nipped at her lips and sucked on her tongue. Liza matched me touch for touch, moan for moan, meeting my passion and desire with equal enthusiasm.

Her hips thrust forward, pushing into my erection with force, with unbridled need. Liza's groan in my mouth was like a heady drink of water, and she swirled her tongue inside my mouth, tugging my shirt away to flatten her smooth hands on my skin.

We moved through her living room, bumping into furniture, crashing into walls, grabbing at one another and growling. Liza released her passion and her aggressions at the same time. I took it all without a moment's hesitation

Her newfound confidence turned me on beyond coherent thought as we allowed ourselves to get lost in the passion.

If I lived to be a hundred, I would never get tired of being with her.

We moved through the living room and crashed into an end table that slid sideways. The lamp on top of it tumbled to the floor and shattered. Liza giggled, which only made me want her more. "It's only a lamp."

I leaned down and found her mouth again, then broke away, this time trailing kisses down her neck to the hollow just above her collarbone.

She caught my face in her hands, pulling me back to her, her mouth merging with mine. This kiss was more frenzied and intense as our bodies pressed against one another.

It took a while, but eventually, we pulled apart from each other, panting heavily. I looked into Liza's eyes and made myself a promise right then and there.

She would be mine. Forever.

Liza stepped back an inch, but it was enough for me to her hard nipples poking through the thin fabric of her T-shirt.

My wolf growled and shouted, *"Mate! Mate!"*

She took my hand without saying a word and led me to her bedroom. This would not be the same as the night we'd shared in my bedroom. This kiss had ignited something more between us. I gazed deep into her eyes. I had to make sure she definitely wanted this. That she wouldn't regret it. I wouldn't take her unless she was positive.

She looked back at me with an intensity that sent shivers down my spine. "I trust you," she said, her voice barely more than a whisper. "I know it hasn't been long, but every instinct in me screams to trust you."

I was an asshole. A liar. A man who knew things about her that he wasn't telling her—things she had every right to and probably needed to know. But I needed her. And I wanted her.

I wanted and needed her to believe in me. To trust that I would never hurt her, and that anything I kept from her wasn't out of selfishness but to protect her, to make sure she was equipped to handle the information. That was what I told myself because I wanted this.

Like I said, I was an asshole.

At that moment, Liza needed something more from me. To feel free. To be herself and give in to her desires and do it without judgment.

And by fuck, she was going to get what she wanted. I didn't care what it cost me.

As we kissed, our hands skimmed and roamed and explored each other's bodies, taking in every inch we could reach while our lips were still fused together. I could sense her desire, feel it growing for me with every passing moment as the scent of her strong pheromones filled the bedroom. Even without them, I wanted her, and I was eager to satisfy her.

I moved us toward the edge of her bed. She still had a few too many clothes on, and I relieved her of all of them with deft fingers and smooth movements, leaving her in nothing but her panties.

I shed my own T-shirt, then wrapped my arms around her so we were skin to skin.

After a kiss that could've peeled the wallpaper, I lowered Liza down onto the mattress. She opened her legs, allowing me to fit my erection snuggly against her warm pussy.

Heat radiated off Liza's body as I ran my hands up and down every inch of her. She was soft and supple beneath my touch, and I had been dreaming of doing this with her since the first night. My heart pounded. My stomach tightened. The moment was finally here.

I kissed her neck and groaned when goosebumps rose on her skin under the pressure of my lips. She moaned, her head tilting back as I dragged my mouth along the vein in her throat. I moved my lips down to her collarbone, nipping lightly at the sensitive skin.

Liza's hands slipped down my chest, tracing the lines of my muscles. Her fingers danced around to my spine,, slipping beneath my jeans and down to my ass.

She scooted one around to the front, but I caught her wrist. "Don't touch me, yet. I'll lose control too soon." It was why I had yet to shed my jeans. I couldn't risk this ending too soon, because when I was with her, I couldn't control myself.

I moved my attention to her thigh, tracing small circles on the inside of her leg with one gentle fingertip. She spread her legs wider in silent invitation.

I pushed myself up onto my knees and looked at her. I'd never seen a woman so exquisite, so beautifully desirable. I grazed the back of my hand gently over her clit through her panties. Her breath caught in her throat, and she angled her hips up, trying to make me touch her again.

"Not yet, baby. Be patient."

She was wet, ready, and I wanted her, but I wanted to make this so good for her that she never wanted anyone else and never so much as thought of another man pleasing her for as long as we lived.

I leaned in, kissing her deeply as I slid my hand up over her belly to cover her full breast. Her nipple stood at attention as I circled it gently with my finger and then rolled it under my thumb.

Liza's nails scraped my skin, digging into my back. "Ty. Please. Your mouth."

"If you say so."

I had waited such a long time for this, I needed a moment to take it all in: the sight of her, the sound of her breath when she begged me for my mouth, the smell of those pheromones. This woman was so fucking intoxicating.

My mouth found her breast, sucking her nipple as deeply into my mouth as I could.

My tongue flicked and teased the hardened tip. Liza moaned and ground her pussy against my erection.

"Do you want me to touch you, Liza?" I needed to hear her say it. Not for consent's sake as much as me wanting those words. They would be mine as soon as she said them, and I would be able to call on them anytime I wanted to recall this exact moment.

"Yes, please, yes." She sighed, nodding imperceptibly, her eyes fluttering closed.

I slid my fingers inside her panties, reveling in the wetness, using her own juices as I explored her folds. Liza moaned softly, her hips bucking in reply to my touch. I continued to stroke her as she became wetter and wetter. I played with every part of her, sliding my finger around her rim, then finally over her clit. She writhed and twisted, trying to move her body so my fingers would find the spot she so desperately wanted to be touched. But I waited. I wanted to drive her crazy.

My cock ached as I caught a whiff of her. She was the best dream I'd ever had.

"Fuck, Liza, you smell so good."

I slipped one finger inside her and watched, chewing my lower lip so I wouldn't cry out with my own need when she tilted her head back and groaned with pleasure.

I couldn't hold back any longer; I needed to taste her. I yanked her panties down her thighs and left a trail of kisses down her stomach, stopping just above her mound. I crouched over her, grabbing her ass and pulling her pussy to my mouth. My tongue traced her clit before I opened wide, pulling in every inch of her center. My tongue encircled her, eliciting a scream from Liza as she writhed beneath me. Her body was coiled, her cries more desperate. She was getting too close, so I stopped.

"Do you want to touch me?" I jerked my jeans down, and Liza's eyes went wide.

"Holy shit, Ty. I don't know if it will fit." And what guy wouldn't want to hear that? She pushed herself up on one arm and stared at my massive erection. "I want to touch you." Just hearing her say it was enough to make my cock drip. I wasn't going to last long.

I moved onto the bed beside her as she reached out and took my cock in both hands. She growled as she inspected every inch, cupping my balls and sliding her fingers up and down my shaft.

She gripped my hips, pulling me forward as she positioned herself between my legs on the floor.

As Liza caressed my body, a shiver ran down my back. I knew what she was about to do, and the anticipation was almost too much to handle. I inhaled slowly, trying for steady. Failing. My breath stuttered in and then out of me.

She kissed my stomach, trailing her lips down until she was kneeling in front of me. Her hot breath blew against the head of my cock, and I couldn't help but let out a low growl.

Liza looked up at me, her eyes dark with desire as she took me in her mouth. The sensation was intense, and I could feel myself growing inside her.

She started slowly, taking just the tip of my cock into her mouth before sliding her lips down farther. Her tongue swirled around me, and I moaned because I couldn't hold it back. The pleasure was too powerful to be denied.

Liza picked up the pace, bobbing her head up and down as she took me deeper into her mouth. Her hand moved up and down my shaft, stroking me as she sucked, and the head of my cock slipped into her throat.

My muscles tensed; my balls tightened. I was too close to the edge, so I gently pushed her away, letting my cock fall from her mouth. I could resist the urge to take things to the next level. I wanted to feel her, all of her, and she was trembling, staring at me as her breasts heaved. A sheen of sweat coated her body. She wanted this, too.

I pulled her back onto the bed, lowering my body onto hers. My mouth covered her, and I kissed her deeply, savoring the taste of her lips as my hands roamed over her exposed skin.

I reached down between her legs. "Damn, Liza. You're so wet for me."

She was ready for me, and I couldn't wait any longer to give her this. I slid my hand up her thigh, her skin soft and delicate beneath my fingertips.

Liza moaned softly, arching her back as I continued to stroke her. I could feel her getting wetter by the second, and I knew it was time. I pulled away from her, breaking our kiss. I groped for my wallet in the pocket of my jeans and pulled out a condom. I ripped the foil packet with my teeth, then rolled the condom onto my length and positioned myself between her legs.

I looked down at her, memorizing the beauty of her in this moment. Her eyes were closed, her chest rising and falling with every breath. She was ready for me, and I was ready to take her.

I slid my hands up her thighs, spreading her legs wide as I positioned myself at her entrance. My own arousal grew stronger as I looked down at her. I wanted her, all of her, and seeing her this way, knowing I was about to get it, was almost more than I could handle without shooting my load into the condom before I'd even felt her clench around me.

Slowly, I entered her, trying to be as gentle as possible, her tight walls gripping me as I slid deeper inside. She moaned softly, her eyes snapping open to look at me. Desire burned in them, and in that moment, there was no doubt that I was doing something right.

I started to move, thrusting slowly at first, then picking up the pace as her body jerked and responded to my touch. Liza's moans grew louder, signaling that she was close. I was closer, too. It wouldn't be long before we both reached our peak.

I continued to thrust, harder and faster. She arched her back, pushing her hips up to meet mine as we moved together in perfect harmony.

"Fuck!" Liza screamed and grabbed my ass with both hands. "Deeper!"

I gave her what she wanted, lifting her hips, thrusting harder. Liza screamed, and I knew I was hitting her G-spot.

The muscles deep inside Liza tightened, and the tension built within her. Her breathing became more rapid, and her moans grew guttural as she neared the edge.

I could feel my own release building, but my focus was solely on Liza. I wanted to bring her to the brink and make her feel everything she had ever desired.

I moved my hand down between us, tracing small circles on her clit as I continued to thrust into her. The sensation was too much for her, and she let out a loud cry as she finally let go.

Her inner muscles pulsated around my cock as she came undone. I increased the pressure on her clit, driving her even higher when she screamed out my name.

Finally, she collapsed against me, her body shaking with the force of her orgasm. I continued to move inside her, riding out my own release as I poured myself into her. I exploded inside of her, the intensity of the orgasm taking me by surprise.

I collapsed on top of her, my heart racing while I tried to catch my breath.

We lay there, our bodies entwined and our breathing slowly returning to normal, and I knew that this was just the beginning of what was to come between us. We were fated mates, two beings destined to be together, and I couldn't wait to explore every inch of her body and soul.

I took a deep breath. Liza's scent had changed. I hadn't claimed her as my own, but something in her scent was different.

She curled into me, sighed, and then she was asleep.

I wasn't surprised at the way we had gone at it. Glancing at the condom wrapper on the nightstand, I silently thanked the gods and my mother for instilling all of those safe-sex ideas into my head for my emergency supply of protection. Otherwise, there was no doubt in my mind that I would've gotten her pregnant.

I sighed, knowing exactly what that would've meant. Liza was an omega. It was in her nature to reproduce. But she'd been so suppressed, and she didn't even know it.

I'd caught a glimpse of that tonight. Her passion. Her needs and her desires.

I gently twirled Liza's hair between my fingers. I didn't want to keep her locked away from herself.

Liza, and the truth about what she was, needed to be set free.

Chapter 24 – Liza

I studied myself in the mirror before work, my eyes widening in shock. My skin looked better than ever. I leaned in closer, peering at my complexion. There wasn't a blemish or pore or spot of red chafed or dry skin in sight.

It had been two days since I'd lost my virginity, and the effects had been incredible. Had I known it would be like this, I would've done it sooner. I'd felt different from the morning after. Not just the cliché mental shift of *welcome to womanhood*, but a peculiar sensation, like my body was strengthening and healing whatever was wrong. I liked it. It was a sensation I wouldn't have minded getting used to.

Physically and emotionally, something inside of me had shifted. I felt amazing. My skin practically glowed, and my eyes were brighter.

As I walked into my client's house, I experienced a boost of confidence that could only have been a result of my night with Ty. Nothing else in my life had changed. Even my spine felt straighter as I held my head high and entered the extravagant home.

"Good morning!" I almost didn't recognize the sing-song voice that left my mouth when I greeted my kitchen staff.

Cassidy poked her head around the stainless-steel refrigerator door and stared at me as I walked by and snapped her ass with a dish towel.

She chuckled. "You sure have a lot of pep in your step for such an early hour."

"It's early? I didn't notice." Grinning, I tied an apron around my waist. "A lot of pep, huh? Oh, yeah. Maybe I do."

She shut the door and looked me up and down, smirking at me. "Something is different about you."

I hadn't thought anyone would be able to tell, but I supposed if I could see it, they would, too. I stopped tying the apron strings and hoped she wouldn't somehow pick up on the fact that Ty and I had fucked.

She was an employee, and I was the boss. We had our roles to play and jobs to do, and I didn't want to discuss all of the details with her. Besides, I wanted to keep those intimate moments between Ty and me.

Cassidy smiled warmly. "I can't put my finger on it, but whatever it is, you should do it more often. It looks good on you."

Do it more often. I giggled. "Maybe my happy disposition will rub off on everyone else."

She glanced over her shoulder at the rest of the staff who were chopping and dicing. "Doubtful."

The morning flew by as we prepped ingredients and cooked a delicious breakfast for my clients. Cassidy and I chatted while we worked, and by the time I was finished, I had a feeling that something good and pure had come into my life.

Thanks to Ty, I felt womanlier than ever before, and it showed in the way I carried myself at work and how I interacted with others. His touch had given me a newfound sense of confidence and power, but also something else I couldn't quite place.

On my way home, I stopped at the grocery store to pick up ingredients for a client later in the week. One of the spices I needed was hard to find, so I'd popped into multiple stores in hopes of finding it.

I snatched a basket from the floor and scoured the seasoning aisle. An elderly couple stopped next to me, their cart clearing me by only an inch.

"Hello, dear." The woman smiled kindly, and her husband nodded.

I racked my brain, trying to place their faces, but after a few minutes, I gave up, confident I'd never seen them before in my life.

"Good afternoon." I smiled and went back to searching for the specific spice as the couple moved on.

They didn't speak to anyone else. Odd. I'd taken them to be one of those lonely couples who used their time at the grocery store to socialize, but they didn't say a word to the other patrons in the store.

It was a bust. The specific spice I needed was nowhere to be found. Not wanting the trip to be a waste, I decided to grab a few non-perishable items I needed at home. Each person I passed went out of their way to make eye contact with me and smile. Some said hello while others nodded in my direction.

Taking a deep breath, I lifted my chin and smiled back at them. All of a sudden, I was approachable, and it certainly hadn't always been this way. It was almost like I had an aura of light around me that drew people in.

Was this the power of love and intimacy? Or had I simply discovered something new about myself?

Either way, it was nice to be considered a friendly face.

After exchanging pleasantries with the teenage cashier, I carried my groceries to the car. I stowed everything in my trunk and glanced at my watch. It was still early enough to visit my parents. I hadn't seen them since our dinner with Ty, and I might have been going through a little Mom-withdrawal. In any case, I wanted to check in on them.

As soon as I walked through the door, Mom took me by both hands. Her brow furrowed when she leaned in, staring at my face from every angle. Without her saying a word, I could tell she was worried about something.

Dad popped his head out from the newspaper he'd been reading and scowled. The newspaper slipped out of his hands as he stared at me.

What the hell? Why were they acting like that?

"Something's different about you, Aliza." Dad took up position next to Mom.

Shit. Everyone in the world knew that when a parent used their child's full name, it meant the child was in trouble.

I forced myself to smile. No way did I want to tell them *why* things had changed. "I'm glad you noticed because I *feel* different, but not in a bad way." I pulled my hands out of my mother's death grip.

"In what way?" Mom asked, worry etched on her forehead, the corner of her eyes, and around her mouth.

"Free. I feel free, Mom." I took a step back and reached over my head, stretching languidly.

My parents shared a look of concern, but neither of them pushed for more information, instead turning the conversation to more mundane things.

I smiled to myself as Mom and Dad chattered on and on about the new flowers they'd planted in the garden beds. The strain from earlier had disappeared, and my parents even seemed glad that I'd found happiness, no matter the reason. I wasn't exactly sure what had caused the sensations of peace and confidence, although I had a feeling it had a lot to do with Ty.

"Do you want to stay for dinner?" Mom's question broke through my train of thought. "I've got a roast cooking in the crockpot, and you could help me bake those rolls you love with the garlic and cheddar seasoning."

"That sounds delicious, Mom." Some of my best recipes came from her. "But I'm pretty tired. I still need to stop by the gas station and fill my car up." I turned to Dad. "The flowers look fantastic, by the way. I noticed them as soon as I pulled into the driveway." I sighed. "I mostly just wanted to stop by and check in with you. Make sure you're doing okay."

Dad beamed with pride over his garden and squeezed my shoulder. "Take care of yourself, okay?"

As I made to open the door, Mom stopped me. "Liza? If there was something going on, you would tell us, right?"

"Of course." It wasn't often that I didn't tell my mother the truth, but this was a lie. Only in the sense that there were some things I would never be able to talk about with my parents.

No way in hell was I ever going to tell them I'd finally lost my virginity and that the sex had been pretty fucking extraordinary. However, if I had concerns about the other areas of my life, I would come to them in a heartbeat. Right now, though, my life seemed to be moving in a positive trajectory.

I smiled back at her. This wasn't a lie that would hurt anyone. Not that I knew of, anyway.

After filling my tank at the gas station, I went inside to pay. I handed the cashier the exact change.

"Thank you so much, Miss. Have a wonderful evening." It seemed as if everyone in town was in a better mood because I'd got laid. I laughed aloud at the thought and shook my head as I walked out of the station toward my car.

I stopped in the middle of the parking lot. Stone Black stood at the rear of my car, his hip resting against the trunk, arms crossed over the wide expanse of his chest. I hesitated, not sure whether I should approach him after the scene at the ice cream shop. Although, I couldn't just stand here all day, and I couldn't get home by ignoring him.

Ty hadn't told me what happened between him and Stone, and I hadn't felt like it was my place to ask about it. I assumed that, as the future alpha, he'd dealt with all kinds of high-stress situations in the past. I figured Stone's issues were business-related since they'd talked in private.

But now he was leaning against my car. It was very odd for us to constantly be running into each other. I couldn't see a reason for it. If he had business with Ty, I wasn't a part of it, but he had no business with me, and it begged the question of whether or not he had followed me here. I couldn't imagine what he wanted with me.

"Hello, Liza." Stone stood up straight and shoved his hands into his pants pockets. A slow smile slid across his face. He was handsome enough, but not my type. I had Ty. "You're waking up."

I cocked my head to the side. I really hated people who talked in riddles and assumed the rest of the world was either on the same page or beneath them because they didn't understand. I sighed. "Excuse me?"

"I hate that it took someone like Tyson Keller to make it happen, but I can look past that." He took a step closer to me, and I backed up a step. I didn't want him near me.

I stared at him in confusion. "What are you talking about?"

He scoffed, then shook his head. He was an arrogant and mostly condescending prick. "You'll figure it out soon enough. Now that you're waking up, you'll start remembering things. The pieces will fall into place, and when they do, I'll be waiting for you. Come find me." He cocked his head, gave me one last look, then started walking.

He didn't give me a chance to let the words sink in enough so I could form a coherent thought, but as he walked past me, his scent washed over me, and I wavered. My wolf jumped to attention as Stone's smell penetrated my memory.

The scent was so familiar that tears filled my eyes. *Why?*

I turned and watched Stone walk away. For a brief second, he'd felt like home. I closed my eyes and waited for the sensation to fade. When it did, I wanted it back, and neither of those things made sense to me—not that he had brought with him a sense of home, and not that I longed for it.

Pulling out of the gas station, my phone buzzed with a text from Ty.

I want to see you tonight. How about a movie?

I couldn't shake the sensation I'd experienced when Stone walked past me, but spending time with Ty would keep me grounded. When I was with him, I was safe.

Yes! I should be home in ten minutes.

Ty showed up shortly after I arrived home, and our hello kiss lasted so long that we barely made it to dinosaur movie in time. We missed the first few previews, but I didn't care. Kissing Ty was much better than watching a movie. But after, when we were in the crowded theater, I kept replaying Stone's words.

What the fuck did *waking up* mean?

No one seemed to know much about omegas outside the ridiculous myths and rumors. Was my special identity somehow connected to Stone's words?

When the movie ended, I simply stared into space as the credits rolled and the lights inside the theater came on.

As the other moviegoers shuffled down aisle to the door, Ty turned to me. "Are you okay? You seem distracted."

"I'm sorry, Ty." I shook my head. Maybe I should have said no to the movie, but I'd wanted to see him. "I'm a terrible date."

Ty pulled one of my hands from my lap and kissed it tenderly. "You don't need to apologize. I just hope that you trust me enough to tell me if something is bothering you."

I cleared my throat and turned, tucking one leg underneath my body. It was the guilt of keeping something from him that made the talking start. "I ran into Stone today. Well, I guess it's more accurate to say *he* ran into *me*. He was leaning against my car at the gas station."

Ty's body tensed, and his eyes narrowed. He was on edge at the mere mention of Stone. There was something more than business going on.

I didn't want to upset Ty, but I deserved to know what relationship he and Stone had. "What's your history with him?"

Ty fidgeted in his seat, obviously uncomfortable with the subject. He hesitated for a few moments, looking everywhere but at me, then answered. "Stone has some unresolved business with my father, and my father is using me as a middleman for negotiations. We're struggling to find common ground, though."

Oh. That made sense, so I didn't push for more details, even though part of me knew there was more to it.

Plus, I was still confused about Stone's interest in me. Ty's father having business with Stone had nothing to do with me or whether or not I was *waking up*.

"Am I in some kind of danger, Ty? Does Stone want to use me to get your father to do what he wants?"

Ty sighed and squeezed my hand. "I don't believe Stone wants to harm you. Even if he tried, I would never let *anyone* touch a hair on your head."

His words were reassuring, but that was all they were: words.

I took a moment to weigh the pros and cons of telling Ty what I'd experienced when Stone's scent had reached me. It was better for him to know.

"There was a moment at the gas station when Stone felt familiar to me."

Ty stiffened. I was onto something. Not that I had any idea what it could be.

"I swear I've never met him prior to our first run-in at the farmers' market." I paused and studied Ty's face, which had gone sickly pale. "I can't explain it, but when he walked past me, his scent even caused my wolf to sit up at attention."

Ty didn't respond, just stared straight ahead. The muscles in his jaws flexed, and I wished I could read his mind.

"There's more," I admitted softly, almost afraid of how he would react.

He released my hand and turned to face me.

"Stone mentioned something about me *waking up*. It all seems odd to me because I have no idea what he's talking about." I was hoping Ty had some answers for me.

He ran a hand through his hair and stood. "It's probably best for you to stay away from Stone." It wasn't a suggestion. His words were forceful, and he waited for me to nod before he continued. "And you make sure you always have your phone with you so you can call me if you ever feel like you're in danger. I don't care what time of day or night it is."

I followed his lead and stood, gathering my drink and purse. "Of course."

He grabbed the popcorn bucket from the floor. "I think it's also best if I put some security around your place until we're mated and we decide where we'll be living."

Hearing Ty talk about us creating a life together made the butterflies in my stomach flutter. "I like that you didn't just assume we'd move to the estate."

"Of course, we'll have to spend some time there. It'll be expected since it is the family estate, and that's where pack business is conducted." He laced our fingers together and smiled at me. "But we're partners, Liza, and that means making important decisions together."

An odd expression crossed his face, something that certainly resembled guilt or regret, and I wished I knew the cause, but then Ty kissed my hand, and the look vanished just as quickly as it had appeared.

He insisted on staying the night with me—and by insisted, I meant he kissed me into a submission he didn't honestly have to work so hard to secure—and I didn't argue. I loved having his warm body against mine, and his strong arms wrapped under my neck and over my waist as we slept.

With him beside me, it didn't take long at all for me to drift off into a deep sleep. I experienced the most vivid dream I'd ever had. Vivid, terrifying, and familiar.

Smoke filled the house as people shouted from outside. "Protect the alpha! Protect the princess!"

I glanced at my hand. I was holding onto the hand of a woman, looking up into her face as she smiled sadly at me.

A man with my coloring and my facial structure spoke quietly and urgently. "We won't be able to hold them off. Get the baby out."

I wanted to protest, to tell them that I was hardly a baby, but I couldn't do more than watch what was happening.

The woman began to cry, but all too soon her tears turned to anger. "I'll kill them all."

A knock on the back door startled the woman. She and the man grabbed weapons, preparing to fight against whoever was on the other side of the door.

"It's only me." It was the voice of a young boy.

They both rushed to open the door, and before I could stop her from dropping my hand, she spun to crouch in front of me. "I love you. You're the most perfect princess. I want you to go with him." She pointed toward the boy. "He'll keep you safe until we can find you again."

The woman's words were reassuring, but her face was wet with tears. She looked so sad and helpless. Again, I wanted to comfort her.

The man touched the boy's shoulder, then gave a sharp, hard shake. "Always remember your purpose. I'm counting on you to keep my girl safe."

The woman wept, choking on her sobs as the man knelt in front of me. He cupped my face, studying every feature. "I love you so much. Always remember who you are, my little princess. You're royalty."

The boy stepped forward and took my hand, leading me out the door. Tears streamed down my cheeks, and I screamed. I didn't want to go. I wanted to stay with the man and the woman.

The boy pulled me along, and I turned to look back at the woman. Her eyes were sad as she watched us walking down a long path that seemed to keep getting longer. She shifted into wolf form just as the front door flew open. A loud bang reverberated through the air, and the wolf fell to the ground.

Something deep within my chest seemed to shred, like a bond breaking. I cried until there were no more tears left to shed.

We ran for what seemed like hours, the boy pulling me toward the snowy woods with fierce determination. I glanced around, trying to make sense of the red-stained snow.

"Don't look! We have to get to the boat!" the boy shouted and tried to distract me from what I was seeing. Death. Blood. All of it so vivid.

I didn't know what he was talking about. He couldn't have been much older than me, but he was bigger. I didn't know how to drive a boat, so it didn't make sense to me that he would. Fear rolled like a little ball in my belly, and I pulled against his hold. But then a chorus of angry shouts came from behind us.

"Get her! Get the girl!" I heard it loud and clear as if whoever was shouting was right next to me.

"Run faster!" The boy tugged hard at my hand, almost dragging me through the forest.

He tripped over a tree root and pulled me down to the ground beside him. He covered his mouth, clearly in pain. His ankle was bent at an unnatural angle. No way were we getting farther. There would be no boat.

"Keep running and hide in the bushes near the flowers." He scowled and reached for his ankle. "I'll find you there, but I need to hide until my leg can heal."

The voices moved closer, and the boy's eyes widened. "Run! Now!"

I did as I was told and ran as fast as I could. I was tiny. I fit through whips of switches and vines that seemed to be growing around me as I ran. But the fear let me ignore the pain and keep moving. I didn't want the men to catch me.

I was sad. So very sad.

When I finally made it to the bushes and the field of lavender, I crouched down and hid. The overwhelming scent of the lavender filled my nose. It tickled.

A long time passed, but I had no way of knowing exactly how long I'd been hiding. I must've fallen asleep because I woke up with a start and discovered an unfamiliar man standing over me.

He squatted beside me. "Don't worry, little one. I'm going to make sure you're taken care of." His voice was soft, sincere, and I wasn't scared anymore.

I squinted, trying to get a good look at the man. Just before his face came into clear view, I woke up.

Sitting straight up, I clutched my chest, my heart pounding.

Ty jolted awake and sat up beside me. "Are you okay?"

The dream lingered, and my heart hurt so badly, I didn't realize I was crying until Ty brushed away the falling tears with his thumbs.

"What's wrong, Liza?" Panic rose in his voice as he tried to understand what was happening. "A nightmare?"

I didn't know how to explain it to him. The pain I felt was so real.

But why?

It was just a dream, but part of me knew it was more.

It was a memory.

Chapter 25 - Ty

It had been a long morning without Liza. A morning I spent worrying, knowing what she'd suffered as I held her, oblivious to the dream that had fractured her sleep and woke her with pain and such a strong, lingering fear that I could smell it on her. My worry for her had stretched into the evening and the night and another morning.

So, when she called me, relief came first and powered through me, right up until I heard her voice. Then the worry slipped right back in. She was coping at best, still suffering at worst, and I wanted to fix it for her. I wanted to make it all go away. Of course, that might've been selfish because if it went away, I would never have to tell her how my father and my pack destroyed her life.

Liza sighed into the phone. "I think I can tell you about it now."

Because I wanted no one to hear my side of the conversation, I stood and closed my office door at the manufacturing plant, then pulled the shade on the window. Liza deserved my full attention, and damned sure, she was going to get it.

I was concerned about her. Even with a couple cups of coffee in her and a shower, she hadn't been herself after the nightmare. She'd been so upset and exhausted that she couldn't bring herself to talk about it. Not even with me. Now, a day later, she was ready to talk.

I slumped into my chair, wishing I could see her face. "I'm all ears."

"It's hard for me to describe it in a way that will do it justice." She paused, probably to gather her thoughts. "It's kind of like the nightmares I've had since I was a young kid, only this time it was different."

"How so?" I asked.

I was afraid to hear her answer. Stone's smug face popped into my head, and I couldn't bear the idea of him influencing Liza's memories—or lack thereof. Had his sudden presence in her life led to this horrific nightmare that was so bad she couldn't even speak about it?

"Sometimes it's only flashes of fire and blood and death. This time, the dream was bigger, longer, and in sequential order." She paused and exhaled loudly into the phone. "There were no missing pieces. I could see and feel and hear everything going on around me like I was actually there—like it wasn't just a dream."

I grabbed a stress ball from my desk drawer and squeezed the shit out of it, preparing myself to hear what I was sure was a memory. After everything I'd learned from Stone and what he'd said to Liza about *waking up*, I could only imagine the horror she'd witnessed in her dream. But then I reminded myself that it was only a dream. Liza was suffering from an insane number of hormones flowing through her body. The hormones had probably made it all the more vivid and realistic.

Even as my thoughts tried to brush away the concerns, Liza continued. "A woman and a man who both looked a lot like me." She paused. "My color, my features...I think they were my parents. They were terrified, trying to decide how to respond to some type of invasion."

"Invasion?" God, I was an asshole, but I needed to know the details.

"Yes. I sensed someone was coming after them. After me." She paused again. "They were afraid someone would harm me, so they forced me to leave with a boy. He also seemed very familiar to me, so I wasn't afraid to go with him, but I didn't want to leave the man and the woman. Before I left, the man told me to never forget that I was… royalty."

Definitely a memory disguised as a dream, which meant I didn't have much time to decide how to tell her I knew what had happened to her, and who and what she really was, because even I couldn't explain this being a coincidence.

Liza continued. "Just as the boy pulled me from our home, I witnessed the woman shifting and then…" Her voice cracked, and she inhaled a shaky and stuttering breath. "She was shot."

I closed my eyes. She had to be speaking about her real parents. "That's awful, Liza. I'm so sorry."

"Thank you. I know." She paused again. "I wish I'd woken up at that point, but I didn't." Liza's tone thinned, becoming softer but shriller. "The boy and I ran through the forest. The snow was soaked red with blood everywhere I turned. I could hear screaming and wailing from those who weren't quite dead yet.

And someone was chasing me, telling others to find the girl."

Fuck. No wonder she couldn't speak after waking from the nightmare.

"The boy helping me fell and broke his ankle, but he insisted that I keep running, not to stop until I reached the lavender field."

I wished I could see her; hold her as she spoke. And I wasn't sure if that was a selfishness on my part because I knew our time was ending or if it was truly for her. To say my motives were unclear was an understatement.

"I did as he said and hid for a very long time. I must've fallen asleep because next thing I knew, a man was standing over me."

She fell silent.

Had she seen my father's face in her dream? Surely if she had, she would mention it. "Did the man talk to you?"

"Yes," Liza's voice lowered. "He said he'd make sure I was taken care of. I tried to focus on his face but then I woke up. I don't know who he was."

Thank the fucking gods. "I can see why you were so upset, baby. That must have been terrifying. Do you have any idea what it all means?"

There was a long pause before Liza finally replied. "I'm not sure. It seemed like a memory"—because it was indeed a memory—"but there's no way any of that could've actually happened, or that I would be able to remember it with such clarity and vivid detail."

Standing, I started to pace the length of my office. She remembered because it had happened. It wasn't a dream. It was a memory of a trauma she'd endured—been forced to endure because of my father and our pack.

She'd been four years old when her parents were killed. I didn't know or understand how she was able to have such perfect recall about the battle my father had described. Her wolf hadn't even been present at the time, so they couldn't be *her* memories. I wanted to believe that so much, to tell myself it was so, but I didn't buy my own bullshit.

Or perhaps having a strong memory was another power of an omega. All of the stories I'd heard about omegas painted them as almost mystical creatures with abilities that went far beyond that of an average shifter.

"Are you still there?" Liza asked.

Fuck. I needed to pay attention. She needed support. I was the man for that. "Yes, sorry. I was just trying to make sense of your dream." I stopped pacing and rested my free hand on my hip. I needed a lie, and I needed it fast. And she would have to forgive me. I had no other choice.

"I was trying to think of what you had for dinner. Sometimes strange foods can give me nightmares." The lie came too easily. I was ashamed.

Liza scoffed. "No, Ty. You don't understand."

"Okay, Liza." I kept my voice calm despite the frustration aching through me. "Make me understand. What are you trying to say?"

She choked back a sob. "I think it was more than a dream. Beyond that, I just don't know." She let out a shaky breath. "Either way, I want to learn more about my family. Not the Mims. My original birth family."

Fuck. I had to stall her while I got to the bottom of everything with Stone. "I think that's a natural desire for someone who's adopted. Listen, let me get through this work day, then we can meet for dinner and talk this through." That bought me about four hours. "Please, try not to worry about it. I know that's easy for me to say since it isn't my life in the gray area, but try not to focus on the dream. It sounded pretty traumatic to me. Dwelling on it will only upset you more."

"I'll try." Liza's voice leveled out and wasn't as highly-strung as it had been a moment before.

We hung up, and I jogged over to the manager's office. "Hey, I'm heading out early." I had to let someone know or there would be questions, and I didn't need more of those.

He popped his head up from his computer. "Everything okay?"

"Yeah, I just need to take care of something back at the estate. Call me if you run into any more issues with the temp employees."

I wasn't scheduled to be at the plant today, but I'd woken up to a text from the temp agency saying that they couldn't fill the scheduled shifts for the day. After many threats to move our business to the agency in the next town over, they miraculously filled our request. I'd still needed to check that things went well, though. With everything else going on, I needed business to be solid.

My mind raced, trying to determine if I had some other option, but I couldn't think of an alternative. I needed to talk to Dad and tell him that my idea to negotiate with Stone hadn't worked out. We had no other option but to take him out, officially removing the threat forever.

After days of waiting for a response from Zephyr, I determined he'd been unsuccessful in finding dirt on Stone. My hands were tied, and I hated having to admit that to my father.

The drive home seemed longer than usual as I imagined the curse-laden lecture I would receive after admitting failure to Dad. He would feel compelled to remind me that he was, after all, the alpha, and that I should've listened to him. He would certainly say he had been around much longer than me and knew what kind of person Stone was, that the guy couldn't be reasoned with or threatened, which had been my plan.

Just as I pulled into the driveway, my phone rang. Zephyr's name flashed on the screen.

A sliver of hope lodged in my stomach. "Speak of the devil, Zephyr. I was just thinking about you."

He chuckled. "I don't know if I should be flattered or creeped the fuck out."

"You're the one who dropped off the face of the earth, man." I tried to keep the annoyance out of my voice, but I couldn't hide the edge to it.

"I'm sorry for the radio silence, Ty." He sighed heavily into the phone.

Shit. That wasn't a good sign.

"You'll understand why it's taken me so long to get back to you once you see what I found. I'm at the tech store." My stomach churned. He wasn't coming to meet me because more than once in history the messenger had not, due to rage inspired by his message, returned.

"On my way." I tossed my phone onto the driver's seat and made a U-turn in the driveway.

By the time I pulled into the parking lot of Techno Trends, I'd run every scenario I could imagine through my head. Maybe he'd found information on Stone that would give me leverage. Not just any type of leverage, though. I needed facts that would send

Stone running with his fucking tail tucked between his legs, never to be seen in Presley Acres again.

I walked straight through to the office, and found Zephyr hunched over his multiple computer screens and keyboard.

"All right, what do you have for me?" I pulled up a chair and leaned forward, prepared for whatever news he had to give.

"Stone Black doesn't exist." Zephyr tossed a sheet of paper in my direction.

I picked it up and stared at a bunch of words that meant nothing to me. "What the hell do you mean?"

"I thought *Stone Black* sounded like a shady, shifty name. The kind someone would make up in one of those old, black-and-white detective movies." Zephyr laughed like he'd told a joke, but I didn't find it funny in the least. "And, sure enough, I was right. Stone's real name is Castro Neal."

"Does that mean he's not from the Wylde pack?" I handed the sheet of paper back to Zephyr and he set it on a pile.

He held his hands up, then rooted through his pile for another page. "Give me a second and I'll explain it all." When he found the page, he scanned it, then looked up at me. "His parents were Lillian and Foster Neal. They, too, originated from Denmark. Their families had a shit load of stocks in oil companies that left them loaded beyond comprehension."

Why wasn't I surprised that we were still dealing with rich motherfuckers? I could only imagine where the rest of their money had come from, considering the history of the Wylde pack. Of course, I couldn't throw stones. My wealth had come far more nefariously than I wanted anyone to know.

Zephyr continued. "Lillian and Foster's parents had been friends with Josef's parents."

"Remind me who Josef is again?" I couldn't keep up with my own pack members' names, not to mention the names of an annihilated pack.

"Josef was the alpha of the Wylde pack."

"Ah, yes." I slapped my forehead. The drugs-and-arms dealer that got our family into this mess. Zephyr didn't need to know that… but he probably did. "Okay. I'm with you now."

"All right, so when Josef's parents decided to immigrate to the States, Lillian and Foster Neal's families followed suit." Zephyr sat back in his chair, tossed the paper on the desk, and rested his hands behind his head. "Foster had been Josef's right-hand man. On the business documents I managed to find, it seemed that Josef had a hand in a lot of business dealings outside of his supposed illegal activities."

The cameras alerted us of a customer bursting into the store, eyes wide with panic. "My laptop crashed again! I need help."

Zephyr and I exchanged a knowing look—it was one of those days. His computer store gave him a great coverup for the real work he did behind the scenes, but there were still actual customers that needed to be dealt with, and it had happened more than once that a customer showed up at the worst time. I needed to finish this business.

He quickly got up from his chair and exited the hidden workstation, greeting the woman with a warm smile. He ushered her over to his repair table and had her fill out a request form, leaving me to mull over what he'd told me.

So, there was even more money that hadn't been accounted for from the Wylde pack. Where could it be? Dad had worked hard to bury everything about

Heather Falls and the Wylde pack. Apparently, he hadn't buried it deep enough since Zephyr had managed to dig it up.

Zephyr returned a few minutes later. "Sorry about that. There's nothing more urgent than a housewife with a laptop issue. Now, where was I?"

"I have no damn clue, but why don't we circle back to Stone?" I suggested.

He nodded. "Castro's birth wasn't documented anywhere. It's like the pack wanted to keep the births of the children a secret… but I did manage to find the names of all the registered members of the Heather Falls residents. I hit firewall after firewall trying to crack the code for the information. Neither Castro nor Liza were registered."

"Then, how did you find Stone's real name?"

Zephyr's detective work never ceased to amaze me, but this particular case blew my mind.

"I only managed to find Castro's information because when he turned eighteen, he returned to Denmark where he received a trust his family left for him under his birth name." That was why I trusted him. He was haggard. A dog with a bone. Didn't give up. Those were exactly the kind of traits one wanted in a PI.

"Money. Of course." I scoffed. "Always follow the fucking money, right?"

"Exactly." Zephyr picked up a new stack of paperwork and laid each piece out on his desk in front of me. "This is the paper trail Castro left behind. He spent an ass load of money on these reports."

I examined the documents. It seemed Castro had been hiring private investigators every year up until about two years ago. All these documents were invoices.

I tapped the last document with my finger. "What happened after this?"

"At that point, Castro disappeared, but that's also when a man named Stone Black started using new accounts." Zephyr chuckled. "These sons of bitches think they're so clever, but they always leave a fingerprint or a piece of paper along the way. No one is ever truly untraceable."

"Interesting. What kind of activity did Stone get up to?"

He tapped his keyboard, then turned the monitor toward me. "This is a property deed purchased by Stone Black. It's a massive amount of acreage. Do you recognize the location?"

I leaned in and squinted at the new tab Zephyr had opened. It was an aerial view of flat, wooded land. "Is that fucking Heather Falls?"

"Ding, ding, ding. Give this man a prize. We have a winner. Stone purchased the land exactly where Heather Falls had once hosted the Wylde pack. It seems he also spent a great deal of money to purchase it."

Holy shit. That acreage wouldn't have been cheap, which led me to believe Stone had a considerable amount of assets at his disposal. I couldn't begin to guess how much, but it would not be a tiny sum.

He looked like some kind of fucking vagabond who roamed from town to town, owning only the shirt on his back. Well, looks were deceiving. "This is unbelievable." And not fucking good, but it wasn't Zephyr's fault. "Great job."

"There's more." Zephyr eyed me and lowered his voice. "Josef Wylde must have known something big was coming because he did the same thing the

Neals did. They set their kid up with a fortune." He tossed me another document.

My eyes bulged like a cartoon character as I stared at the massive numbers. There were a whole lot of zeros and commas on the left side of the decimal point.

I didn't buy it.

"This can't be right."

"Bet your ass it's right." Zephyr chuckled. "The account hasn't been touched, so it's accumulated a shit load of interest over the years." A shit load. Of course. There were about ten zeroes to that, too. "An offshore account made auto deposits up until last year. And there's a safety deposit box registered in their names." He ran his tongue over his teeth. "But the trust was left under the name Aliza Wylde."

I'll be damned. Dad had taken everything from Liza except her first name.

"The whole thing is fucked up, Ty." Zephyr massaged his temples with both hands as if to stave off a headache. "It was all heavily encrypted. Banking usually is, but this was over the fucking top. I had to quickly erase any backtrace that might lead to me. Whoever your father hired to cover his tracks did a damn good job of it." He smugly smiled now. "Unfortunately for them, I'm not the average hacker. Either way, I didn't want them to catch wind that I was on their trail or that I'd cracked their code, so to speak."

"Thank you for doing all of this, Zephyr." It wasn't like I didn't pay him, but he'd given me a lot of information.

"No problem." He paused. "I have to ask, what are you going to do now that you have all of this information?"

"Hell if I know." I stood and pulled my wallet from my back pocket. "Here's a deposit for all your hard work. I'll wire the rest to your account tonight."

I tossed a stack of cash onto the desk and gathered up the documents.

I walked to the car, trying to make sense of the information Zephyr had dumped in my lap. There was no way I could sit quietly after this. Liza had a fortune waiting for her. A fortune her parents had set up for her. A fortune that would see her, her kids, and her grandkids all set up for life.

I had no idea what my next move should be, but it seemed the decision was being made for me when a text message from Dad popped up on my phone screen.

We have a problem.

Instead of wasting time texting Dad back, I dialed his number and waited for him to answer. This was better done with a phone call.

"Hey, Ty. I know you're at work and you have shit to do, but we have a situation." I didn't miss the urgency in his voice.

I sighed. "Yeah, Dad. I just got your text. What's going on?" Whatever it was, I'd just add it to the list of shit I already had going on.

"Stone Black has made a move. I guess he's tired of us dragging our feet."

Well. Fuck. "What kind of move?" I buckled my seatbelt and pulled out onto the road, heading in the direction of the estate.

"I've just been made aware that the Heather Falls property is currently being developed."

"Developed? Into what?" Not that it mattered.

Fuck! Stone's mission was clear, which I should've expected. He'd said as much when we chatted outside the ice cream shop. Stone had big plans, and he wasn't waiting around to move forward with them.

He was going to rebuild the Wylde pack and restore them to their former glory, and he couldn't do that without Aliza, their omega princess.

This was going to get ugly.

Chapter 26 - Liza

The scent of lavender always made my stomach turn, though I was standing in the middle of the banquet hall kitchen without so much as a sprig of lavender in sight.

It had been many long days and a few longer nights since I'd suffered through that awful dream, but I hadn't been able to shake it. The details continued to linger, and I often found my thoughts drifting back to that snowy day when screams had filled the air, when I'd stood by and watched the kind woman shift before falling to the floor.

No matter how many times I tried to shift my focus and think about pleasant memories or what I needed to do that day, the dream always streamed back into the forefront of my mind.

Ty had suggested I not dwell on it, that it wouldn't change anything and only make me more miserable, but the emotions that consumed me were damn near impossible to ignore.

I'd imagined every possible explanation for the vivid nightmare, and all I could come up with was that it wasn't just a dream. There was something much bigger to it, and I wanted answers. I wasn't going to get a good night's sleep until I figured it out.

I also couldn't help but feel like something was off with the dream and like I was missing a few pieces of a puzzle. I didn't know the names of any of the people, and I also couldn't focus on the man's face at the end of the dream. My gut instinct told me those were important facts I needed to discover.

Last night, I tried to will myself into the dream to no avail. Though it had been seriously traumatic the first time, I thought experiencing it again would provide the missing clues. If I could only force myself to ask questions in the dream, maybe I would unlock the mystery of my past.

I'd been hired to cater a banquet for a local banking group tonight. Even though my mind was heavy, I still had a job to do. I couldn't afford to let this consume my life and ruin the business I'd worked so hard to build. There was no need to be losing customers just because I couldn't snap out of my repetitive train of thought.

"Adam, once those vegetables are chopped, I need you to keep an eye on this bread. It should be ready in about two minutes."

Adam nodded and continued to slice and dice multiple cucumbers and tomatoes for the salads.

"Shit!" Sabrina yelled from across the kitchen. "I just sliced my damn finger open."

Holy fuck. If it wasn't one thing, it was another. I was tired of *things*.

I grabbed the first aid kit from under the sink and moved Sabrina out of the kitchen. She held a paper towel around the wound, but she hadn't caught all of the blood in time.

"Someone sanitize her area while I fix her up!" I shouted over my shoulder as we pushed through the swinging kitchen door.

We took a seat at the closest table in the main dining hall. Digging through the first aid kit, I pulled out several band aids, some antiseptic, and an antibiotic ointment. "How'd it happen?"

"Sorry. I just wasn't paying attention. I'll be more careful," she grumbled and gritted her teeth together while I cleaned the cut.

I focused on the task at hand while visions of the woman's sad eyes from my dream flashed in my mind. There'd been so much blood then, too.

"Liza, why are you crying? It's just a cut; I'll be fine." She was staring at me as if she thought I might be having a mental incident.

"Crying?" I swiped my free hand over my cheeks. Sure enough, they were wet. I was, indeed, having a mental incident, and I needed very much not to have it here and now. But there really wasn't much I could do to stop it. My emotions were spilling over, and I hadn't even noticed. "I'm fine."

"I don't believe that." Sabrina tapped her fingernails on the tabletop. "Is there trouble in paradise?"

A chuckle escaped my throat despite the tears that continued to spill down my face. "No, not at all. Ty is perfect."

I didn't notice one of my tears fall onto Sabrina's wound until she caught my attention with her panicked voice. "Liza? What the hell?"

She pointed to her hand, and I stared as Sabrina's finger which had healed right in front of our eyes, her skin merged now together.

We stared in awe as the wound scabbed over within a matter of seconds. Shifters healed fast, but this was like fast had been sped up times ten, and Sabrina was human.

"What the hell just happened?" Sabrina's voice went shrill as she stared at me with wide eyes.

I swallowed thickly. Sabrina didn't know anything about omegas, and I had never felt the need to tell her.

"Are you some sort of supernatural superhero and didn't know it?" I asked. I was this far into it, might as well keep it up. "Are you wearing a cape under your apron?"

It was gaslighting and I knew it, but I didn't want her to ask questions or freak out and draw attention. I couldn't explain this to her.

"No, of course not." Sabrina shook her head. "My parents are a hundred-and-ten percent human. You know that."

Panic crept from my belly up to my chest, and my heart pounded in response. It pounded so hard, as a matter of fact, it hurt. I put my hand over my heart and willed the pain to stop.

How could I keep hiding the truth from everyone, especially my best friend? Was this an omega ability? I had no fucking clue, but surely Sabrina would recognize that I wasn't a normal shifter.

Michael when he'd injured his arm and I'd cried, then again with the rabbit, and now with Sabrina. I'd cried over each of them, and they had healed. That was... weird, at best, if I was looking at it from her point of view, and this wasn't best. This was the opposite. It was confusing. And scary. And fuck... so many things I couldn't comprehend, how could I expect her to understand?

The weight of a thousand thoughts came crashing onto my chest, pushing the air from my lungs. Every breath I tried to draw was short and shallow as I struggled to refill my lungs with much-needed oxygen.

The room dimmed, and I grabbed my head, hoping to keep the world from spinning. An elephant seemed to be sitting on my chest. My fight-or-flight response kicked in. I needed to get out of the banquet hall immediately.

I stood, but the dizziness knocked me back into the chair. I slumped forward, trying to catch my breath and trying to make sense of my life.

"Hey. Calm down, Liza. It's all right." Sabrina stood and fanned me with her hand, which didn't help at all and probably looked as ridiculous as it felt, but I didn't have enough oxygen or energy to tell her to stop.

I was in the middle of a full-blown panic attack. All I could think about was my powers and the people around me finding out exactly what I was.

My thoughts were so loud, so all-consuming, I didn't even notice Sabrina rushing away and grabbing her phone.

I couldn't keep all of this inside for much longer. I dropped my head between my legs, not sure if it would actually help. I'd seen someone else do this on a lawyer TV show once. It had something to do with getting enough blood to your head.

Why did I have to be like this?

"Why couldn't I have been born normal?" I didn't recognize my own voice. It was so high-pitched and shrill.

"There's no point in being normal when you were born to be so special." A voice I didn't recognize broke through my anxiety-ridden mind.

I looked up to find Stone leaning against wall next to the swinging kitchen door.

"What are you doing here?" Wiping my face, I tried to regain my composure. I didn't know him very well, but I also didn't want him to see me like this: weak, sinking into my own tragedy.

Unfortunately, trying to act as if he hadn't already seen me with my head between my legs and crying like a baby probably wouldn't do much to convince him of my mental stability.

"I'm accompanying a friend to the banquet tonight. Her parents are on the advisory board for the bank." He paused and glanced across the room at Cecily, who stared at me with contempt.

I should've known.

Stone turned his attention back to me. "I was on my way to the restroom and saw you having a moment. Or should I say, a meltdown?"

"Not very gentlemanly to point it out," I said. I shook my head, then cleared my throat and smoothed my hair back from my face. "I'm fine, thanks for your concern. You can go away now."

Instead of leaving, he sat down next to me. "What happened?"

I turned away, clamping my lips together. Who did this guy think he was?

He sighed loudly, but when I turned to look at him, his gaze smoldered as if he was trying to entice me. "Someday soon you're going to seek me out on your own, and I'll be waiting with open arms."

I held his gaze, unaffected, and proud of it. "I wouldn't bet on it."

Stone smiled and stood. "Your scent is getting stronger."

His words made me stiffen. It was weird when someone randomly came up to me and mentioned my scent. It made me wonder if I needed stronger deodorant or different medicine. This time, I knew the answer.

He scoffed almost happily "You'll be fully aware of everything soon. I'm sure of it."

Stone turned to walk away.

"Wait." I got to my feet. I couldn't let him walk away without trying to get to the bottom of his cryptic words. "What are you talking about? What exactly do you know that I don't?"

His gaze held mine, and my breath caught in my throat, the hairs on my arms standing at attention. As I looked at him, I saw something familiar in his eyes. I couldn't place it, but I had the distinct impression I'd seen them before. A long time ago.

He held me in place with that piercing gaze. "I know everything. So does lover boy." He turned and stared out the window. "Wait for the full moon, Liza. The full moon should finally do it."

I followed his gaze and noticed the moon shining brightly. What did the full moon have to do with anything? He spoke in riddles. So many fucking riddles, and because of that, nothing this man said made sense to me. Maybe that was his game. He wanted to confuse me in hopes of me giving him insider information about the Keller family businesses.

Stone interrupted my thoughts. "Liza, are you still taking your medication?"

It was as if I had been doused with ice water. I hadn't told anyone except Ty that I'd stopped taking my meds. I'd made the decision after we'd slept together. It wasn't that I wanted to get pregnant or anything, but something inside told me I no longer needed them. I followed my instincts, and my wolf seemed to be in full agreement not to take the pills.

"How the fuck could you possibly know that? Have you been following me? Spying on me?" I punched my hands onto my hips and narrowed my eyes. This bastard knew way too much.

A sly grin spread across his face. "Your true nature is making itself known. I'll be the one to fully bring you to your glory."

Just like all the other times I'd interacted with Stone, I had no damn clue what he meant. I didn't have another chance to ask because suddenly Ty was there. I recognized his aura before I saw him.

He moved quickly across the banquet hall. Growling, he shifted right there in the middle of the room, not caring who saw.

Stone didn't even flinch. "Ty, good to see you. You'll be happy to know that everything is going as planned and that I won't be able to keep your secrets for very much longer. Her wolf is truly awakening, and when she finally breaks free, you'll no longer be able to hide your deception."

Secrets? Ty?

Ty didn't hesitate. He charged toward Stone, who stood his ground, again not showing even an ounce of fear.

"No, Ty! Stop!" I tried to jump in between them, but I was too woozy to move fast enough.

Bryce came out of nowhere and slammed his shoulder into Ty's body. "This isn't the time or the place."

Ty turned his feral eyes on Bryce. He didn't have to talk for us to know his goal. He wanted to kill Stone.

Stone glared at Ty, who snarled, baring every tooth. "I've given you time to decide, and I'm tired of waiting. You know exactly why I'm here, and I won't wait for you to give it to me."

Ty snarled viciously as Bryce dug his heels into the floor, trying to hold Ty back from completely ripping Stone to shreds in the middle of the banquet hall.

"Sorry to say that your time is up, Ty." Stone took a step forward, mocking Ty. "You need to decide by the end of the full moon, or a decision will be made for you."

Stone turned and walked back to Cecily. She cocked her head and slapped Stone's chest. "What the hell is so special about *her*? Was it really necessary for you to give her that much attention?" Her loud voice carried across the hall, and I cringed.

Stone shrugged and put his arm around Cecily's waist. "It's time for us to go."

He took one last look at me before turning and leading her away. I stood there speechless as Bryce released Ty from his grip.

He stayed close in case he decided to go after Stone again. "Calm down, man. He's gone."

Ty growled, but the fight left his body.

"Remember why we came here in the first place," Bryce murmured in Ty's ear. "You can't shift back now, you idiot. If you do, you'll be as naked as the day you were born." He shook his head at me. "His clothes are shredded."

Ty glanced back at me. I was too stunned to speak. Everything had happened so quickly, and I was still recovering from my panic attack. I hadn't expected this sort of reaction out of Ty.

Something told me Stone wasn't in town for a business deal, which only raised my suspicions.

Stone's words settled deep within me as I tried to make sense of them. What did he mean by *her wolf is awakening*? Why was Ty so intent on keeping me in the dark?

Questions raced through my mind, and I had no idea how to find the answers. All I knew for sure was that something strange was going on, and it seemed to have everything to do with me.

Bryce went to get a change of clothes from his car, and when he came back, he and Ty went to the restroom. Shaking my head to return to some semblance of normalcy, I headed back to the kitchen to check on my staff.

"Liza? Is everything okay?" Sabrina walked to my side and laid a hand on my arm. "I hope you don't mind me calling Ty. You were freaking the fuck out and I didn't know what to do. I figured he could calm you down."

"Well, he certainly got my mind off the panic attack."

Adam pretended like he hadn't been listening and turned from the stove.

"It sounded like a full-blown brawl out there. Did Ty win?"

I shook my head. "Nobody won." That included me. I squeezed the bridge of my nose and closed my eyes. My energy had been zapped right out of me. I couldn't think straight. No way I'd be able to manage an entire kitchen tonight.

Just then, Ty popped his head into the kitchen.

"Oh, good." Sabrina motioned for him to come in. "You're just in time. I was about to tell Liza to go home. She looks pale."

I glanced at Ty, and he reached for my hand.

"Max can take care of it!" Sabrina shouted so that my head chef could hear over the blender.

He gave me a thumbs-up and smiled, which was enough confirmation for me.

I turned back to Ty. "Can you drive me home? I don't feel like driving." I really didn't feel like doing anything but finding out what the hell Stone had been talking about.

"Of course, baby." Ty squeezed my hand. "Anything you need."

I shot a half-smile at Sabrina. I was going to have to give her—all of them—a big raise. "Thanks. Call if you need me."

When we walked outside, I looked for Ty's car, but he shook his head like he was reading my thoughts. "We'll have to take your car. Bryce drove me."

I nodded and handed Ty my keys.

My hands were shaking, and my head still felt like someone had tried to knock me out with a cast-iron skillet. I was on edge, and there was no hiding it. I was sure Ty could sense my mood. As soon as he had the car in drive, he reached for my hand, stroking my skin with his thumb.

Ty was quiet on the drive to my house, waiting for me to talk, like he thought there might come a time when I was ready. I didn't know about that.

"We need to have a serious conversation." I pulled my hand out of his grasp and clasped my hands together in my lap.

"Okay, sure." He wasn't bothered. He put his hand on my leg, rubbing my skin reassuringly.

"Not in the car, and not at my house." I stared out the window. "Is there somewhere else we can go? Somewhere we can get some fresh air?"

"I know just the place." Ty turned onto the highway, heading away from my house. "There's a clearing at the estate that is beautiful in the moonlight."

"Sounds perfect." I didn't need beauty. I needed quiet. I needed seclusion. Most of all, I needed fucking answers.

The rest of the ride passed in silence, but it was comfortable. I wondered if Ty knew what I planned to ask; if he had the slightest inkling. I had no idea how much he'd heard. He could've been there even before I sensed his aura. I'd been so distracted. He was unusually quiet, but there was a chance he was still reeling from his stand-off with Stone.

He parked the car at the top of his long driveway and came around to help me out. I didn't take his hand, instead folding my arms over my stomach as we walked down the narrow path.

When we reached the clearing, my anxiety slowly faded away. The stars sparkled above us, and a gentle breeze blew through the tall trees surrounding the clearing.

Ty's aura spilled over, tension radiating off him in waves. His run-in with Stone had affected him more than he was letting on, but his aura didn't lie.

I raised my head, allowing the light from the full moon to wash over me. For the first time in my life, I felt a tingle penetrating deeply into every nerve of my body. The sensation was undeniable. It was the pull of the moon.

I suddenly felt powerful, like I was a part of something bigger. Something that went beyond my current circumstances or my anxiety over my dreams.

Closing my eyes, I took a moment to enjoy the overwhelming sense of peace and power. The moon called me, tugged at my soul, and compelled me to answer its call. Maybe I needed to shift before we had this talk. Run to clear my mind. But I didn't shift. Didn't run. I only stood under the rays of moonlight and waited.

A few moments later, I opened my eyes, refreshed, ready to have a conversation that probably wouldn't go well.

Ty watched me, his gaze soft as if he understood and was trying to comfort me. He reached for my hand, intertwining our fingers as he smiled knowingly at me. "Ready to talk?"

I asked the question that had been burning inside me since Stone spoke his mysterious words: "Are you keeping something from me?"

Chapter 27 - Ty

If I had the ability to freeze time, I would have done just that. I watched as Liza stood in the moonlight, her platinum blonde hair reflecting its beams as she closed her eyes. A peaceful smile spread across her face. Her arms were outstretched, her face raised to the sky as if she were calling on a higher power. Were I an artist, this would be my masterpiece, and I would title it *Serenity*.

Warm contentment swelled deep within my chest as I watched peace wash over her. I didn't dare attempt to interrupt her.

After a moment, though, she opened her eyes, and reality set in, the gravity of our situation returning. I had nearly ripped Stone's throat out when I spotted him with Liza. I'd sure as fuck intended to. He had no right to corner her, and it wasn't the first time he'd done so.

Stone was smart—not smart enough to know to stay away, though— and he wasn't fucking around. He knew exactly what he wanted. Since he had me by the balls, he was forcing my hand.

My mind swirled with the possible outcomes of my situation with Stone. If I stood by and did nothing, he would tell Liza the truth. Then he planned to take her for his own. Hell, she would probably go willingly when she found out I'd kept the truth from her.

He'd given me an ultimatum, and even though I wasn't one to be bossed around, I didn't really have a choice. He had a card to play, and I was certain he was going to play it soon. I had to make the next move, and quickly.

Liza, snapped out of her meditative state and frowned at me. "Are you keeping something from me?"

My heart pounded a thousand beats per second as I let Liza's question sink in. I wasn't ready for this conversation. I stared into the trees at the edge of the clearing, hoping to spot some type of distraction or interruption. I needed more time to gather my thoughts and figure out exactly how to explain everything to her.

The forest was still, almost as if the other animals knew that the alpha and the omega were preparing to have a serious conversation. One that required privacy and the utmost respect.

I was certain of only one thing: I had to get rid of Stone. That was my priority, but I couldn't very well leave Liza in the middle of the woods to go handle it, especially after she'd point-blank asked me if I was hiding something from her.

I sighed. I had to tell her something. Finally, I decided on the lesser of the two evils. She'd be pissed at me either way. Me keeping facts from her while she had been struggling to understand why she was different from other shifters was the lesser offense. I believed she could forgive me for that and hopefully see that I only wanted to protect her. We might be able to come back from that.

Me telling her that my family murdered her pack and basically kidnapped her, on the other hand, was unforgivable. She would never trust me again. It would end us.

I took a step toward Liza and met her glare. "I was curious about you, Liza. You piqued my curiosity, first with your light hair and skin, then with the pheromone situation at the coffee shop." This was harder than I'd thought, not for any reason other than I wanted to tell her everything. And because I didn't want to lose her, I couldn't tell her. It was killing me.

She pursed her lips. "It makes sense that you were curious about me." She paused, and the silence stretched because I didn't want to go on. "There's more, though, isn't there?"

I nodded. "I looked into your past, but there was nothing to find. Literally. Nothing."

Liza crossed her arms. "What do you mean you *looked into me*?" She shook her head once.

Shit. This wasn't the part I thought she would stick on, but it was the easiest to explain. I didn't want to tell her I'd hired Zephyr, but I also didn't want to lie right to her face. "I have a guy on the payroll. And investigator of sorts." She didn't balk or flinch or get pissed off at my answer, so I continued. "Bryce and I had conversations about you. You know how men talk." She had brothers. Of course, she knew. "And Bryce has been my best friend for ages."

"Yeah." She sighed loudly, and I couldn't tell if she was already pissed or just bracing for whatever I was about to admit.

"Bryce had his suspicions about you from the beginning." I held up my hands as her gaze narrowed. "Not in a malicious way. He just noticed your differences, your hair, your eyes, and he… and I—that is, *we*—wondered if there might be something special about you aside from what I could already see." I wasn't a stammering, stuttering kind of guy, but I had a feeling I was standing at the beginning of the end.

"Special?" Liza asked.

I rubbed my chin. Fuck, this was more awkward than I had imagined it would be. "Yeah. I told him about the incident with the rabbit in the woods that night when we shifted for the first time. It only spurred him on. He was always chirping about it. He couldn't stop talking about how you were even more special than he initially realized."

I didn't want to mention Stone because then I'd have to explain why he knew who Liza was. That would lead to the premature beginning of the conversation we would have to have at some point down the road. I absolutely planned on telling her the truth about her family and mine, but not yet. Later. I sure as hell couldn't do it right now with the anger flaming in her eyes, and certainly not while she was standing with her feet apart and her arms crossed like she was ready for battle. I didn't want that battle to start with me. Unfortunately, she was already suspicious of Stone, so I couldn't leave him out completely.

    I thought fast and settled on the direction of my explanation. "Stone overheard a conversation between Bryce and me. I was in the middle of telling him about the conversation I had with your parents the night we had dinner with them." I was using all the tricks, trying to bring her parents into it to soften her anger—nope, it was rage.

    And I felt worse because I'd just told her a blatant lie, but I was backed into a corner. I silently hoped Liza wouldn't ask for more details because I didn't want to make any more shit up.

    She hadn't moved or spoken, so I continued. "Stone threatened to reveal everything to you before I was prepared to have this conversation."

    Liza scratched her forehead, her hand visibly shaking. "What the hell is so secretive about me that everyone has chosen to keep it hidden?" And louder, with more emphasis, she added, "From me."

    My throat tightened as I shakily cracked my knuckles. Liza was an observant woman who, no doubt, could see how nervous this discussion was making me. There was no turning back now, though. I had no choice but to tell her the truth about what she was. Stone had taken that choice from me.

Another reason I wouldn't mind killing him.

"Your parents confirmed my suspicions..." I trailed off, as much because I needed a break as to let her prepare herself. It wasn't bad news that she was extraordinary, but it was big news that had been kept from her.

"For fuck's sake, Ty. Just say it!" Liza popped her hands onto her hips, her cheeks flushed, and eyes dark with an untamed fury.

"Your parents said Bryce was right." I averted my eyes. "You're an omega."

I held my breath, waiting for Liza's reaction of disbelief.

She didn't react. She stood perfectly still, staring a hole through me. Then her lips twitched, and she started to laugh. Her laughter quickly turned into an all-out cackle.

Well, fuck. That wasn't the reaction I'd anticipated.

Liza continued to laugh until she doubled over, clutching her stomach and wiping tears from her eyes.

She finally stood up and looked at me, gasping for breath. "I know what I am."

My jaw dropped. Too stunned to speak, I stared at Liza as she recovered from laughing so hard. She already knew? Not only that, but Liza had chosen to keep that part of herself a secret from me. I clenched my jaw so hard I thought my teeth would crack. "What do you mean you know what you are?"

She glared at me. "You're not seriously pissed off at me right now. Because let me tell you something, buddy, you of all people have no right to be upset with me. You're the one who's had your fucking '*man on the payroll*'"—I could've lived without the air quotes—"digging around, trying to find out information about me. And don't forget all these conversations you and your BFF Bryce had behind my back." She shook her head, her glare striking me right in the heart. "You told him private details that should've stayed between us. I don't… can't even fucking imagine what made you think it was a good idea to hash out the way I look and act with Bryce, then with my own fucking parents."

She was past angry now. Past furious. This was a kind of rage I hadn't seen before.

"All you had to do was come to me. You should've asked me, Ty." Her voice softened, but the fury was easy to spot in her red cheeks, the dark eyes, and her lowered tone.

I growled in frustration as I ran a hand through my hair and paced the edge of the clearing. "Fuck, Liza. You make it sound like it was that simple. I didn't even know if it was a possibility. I'd always thought omegas were a fucking legend." And she hadn't trusted me enough to tell me, even though she'd said she trusted me. I stopped and whirled around. "How could you keep something like that from me?"

Liza scoffed. "It's none of your fucking business."

My mouth fell open. "Are you fucking serious? Not my business? You have no idea how much I've agonized over having this conversation with you. It's been tearing me apart." I raked my hand through my hair and stared at her before looking away. I considered all the scenarios that had run through my mind up to this point. "You were so worried about your hormones and wondering why you were so different from everyone else. Can't you understand that I was worried about being the one to tell you? In my mind, you were an omega, and your parents and everyone else in your life had kept it from you, even going so far as putting you on hormone pills to conceal your true identity." I'd thought telling her would destroy relationships. Hurt her. I didn't want to be the one to do that.

"They didn't keep it from me. They protected me from it. Taught me how to protect myself because I had to." Liza held up a hand and cut me off. "I've had to protect myself from being who I am since I was thirteen years old, at which point I was almost sexually assaulted by my fucking neighbor." She shook her head and choked back a sob as the anger immediately seeped out of my body.

Maybe I was an asshole. "Liza." I reached for her, but she jerked away. That was a bad sign.

Her voice cracked as tears spilled onto her cheeks. "I can't describe to you the struggles I've lived with. Once I realized the weight I carried on my shoulders as an omega, my life was never the same."

I opened my mouth, but no words came out. My fury over Liza keeping her identity from me had completely dissipated. I stared at my fated mate as she let her walls crash down. I wanted to pick up every piece and toss it for her. She didn't need walls with me.

She sobbed into her hands, releasing the emotions she'd held back from me for the entirety of our relationship. "My parents were scared out of their minds after the attack. It took a while—some consultations with the doctor and some long talks with me—before they realized the truth about why it had happened in the first place. They kept it a secret from everyone because they wanted to protect me." She blew out a breath.

I wanted to go to her and hold her, but I wasn't sure she would accept the comfort from me right now. "Oh, Liza."

"They were worried that if word got out, I would be a target for multiple reasons." Her icy blue eyes were even more striking from the tears. "I was going to tell you when the time was right. There's no way I'd allow us to officially mate without filling you in on something of this magnitude."

I nodded. I believed her.

"You have to realize that I had reason to be cautious. You said yourself that you thought omegas were just a legend, so surely you remember the myths. Omegas have always been depicted as overly sexualized wolves who just want to get fucked and pregnant." She shook her head and stared off into the distance. "Can you imagine the number of people who would want to take advantage of me based on that stupid myth alone?"

The sound of a snapping branch interrupted our conversation. I turned and crouched low, searching the forest floor for the culprit. A deer stopped, turned its head our way, and stared at the two of us.

Liza's emotions were powerful. I'd seen her tears heal a dying rabbit. It made sense that the animals were curious, and I was relieved we weren't being followed. The last thing we needed was another shifter hearing us talk about Liza's true identity as an omega. Gossip, especially when it was true, was dangerous.

I turned back to Liza to see her whole body shaking now. Her emotions hit me like a ton of bricks. "Liza, I'm so sorry for looking into you without your consent, and I apologize for keeping the omega suspicions and information from you instead of just coming directly to you about it." I took a step closer because I needed to touch her. "Please forgive me for getting upset. You're right, I had no reason for getting mad. I can't imagine what you've been through. You have every reason to be cautious." I brushed a strand of hair from her face and tucked it behind her ear. "I'm your mate, though. You should know that I would never do anything to harm you."

Liza's shoulders shook violently as a new wave of emotion washed over her. It was impossible for me to keep my distance, so I pulled her close against my chest and wrapped her in my arms.

She buried her face in the hollow of my shoulder. "I never wanted any of this. I spent so many nights wishing it would all just disappear."

She was trembling, so I held her tighter.

"I always worried what might happen if someone found out." She pulled away from me and froze. "Stone knows. Oh, fuck. He fucking knows what I am. Is that why you've been so angry with him? And why you almost ripped him to shreds back at the banquet hall? He's been threatening to expose what I am if he doesn't get what he wants from you. Am I right?"

My heart dropped into my stomach. After what just happened, I should have told her everything and got it out in the open so we could figure out what to do about it, but I wanted her deeply in love with me before I told her the absolute worst thing I'd ever had to tell anyone.

This was my chance to tell her the truth, but instead I was spinning an entirely new lie to feed her. I was such a piece of shit. In my defense, this was the only way I could prevent her from learning the truth of what my father had done to her family. I had to figure out how to tell her without losing her. I wouldn't survive losing her.

I nodded. "Yes, Stone wants money. A lot of it. He's been threatening to reveal your secret to anyone who will listen if he doesn't get what he wants. That's why I wanted you to stay away from him." I wished she would see through me, call me a fucking liar, and demand I tell her what I was hiding. When she didn't, though, I kept going. "When I saw him hovering over you tonight, I couldn't contain my wolf. That son of a bitch shouldn't be stepping within a mile of you."

Liza nodded slightly and stepped back into my embrace. I stroked her back in soothing circles.

"I promise I won't let Stone tell a soul. Your secret is safe with me, and I'll make sure it's safe with Stone. That motherfucker knows better than to open his damn mouth." I paused and held her at arm's length. I wanted and needed to look into her eyes. "I will always protect you, Liza. You're my mate, and I would do anything to keep you safe and well. I mean that with every ounce of my being." At least that much was true.

Liza smiled weakly and kissed my cheek before resting her head against my chest. I held her close, never wanting to let go. It seemed like everything was finally falling into place for us now that the omega secret was no longer between us. We had a chance at a real future together, one that would be filled with safety, security, and love.

Dragging out the truth about our families would only piss Liza off later down the line. I knew that, but I had no choice. Stone needed to be handled. I needed him out of the way and out of our lives for good. That was the only way Liza and I had a chance at a real future together.

Once Stone was out of the picture, I could figure out the best way to get Liza what was rightfully hers. Then, one day, I'd tell her the truth about Heather Falls and her true identity.

I walked Liza back to the estate, my arm wrapped protectively around her shoulders. I wanted to make sure she felt safe and secure, that she knew I was and always would be there for her. She was still trembling from our confrontation and her worries about Stone and anyone else who might learn about her being an omega.

Even though it had been a difficult night, we'd needed it. Having the truth out in the open had brought us closer together and deepened our bond. I only hoped that Liza could forgive me when I finally told her about the Wylde pack and how she was a princess who had been stripped of her place as heir.

"Are you okay to drive?" I brushed my lips over Liza's cheek and studied her face.

Her tear-stained cheeks were paler than usual, and she had dark circles under her eyes.

"Yes, I'll be fine." She squeezed my hand. "I'll text you when I get home."

I kissed her softly. "Please do. Let me know if you made it okay."

Liza buckled her seatbelt and reached to close her door, but I caught it before she could. "Remember, if you need me, I'm just a phone call away."

She nodded, then pulled her car door shut. I watched her drive away until her taillights were out of sight.

Someone cleared their throat behind me, and I spun around, poised and ready to fight to the death. The evening had put me on edge, and I already had Stone on my mind.

"Whoa, killer." Dad took a step back. "No need to attack unless you think an old man like me needs to be taken out."

I breathed a sigh of relief and followed him inside.

"What's going on?" he asked.

Lowering my voice, I said, "You'll be happy to know that the Stone situation will be handled very soon."

Dad nodded.

I studied him, really staring at him, taking in the gray at his temples, and the bags under his eyes. He seemed tired. "Are you okay?"

He sighed. "I'm not about to kick the bucket, if that's what you're asking."

I shrugged and chuckled. "No, I'm not saying you look like death, but you do seem more tired than normal." I glanced at my watch. "Didn't the doctor say you needed to be in bed by nine every night?"

"He might have, but you know as well as anyone that I'll do whatever I damn well please. I'll sleep in tomorrow." He leaned against the wall. "All of these secrets have been weighing on me for a long time, Tyson. I've done a lot of things, some legal, some not, to keep those secrets hidden. Now the people around me are being weighed down by the skeletons in my closet." He glanced up the stairs, where I assumed Mother was sleeping.

I would've been tired, too. "That's enough to make anyone tired, Dad. I get it."

He then did something he'd never done my entire life. He grabbed my hand and let his guard down, showing more emotion than any alpha should. "I'm sorry all of this has fallen on your shoulders."

His apology shocked me, but I appreciated it. "I accept your apology, Dad, and I promise I'll handle this so you can finally rest easy."

I knew what I needed to do. There was no other option.

Stone had to die.

Soon.

Chapter 28 - Liza

Last night had been horrific and beautiful all at the same time. My argument with Ty had reminded me of the times in my life when I'd felt completely out of control and vulnerable and had acted out because of it. But last night, I'd controlled my anger. Hashing it out had brought us closer together than ever before.

But with the good came the bad, or so it seemed in my life. The truth about my identity was out in the open, and Ty was determined to ensure Stone paid for his crimes against me. I wouldn't have bet that piece of shit was smart enough to find his way home with GPS and a map, yet here he was, creating a blackmail scheme, threatening to out me if he didn't get paid. It spoke of his character. Spoke volumes.

Ty promised he'd find a way to keep me safe and assured me that Stone wouldn't breathe a word about me being an omega. I couldn't help but worry about what Ty might have planned, but I trusted him to take care of the situation.

The truth was out, which meant I needed to talk to my parents. Ty had agreed to meet me at their house.

I woke up with a renewed sense of peace that morning after sleeping a full ten hours. Between the anxiety attack, witnessing Ty shift in front of a crowd and almost taking Stone out, not to mention the argument and emotional toll of my conversation with Ty in the clearing, it had all been mentally draining.

From the age of thirteen, I'd spent my life trying to hide what I was, to keep it buried deep with the aid of hormone medication and a long line of lies and half-truths.

I'd planned on telling Ty that I was an omega, but I'd been terrified he'd reject me. He was the next alpha, for God's sake. I assumed he'd at least feel somewhat threatened to have an omega as his mate. I wasn't stronger than he was, but I was a badass in my own right, possessing special skills he didn't. It could've been intimidating. It would have been to any other shifter, certainly.

Once again, though, he'd surprised me with his understanding and gentle nature. Sure, he'd been pissed when he discovered I had kept it from him, but once I explained my past and how being an omega was a burden, he'd been quick to comfort me, and his promise to protect me carried some weight.

I held Ty's hand as we sat across from my parents in their living room.

Mom wrung her hands together nervously as Dad sipped his freshly squeezed lemonade. "What happened, Liza? Something's wrong."

Poor Mom. She'd always been the highly strung one in the family, always anticipating the next disaster that might befall one of her precious children. But she had an undeniable sixth sense about us. My mother always knew when I was upset.

I smiled. "Mom, calm down. Everything's fine." I shot Ty a look.

He took my cue and set his glass on a coaster on the table. "Liza and I had a conversation last night about her being an omega." He looked at my father. "I didn't realize she was aware of her... abilities, but she assured me she's known since she was thirteen."

Mom let out the breath she'd been holding for far too long and slumped back against the chair. "Good heavens, maybe you could've led with that. I thought you were going to tell me that her medication had stopped working again." She shook her head in annoyance, but was she was smiling.

Dad took another sip of his drink. As usual, he was completely unfazed by the conversation.

"So, the truth is out." I crossed my legs, suddenly relaxed. "Ty said you all discussed this. That you led him to believe I was oblivious." I didn't need to say more. They were appropriately chastised for their fib. Mom looked away.

Dad cleared his throat. "Liza, we didn't mean to mislead Ty, but we felt like it was your place to tell him, not ours."

"No need to apologize to me. I'm not angry." Ty nodded in Dad's direction. "I completely understand. You were protecting Liza while also giving her the chance to tell me herself. No harm done."

My parents shared a look, and Ty picked up on their anxiety.

"You don't need to worry, Mr. and Mrs. Mims. I'll keep Liza safe." He squeezed my hand. "I know you've carried the burden of her safety since she was thirteen, but I won't let anyone harm a hair on her head. Her secret is also safe with me. There's no real reason for others to know that she's an omega. Unless, of course, Liza chooses to share that information."

Mom held a hand to her chest. "Thank you, Ty. That means a lot to us. Liza is a very special woman, and she deserves to be protected and cherished."

Ty's eyes crinkled at the corners. "Absolutely."

"We can chat more over dinner." Mom stood and rubbed her hands together. "I made pulled pork in the slow cooker."

There wasn't much in life better than Mom's pulled pork, and I savored the juicy taste as I thought about the full moon. It had been extremely bright the night before, but Ty had said it would be at its fullest tonight. I had been on edge all day, wondering how my wolf would respond, especially after I'd felt such a strong tug last night.

Dad cleared his throat loudly, interrupting my thoughts. "Liza, are you still taking your medication?"

Ty inclined his head toward me, urging me to be honest with my parents. I was embarrassed about having to talk about my hormones and Ty *handling* my sexual cravings, but my parents deserved to know the truth. After all, they always had my best interests at heart.

I sighed. "Uhm, no. I actually stopped taking them recently."

Mom choked on her wine, spluttering, coughing, and slapping her chest. Once the spluttering stopped, she stared at me with wide eyes. "Why would you do that, Liza? Didn't the doctor double your dosage to keep you safe? Prescribe new medication?" My safety was always foremost in her mind, and I loved her all the more for it.

I twisted my mouth to the side, trying to think of a delicate way to say it. "I don't feel the need for them anymore now that I'm with Ty."

One of the main reasons for the medication was to calm down any hypersexual cravings I might have developed during puberty. Since I'd been on the medication, I didn't know if such a thing had occurred or not. Now I had a mate who could handle... *it* for me. It was an embarrassing dinner topic, but I needed to explain, otherwise my mother wouldn't sleep until I did.

"Ty handles my, uh, cravings."

Dad's face reddened as he shoved a forkful of pulled pork into his mouth and chewed without speaking, but he narrowed his eyes at Ty. I was still his little girl.

I'd felt some cravings brewing deep inside since I was a teenager, but they were like an itch I couldn't scratch, and nothing so severe as the doctor had predicted. They were too far out of reach, even when I took matters into my own hands. It just wasn't the same.

Mom cleared her throat, leaned closer to me, and lowered her voice. "So, what you're saying is that your hormones have leveled off now that you're with Ty?"

"Exactly." I took a sip of water because my entire body, but mostly my face, was on fire with shame. This wasn't a conversation any woman should have to have over pulled pork in her mother's dining room. "With my desires being met, my hormones are much more balanced."

"I'll just finish this in the other room." Dad stood and carried his plate into the kitchen.

I stifled a laugh as Mom whispered across the table, "Your father isn't exactly a sexually liberated man. You'll have to excuse his prudence."

Ty chuckled. "I don't think I'd want to discuss any of this with my daughter, either."

The mention of a daughter stirred something deep within me. I didn't want to play into the myths about omegas only wanting to procreate, but the thought of having a child with Ty made me happy. He would be an amazing and protective dad. A daddy any little girl would be proud to call her own.

Mom stood and grabbed our plates, following Dad into the kitchen.

Ty rubbed my back. "I will never dictate what you do to your body, but if it seems like you're going to send the entire male population of Presley Acres into a rut, you'll need to go back on your meds."

I nodded. "I can agree to those terms."

"Good. I'd rather not have to take on the entire male population of our pack to defend you." Ty laughed as we stepped into the kitchen.

We spent a few more minutes making small talk with my parents before saying our goodbyes. It was already dusk, and Ty didn't want to be late arriving at the Keller Estate.

It was the first full moon, which meant I would have my first run with the upper-class wolves. This full moon would be different for me, though. I could feel it in every inch of my being. I would finally experience what the other shifters had enjoyed their entire lives—the rush of freedom and of running under the full moon without the drugs hazing my joyousness. The thought of it was liberating.

Cars lined both sides of the estate's long driveway and spilled out onto the street below. Ty had called all members to this run, not just the upper-class. No segregation. No class differences. Just the pack.

Holding my hand, Ty led me to the clearing where everyone had gathered, waiting for their alpha to speak. I stood next to him as the members of the pack stared up at the royal family of the south.

Dominic Keller stood before his pack, scanning the group of loyal wolves gathered in the clearing under the bright light of the full moon.

He raised his hands, instructing the pack to quiet down. His voice, strong and commanding, filled the air as he began to speak. "Welcome, everyone. Family is everything to us. We have been passed down through generations, from one alpha to the next. We are connected by blood, by the bonds of loyalty and love that we share."

The pack listened with rapt attention, hanging on to their alpha's every word.

"Tonight, we celebrate a new chapter in our pack's history," Dominic announced, pride emanating from his voice. "My son Tyson has found his mate, Liza. They will take on the responsibilities of leadership and become the future of our pack."

The announcement was met with an excited murmur. It went without saying that this was a momentous occasion, a changing of the guard that marked passing the torch from one generation to the next.

I was shocked that he'd publicly acknowledged me after having been so against our pairing. Did he know I was an omega?

"Tyson has proven himself to be a worthy successor. He will make a strong king, one who will lead our pack with loyalty, wisdom, and compassion," Dominic continued, his chest swelling. "And Liza is a powerful and intelligent wolf. Together, they will be a force to be reckoned with."

The anticipation among the pack members grew. This was the beginning of a new era for their pack, and the excitement was palpable.

"I stand before you tonight to announce my intention to renounce my title as alpha once Tyson officially takes Liza as his mate," he declared with a sense of finality in his voice. "It is time for me to step down and for my son to take his rightful place as the leader of our pack."

The pack members nodded in agreement, showing their support. They knew he had served their pack well and that it was time for him to enjoy his well-earned rest.

The clouds shifted, revealing the full moon in all its splendor. My wolf lunged, causing me to react almost violently to the pull of the moon. Ty held my arms and stepped in front of me, blocking my view from the others as I trembled. I'd never felt this way.

"I know this is new for you. It can be overwhelming." Ty put his lips against my ear and whispered, "Remember that the moon is our guide, our strength, our source of power. We draw from it, but we don't let it control us."

His words reassured me, and I soon found myself calming down, better able to control my body's reaction to the glow of the moon.

Just then, Dominic raised his head to the full moon above and let out a long, piercing howl. It was a signal to the pack that it was time to shift and run together, celebrating their unity and strength. The pack quickly shed their clothes and shifted, taking off in all directions.

Ty kissed me on the forehead. "Are you ready for your first *real* run?

"As ready as I'll ever be." I smiled at him as anticipation shivered through me.

I closed my eyes and allowed my wolf to move forward, no longer holding her back from what she desired. My muscles twitched with anticipation when the familiar feeling of transformation took over. As I shifted, my senses sharpened, allowing me to see and hear with a clarity I had never experienced. My wolf also seemed more alert than she'd ever been before.

I ran through the clearing, not stopping to worry about Ty. My instincts kicked in and the moon was my guide, pulling me deeper into the forest.

The leaves rustled beneath my paws as I ran through the woods, feeling the cool breeze on my fur. Every sound, every scent, was magnified, and the woods came alive around me. I could hear the soft rustling of leaves, the chirping of crickets, the hooting of an owl in the distance.

I kept running and running, the trees passing by in a blur. It was almost as if I didn't have control over my speed or direction.

Ty growled behind me, like he was telling me to stop.

I couldn't.

I ran for what felt like hours, though it had probably not been longer than forty minutes, but instead of continuing to streak through the fields and the woods, my wolf came to an abrupt stop.

I panted, trying my best to force oxygen into my burning lungs. My entire being froze. My shift was immediate, and I stood completely naked, trying to take in my surroundings.

I stood in a field of lavender. My nose pricked from the strong scent as my mind whirled, trying to make sense of my location.

My knees shook when I heard, "Liza," in Ty's warm rich voice, though it was a whisper from just behind me. I ignored him and continued to walk, stopping in front of the brush of bushes, my breath hitching in my chest as my heart pounded.

"We shouldn't be here, Liza. It's not our territory. Let's go home," Ty pleaded a little louder, as though he thought I hadn't heard him call my name. Still, I ignored him.

There was no turning back now.

I didn't know where I was, but I couldn't leave.

I had no idea what was leading me or pulling me, but I was on autopilot, neither seeing nor hearing, only feeling as I navigated through the dark woods. The moonlight illuminated my path as my heart beat faster and harder with a sense of anticipation.

My hands instinctively reached out, caressing the trees as I passed. They seemed to be singing to me, welcoming me. The words *home, home, home* echoed like a siren in my mind, calling me to where I needed to be. To where I was *meant* to be.

The moon seemed to shine even brighter as it rose higher in the sky, casting a silvery light on the trees and illuminating the path ahead of me. The night was alive with energy, and I felt strangely connected to the earth beneath my feet.

Suddenly, images filled my head. I was running through these exact trees while a beautiful woman with my face chased me. She laughed and told me that princesses weren't meant to get so dirty, but her smile was wide, and she wasn't chastising me. She loved seeing her little princess this way, so wild and free.

I frolicked, giggling, leaping high, attempting to grab the tree limbs above me. I was happy and safe.

My breath caught somewhere between my lungs and my throat as I continued to walk. I picked up speed, certain I was getting closer to my destination.

More images popped into my mind. There was a bright full moon. Several people sat in its glow, feasting and laughing together. I sat in the middle of the table, surrounded by love.

A handsome man leaned down and spoke in a soft voice, telling me how blessed they had been with their princess, their honor, and their joy.

A sob escaped my throat, and tears streamed unbidden down my cheeks. I could sense Ty walking by my side, but he no longer tried to stop me. He had to know it was no use. Something greater was happening here.

I broke into a run as several more memories flooded back into my mind. They came in waves, almost overwhelming me. Clutching my chest, I squinted, trying to see where I was going through the tears that wouldn't stop coming.

I broke through the trees and fell to my knees. My emotions overwhelmed me because I finally understood where I was. I wasn't lost at all. I knew exactly who those people were in my memories and in the dreams that had haunted me since the age of four.

I remembered everything as I stared at the house in front of me. It wasn't quite the same as my old one. The coloring was different, but the design was the same.

It was a home fit for a royal family. A home fit for *my family*.

A man was silhouetted on the back porch. As my eyes focused, I realized that I knew him. Not the man, but the boy he used to be. He'd come to our house every day to play with me. My parents had told me he'd always protect me. It was the boy who had taken my hand and fled with me into the woods to escape being killed by the bad men who had attacked our home.

That boy was now a man. My voice cracked as I said his name. "Stone."

But that boy had a different name. He had been Castro. I couldn't believe I'd forgotten him.

I covered my face with my hands as I suddenly saw the man at the end of my dream. His words rang in my ears. He would make sure I was okay.

The face became clearer, and I slowly turned to Ty.

My heart felt as though it was shattering into a million pieces. This couldn't be real. This couldn't be fate's design.

Something wasn't right.

I remembered the face of the man with the bloodied hands that had reached for me and taken me far from my home.

His face was now crystal clear.

That man had been Dominic Keller.

Chapter 29 - Ty

Watching Liza shift and follow the pull of the moon had been fascinating. Her wolf took over and fell into line with all the other shifters who lived for the full moon.

She had taken off so quickly, I'd struggled to keep up with her, and I was one of the fastest shifters in the pack. I knew every inch of these woods. She'd twisted and turned on a dime, so much so that my senses had become confused. I wasn't paying attention to my surroundings and only had my sight locked on Liza.

With this being her first full moon run without the desensitization of her hormone pills, I was worried she might run off into a dangerous area where shifters weren't protected.

Soon, though, her wolf halted, and then I smelled the lavender. Liza shifted, and I followed suit, turning in circles, trying to figure out where we were.

Then it came to me.

It was the place Liza had described from her dream. We were in the old Heather Falls territory where the Wylde pack had met its end.

Fuck.

The moment I stepped into the clearing, my senses heightened, and every little thing seemed to be alive with energy. It was as if the forest had been waiting for her to arrive. The trees waved harder in the billowing breeze, and the crickets chirped louder. A frog croaked somewhere nearby, and the night birds sang.

Moonbeams bounced off her pale skin as she walked. I begged her to come back, to run home with me, back into our safe territory.

She ignored me and moved forward through the tall grass and lavender. The fucking lavender.

By the time we reached the newly constructed house, I was positive that Stone would be close by. Sure enough, there he stood, smirking on the back porch of a home I presumed he'd built for himself … and for Liza to replace the one her family had lived in before.

I turned my attention back to Liza and watched as she fell to her knees, heavy sobs escaping her throat.

She eventually turned to face me, her eyes wild with a mixture of confusion and hurt. My heart inched up into my throat, and I swallowed hard. I was going to lose her. My soul ached.

"Did you know?" Liza's voice was thick, hoarse, and broken from the uncontrollable sobs that shook her body.

I stood frozen like a deer in headlights. "Know what? What are you talking about?"

I played dumb, unable to read her mind or understand exactly what she'd remembered. It was another asshole move, but I held tightly to the last shred of possibility. There was an ever-so-slight chance that Liza wasn't referring to my father or his slaughter of her family.

Liza's hands balled into fists as she lunged for me and pounded her fists on my chest. "Did you know?" she screamed at me, tears falling down her face.

She didn't give any more details. She didn't have to. The anger in her voice said as much as the words she'd spoken, and it all meant that she already knew the answer to her question.

I didn't answer her right away because my mind was working frantically as I tried to come up with an excuse that would make sense. I couldn't lose her, and the truth would tear her apart. I needed more time to fix it, to figure out how to tell her the truth myself.

But in the face of Liza's pain and hurt, all my excuses were futile. I had to find the strength to admit everything and to tell Liza that my father was to blame for the deaths of her parents.

"He knew." Stone's voice was concrete as he walked down the steps, carrying a large blanket.

He wrapped it around Liza's shoulders, covering her naked body.

Liza didn't take her eyes off me, not even acknowledging that Stone had moved to her side. "Why? Why would you keep this from me? Why didn't you just tell me the truth?"

There was no point in lying anymore. I'd done enough of that during our time together, and I could see now what I hadn't seen when I thought lying was the only way forward. Not telling her had only made things worse.

"Because I care so much for you, Liza." The words barely left my mouth before I felt her pull away completely—body, mind, and soul. "I wanted to keep you safe from all of this. If I had told you the truth, would you have been able to look me in the eye? Or would you have done as you're doing right now… blame me for the sins of my father?"

My words seemed to hit something deep inside Liza because her body jolted once I finished speaking. She pulled the blanket tightly around her shoulders, her body shaking from either the pain or the shock of hearing it all. Of knowing it was fact.

Stone stood still beside her, ready to catch her as soon as I sent her toppling, watching and waiting. No doubt he wanted to give me the chance to hammer the proverbial nail in the coffin. That son of a bitch expected my words to destroy my relationship with Liza, and all he had to do was stand by and wait for her to fall into his arms.

"Liza, please understand." I stood before her completely naked, stripped of any and all the secrets I'd once held, pleading for her to actually hear me. "I didn't want you to look at me and see the son of a murderer. I wanted you to look at me and see your mate." God, I sounded fucking pathetic and I couldn't fucking stop. "I wanted you to see the man who is ready and willing to move Heaven and Earth to make you happy. I'm not proud of keeping this secret from you, and I'll be the first to admit it was selfish of me, but none of that changes the way I have grown to care for you. If you can look past your hurt, you'll know I'm being honest."

Liza opened her mouth, and I held my breath, prepared to throw myself at her feet.

Before she could speak, Stone cleared his throat and spoke up. I growled, wanting to dig my claws into the man's face.

"Liza, you don't need to answer him. You don't owe him anything. Right now, you need to walk away. You're hurt and confused," he said reassuringly, moving closer to her side. "You just need time to process all this and make the decisions that are best for you. The decisions that best honor your parents and the Wylde pack."

His words were a reminder of how far away I was from gaining Liza's trust again. My stomach clenched. It would take more than words to make things right between us. Even then, she'd very likely tell me to go fuck myself, but I held onto the small hope that she'd forgive me and find her way back into my arms. That no matter what had happened between our families in the past, we could still have a future together.

"Your future in-laws knew exactly what treasure they'd stumbled on in that field." He pointed to the lavender growing behind us. Stone nodded his head in my direction. "Ty knew, as well. And don't think it was fate. He probably slipped you laudanum."

Shifter poison. "How the fuck would that make her think and feel all the things being my mate gives her?" He was grasping, making up details that fit his narrative. Everything I felt, everything she felt, was real. She had to know that.

"They hoped you would give them powerful offspring, so why would *he* tell you the truth? It wouldn't benefit him in the slightest, and we all know how the Keller family does whatever leaves them on the winning side." He nodded like a fucking preacher.

"That's a fucking lie," I barked in response. "My father doesn't even know that Liza is an omega. Liza, listen to me. He's making this shit up. He's spewing lies to get in your head."

Stone spoke over me, his eyes boring into Liza's. "You can't begin to understand how many years I spent trying to find you. I was too young to know who the bad men were that took you away, but I had to keep looking." He took her by the shoulders, touching her skin. I was about to kill him, to get rid of him now before he did any more damage. "For all I knew, they'd come from another country. I had no idea they were in our own backyard. How could I have guessed that you would only be forty minutes away?"

Liza blinked rapidly. From my vantage point, I couldn't tell if she was buying his lies or if she was questioning his motive… or mine.

Stone continued. "When it all happened, after I couldn't find you, I found shelter with a pack an hour away. It's not that I didn't want to find you, but everyone in our pack was dead, and I had no choice but to move forward, to survive. I was just a kid left in the forest alone with a broken ankle." Stone paused for dramatic effect, and it was as effective as he'd probably hoped. "The pack kept me and my true identity hidden, which I'm eternally grateful for, but I never stopped thinking about you and waiting anxiously for the day when I could make my move to find you and reunite the future alpha and omega."

"You were waiting to make a move, huh?" I didn't even pretend not to hate him. I spat my words and snarled, flashing my teeth in warning.

Stone ignored me, not taking his eyes from Liza. "I knew my parents had left me a great deal of money. I spent a lot of it hiring private investigators in hopes of finding you, Liza. For years, they searched tirelessly with not even a small clue as to where you were. For all we knew, you were dead. It was just pure luck that your name popped up in an article in the Presley Acres Country Club magazine for your catering business. When I saw your gorgeous face, I knew immediately that you were my Aliza. I had finally found you, so I set my plan in motion." Stone turned and gestured to the house behind him. "I bought this land where our pack once lived in harmony before they were slaughtered, and I began rebuilding our home."

Stone reached out and took both of Liza's hands, and I snarled again. My wolf raged inside, but I instructed him to wait. It wasn't time.

"Your parents chose me for you. That was their wish for you, Liza." He smiled and kissed one of Liza's hands. "They wanted us to create the next generation for the Wylde pack."

Liza's body locked up. She no longer gazed at Stone with interest, but dropped her gaze to the ground. She angled her body away from him, and my protective instincts kicked in.

Whether Liza was angry at me or not, I wouldn't stand by and allow any harm to come to her, physically or emotionally. I grabbed Liza and shoved her behind me before Stone even realized what was happening.

Liza didn't fight me. She seemed eager to not be near Stone, her muscles relaxing as she stood close to me.

Stone glared at me. "You know what will happen if you try to interfere, Ty. The world will know exactly what your father did to my pack." He grinned wickedly. "I have enough proof about the Kollor family and their shifty background to send your family's entire financial portfolio into the ground. You'll be an absolute mockery, and I will relish in your misery. It would only be a fraction of what you deserve for taking fucking everything from me."

My mother's face flashed through my mind, and her desperate pleas to make things right. She had stood by Dad through every moment of heartache, during the fallout of each of his bad decisions regarding the Wylde pack. Both of my parents were looking to me to preserve the family name and to keep the Keller pack in good standing amongst all the other packs. Dad had said himself tonight that he was proud of me, that Liza and I would lead our pack faithfully and triumphantly, yet here I stood at a crossroads.

It was Liza or the pack.

"I'm not handing Liza over to you, Stone."

Stone laughed. "You don't have to. I'm pretty sure Liza wants to come on her own. She now knows that *your* family is responsible for murdering her family." He paused and stepped to one side, locking his eyes on Liza. "Remember, it was your parents' wish for us to be mated."

Stone stepped closer to me, and I tensed, prepared to shift and fight. I didn't have to.

A quiet voice behind me stopped both of us in our tracks. We both glanced at Liza, the blanket wrapped tightly around her body. She stared at Stone, breathing rapidly. She looked at him as if she were seeing a monster, her lips curled back in disgust.

Her reaction put me on high alert as I turned to face her fully. She never took her eyes off Stone.

"What's wrong?" Stone cocked his head to one side. "Why are you looking at me like that, Aliza?"

Liza suddenly gripped her head and grimaced.

I cupped her face. "What's wrong? Liza? Are you hurting?"

Her breathing was uneven, and she shook her head. "My parents didn't want me to do that… to mate with you." She pointed a shaky finger at Stone.

I glanced over my shoulder at Stone to see his face contorted. His smile wasn't genuine, it was predatory.

A loud growl ripped through the quiet night, my warning to Stone.

Stone scoffed, his sly grin still plastered across his face. "You were too young to remember, Aliza. I was there for all of the adult conversations. They talked a lot about the infertility of the pack and how you, the omega princess, were the answer to their prayers. I was the only other child in the pack at the time. It made sense for them to choose me."

Liza glared at him.

Stone held up his hands in defense. "This is our destiny, Aliza. You were meant to be with me, to birth my children, and bring the Wylde pack into a new era!"

Before I realized what was happening, Liza had a hold of my shirt, squeezing so tightly that her knuckles turned white. "I remember something." Her voice trembled as she closed her eyes, trying to make sense of the memory.

Stone stared at her, his eyes hard with indifference. His voice was gruff when he issued his final threat, hoping to play on Liza's emotions. "Do you want to shit on your parents' final wishes before they met their demise at the hands of the Kellers?"

Chapter 30 - Liza

Stone's question rang in my head as I tried to focus on the memories. I compared them to my dreams, the recurring ones I'd had since I was a young child, and the nightmare I'd had a few nights ago.

My dreams had always been a bit distorted, fuzzy, and out of focus. The ending had remained the same, though. The boy took my hand and led me into the forest... but there was another part I'd never dreamed about. Suddenly, it was clear as day to me.

My parents had never liked Castro. There was something different about him... something off. One time, they found him in the woods completely covered in blood. He had killed a deer, which was normal for wolves. The difference was that he did it for fun, just because he wanted to. I had overheard my parents talking about the way they'd found him, his hand gripping the deer's neck and blood dripping down his face. He was in human form, not even attempting to eat the deer meat, just ripping the carcass to shreds for the hell of it. His eyes had been wild, and it had stirred something inside my mother.

After that, they never left me alone with Castro. I'd see him multiple times a week, but my parents assigned one of the household employees to keep watch over us as we played in our large backyard or in the playroom that was filled to the brim with toys.

Castro's parents came over to our house unexpectedly one evening for a visit. They talked with my parents about their concern for Castro. They questioned why he was the way he was, and they admitted to being afraid of him. I couldn't remember the details of that conversation but knew his parents had laid out multiple examples of Castro doing inappropriate things or saying hurtful words to them.

By the time Castro reached the age of twelve, most of the pack was afraid of him. They avoided him like the plague because he was unpredictable and couldn't be controlled.

Not me, though. He went out of his way to be nice to me, doting on me, bringing me gifts. I remembered him being mean to the other kids. He would beat up the boys who got too close to me, and be hateful to the girls who played with me.

Before I knew it, I didn't have any friends except Castro. I was so young that I didn't think much about it. After all, when I was with him, we had a great time. He always made me laugh and played with my dolls, making funny voices, and creating silly scenarios that left me in stitches.

His bullying became too much for the families of Heather Falls, though. Within a year, they left out of fear for their children's lives.

It was confusing for me because even though I heard what people said about Castro, his actions toward me didn't match up.

One night, I'd snuck out of bed and stood at the top of the staircase, clutching my stuffed bear to my chest while I eavesdropped on my parents. My father told Castro's parents that they no longer felt Castro was suitable to be my future mate, even though we had been betrothed since the day I'd been born. His parents sobbed and pleaded with my parents, promising them that Castro could change and that they could crack down on his behavior and whip him into shape. But my parents stood firm in their decision to protect me from the boy they believed to be a crazed, erratic, unstable shifter.

Castro's parents finally admitted that they understood and that they would have done the same thing in my parents' position.

My parents loved me above all else, and they only cared about keeping me safe. They felt Castro was a danger to their daughter—their princess.

After a long discussion, my father asked Castro's parents to leave the pack and take Castro far away from me. My mother apologized profusely and held Castro's mother as she sobbed. They had no choice, though. My father was the alpha, and his final decision was law. They couldn't stay in Heather Falls, and they could never come back.

My memories of the night of the attack had been distorted, and I suddenly realized how the brain had a funny way of protecting a person from the trauma they'd experienced. Now I could see everything clearly, and it had me shaking down to my bones.

I tried to steady my breathing, but my teeth chattered as the truth came rushing back to me.

Ty held me close, his strong arms only bringing me a minuscule amount of comfort. There was a war raging in my mind as the past and present collided, leaving me to reconcile fact from fiction, true memories from reimagined scenarios.

"What's wrong, Liza? Talk to me," Ty asked.

I stared at the monster who stood only a few feet from me. "Ty, your father might have killed my pack, but he didn't kill my parents because they were already dead when he got to them. Weren't they, Castro?"

Ty stiffened and held me at arm's length. "What are you talking about?"

Castro's eyes narrowed on me. He no longer tried to hide his true personality, and his kind smile contorted into a sly grin that made the hair on the back of my neck rise.

Fear consumed me. Castro was a sick bastard, and there was no telling what he'd do to get what he wanted. In this case, he wanted me.

I clutched my chest, gasping for air. Another panic attack tried to pull me under. I closed my eyes, attempting to focus on my breathing and not allow Castro to dictate my emotions.

My true memories came to the surface, my wolf whining and whimpering. She tried to comfort me and calm down my racing heartbeat, but it was no use. It was as if I had just lost my parents all over again, and the grief threatened to consume me.

Ty squeezed my shoulders gently, pulling me out of my head. "Liza, what *are* you talking about? Please. Talk to me."

My eyes burned with tears, though I wasn't sure how I had enough water left in my body to cry anymore. "Castro came to my house covered in blood. He said his parents were dead. That bad men had gotten into the house and killed them. We could hear the noise coming from the other houses and smell the smoke in the air."

I took a breath, trying to process the memories before I spoke them out loud. Thinking of them was one thing, but putting them out into the universe was another. I had to be sure that I was getting it right.

"My dad cursed and told Castro not to worry. He said our family would protect him, keep him safe. He told us to stay put while he handled the situation. I hid behind my mother's legs while my father made a phone call. He said that the pack was being attacked and instructed his army to make a move immediately." I looked up at Castro and forced myself to recall the worst moment of my life. "I hadn't seen it until it was too late. Castro had a gun. My mother had turned the corner, her eyes wide with panic. She asked my father what they needed to do because they had to keep me, their princess, safe… no matter the costs."

I stopped talking, closing my eyes as I remembered that moment, the scene playing out in front of me like a movie.

"You all need to go to the boats. Wait for me there," Dad instructed us from across the room, his face flushed with apprehension. "I'll take care of everything. Don't worry."

But we wouldn't make it to the boats. Not because the bad men had arrived at our front door, but because Castro had shot both of my parents.

I looked down and saw Mom on the floor, trying to cover her stomach wound as she bled out. "Run, Aliza!"

She wanted me to run from Castro, to run for my life. So, I did.

I ran. My heart broke, and fear consumed me, but I ran as fast as my short legs would carry me. Branches smacked me in the face as my tears distorted my vision. The screams of our dying pack members rang in my ears, and all I could see were my parents dying on the floor of our living room in the home that used to bring me such a sense of security.

It was the only home I ever knew, and I could never go back.

Instead, I ran for my life.

Glancing over my shoulder, I caught a glimpse of Castro as he closed the gap between us. He was much older and taller, so it didn't take him long to catch up to me.

He grabbed my hand, holding it so tightly that I didn't stand a chance of pulling away from him. We both ran, attempting to outrun the bad men who seemed hell bent on killing every person in Heather Falls.

Castro's ankle didn't break by accident. I saw an opportunity and I took it. Even at the age of four, I knew I couldn't hesitate when an opportunity presented itself. I let my instincts guide me when I noticed a hole in the ground. With every ounce of energy in my tiny four-year-old body, I shoved him toward it. He stepped in and twisted his leg, immediately falling to the ground and crying out in agony.

He was so angry at me, cursing and yelling, "You are mine, Aliza! Come back!"

I ran, never looking back, as far as I could, finally hiding in the brush when my body gave out from sheer exhaustion.

I opened my eyes and stared up into Ty's face. "Castro killed my parents, then tried to take me as his own."

Ty's eyes widened. "Are you sure? Dad never mentioned that."

I shook my head. "He probably thought one of his men got to my parents before he could."

I'm sure Ty was relieved that his dad hadn't killed my parents, but if Castro hadn't shot them, someone from Dominic's army would've taken them out. They never stood a chance.

Castro grunted and started slow clapping, shifting his weight from one leg to the other. "I'm surprised you remember so much, Aliza. You were only four at the time. I'd always wondered how much you would actually recall from that night, seeing as you were practically a toddler. But when you didn't instantly recognize me that day at the farmers' market, I figured you had no memory of what happened, which was good for me. It made my plan so much easier."

I pulled myself from Ty's embrace and stood tall, staring at Castro. I willed my body to stop shaking, pulling the blanket tighter around my naked body. Now that the initial shock had worn off, I needed to show him that he couldn't scare me with his words. He couldn't intimidate me. I was no longer the scared little girl, powerless and small in comparison.

I was a fucking omega.

Castro looked at me and raised one eyebrow but continued his rant. "I had hoped when your wolf fully awoke that your omega powers would lead you to your heart's desire. And they did. They led you home, and I was waiting with open arms just as I promised you I would be. The one snafu in my plan was that I didn't expect you to remember every little detail, Aliza."

His face twisted as anger overtook him. "Your sudden burst of memory throws a bit of a wrench in my plans, but there's no need to worry. I'm not the least bit concerned. I don't need you to love me, Aliza. It is your *duty* as the princess of the Wylde pack to restore the pack to its former glory. It's our duty as the only survivors to bring forth a new generation and honor our ancestors."

Castro's eyes were wild as he took one step closer. "My father told me it was my duty. I'd grown up hearing my parents discussing my rightful place at your side, the one who would bring forth a new generation. Then my father took all of that from me the night he told me we were leaving Heather Falls for good. He said I'd no longer be able to see you, Aliza. It was a permanent move."

Castro paced back and forth, cracking his knuckles, breathing rapidly. "I was out when the attack happened. I knew we were all about to die, but I couldn't stand the thought of my precious Aliza dying. I didn't want to leave you. I refused. So, I did what had to be done. I killed my parents. For you! With them gone, they couldn't take me from you. I killed your parents for the exact same reason. And now, I'll do the same to your mate, and anyone else who gets in the way of us achieving our dreams. Together."

Ty slowly pushed me behind him once more. "Stay back, Liza." It was a command, and his aura was so strong that I nearly folded from the force of it.

Castro narrowed his eyes on me. "You will be mine, Aliza. I just need to handle this pest first."

Chapter 31 - Ty

The shift took over, adrenaline coursing through my veins. Unable to hold my wolf back any longer, the transformation was almost instantaneous. He burst forth so quickly that it took me a moment to focus on my surroundings. The woods blurred around me, but I quickly set my sights on the only thing that mattered: protecting Liza from Castro.

Castro's wolf looked very similar to Liza's, with the light fur and pale, gray eyes. The hair on his back stood on end as he crouched low, ready to attack.

He would be a formidable opponent. It wouldn't be an easy fight. His snarling face and flashing teeth made it clear that he was here to win and would do anything to come out on top. He'd already made it abundantly clear that he would do anything to get what he wanted. The motherfucker had murdered his own parents.

We circled one another, our growls filling the air as we prepared to strike. Castro lunged first, his claws extended, teeth bared. I dodged to the side, snapping at his flank. We danced around each other, looking for an opening.

Castro fought dirty, trying to use every trick in the book to take me down. He feigned weakness, only to launch a surprise attack when I was off guard. But I was skilled and knew how to handle myself in a fight. I managed to keep him at bay, using my speed and agility to dodge his attacks and counter with my own.

As the fight raged on, I could see that Castro was tiring. His movements were slower, his attacks more predictable. This was my chance. I lunged forward, sinking my teeth into his shoulder. He howled in pain, thrashing wildly in an attempt to throw me off, but I held on; my jaws locked tightly around his flesh. His warm blood coated my mouth. Now I had the upper hand. I could taste victory on the tip of my tongue.

Suddenly, a sharp pain penetrated deep into my side. Castro had managed to get a claw in, and I stared in disbelief as blood poured from the wound. I howled in pain, but I refused to let go. I tightened my grip on his shoulder, determined to finish the fight.

The blood loss weakened me. Castro twisted and sank his claw deep into the existing wound, bringing me to my knees. I blinked hard, my vision blurring. Just when I became light-headed, a familiar scent filled the air. I knew that scent.

I could handle it—could fight against it. Castro, however, responded immediately. He lifted his head, cocking it to one side as his eyes glazed over like a teenager in heat.

Liza had unleashed her pheromones to distract Castro, and it worked.

He was sidetracked, staring at Liza as if she were a fresh piece of meat. Now was my chance to end his life, but as I gripped his neck, I decided against it. I would give him grace, even though he was undeserving of it.

Castro would face his crimes and would be punished accordingly.

Summoning what little energy I had left, I slammed Castro's head onto the hard ground. His eyes rolled to the back of his head, his body going limp. He wasn't dead, but I had rendered him unconscious.

He transformed back into his human state. Castro was lifeless, naked, and completely vulnerable. From my vantage point, he suddenly didn't seem like the fucking monster he truly was. But looks could be deceiving, and I shuddered at what he would've done to my precious Liza if he had succeeded in getting his hands on her.

I glanced down at the gash in my side as I collapsed, breathless. My injury was serious, so I howled, hoping the other pack members would hear and respond. Within seconds, a return howl reached my ears, and I breathed a sigh of relief.

Using what little energy I had left, I shifted back into human form and covered the wound with my hands, pressing tightly and hoping I could slow the blood loss.

My head was spinning, my vision fading in and out. Fighting the urge to pass out, I kept my eyes on Castro. Even though I knew he'd be out for a while, there was no way I'd allow myself to faint and leave Liza alone with that fucking psycho.

Liza fell to the ground and held my head in her lap.

"That was a dangerous move, Liza." I paused to catch my breath. "You should've let me handle it. What if he'd turned on you? I was in no position to protect you with his fucking claw in my side."

She ran her fingers through my hair. "I wasn't going to stand by and watch that maniac take someone else from me." A sob escaped her throat as she whispered, "He killed my parents."

Her words shattered my heart. Reaching up, I cupped her face and pulled her forehead to mine. "I'm so sorry. Castro will pay for his crimes."

I drifted in and out of consciousness for at least forty-five minutes, but the sound of stomping in the distance brought me back to full alert. Sighing deeply, relief washed over me at the familiar feeling of my pack moving into the area.

The pack elders descended upon us, quickly assessing the scene and moving into action. They'd come prepared with medical supplies and didn't waste any time covering me with a blanket and attending to my wound.

My body was ready to give up. I couldn't fight against the darkness that was filling my peripheral vision. Before I passed out, I pointed to Castro. "Tie this man up and put him in a cell."

My last thoughts were of Liza and her safety, putting my trust in the pack to keep Castro far from her. Before I could give any more orders or explanations, the darkness consumed me.

I found myself running through the forest, my heart pounding in my chest as I chased after Liza. She was just ahead of me, always just out of reach, and every time I thought I was close enough to catch her, she slipped away.

She laughed at first, her voice ringing out through the trees. But then, suddenly, she started to cry, her tears streaking down her face as she cried out for her family.

I pushed myself harder, my legs pumping as I tried to catch up to her. But every time I got close, she slipped away again, her form twisting and turning as if she were made of smoke.

The forest around us was dark and eerie, the branches reaching out to grab at us as we ran past. Wind howled through the branches, carrying with it the sound of Liza's sobs.

As I ran, a growing sense of panic filled my chest. I didn't know what was happening to her, but I had to catch her before it was too late.

Finally, after what felt like an eternity, I caught up to her. She was standing in the clearing, her back to me, her naked body shaking with sobs.

I reached out to touch her, to comfort her, but she slipped away again, vanishing into the darkness, and as she disappeared, my eyes fluttered open.

I clutched my chest, trying to slow my heartbeat. Glancing around the room, I breathed a sigh of relief. I was at the estate. An IV bag hung above my head, so I concluded that I was in the medical wing. To my left, Mother hovered, her face twisted with worry.

A soft squeeze of my hand pulled my eyes to the opposite side of the bed where Liza sat, holding my hand, and smiling weakly.

Dad cleared his throat. He stood at the end of the bed, his arms crossed over his chest, staring at me with concern.

They all let out a sigh of relief.

I narrowed my eyes on Dad. He looked as if he'd aged another ten years during the night.

"You can never scare me like that again, son." Dad patted my leg and swallowed hard, trying not to get emotional.

Mother leaned over the side of the bed and kissed my cheek. "I was so worried about you, Tyson. You've been unconscious for a few days."

"A few days?" My voice was hoarse, my throat scratchy. I coughed.

A nurse appeared and handed me a glass of water. She helped me sit up, then placed a few pillows behind my back.

"I'm so sorry to put you all through that." I took a small sip of water, realizing how dry my mouth was. "I certainly didn't plan for things to go this way."

Dad held up a hand. "You don't have to explain, just conserve your energy. Liza already filled us in."

My gaze drifted to Liza. It looked like she hadn't slept in days. Her eyes were swollen and red-rimmed, her hair a tangled mess on the top of her head.

"I'm glad you're okay." She dropped my hand and stood, turning to leave.

"Where are you going?" Why would she leave me just as I woke up?

There was so much I wanted to say to her, and I needed to make sure she was okay. The whole situation with Castro had left her with a heavy burden to process, and I was concerned for her well-being.

Liza turned and clasped her hands in front of her chest. "I have to think about my next steps, Ty. Even though your father didn't kill my parents, it was his actions that caused the destruction of my home."

Dad hung his head, unable to look Liza in the eyes.

She continued. "I know why you chose to keep everything from me, and you were absolutely right. If you had shared all the gory details with me, I would have blamed you for the sins of your father, not being able to see you for who you are. But right now, I want to mourn my parents in peace because I was never given the chance."

I opened my mouth to protest. To apologize again.

Liza held up a hand. "No, Ty. It's time for me to speak and for you to listen. I have to dig deep and find it in me to forgive you for everything you kept from me. Right now, I'm not sure I can do that."

She stopped in the doorway, looking back at me with her gorgeous eyes penetrating my soul. "Get well soon, Ty."

Liza walked away. Had I just lost my mate?.

Dad watched her go. "I can't blame her if she never wants to lay eyes on me again." He sat in the chair she'd just vacated and rested his elbows on his knees. "I honestly had no idea who had ended Josef and Portia's lives. When Liza told me everything she'd witnessed, it wrecked me, Ty. It's devastating what that child went through." He pinched the bridge of his nose.

I patted his arm. "What's done is done, Dad. We can't go back and change things. Our actions moving forward will show everyone involved what values the Keller family holds. That's all we can do... move forward with integrity."

Dad lifted his gaze. "You might not want to hear this right now, considering that you just woke up, but our family secret won't be getting out. Castro succumbed to his injuries."

My jaw dropped. "He's dead?"

Dad nodded. "Apparently, you did more damage to Castro than he could heal from. You punctured a major artery. He couldn't recover."

I closed my eyes, recalling the fight. I had been so focused on my own wound that I hadn't realized I'd punctured his neck when I had my paws wrapped around him.

Shit.

"I didn't want to kill him. He needed to be tried for his crimes and punished accordingly."

Dad sighed. "Good riddance is all I'll say. Although, I can understand Liza feeling jilted since her parents won't ever get the justice they rightfully deserve. Honestly, I wouldn't be surprised if she decides to give us all a big fuck-you and tell the entire world our secrets."

I cleared my throat. "No. Liza isn't like that."

He nodded. "Yeah, that's the impression I got when we discussed everything. She just wants to move on." Dad rose to his feet and shoved his hands in his pants pocket. "That reminds me. There's something I'd like to do for Liza once you're back on your feet. Maybe it can be an offering of peace."

The next three days were torture while I waited to be released from the medical ward. I was bored and anxious to get back to some sort of normalcy.

The nurses and Dr. Anderson took good care of me, but as the future alpha, they went over the top in assuring I was healing as I should be. Anyone else would've been released after day two, but not me.

My parents had spent a lot of time with me, playing cards and chatting about random happenings within the pack, but Liza never came back. Bryce even showed up one day with a bouquet of bacon that had been twisted into the form of roses, but no Liza.

At the end of the third day, I was ready to get the hell out of there. I had to sign a shit load of medical release forms before Dr. Anderson would agree to discharge me.

Standing on my own two feet again was painful since the gash in my side was still healing, but I didn't care. I only had one mission in mind. I had to make things right with my mate.

After showering and trading a hospital gown for normal clothes, I drove straight to Liza's house. She wasn't there, so I drove to her office.

Sabrina met me at the front door. "Oh, hey, Ty."

"Where's Liza?" I didn't have time for niceties.

I'd spent the past three days mulling over what I needed to say to Liza, and I could only hope that she hadn't already concluded that she wanted nothing to do with me or my family.

"I'm sorry. She's not here." Sabrina looked at me with pity. I assumed Liza had told her everything.

"Where is she, then?" I tried not to sound too desperate, but it was useless.

Sabrina sighed. "She decided to take some vacation time, but I don't know where she is right now. Sorry."

"Fuck!"

I pulled my phone from my pocket as I jogged back to my car. Liza didn't answer, which wasn't shocking. I'd been trying to call her for the past three days and my calls always went straight to voicemail every time.

Then a thought occurred to me as my tires squealed out of the office's parking lot. I hung a left and drove in the direction of Heather Falls.

I parked near the house Castro had built and walked past the site where I had fought him to his death.

Following the same path we'd taken a few nights earlier, I found Liza standing in the lavender field. She didn't turn to look at me, but she could sense my presence.

"It's funny how my allergy is gone now that I remember everything." She took a deep breath. "I think my subconscious reacted to lavender because of the bad memories associated with this field. Every horrific thought was connected to the flowers."

She sat down, and I followed suit, not sitting too close. I didn't want to make her uncomfortable.

I waited a few moments before speaking up. "Liza, I'm sorry. Not just for the lies, but for all the pain and suffering my family has caused you. I know money can't fix any of it, but there's something you need to know about."

Liza looked at me, one eyebrow raised in interest.

"Your parents set up a trust fund in your name. It's been accruing interest for many years, and they were well-versed in the art of making smart investments. You are a very rich woman." I pulled a folded piece of paper from my back pocket and handed it to her.

She unfolded it and stared for a moment. Eventually, her mouth dropped open in shock as she made sense of the long string of numbers at the bottom of the sheet.

"The bank is already aware of your name change, so you have full access to the money. There's a safety deposit box in your name, as well. The president of the bank assured me that they can unlock it for you when you're ready."

Liza stared at the paper in disbelief.

"Oh." I pulled another piece of paper from my pocket. "I have one more thing to give you."

I handed over an address written in my dad's handwriting. "This is where your parents are buried."

Liza's eyes widened. She was stunned.

"Dad wanted me to share a message with you. He said that greed tends to make people blind, and that sometimes the outcome of greed lives with you forever. Your parents were not bad people, despite their way of life. They loved their daughter and their pack. They deserved a proper burial."

Tears streamed down Liza's face, and I ached to hold her. I scooted closer, and she instinctively fell against my chest, releasing the emotions overwhelming her.

After a few minutes, she pulled her soaked face from my chest. "You still aren't forgiven."

I didn't let go.

Liza wept on my chest. "I miss them so much."

I held her even tighter, refusing to let go.

She wrapped her arms around my waist, hugging me back. "I'll sic my brothers on you if you ever lie to me again."

I kissed the top of her head. "I'll gladly take the beating."

Once her tears stopped, we sat in silence, looking out over the lavender field. It was peaceful and beautiful. A far cry from the darkness that had hung over it only a few nights before.

Liza broke the silence with her soft, quiet voice. "I'm so pissed that Castro won't face his crimes. I hope he's burning in Hell."

I took her hand and kissed it. "Karma always has a way of giving people what they deserve. An eye for an eye. Maybe this was the justice fate felt he deserved."

She sat in quiet contemplation for a moment and then smiled weakly. "You may be right. Fate always seems to be one step ahead."

She nestled her head back against my chest, and we sat in silence, watching the sun set over the lavender field.

We finally stood to go. Before we made it to Liza's car, she turned and took one last look at the home Castro had attempted to recreate.

"Goodbye," she whispered to her past.

Chapter 32 - Liza

Two Months Later

"Tell me again why you haven't gone to the bank to claim your millions?" Sabrina eyed my car as I pulled into work. "If I were you, I'd be driving a brand-new car and wearing a diamond necklace when I walked to the mailbox."

I laughed. "I bet you would."

"I'm serious, Liza. You do realize that with that kind of money, you don't have to work another day in your damn life, right?"

I waved her off with a smile. "I have no use for it right now because I already have everything I could possibly need."

"All right, then you can slip me a few million since you're just letting it go to waste." Sabrina flipped her hair behind her back and strutted into the venue.

I wouldn't know what to do with that kind of money, so I had decided to just leave it alone. I wasn't being penalized for not withdrawing it, and the amount continued to earn interest without me lifting a finger. I knew it was there for rainy days or if, God forbid, my business tanked, and I ended up jobless. But I didn't think that would happen.

Sabrina said I didn't need to work, which was true. What she didn't realize, though, was that I enjoyed my job. I'd built my company from the ground up, and I took pride in the service we provided to the people of Presley Acres.

My business was more to me than a paycheck.

Before putting on my apron, I looked at my calendar app. My heart became heavy. I'd been trying to avoid the upcoming date, but it was impossible to ignore.

I glanced out the window at the sky. It was gray with a thick cloud cover. Snow would be coming soon.

A few days later, Ty stopped by my place with a bouquet of flowers, coffee, and a box of pastries for breakfast. I wasn't as angry at him anymore. After much contemplation and soul searching, I understood his reasoning for keeping everything from me, and I had somewhat forgiven him.

Ty had worked hard to regain my trust. He put me first, sometimes even before his work engagements. He was there whenever I needed him, providing a steady shoulder to lean on whenever the weight of my grief consumed me.

Even his parents tried to make amends, going out of their way to invite me to family functions, having real heart-to-heart conversations with me and apologizing profusely for their sins against my family.

I still had a lot of healing to do, which was why I decided to take the next step. Over breakfast, I turned to face Ty. "Will you go with me to see my parents?"

Ty's eyes widened when he realized I wasn't talking about my adoptive parents. "Of course, baby." He kissed me softly on the cheek. "I'd be glad to."

After we cleaned up the breakfast dishes, we bundled up and took the long drive to where my parents were buried.

Ty knew I was anxious about seeing my parents' graves, especially on the anniversary of their deaths. So, he was quiet on the drive, letting me choose whether or not we'd chat on the way. It was about a ninety-minute drive, and we sat quietly, listening to soft jazz music as we drove through the countryside.

I tried my best to prepare my heart and my mind for the sight of their names written across the cold, hard headstones, but no amount of preparation could have helped. I immediately fell to my knees, weeping over their graves. The names were fake—another attempt Dominic had made to try and cover up the existence of Heather Falls.

I wanted to be mad and to scream at Ty and let all my frustration out on him. I wanted to beat my fists into his chest and scream, ask him why life had to be so cruel.

But I couldn't. I didn't

I was too exhausted from all the anger.

Ty stayed back while I sat and placed my hands over their graves. "Momma, Daddy, I'm here. I found you." My tears fell onto the perfectly manicured grass that covered their burial sites. "I remember now. I remember everything. I was your princess, your baby girl. You would've moved Heaven and Earth to keep me safe, and I'm so sorry you had to die not knowing if I was safe."

I pulled my knees to my chest and buried my head in my hands, remembering the look on my mother's face as she lay on the ground, bleeding to death, pleading with me to run and save myself.

"I survived, and not only did I live, I've had a wonderful life not far from Heather Falls. I run my own catering business, and I'm happy. You need to know that I'm happy. But I miss you so much."

I slumped over and allowed all of my sadness and grief to bubble to the surface, letting my emotions release in whatever form they chose. My wolf whimpered, sharing my grief, and attempting to console my broken heart.

After an hour, I stood to my feet and rested my hands on their gravestones. "I love you."

I walked away feeling lighter. The weight of not having a final conversation with my parents had been lifted.

Ty took my hand and silently walked by my side to the car.

The drive home was even quieter. Ty didn't turn any music on, and I laid my head against the headrest, closing my eyes and allowing happy memories of my childhood to fill my mind.

I'd had wonderful parents, and I was blessed to have had four amazing years with them, and the rest of my life with another set of parents who also loved and cherished me. It didn't work out that way for everyone, and I was grateful I'd been one of the lucky ones.

Ty walked me into the house and stood at the door. I assumed he was waiting to see if I wanted him to stay, and I wasn't sure what I wanted to do... what I could do.

"Thank you for coming with me." My voice was soft, and I tilted my head to look at him.

"Of course, Liza." He sighed. "I would do anything for you." There was such sincerity in his tone, I didn't doubt the words, but there was a lot between us that needed fixing.

I studied him for a long time. His eyes were kind and contemplative. The more skeptical part of me—the part that hadn't forgotten that Ty had already burned me—wanted to twist his words and find the fucking lie I knew had to be there, but I saw nothing except truth in his declaration.

He stepped closer and hugged me tightly. "You're my family now."

I smiled, resting my head on his shoulder. He was the kind of man I'd always dreamed of finding.

Someone who loved me unconditionally, without judgment or expectation. Someone to share both the good and the bad with.

"Thank you," I whispered, tightening my hold on him.

It had been a long two months, and Ty's hard body pressed against mine stirred something deep within my core. Desire pooled in my belly, and I wanted more of him than a goodnight or goodbye kiss. I wanted *him*. I would always want him, and there wasn't a fucking thing I could do or wanted to do about it.

My wolf had recognized my grief and had kept her base instincts on lockdown. But now, my inner Pandora's box seemed to have opened back up. My wolf was over waiting for me to make up with Ty. Either I did it now, or she would force me to pounce on him. If that happened, it would be a battle to take back control, assuming I wanted control back.

Ty pulled back, holding me at arm's length. He cocked his head to the side as he inhaled a whiff of my scent. I hoped he saw the lust in my eyes, in the shallow, short breaths I was taking, in the soft, coy smile, and in the way I inched closer.

He growled, staring at me hard, trying to decide what to say. Honestly, nothing he said or didn't say mattered. I wanted him, and that was the entire truth of it. "I'll ravage you, Liza. So, if this is what you want, you'd better want all of it."

Oh, I did. But instead of speaking, I looked up into his beautiful dark eyes and jumped into his arms, wrapping my legs around his waist.

He shifted position, pinning me to the wall with his hips as his hands roamed my breasts, my face, then my ass. His kiss was deeper, harder, more powerful than any other kiss we'd shared. His mouth punished and soothed, caressed and abused. His tongue battled with mine as he pushed my hands over my head and held them there.

I wanted to rake my hands down his back, touch his skin, and feel the heat of him under my palms, but when I wriggled and struggled to break free, he tightened his grip.

Ty let me slide down his body, then swung me into his arms and made for the stairs. As he carried me up to the bedroom, he kissed me harder and deeper with every step. Without breaking the kiss, Ty set me on my feet.

I wanted to be ravaged, possessed, claimed, and owned. Much the same as I wanted to ravage and possess and claim and own him. I was anxious, needy, and yearning, but he didn't move in right away. He looked first, took his fill, and smiled. "You're so fucking beautiful, Liza."

Yeah, so was he, and there was plenty of time later for compliments and sweet talk. Right now, I wanted down and dirty, and before I could open my mouth to tell him what I wanted—it was a turn-on for each of us when I did—he slid my pants down and knelt in front of me.

I curled an arm around the post at the corner of the footboard and held on as he flicked his tongue out and caught my clit. I gasped. There wasn't enough oxygen on the planet, and I moaned when he sucked the already tight nub into his mouth and teased me with his tongue, his hand sliding up my thigh. Without warning, he thrust a finger inside me, and I groaned.

I was wet already. I'd wanted him since the car ride home. I'd wanted to ask him to pull over then and take me in the backseat or even on the hood of the car.

It had been a while, and I needed the connection, the heat of his body, and the power in his cock.

But now he was kneeling in front of me, licking my pussy, tilting my hips, fingering me so deftly that my knees were weak, and my body was coiled, cells ignited, and I was ready to explode.

He moaned against my clit, and that was enough. My knees quivered, and I was relying solely on his strength, his hand, his mouth to keep me from crashing to the floor. My orgasm pulsed through me, wave after wave, and I cried out, curling my fingers in his hair as he looked up at me.

There was nothing more erotic than this moment. Although I'd felt that before, I was certain another moment would never compare to this one, and just when I thought it was over, he slid another finger inside me, and continued licking and sucking until I could do no more than tremble from another orgasm.

"Ty! Fuck!" I'd meant to ask him to fuck me, but this was okay, too. I could wait until the passion subsided for him to fill me with his cock. Probably.

When the spasms stopped, he pulled his fingers out of me. With a wicked grin, he nudged me backward and spread my legs. He kept his eyes locked on mine as he shed his pants, and then he was inside me in a single thrust. He was hard, thick, and long, and my body stretched to accommodate him. Then he started moving, slow but deep, his hips sliding against mine.

But I wanted more. I wanted hard. I wanted fast. I quickly pulled my hips back, then slammed back.

"You want more, baby?" He pulled nearly all the way out, until only the tip of his cock was inside me.

He knew exactly how to tempt and tease. How to make me gasp and cry out. He looked down at me, grinning as he pushed in deeper, thrusting harder.

I raked my fingers down his back, then grabbed his ass and dug my nails into his flesh. He started moving again, faster and faster. I curled my legs around his hips.

He rammed his cock harder, deeper, and I panted and moaned, clinging to him, and when he lowered his head and used his tongue to mimic the moves of his cock, I whimpered with need.

I uncurled and curled my fingers into the soft flesh of his ass, and he tightened his glutes. I could've snapped a quarter off his ass, it was that perfect, and I was glad for it. I pushed him closer, or tried, but he was teasing me again, building my need to a new level until there was no going back.

I was spiraling out of control with no conscious thoughts except those that escaped my mouth. "Ty!" and, "Oh fuck, Ty!" and, "Ty! I'm coming!"

My legs clamped around him, and I held on while he continued pumping in and out of me until his body went rigid. He grunted and buried his face in my shoulder.

He rolled away and lay on the pillow beside me while we caught our breath.

I must've dozed off because when I opened my eyes, Ty was no longer in bed next to me. The running shower told me he hadn't left, though, so I stretched and let out a loud yawn.

I pushed myself up with one arm, my head spinning slightly. I was lightheaded, no doubt from the multiple orgasms and from not having eaten lunch.

A knock at the door caused me to jump. I glanced at the clock. It was almost five p.m., and I couldn't think of anyone I should have been expecting. In the age of cell phones, text messages, and emails, who the fuck came over unannounced?

I hurriedly tossed on my clothes and peeked out the window. Whoever had knocked was already gone, but there was a small package on the step on the front porch.

I opened the door and snatched up the manila envelope. I looked around but didn't see anyone, not even a vehicle parked in the driveway or up the street.

"Ty? Did you have something delivered here?"

I locked the door as Ty came downstairs. He was freshly showered, moisture glistening on his muscular chest, and a small towel wrapped around his waist.

For the love of all things masculine, he should have been somewhat aware that seeing him mostly naked, and knowing that if I grabbed the towel and tugged, he would be wholly naked, brought out something feral in me. It took every ounce of strength and willpower I had to keep me from ravaging him again.

I held up the envelope instead. "Someone left this on the doorstep."

He stared at the envelope and frowned. "It's not anything I ordered. Are you sure you haven't been tapping into that money and going on an online shopping spree?"

"An online shopping spree wouldn't fit in an envelope." He obviously knew nothing about designer bags and shoes. I rolled my eyes. "Besides, I didn't order anything."

We both stared at the envelope, and an eerie sensation came over me. My gut told me I wouldn't like what was inside. There was no return address and no indication that it was even meant to be delivered here. Only my name was scrawled on the front.

My feelings were at least validated when Ty crossed the room and snatched the envelope from my hand. He ripped it open and pulled out a letter.

The room seemed to shrink under his anger as he clenched his jaw and his eyes narrowed at the words.

"Ty? What is it? What's wrong?" I walked to his side and tried to catch a glimpse of the words over his shoulder.

He pulled the letter to his chest and gave me a defeated look, his eyes burning with anger. "No matter what, I'll keep you safe. Please remember that."

Fuck. That didn't bode well.

I took the letter from him and scanned the scribbled handwritten words. All the blood drained from my face when I read the words: *What was designed by fate can never die.*

My blood ran cold. Those were the words Castro had uttered in the hospital just before he passed out. Dominic had told me how the doctors tried to save him, but he'd lost too much blood. One of his arteries had been punctured and there was nothing they could do.

But just before he succumbed to death, he'd whispered those same words.

My whole body shook as I grabbed Ty's arm. "Did you actually see Castro's dead body?"

He shook his head. "My father saw it, and the coroner reported him dead. There's no way. This can't be from him." Like he wasn't completely certain, he added, "Dead men don't send letters."

I snatched the envelope from Ty and reached inside, pulling out another sheet of paper. My stomach clenched as I stared at the coroner's report along with a receipt for a transaction. Someone had written a small note at the bottom of the receipt.

It's amazing the things money can buy nowadays.

Ty took the papers from my hands as I covered my mouth to keep from screaming.

No. It couldn't be.

Ty was on the phone immediately, barking orders. "Bring the coroner to me. Now!"

It was useless. Ten minutes later, Ty got the call saying that his men had found the coroner's house empty, completely cleaned out except for a simple note that read: *I'm sorry.*

My knees gave out, and I slumped onto the floor as Ty let out an angry howl.

This wasn't over. The nightmare hadn't ended. Castro Neal was still alive.

Thank you for reading Wolf Prince. I hope you loved it! Find out what happens next when Liza is targeted by a rogue wolf from her past, and Ty is under increasing pressure to claim his mate....

Get Wolf Prince 2 Today!

Our fated bond is doomed from the start...

Our packs are sworn enemies, and those closest to me claim that Liza cannot be my mate. Even with the odds stacked against us, my wolf is certain that she's the one I've been waiting for.

But first I must stop the rogue wolf from Liza's past who is obsessed with her. If I don't hunt him down fast, he has the power to destroy our pack and my bond with Liza completely.

And with my father becoming weaker by the day, the pressure is intensifying for me to claim my mate and become alpha. Only Liza's wolf is growing more unpredictable, and she's starting to question if I'm acting with my heart or out of duty.

I'll risk everything to be with her because I know exactly how special Liza is. But if the wrong people find out who she really is, it could be a fate worse than death...

Get Wolf Prince 2 Today!

Wolf Prince
The Royals Of Presley Acres: Book 1

Roxie Ray
© 2023
Disclaimer

All rights reserved. No part of this publication may be reproduced, distributed, or transmitted in any form or by any means, including photocopying, recording, or other electronic or mechanical methods, without the prior written permission of the publisher, except in the case of brief quotations embodied in critical reviews and certain other noncommercial uses permitted by copyright law.

This is a work of fiction. Names, places, characters, and events are all fictitious for the reader's pleasure. Any similarities to real people, places, events, living or dead are all coincidental.

This book contains sexually explicit content that is intended for ADULTS ONLY (+18).